# WUTHERING
## BITES

# WUTHERING
# BITES

### SARAH GRAY

KENSINGTON BOOKS
www.kensingtonbooks.com

KENSINGTON BOOKS are published by

Kensington Publishing Corp.
119 West 40th Street
New York, NY 10018

All Kensington titles, imprints, and distributed lines are available at special quantity discounts for bulk purchases for sales promotion, premiums, fund-raising, educational, or institutional use.

Special book excerpts or customized printings can also be created to fit specific needs. For details, write or phone the office of the Kensington Special Sales Manager: Kensington Publishing Corp., 119 West 40th Street, New York, NY 10018. Attn. Special Sales Department. Phone: 1-800-221-2647.

Kensington and the K logo Reg. U.S. Pat. & TM Off.

ISBN-13: 978-0-7582-5408-5
ISBN-10: 0-7582-5408-3

First Kensington Trade Paperback Printing: September 2010
10  9  8  7  6  5  4  3  2  1

Printed in the United States of America

# WUTHERING
# BITES

# Chapter 1

*1801*

I've just returned from a visit with my landlord—the solitary neighbor, rumor has it, is a vampire. It is truly a pity, really, this infestation of unholy bloodsuckers, because this is certainly a beautiful country, the moors of England. I do not think I could have picked a place more solitary or removed from the stir of society. It is a perfect misanthrope's heaven . . . at least it will be so long as I do not have the misfortune of being bitten by said neighbor—or any of the other unnatural beasties that roam the countryside.

I think Mr. Heathcliff and I are a suitable pair to share this desolation. A capital fellow! I do not think he realized how my heart warmed to him when I beheld his suspicious black eyes as I rode up. Who knows? Maybe we are both the subject of unfounded rumor and he has been warned that I am vampire!

As he stared at me, I asked, "Mr. Heathcliff?"

He nodded.

"Mr. Lockwood, your tenant, sir." *And most unquestionably not a vampire,* I thought, but did not say. "I do myself the honor of calling as soon as possible after my arrival. I hope I did not inconvenience you when I persevered to solicit occupation of Thrushcross Grange. I—"

"I do not allow anyone to inconvenience me if I can prevent it," he interrupted. "Walk in!"

His last words seemed expressed with the sentiment *May your flesh be sucked dry* and the hair rose on the back of my neck. But despite the inkling of fear for wonder if the rumors about him could possibly be true, I was curious enough of his reserved nature to follow his bidding.

"Joseph, take Mr. Lockwood's horse," he ordered as we entered the court.

Joseph was an old man, though hale and sinewy. His skin was paler than the palest moon and his eyes red, rimmed in dark shadows. Around his neck, he wore a long scarf that he tied high beneath his ear, a peculiar accessory, indeed, for a manservant.

"The Lord help us!" he whined, taking my horse. Why we needed the Lord's help I was unsure, but I dared not speculate.

Wuthering Heights is the name of Mr. Heathcliff's dwelling, though I have heard that all in the countryside refer to it as Wuthering *Bites*. A poor, unimaginative jest, I know. "Wuthering" is an adjective referring to the atmospheric tumult to which the house is exposed in stormy weather. By the look of the excessive slant of a few stunted firs and tangled briars at the end of the house, I can only guess at the power of the north wind that must blow over the edge. Happily, the architect had the foresight to build the structure strong; the narrow windows are set deep in the wall and the corner is defended by large, jutting stones.

Before I passed the threshold into the house, I paused to admire the grotesque carving lavished over the front of the principal door. Among crumbling griffins and what appeared to be cloaked figures, their faces obscured, I detected the date "1500" and the name "Hareton Earnshaw." Curiosity tempted me to ask about the history of the place from my surly, pale-skinned, black-haired owner, but his curt attitude at the door suggested he wished a speedy entrance or complete departure, so I hurried after him.

Without a lobby or passage, one step took us into the family sitting room. They called it "the house." It included the parlor and the kitchen in the back, from where I could distinguish a chatter of tongues and a clatter of culinary utensils. At one end of the parlor stood the massive fireplace, flanked by ranks of pewter dishes that reflected both light and heat, interspersed with jugs and tankards. On a vast oak dresser was a frame of wood laden with oat cakes and clusters of legs of beef, mutton, and ham.

They say vampires take no nourishment but blood, so the sight of the feast encouraged me. Surely the sign of abundant foodstuffs was proof enough that the master was no such creature! . . . Unless the spread was meant to disarm and persuade me that all here was as it should be in a decent household.

Above the chimney were sundry villainous old guns, a couple of horse pistols, and three gaudily painted canisters on the ledge. The floor was smooth, white stone unsoiled, I noted, by bloodstains; the chairs, high-back, primitive structures painted green. In the arch under the dresser was a huge liver-colored bitch pointer, surrounded by a swarm of squealing puppies, and more dogs haunted other recesses.

The parlor and furniture would have been nothing extraordinary for a simple northern farmer among these hills and moors, but Mr. Heathcliff formed a contrast to his abode. Despite his dark-haired, dark-eyed gypsy looks, in dress and manners he seems a gentleman country squire. By his appearance, some might suspect a degree of underbred pride; gypsies are known for such arrogance, and I wonder if he could be one of them. Since the infestation of the vampires, the gypsy vampire slayers have become bold in their haughtiness. With some right, as it is their skill and courage that keep the beasties from devouring all of us and taking over our fair country. But I am running too fast, bestowing attributes on Mr. Heathcliff that might be unfounded.

I took a seat at the end of the hearthstone opposite my landlord and filled up the interval of silence by attempting to caress the pointer bitch that had left her pups and was sneaking wolfishly to the back of my legs.

My caress provoked a long, guttural snarl. At closer glance, I saw that this creature was half again as large as one of her kind, with great ivory fangs and a fierce eye. Her throat, I noted, was protected by a thick leather collar studded with spikes, no doubt to keep her from being drained of blood by a vampire.

"You better let the dog alone," growled Mr. Heathcliff, punctuating his words with a punch of his foot. "She's not a pet!"

He strode to a side door and shouted again. "Joseph!"

The old man mumbled indistinctly from the depths of the cellar but gave no suggestion of ascending, so his master went down, leaving me with the monstrous bitch and a pair of sheepdogs.

Not anxious to come in contact with their fangs—or anyone's, for that matter—I sat still. Unfortunately, I indulged myself by making a face at the dog, and she broke into a fury and leapt for my throat. I hastened to put the dining table between us, this action rousing the whole pack. Half a dozen four-footed fiends of various sizes and ages issued from their hidden dens and I felt my heels and coat-laps subjects of assault. I parried off the larger dogs as effectually as I could with a fireplace poker, but was forced to call for assistance from the household when a yipping terrier slipped beneath my guard and latched onto my knee. He was hedgehog small but keen of tooth, and I felt each tiny dagger dig into my flesh until warm drops of blood ran down my boot.

Mr. Heathcliff and his henchman climbed the steps, slow as molasses running off a block of ice. Fortunately, an inhabitant of the kitchen came running; a lusty dame with tucked-up gown, bare arms, and flushed cheeks rushed into the midst of us, flourishing a frying pan, and used the weapon to such purpose that the storm magically subsided, leaving her heaving like a sea after a high wind when her master entered the scene.

"What the devil is the matter?" he asked, eyeing me in a manner I could barely endure after such inhospitable treatment.

"What the devil, indeed," I muttered, collapsing into a chair, trying to pry the still-clinging terrier from my wounded knee. "A herd of possessed swine has better manners than those animals of yours, sir. You might as well leave a stranger in a hive of vampires!"

He put a bottle of spirits down in front of me. "The hounds do right to be vigilant. We all do, considering what roams the moors. A glass of wine?"

"No, thank you." The terrier released my knee long enough to bite my thumb and went back to the knee with undisguised glee.

"Not bitten, are you?"

"By the son of Lucifer!" I replied, trying to shake the little dog off. "If blood loss be any measure—"

"Vampire bitten," Heathcliff corrected.

I could not suppress a shudder, as I knew the meaning of the phrase was far broader these days than it had once been. "If I had been, I would have set my silver dagger on the biter," I responded, laying my hand on its sheath at my waist, my meaning equally broader than it might once have been.

In these times of roaming vampires, both gentlemen and

gentlewomen had taken to carrying weapons to fend the beasties off. Pure silver made up for the small size of the dagger and my lack of vampire fighting skills, I was assured by the salesman when I made the purchase in London. Well worth the extraordinary cost, I was promised.

The vicious terrier continued to rend my poor knee until the kitchen wench with her flushed cheeks and noble frying pan put her fingers to her lips and emitted a sharp whistle. The canine fury's pointed ears perked up and his gaze fixed on the skinned rabbit the dame dangled from one hand. With one final nip, the dog unclenched its jaw and dove for the rabbit. She sliced off the head and tossed it, bringing all the hounds to full cry and chase. The small devil that had so harried me reached the meat a paw's length ahead of the pointer bitch and carried his prize to the top of a sideboard and hence to a lofty shelf to devour the bunny head, to the sorrow of those companions left supperless.

Heathcliff's countenance relaxed into a grin, surprising me. "A noble beast. A first-rate terrier. I've lost count of his bloodsucker kills. Of course, his mother was a badger, his father a noble hunter of vermin. Still, I doubt you've seen the like in your travels."

"No, I can't say I have." I unwound my second-best stock from my neck and used it to stanch the worst of the bleeding.

"Come, come, you are flurried, Mr. Lockwood. You look pale."

The massive pointer bitch had crept closer to lap up the droplets on the floor around my boots. "I have lost blood," I pointed out.

"Naught but a spoon or two. Nothing to grouse about. Take a little wine. Welcome guests are so rare in this house that I and my dogs hardly know how to receive them. To your health, sir!"

I bowed, beginning to realize it would be foolish to sit and sulk over the misbehavior of a few curs and unwilling to yield my host further amusement at my expense.

He—probably persuaded by the realization he should not offend a good tenant—relaxed a little and introduced a subject of interest to me, my present state of retirement. I found him very intelligent, and before I went home, I volunteered another visit tomorrow. He evidently, however, wished no further intrusion and expressed such.

It is astonishing how sociable I feel myself compared to him.

# Chapter 2

The next afternoon set in so misty and cold that I had half a mind to spend it by my study fire instead of wading through mud, risking my life in tempting the demons that course the moors—to Wuthering Heights.

Walking down the hall with this lazy intention, I spotted a serving girl on her knees and stepped into the room thinking I might greet her. Settled in front of the fireplace, she was surrounded by brushes and coal scuttles and raising an infernal dust as she extinguished flames with heaps of cinders. When she looked up, startled by my intrusion on her work, I noticed two distinguishing puncture marks on her pale neck. The spectacle drove me back through the doorway, and she watched with the oddest little smile on her face.

I resolved to place a chair in front of my bedchamber door at night and keep a vigilant eye on this saucy jade. It was well-known that maidens of the lower sort often traded virtue for the thrill of sexual congress with the fanged ones. Male vampires were said to possess extraordinary physical attributes such as to render foolish females incapable of moral judgment. Who knew if she was an innocent seized on her way home from church or a lusty wench who sought her own downfall among the beasts? In

any case, she would bear watching, and if I sensed anything amiss, she would find herself dismissed without a letter of recommendation. She might be happier dancing half
naked and exposing her slender throat in some vampire-
friendly tavern than emptying chamber pots in an honest
man's house.

Without lingering, I took my hat and made the four-
mile walk to Wuthering Heights. Fortunately, on my journey, I encountered no sign of cloaked and bloodthirsty
predators. In fact, I had not seen one since my arrival. Just
as I made my way to the garden gate, however, I thought I
spied what seemed to be shadows of the enemy through
the first feathery flakes of a snow-shower.

On that bleak hill-top, the earth was hard with black
frost and the air made me shiver through every limb as I
blinked, unsure if the shadows were real or mirage. Vampire or swaying grass? Unwilling to wait out the answer, I
ran up the causeway and knocked for admittance, keeping
a look over my shoulder.

When there came no immediate answer from within
save for the howl of dogs, I grasped the latch and shook it
vehemently. Vinegar-faced Joseph projected his head from
a round window of the barn.

"What ye want?" he shouted, adjusting the scarf
around his neck. "Go round if ye want the master."

"Is there no one to open the door?" I responded, looking again over my shoulder. Yes, something was definitely
there . . . and there! I recalled the poor maid's wound and
went on faster. "Open to me, Joseph, for pity's sake! 'Tis
not safe for man untrained in vampire repelling to stand
out in this weather."

"There's nobody but the missus, and she'll not open the
door. Not for King Georgie himself."

"Why?" I peered up at him, shivering inside my coat.
"Can't you tell her who I am?"

The head vanished and I was left in the snow, which had begun to drive thickly. I had the sense that I was being watched, a feeling so strong that I feared to turn and look over my shoulder. I had just seized the door handle to give another try when a young man shouldering a pitchfork appeared in the yard behind. He hailed me to follow him, and I, glad for flesh and bone of any human kind, trailed after him through a washhouse and a paved area containing a coal shed, pump, and pigeon cote. I gave a sigh of relief as we arrived in the warm, cheery apartment and I was formally received.

The room glowed delightfully with the radiance of an immense fire built from coal, peat, and wood. Near the table, laid for a plentiful meal, I was pleased to observe the "missus," whose existence I had not previously suspected.

I bowed and waited for her to offer me a seat, quite relieved to have arrived unscathed. Leaned back in her chair, she looked at me, remaining motionless and mute.

"Rough weather and beasties lurking!" I remarked. "I'm afraid, Mrs. Heathcliff, I had to work hard to make myself heard at the door. It was a near thing."

She never opened her mouth and I glanced at her neck, wondering if, like the maid at Thrushcross, she had fallen victim to one of the vampires I thought I had seen in the snowing mist. She kept her eyes on me in a cool, regardless manner. I saw no bite marks, but that was no guarantee; women in particular were good at hiding them when they wished to.

"Sit down," said the young man gruffly. "He'll be in soon."

I obeyed, keeping one eye on Mrs. Heathcliff while calling the villain canine, Juno, the pointer bitch, who moved the extreme tip of her tail in token of owning my acquaintance. To my relief, the tiny terror was nowhere in sight.

"A beautiful animal," I commenced. "Do you intend parting with the pups, madam?"

"They are not mine," said the hostess, more unkindly than Heathcliff himself could have replied. "You should not have come. It is not safe." She rose, reaching for the mantel for two of the painted canisters. "Vampires are thick on these moors on such sunless days."

*As if one needed reminding. . . .*

Her position before was sheltered from the light; now, I had a distinct view of her figure and countenance. She was slender and barely past girlhood, an admirable form and the most exquisite little face I have ever had the pleasure of beholding. With flaxen ringlets hanging loose on her delicate neck, she had small features that, had they been in agreeable expression, would have been irresistible. Fortunately for my susceptible heart, the only sentiment they evoked hovered somewhere between scorn and a kind of desperation.

The canisters were almost out of reach, and I made a motion to aid her.

"I can get them myself," she snapped.

"I beg your pardon?"

"Were you asked to tea?" she demanded, tying an apron over her neat black frock and standing with a spoonful of leaf poised over the pot.

I detected the sharp scent of garlic, a common ingredient in English teas, as of late. It is said to ward off vampires; they detest it. Some, like my housekeeper, have even taken to wearing garlic on their persons—a foolish notion, I think. "I'll be glad to have a cup," I said. *Perhaps two, if it will get me home with the eight imperial pints of blood I possessed when I left Thrushcross Grange today,* I thought.

"Were you invited?" she repeated.

"No." I half smiled. "You're proper to ask, though. No telling what sort of strangers will try to make their way into your home these days. A cousin of mine told me that only last week a vampire pretending to be an old acquaintance tried to invite himself into my cousin's household for tea."

She flung the tea back, spoon and all, and returned to her chair in a pout, her under-lip pushed out, like a child's ready to cry.

Meanwhile, the young man had slung on a decidedly shabby upper garment, stained with blood. I wondered if, like many young men in the country, he was training to fight the dark devils. I nearly asked him myself, but then he looked at me from the corner of his eyes as if there were some mortal feud unavenged between us, and I swallowed my question. His thick brown curls were rough and uncultivated, his whiskers encroaching bearishly over his cheeks, and his hands were embrowned like those of a common laborer. Yet I began to wonder if he was a servant or not. His dress and speech were entirely devoid of the superiority one could observe in Mr. and Mrs. Heathcliff, but his bearing was free, almost haughty, and he showed no respect to the lady of the house.

In absence of clear proof of his place in the household, I deemed it best to abstain from noticing his curious behavior; five minutes later, the entrance of Heathcliff relieved me from my uncomfortable state.

"You see, sir, I've returned as promised," I exclaimed. "But I fear I shall be weather-bound. I trust you can afford me shelter." Then I cleared my throat, feeling it my duty to warn him. "Are you aware of the creatures that presently linger on your property?"

"Afford you shelter? For the night?" he said, seeming to ignore my reference to a possible vampire infestation, the more pressing issue of the conversation, I thought.

"I wonder you should select a snow-storm to ramble about in. Do you know that you run the risk of being murdered in the marshes? People far more familiar than you with these moors often miss the road on such a day and are never seen again."

So he was aware. . . . "If staying here would be an imposition, perhaps I can get a guard from among your lads to escort me home, and he might stay at the Grange until morning. With weapons, perhaps? I fear I'm not so good with a sword." I laid my hand on the tiny silver dagger I wore on my belt. Little protection should a swarm descend upon me. Perhaps I should reconsider the benefits of a garlic necklace. Who was I to question wiser heads who had known and feared vampires for generations?

"No, I could not."

"Indeed?" I drew back, surprised by his reply. "You would turn me out to certain death?"

"Are you going to make the tea?" demanded he of the shabby coat.

"Is he going to have any?" she asked, appealing to Heathcliff. "I see no need to waste good tea if he's to walk out into the moors and be drained of every drop of—"

"Get it ready!" Heathcliff uttered so savagely that I felt no longer inclined to call him a capital fellow. I wondered if I needed to consider the rumors again. Had I stepped from fang to fang?

When the tea preparations were finished, he invited me to join the others around the table. There was an austere silence while I watched Mrs. Heathcliff make a separate pot of tea from a second container for Mr. Heathcliff. I wanted to sniff it for garlic, fearing it contained naught, but I dared not. Instead, we all digested our meal: a dry wedge of cheese that bore teeth marks of mice, a crock of jellied eels, hardtack at least as old as Joseph, and a splendid length of blood sausage.

Afraid I had caused the cloud of grim silence, I thought I should make an effort to dispel it, and after a false start, I began. "It is strange," I said between swallowing the last of one cup of tea and receiving another. Heathcliff, I noted, took food on his plate and added sugar to his tea, but he neither drank nor ate. "Odd," I continued, "how custom can mold our tastes and ideas. Many could not imagine the existence of so isolated a society, surrounded by hostile hives of vampires, Mr. Heathcliff. Yet I venture to say, that surrounded by your family and your amiable lady—"

"My amiable lady!" he interrupted with an almost diabolical sneer.

For a moment, I feared he would bare fangs.

"Where is she, my amiable lady?"

"Mrs. Heathcliff, your wife, I mean."

"So you suggest her spirit has taken the post of ministering angel and guardian of Wuthering Heights, even when her body is drained of blood and gone? Is that it? She watches us from the grave?"

Perceiving my blunder, I attempted to correct it. I should have seen that there was too great a disparity of years between them. He was forty. She looked no more than seventeen. Then it flashed upon me. The clown in the bloody coat was her husband. Heathcliff, junior, of course.

"Mrs. Heathcliff is my daughter-in-law," said Heathcliff, corroborating my surmise. He turned as he spoke, a look of hatred in his eyes as he gazed at her.

"Ah, certainly," I stumbled on, turning to my neighbor. "I see now; you are the favored possessor of the beauteous lady."

This was worse than before; the youth grew crimson and clenched his fist and I began to have second thoughts as to whose blood it was upon his coat. Rather than a vampire's, did it belong to the last neighbor who came for tea?

"Poor conjecture, again, sir!" observed my host. "Neither of us have the privilege of owning your fair lady. Her husband is deceased."

"And this young man is . . ."

"Not my son, assuredly!"

"My name is Hareton Earnshaw," growled the young man.

"I meant no disrespect," I said, noting the dignity with which he announced himself. Perhaps he was a vampire slayer, a good one, and thus the conceit.

Earnshaw fixed his eye on me longer than I cared to return the stare for fear I might be tempted to box his ear, and then he would be tempted to run me through with a sword meant to impale blacker hearts than mine.

The business of eating being concluded, and no one uttering another word of sociable conversation, I glanced out a window to examine the weather and take in the sights, worldly or otherwise.

I saw before me the dark night coming in prematurely, sky and hills mingled in bitter wind and suffocating snow. It was a perfect haven for vampires in search of heat and nourishment of human blood!

"I don't think it possible for me to get home now, with or without a guard," I exclaimed. "The roads are buried already, and I could scarcely distinguish a foot in front of me. I could walk right into the arms of one of those beasts and not know it until their hellish fangs pierced my throat."

"Hareton, drive the sheep into the barn porch. They'll be fed upon if left in the fold all night," Heathcliff said. "I don't care to go out again tonight and we've lost two this week, already."

"And what must I do?" I rose with irritation. How was it that my host was so protective of the blood of sheep and not a paying tenant? "How am I to get home safely?"

There was no reply to my question as Mrs. Heathcliff leaned over the fireplace, restoring the tea canisters to their place, and Joseph entered with a pail of porridge of sheep bones and hooves to feed the dogs.

"I wonder how ye can stand there in idleness, when all

of them gone out!" Joseph cried. "But you'll never mend yer ill ways, but go right to the devil, like yer mother before ye!"

For a moment, I thought this piece of eloquence was addressed to me, and enraged, I stepped toward the aged rascal, my hand upon my tiny dagger with the intention of piercing him.

Mrs. Heathcliff, however, checked me by her answer.

"You scandalous old hypocrite!" she replied. "Are you not afraid of being tossed among the bloodsuckers? I warn you not to provoke me, or I'll turn you out of this house myself and then we will see how far you get."

"Wicked! Wicked!" Joseph declared. "May the Lord deliver me from evil."

"Too late for that." She pointed to the window. "Be off, or I'll hang you by your thumbs from the outer wall and let them feed on you until you are fully drained. They will do it if he lets them, and let them he might. You know I speak the truth!"

The woman put a malignity into her beautiful eyes, and Joseph drew back in sincere horror and hurried out.

I didn't know quite what she meant by all of that, but wanting to be on my way, I pleaded, "Mrs. Heathcliff, could you point out some landmarks to guide me home?"

"Take the road you came," she answered, dropping into her chair. "It is as sound advice as I can give."

"Then if you hear of me being discovered dead in a bog or pit of snow, sucked dry of my fluids, your conscience won't whisper that it is partly your fault?"

"Certainly not. Do you expect me to provide you safe passage, wielding my sword?" she mocked.

*As if women carried swords!*

"Surely there are men here in training who can fend off if not kill, should the necessity arise," I questioned.

"Who are these *men in training?* There is himself, Earnshaw, Zillah, Joseph, and I, and I guarantee you the master of this abode would not step across the lane to save your neck."

"Are there no trained boys at the farm? Living in such an isolated place, surely—"

"No trained boys. Just us."

"What of Joseph? He knows the way."

"Not Joseph!" Her head snapped up. "Not after dark. Nay, you do not want Joseph after dark. Trust me, good sir."

Her remark was odd, but I was entirely too vexed to consider her meaning. "Then, welcome or not, I am compelled to stay."

"That you must settle with your host. I have nothing to do with it."

"I hope it will be a lesson to you, to make no more rash journeys on these hills, without first finding your own guard," cried Heathcliff's stern voice from the kitchen entrance. "As to staying here, I don't keep accommodations for visitors; you must share a bed with Hareton."

"I can sleep on a chair in this room," I replied.

"No, no. A stranger is a stranger, be he rich or poor. It will not suit me to permit anyone to roam my home in the middle of the night!"

My patience was at end. In disgust, I pushed past him into the yard, running against Earnshaw in my haste. It was so dark I could not see the means of exit, but I smelled the blood upon his coat, thick and cloying.

At first, the young man appeared about to befriend me.

"I'll go with him as far as the park," Hareton said. "Past the worst of them."

"And you'll go with him to hell!" Heathcliff flung back. "You are not up to the fight of such numbers. You never will be! And who is to look after the horses, then, eh?"

I drew myself up indignantly. "A man's life is of more consequence than those of horses."

Heathcliff did not seem to hear me, for he was still upon

the boy. "They will not kill you, you know; they will make you one of them!"

"Well, somebody must go," murmured Mrs. Heathcliff, more kindly than I expected. "For this is poor hospitality to a neighbor and tenant."

"Not at your command!" retorted Hareton.

"Then I hope his pale ghost will haunt you; and I hope Mr. Heathcliff will never get another human tenant, till the Grange is a ruin and swarming with the devils!" she answered sharply.

Joseph, toward whom I had been steering, muttered something under his breath. He sat within earshot, milking the cows by the light of a lantern, which I seized unceremoniously. Calling out that I would send it back on the morrow, I rushed to the nearest door.

"Master, he's thieving the lantern!" shouted the ancient.

On opening the little door, two cloaked vampires flew at my throat, bearing me down and extinguishing the light. As I flailed on the ground, trying to protect my neck, I heard a mingled guffaw from Heathcliff and Hareton.

Fortunately, the creatures seemed more bent on taunting me and tearing at my clothing than devouring me alive. *Well-fed vampires at Wuthering Heights?*

But, oh, the stench of the creatures! When recounting a tale of attack and escape, victims fail to mention the foul scent of rotting flesh, putrid blood, and black, wet humus that wafts from them. "Help me!" I managed. Tucking in a ball to further protect my jugular, I was forced to lie till the malignant master of the abode pleased to deliver me. One bark of Heathcliff's voice and the beasts leapt off me and disappeared into the snow-driven swirl of darkness, curls of smoke, gone as fast as they had come. Then, hatless and trembling with a mixture of fear and wrath, I ordered the miscreants to let me out—on their peril to keep me one minute longer.

The vehemence of my agitation brought on copious bleeding at the nose, and still Heathcliff laughed, and still I scolded, made bold by my first true escape from death. I don't know what would have concluded the scene had there not been one person at hand rather more rational than myself, and more benevolent than my entertainer. This was Zillah, the stout housewife, who entered the room to inquire into the nature of the uproar.

"Are you going to allow folk to be murdered on our very door-stones? Look at the lad, he's fair choking! Wisht, wisht!" She waved to me. "Come in, and I'll see to that. There now, hold ye still."

With these words she splashed a pint of icy water into my face and pulled me into the kitchen. Mr. Heathcliff followed, his accidental merriment expiring quickly in his habitual moroseness.

I was dizzy and faint, realizing I had not even drawn my dagger to defend myself. What man was I! In this state, I was compelled to accept lodgings under Heathcliff's roof. He told Zillah to give me a glass of brandy, and then passed on to the inner room, whereby I was somewhat revived and ushered to bed.

# Chapter 3

While leading the way upstairs, Zillah recommended that I should hide the candle and not make a noise, for her master had an odd notion about the chamber she would put me in, and he never willingly let anybody lodge there.

I asked the reason.

She didn't know for certain, but the girl in the kitchen had told her that the ghost of a lady vampire haunted it. Zillah doubted the story because the silly chit was a known liar. Zillah said she'd only lived at Wuthering Heights a year, and they had so many queer goings-on with the vampires hanging about the outbuildings and peering in the windows that she wasn't sure she cared to know the truth about the room. She said this position was far better than her last near London, where the vampires actually entered the dwelling and killed a kitchen maid and the master's ugliest daughter. Zillah went on further to tell me, as we climbed the dark, dank-smelling stairwell, that it had been her experience that the vampires here at Wuthering Heights rarely attacked, and when they did, the injury was almost never fatal. There were whispers that the Master Heathcliff had some nature of power over them.

"Of course, then there is the matter of Joseph to keep

them somewhat content," she uttered, glancing over her shoulder at me.

I held a rag to my bloody nose. "What of Joseph?"

"Some things are better left alone."

And alone she left me. Zillah took her leave and I fastened my door and glanced round for the bedchamber, wondering if I should expect a coffin. But surely she would have warned me had there been a coffin instead of a bed. Fortunately, the whole furniture consisted of a chair, a clothespress, and a large oak case, with squares cut out near the top, resembling coach windows. The chamber had a thick dampness about it, and deep shadows draped in folds against the walls. My candle cast a feeble light against the gloom. I held it high and peered around me, fearing the worst.

No coffin.

Approaching the odd structure, I looked inside and discovered it to be a singular sort of old-fashioned couch, very conveniently designed. The clever piece formed a little closet, and the ledge of a window, which it enclosed, served as a table.

I slid back the paneled sides, got in with my light, pulled them together again, and felt secure against the vigilance of Heathcliff and anyone and everyone who might be lurking. I couldn't call the space cozy, but I liked it far better than the parlor. Here, no hounds were ready to rip me apart, and no Joseph with who knows what evil plot simmering in his black heart. And here, I had shelter both from the snow and the ever-present danger of the vampires that apparently roamed at will here in the moors.

The ledge, where I placed my candle, had a few mildewed books piled up in one corner, and it was covered with writing scratched on the paint. This writing, however, was nothing but a name repeated in all kinds of characters, large and small—*Catherine Earnshaw*, here and there varied to *Catherine Heathcliff,* and then again to *Catherine Linton.*

Listlessly, I leaned my head against the window. My nose having ceased bleeding, I tucked away the rag for possible later need. Staring at the writing in the paint, I continued spelling over Catherine Earnshaw—Heathcliff—Linton, till my eyes closed; but they had not rested five minutes when a glare of white letters, dripping blood, started from the dark, as vivid as specters—the air swarmed with Catherines. Rousing myself to dispel the obtrusive name, I discovered my candlewick reclining on one of the antique volumes and perfuming the place with an odor of roasted calfskin.

I snuffed it off, and, very ill at ease under the influence of cold and lingering nausea, sat up and spread open the injured tome on my knee. It was a Testament, in lean type, and smelling dreadfully musty: a flyleaf bore the inscription "Catherine Earnshaw, her book," and a date some quarter of a century back.

I shut it, and took up another, and another, till I had examined them all. Catherine's library was select, and its state of dilapidation proved it to have been well used, though not altogether for a legitimate purpose. Scarcely one chapter had escaped a pen-and-ink commentary—at least, the appearance of one—covering every morsel of blank that the printer had left.

Some were detached sentences, other parts took the form of a regular diary, scrawled in an unformed, childish hand. At the top of an extra page, I was greatly amused to find an excellent caricature of my friend Joseph, rudely yet powerfully sketched in the form of a hideous bloodsucking creature with fangs that nearly reached his waist.

An immediate interest kindled within me for the unknown Catherine, and I began to decipher her faded hieroglyphics.

\*   \*   \*

*An awful Sunday!* commenced the paragraph beneath. *I wish my father had not succumbed to that last nasty vampire attack and were back again. Hindley is a detestable substitute—his conduct to Heathcliff is atrocious— he has no idea what or who he is crossing. H. and I are going to rebel—we took our initiatory step this evening.*

*All day had been flooding with rain; we could not go to church, so Joseph got up a congregation in the garret. While Hindley and his wife basked downstairs before a comfortable fire, doing anything but reading their Bibles, Heathcliff, myself, and the unhappy plough-boy were commanded to take our prayer-books. We were set in a row on a sack of corn, groaning and shivering, and hoping that Joseph would shiver, too, so that he might give us a short homily. A vain idea! The service lasted precisely three hours, and yet my brother had the face to exclaim, when he saw us descending—*

*'What, done already?'*

*On Sunday evenings we used to be permitted to play, if we did not make much noise; now a mere titter is sufficient to send us into corners!*

*'You forget you have a master here,' says the tyrant. 'I'll demolish the first who puts me out of temper! I insist on perfect sobriety and silence. Frances, darling,' he said to his wife. 'Pull the boy's hair as you go by.'*

*Frances pulled Heathcliff's hair heartily, and then went and seated herself on her husband's knee, and there they were, kissing and talking nonsense by the hour.*

*We made ourselves as snug as our means allowed in the arch of the dresser. I had just fastened our pinafores together, and hung them up for a curtain, when in comes Joseph, on an errand from the stables. He tears down my handiwork, boxes my ears, and croaks—*

*'Your own father just buried and the Sabbath not over, and you dare play your silly games. Shame on ye! Sit*

*down. There's good books to be read. Sit down, and save yer souls!'*

I could not bear the employment. I took my dingy volume and hurled it into the dog kennel, vowing I hated a good book.

Heathcliff kicked his to the same place. Then there was a hubbub!

'Master Hindley!' shouted our self-made chaplain. 'Master, come quick! Miss Catherine's ripped the back off The Helmet of Salvation, *and Heathcliff's put his foot into the first part of* The Broad Way to Destruction! *The old man would have beat them soundly for such a crime—but he's gone!'*

Hindley hurried up from his paradise on the hearth, and seizing one of us by the collar, and the other by the arm, hurled both into the back kitchen.

I reached for this book, and a pot of ink from the shelf, and pushed the house door ajar to give me light, and I have got the time on with writing for twenty minutes. Heathcliff is impatient, though, and proposes that we should appropriate the dairy woman's cloak and have a scamper on the moors, where he can practice the deadly arts he is secretly acquiring.

I suppose Catherine fulfilled her project, for the next sentence took up another subject.

How little did I dream that Hindley would ever make me cry so! *she wrote.* My head aches, till I cannot keep it on the pillow, and still I can't give over. Poor Heathcliff! Hindley calls him a vagabond and won't let him sit with us, nor eat with us anymore. He says he and I must not play together. Most tragic of all, he has forbidden Heathcliff to practice the skills necessary to fight the vampires running rampant on the moors. My brother threatens to turn him out of the house if we break his orders.

*He has been blaming our father (how dared he?) for
treating H. too liberally, and he swears he will reduce him
to his right place.*

I began to nod drowsily over the dim page, hearing the
sound of a branch of a fir tree touch my window as the
blast wailed by and rattled against the panes. I listened an
instant, detected the disturber, then turned and dozed, and
dreamt.

I remembered I was lying in the oak closet, only it was
now a silk-lined casket, and I heard distinctly the gusty
wind and the driving of the snow. I heard, also, the fir
bough repeat its teasing sound, but it annoyed me so much
that I resolved to silence it. I rose from my grave and endeavored to unhasp the casement. The hook was soldered
into the staple, a circumstance observed by me when
awake, but forgotten.

"I must stop it, nevertheless!" I muttered, knocking my
knuckles through the glass and stretching an arm out to
seize the branch, instead of which, my fingers closed on
the fingers of a little, ice-cold hand!

The intense horror of nightmare came over me. I tried
to draw back my arm, but the hand clung to it, and a most
melancholy voice sobbed—

"Let me in—let me in!"

"Who are you?" I asked, struggling to disengage myself.

"Catherine Linton," it replied shiveringly. "I'm come
home. I'd lost my way on the moor and been chased by the
bloodthirsty devils!"

As it spoke, I discerned a child's pale face, her neck
punctured and bleeding freely, staring through the window. Terror made me cruel, and, finding it useless to attempt shaking the creature off, I pulled its wrist onto the
broken pane and rubbed it to and fro till the blood ran
down and soaked the bedclothes. Still it wailed, "Let me

in!" and maintained its tenacious grip. Horror gripped me at the icy touch of the unholy thing!

"How can I!" I said. "You must let *me* go, if you want me to let you in!"

The fingers relaxed, I snatched mine through the hole, hurriedly piled the books up in a pyramid against it, and stopped my ears to exclude the lamentable prayer.

I seemed to keep them closed above a quarter of an hour; yet, the instant I listened again, there was the doleful cry moaning on!

"Begone!" I shouted. "I'll never let you in, not if you beg for twenty years."

"It is twenty years," mourned the voice. "Twenty years. I've been a fed-upon for twenty years! Dead but not dead."

The feeble scratching outside began anew, and the pile of books moved as if thrust forward.

I tried to jump up, but could not stir a limb in the tight confines of my death chamber, and so I yelled aloud, in a frenzy of fright.

To my confusion, I discovered the yell was not ideal. Hasty footsteps approached my chamber door; somebody pushed it open with a vigorous hand, and a light pierced the top of my coffin, which had transformed into a bed again. I sat shuddering and wiping the perspiration from my forehead. The intruder appeared to hesitate, and muttered to himself.

At last he said in a half-whisper, plainly not expecting an answer, "Is anyone here?"

I opened the panels to confess my presence, and I shall not soon forget the effect my action produced.

Heathcliff stood near the entrance, in his shirt and trousers, with a candle dripping over his fingers, and his face as white as the wall behind him. The first creak of the oak startled him like an electric shock: the light leapt from his hold to a distance of some feet, and his agitation was so extreme that he could hardly pick it up.

"It is only your guest, sir. I had the misfortune to scream in my sleep, owing to a frightful nightmare. I'm sorry I disturbed you."

He blinked and seemed to fall from his trance. "God confound you, Mr. Lockwood! Who showed you up to this room?" he demanded, crushing his nails into his palms and grinding his teeth. "Who was it? I've a good mind to turn them out of the house this moment!"

"It was your servant, Zillah," I replied, flinging myself out of the bed and pulling on my coat. "I should not care if you did, Mr. Heathcliff; she richly deserves it. I suppose that she wanted to get another proof that the place was haunted, at my expense. Well, it is—swarming with ghosts and goblins! You have reason in shutting it up, I assure you!"

"What do you mean?" asked Heathcliff. "And what are you doing? Lie down and finish out the night, since you are here. But for heaven's sake, don't repeat that horrid noise. Nothing could excuse it, unless you were having your arteries sapped!"

"If the little fiend had got in at the window, she probably would have bitten me!" I returned. "I'm not going to endure the persecutions of your hospitable ancestors again. That minx, Catherine Linton, or Earnshaw, or however she was called—she must have been a changeling—human turned vampire—wicked little soul! She told me she had been walking the earth these twenty years, a just punishment for her mortal transgressions, I've no doubt!"

Scarcely were these words uttered, when I recollected the association of Heathcliff's with Catherine's name in the book, which had completely slipped from my memory. I blushed at my inconsideration, but, without showing further consciousness of the offense, I hastened to add—

"The truth is, sir, I passed the first part of the night in spelling over the name scratched on that window ledge. A monotonous occupation, calculated to set me asleep, like counting or—"

"What *can* you mean by talking this way to *me?*" thundered Heathcliff with savage vehemence. "How—how *dare* you, under my roof?" And he struck his forehead with rage.

I did not know whether to resent this language or pursue my explanation, but he seemed so powerfully affected that I proceeded with my re-telling of my dream.

Heathcliff gradually fell back into the shelter of the bed as I spoke, finally sitting down almost concealed behind it. I guessed, however, by his irregular and intercepted breathing that he struggled to vanquish an excess of violent emotion.

"Not three o'clock yet!" I remarked, continuing to dress. I was unsure of where I was going, but quite sure I would not stay there. "I could have taken oath it had been six. Time stagnates here; we must surely have retired to rest at eight!"

"Always at nine in the winter, and always rising at four," said my host, suppressing a groan. "Mr. Lockwood," he added. "You may go into my room. You'll only be in the way, coming downstairs so early, and your childish outcry has sent sleep to the devil for me."

"And for me, too," I replied. "I'll walk in the hall till daylight, and then I'll be off. I am now quite cured of seeking pleasure in society, be it country or town. A sensible man ought to find sufficient company in himself."

"Take the candle, and go where you please, then," Heathcliff muttered. "I'll join you directly. Keep out of the yard, though. The dogs are unchained to keep back the uninvited."

I obeyed, leaving the chamber, but unsure as to which

way to go, I turned back and found myself an involuntary witness to the rather strange behavior of my landlord.

Thinking himself alone, no doubt, he got onto the bed and wrenched open the lattice, bursting, as he pulled at it, into an uncontrollable passion of tears.

"Come in! Come in!" he sobbed. "Catherine, do come. Oh do—*once* more! Oh! My heart's darling! Hear me *this* time, Catherine, at last!"

The specter showed a specter's ordinary caprice. It gave no sign of its existence, but the snow and wind whirled wildly through, even reaching me and blowing out the light.

There was such anguish in the gush of grief that accompanied Heathcliff's raving that my compassion made me overlook its folly. I descended cautiously to the lower floor and landed in the back kitchen, where a gleam of fire enabled me to rekindle my candle. Nothing was stirring except a brindled, gray cat, which crept from the ashes and saluted me with a mew.

Two benches, shaped in sections of a circle, nearly enclosed the hearth. I stretched myself on one, and the cat mounted the other. We were both of us nodding off when Joseph shuffled down a wooden ladder that vanished in the roof, through a trap. He cast a sinister look at me and swept the cat from its bench, and bestowing himself in the vacancy, began stuffing a three-inch pipe with tobacco. I let him enjoy the luxury undisturbed. After sucking out the last wreath, and heaving a profound sigh, he got up and departed as solemnly as he came.

A more elastic footstep entered next, and I opened my mouth for a "good morning," but closed it again. Hareton Earnshaw was directing a curse at every object he touched while he rummaged in a corner. He glanced over the back of the bench, dilating his nostrils, but made no more attempt at exchanging civilities than the cat had.

When he came up with a spade, I guessed that he meant to use it to dig through the snow. Thinking that I was about to be escorted home, I made ready to follow him. He noticed this and thrust at an inner door with the end of his spade, intimating that there was the place where I must go.

It opened into the house, where the females were already astir. Zillah was urging flakes of flame up the chimney with a colossal bellows, and Mrs. Heathcliff, kneeling on the hearth, read a book by the aid of the blaze.

She held her hand interposed between the furnace heat and her eyes, and seemed absorbed in her occupation. I was surprised to see Heathcliff there also. He stood by the fire, his back toward me, just finishing a stormy scene to poor Zillah.

"And you, you worthless—" he broke out as I entered, turning to his daughter-in-law and employing an epithet. "There you are, at your idle tricks again? The rest of them earn their bread, but you live on my charity! Put your trash away, and find something to do, you damnable jade."

"I'll put it away because you can make me, if I refuse," answered the young lady, closing her book and throwing it on a chair. "But I'll not do anything else, except what I please!"

Heathcliff lifted his hand, and she sprang to a safer distance, obviously acquainted with its sting.

Having no desire to be entertained by a cat-and-dog combat, I stepped forward briskly, as if eager to take in the warmth of the hearth. Each had enough decorum to suspend further hostilities. Heathcliff placed his fists out of temptation, in his pockets. Mrs. Heathcliff curled her lip and walked to a seat far off, where she remained silent during the remainder of my stay.

That was not long. I declined joining their breakfast, and, at the first gleam of dawn, took the opportunity of escaping into the free air, now clear and still, and cold as impalpable ice.

My landlord hallooed for me to stop, ere I reached the bottom of the garden, and offered to accompany me across the moor. It was well he did, for the whole hill was one billowy white ocean. The snow had filled the swells, reshaped the rises, blotting out the chart which my yesterday's walk left pictured in my mind.

The day before, I had noticed on one side of the road, at intervals of six or seven yards, a line of upright stones, continued through the whole length of the barren. But, excepting a dirty dot pointing up here and there, all traces of their existence had vanished, and my companion found it necessary to warn me frequently to steer to the right or left, when I imagined I was following, correctly, the windings of the road.

We exchanged little conversation, saw no sign of any vampires, and he halted at the entrance of Thrushcross Park, saying I could make no error there. Our adieux were limited to a hasty bow, and then I pushed forward, trusting to my own resources.

I managed to make my way to my door, losing myself among the trees several times, but fortunately, not falling into a nest of sleeping vampires or sinking up to the neck in snow. At any rate, whatever were my wanderings, the clock chimed twelve as I entered the house.

My housekeeper and her staff rushed to welcome me, exclaiming that they had completely given me up. Everybody conjectured that I had been drained of my blood last night, and they were wondering how they must set about the search for my remains or if the vampires would even have bothered to leave a morsel behind. I bid them be quiet now that they saw me returned unbitten and unscathed, and, benumbed to my very heart, I dragged upstairs.

# Chapter 4

What vain fools we are! Determined to be content with my own company and scorn social interaction, I settled in a remote place. But, after maintaining till dusk a struggle with low spirits and solitude, I was finally compelled to summon Mrs. Dean, for I was frightfully bored. I hoped she would prove a regular gossip while I ate the supper she brought me, and either rouse my interest or lull me to sleep by her talk.

"You have lived here a considerable time," I commenced. "Did you not say sixteen years?"

"Eighteen, sir. I came when the mistress was married, to wait on her. After she died, the master retained me for his housekeeper."

"Indeed."

She paused and I feared she was not a gossip. Unless about her own affairs, and those could hardly interest me. What I wished to know was what history rested upon Wuthering Heights and the odd crew who lived there under the stern hand of my landlord.

However, she studied me for a moment and then, with a fist on either knee and a thoughtful look on her weathered face, she spoke. "Ah, times are greatly changed since then!"

"Yes," I remarked. "Those early days must have been

peaceful and quiet, before the vampire infestation. You've seen a good many changes, I suppose?"

"I have. And troubles, too," she said.

*Oh, I'll turn the talk on my landlord's family now!* I thought to myself. *A good subject to start—and that pretty girl-widow, I would like to know her history.* With this intention, I asked Mrs. Dean why Heathcliff left Thrushcross Grange and preferred living in a situation and residence so much inferior. "Is he not rich enough to keep the estate in good order?" I inquired.

"Rich, indeed!" she returned. "He has nobody knows what money, and every year it increases. Yes, yes, he's rich enough to live in a finer house than this."

"He had a son, it seems?"

"Yes, he had one—he is dead."

"And that young lady, Mrs. Heathcliff, is his widow?"

"Yes."

"Where did she come from originally?"

"Why, sir, she is my late master's daughter; Catherine Linton was her maiden name. I nursed her, poor thing! I wish Mr. Heathcliff would have come here and then we might have been together again, she and I."

"Catherine Linton?" I exclaimed, astonished. *Surely not the ghostly Catherine.* A chill skittered down my spine. If only I could tell this good woman what I had seen. . . . "Then my predecessor's name was Linton?"

"It was."

"And who is that Earnshaw, Hareton Earnshaw, who lives with Mr. Heathcliff?"

"He is the late Mrs. Linton's nephew."

"The young lady's cousin, then?"

"Yes. Heathcliff married Mr. Linton's sister."

"I saw the house at Wuthering Heights has 'Earnshaw' carved over the front door. Are they an old family?"

"Very old, sir, and Hareton is the last of them, as our Miss Cathy is of us—I mean the Lintons."

"What of the cloaked figures carved over the door? They could not possibly be vampires, could they? Not with a date so long ago. The bloodsuckers have only come to England in the last, what, forty years?"

"I can give you no explanation of the carvings," she said, tight-lipped. But then her manner changed. "So you have been to Wuthering Heights? I beg your pardon for asking, but I should like to hear how she is."

"Mrs. Heathcliff looked very well, and very handsome, yet, I think, not very happy."

"Oh dear, I don't wonder!" She narrowed her gaze. "And how did you like the master?"

"A rather rough fellow, Mrs. Dean."

"Rough as a saw-edge, and hard as whinstone! The less you meddle with him, the better."

"He must have had some ups and downs in life to make him such a churl." I thought about the rumors of him being vampire. Of his aversion to the garlic tea we had partaken. But I didn't dare ask outright. Maybe because I didn't want to learn the truth, or maybe because I was enjoying too greatly the unraveling of the mysteries of Wuthering Heights and my surrounding countryside. "Do you know anything of his history?"

"I know all about it, except where he was born, and who were his parents. No one knows that but the devil, I think."

"Well, Mrs. Dean, it will be a charitable deed to tell me something of my neighbors, so be good enough to sit and chat an hour."

"Oh, certainly, sir! I'll just fetch a little sewing, and then I'll sit as long as you please."

The woman bustled off, and I crouched nearer the fire. My head felt hot, and the rest of me cold, but I was excited by the prospect of hearing the sad tale of Wuthering Heights and its occupants.

The housekeeper returned, bringing a basket of work, and drew in her seat, evidently pleased to find me so companionable.

"Before I came to live here," she commenced—waiting for no further invitation to her story—"I was almost always at Wuthering Heights. My mother had nursed Mr. Hindley Earnshaw, that was Hareton's father, and I got used to playing with the children. I ran errands, too, and helped to make hay, and hung about the farm ready for anything that anybody would set me to. Those were good days, before the beasties set upon us.

One fine summer morning Mr. Earnshaw, the old master, came downstairs dressed for a journey. After he had told Joseph what was to be done during the day, he turned to Hindley, and Cathy, and me—for I sat eating my porridge with them—and he said, speaking to his son,

'Now, my bonny man, I'm going to Liverpool today. What shall I bring you? You may choose what you like, only let it be little, for I shall walk there and back. It's sixty miles each way and a long spell!'

Hindley named a fiddle, and then he asked Miss Cathy. She was hardly six years old, but she could ride any horse in the stable, and she chose a whip.

He did not forget me, for he had a kind heart, though he was rather severe sometimes. He promised to bring me a pocketful of apples and pears, and then he kissed his children, said good-bye, and set off.

It seemed a long while to us all—the three days of his absence—and little Cathy often asked when he would be home. Mrs. Earnshaw expected him by supper-time on the third evening, and she put the meal off hour after hour. There were no signs of his coming, however, and at last the children got tired of running down to the gate to look. Then it grew dark and she would have put them to bed, but they begged to be allowed to stay up. Just about eleven o'clock, the door latch raised quietly and in stepped the master. He threw himself into a chair, laughing and groaning, and bid them all stand off, for he was nearly killed. He said he would not have such another walk for the three kingdoms.

'I was near frightened to death!' he exclaimed. 'It's true, the rumors. The vampires have set upon our country. Twice, no, three times, I encountered them on my way home, and it was only by my luck and the bad luck of others that I was not attacked.'

'My dear husband, you must tell me what happened!' cried the lady of the house.

'Not here. Not now.' He eyed the children. 'Later.' Then he opened his great-coat, which he held bundled up in his arms.

We crowded round, and over Miss Cathy's head I had a peep at a dirty, ragged, pale, black-haired child, big enough both to walk and talk. His face looked older than Catherine's, yet when he was set on his feet, he only stared round, and repeated over and over again some gibberish that nobody could understand. I was frightened, and Mrs. Earnshaw was ready to fling him out of doors. She demanded of Mr. Earnshaw how he could bring that gypsy brat into the house when they had their own bairns to feed and fend for? Those were the days before it was widely known that the best vampire slayers were gypsies and that the gypsies had some sort of powers over the vampires.

Mrs. Dean held up a gnarled finger. "But Mr. Earnshaw, he was a wise man. A learned man he was, and he read books about the blood-seeking creatures and the threat they posed in various regions. He knew what was coming.

"The master tried to explain the matter without frightening his wife with tales of vampires, I think, but he was really half dead with fatigue and did not have the patience for her. All that I could make out, amongst her scolding, was a tale of his seeing the boy starving and houseless in the streets of Liverpool. Not a soul knew to whom he belonged, he said, and both his money and time being limited, he thought it better to take the child home with him at once.

The conclusion was that my mistress grumbled herself calm, and Mr. Earnshaw told me to wash the boy, give him clean things, and let him sleep with the children.

Hindley and Cathy contented themselves with looking and listening till peace was restored, then both began searching their father's pockets for the presents he had promised them. Hindley was a boy of fourteen, but when he drew out what had been a fiddle, crushed to morsels in the great-coat, he blubbered. And Cathy, when she learned the master had lost her whip in attending to the stranger, showed her humor by spitting at the little boy. That bit of nasty behavior earned a sound blow from her father. 'Rather you should love him,' said the master. 'For it was his warning that saved me. While traveling home, our traveling party was ambushed. Together, he and I hid in a haystack until the fiends had sucked the life's blood from my other companions.'

Mrs. Dean looked at me earnestly. "I remember clearly, sir, as if it had only just happened. The master believed the boy had saved his life and that it was the great spilling of blood that kept the vampires from sniffing them out. They say the beasties smell the way they hear, with supernatural powers!"

"Really?" I asked, enthralled with the tale. "Master Earnshaw believed the gypsy had saved him? Shouldn't that have changed his wife and family's opinion of the foundling?"

"Should and would are often far apart," she replied

philosophically as she began to stitch a nightcap, drawing
her needle in and out as she continued her story.

"The Earnshaw children entirely refused to have the
gypsy boy in bed with them or even in their room, so I put
him on the landing of the stairs, hoping he might be gone
on the morrow. Instead, he crawled into Mr. Earnshaw's
bedchamber and was found at the foot of the bed when
daylight came.

They christened him 'Heathcliff.' It was the name of a
son who died in childhood, and it has served him ever
since, both for Christian and surname.

Miss Cathy and he became very thick, but Hindley
hated him, and to say the truth I did the same. In those
days, we didn't realize how badly the moors would become infested with the vampires, or how greatly we would
need the slayers."

"So the boy was of slayer stock?" I exclaimed. "I knew
it!" I wanted to ask how the rumor could have started that
he was a vampire, if all knew he was a gypsy, but I didn't
dare.

"No one knew for sure what he was, except us, below-
stairs." She looked up at me. "A matter of speech, you understand, sir, for no one could abide long in the cellars of
Wuthering Heights. There are dark tunnels there, you see,
and a great, dark hole covered with an iron slab. Some say
the hole leads to hell." She began to stitch again. "Not
that I'm superstitious, you understand, but some do say
it."

"Well, it certainly makes sense. The gypsy orphan knowing to hide in the haystack whilst the others were slain," I
agreed. As for the entrance to hell she described, I was unsure what I thought, but I was too eager to have her continue to allow her to digress too far. "Tell me more about
the child Heathcliff," I urged, sliding up in my comfortable chair.

He seemed a sullen, patient child who had an aversion to the few sunny days we saw on these moors. He was hardened, perhaps, to the ways of his people, we would guess later. He would stand Hindley's blows without winking or shedding a tear, as if he had hurt himself by accident and nobody was to blame.

This endurance made old Earnshaw furious when he discovered his son was persecuting the poor, fatherless child. He took to Heathcliff strangely, believing all he said. There seemed some bond between them we did not understand.

So, from the very beginning, Heathcliff bred bad feelings in the house. At Mrs. Earnshaw's death two years later, the young master had learnt to regard his father as an oppressor rather than a friend, and Heathcliff as a usurper of his father's affections, and he grew bitter with brooding over these injuries.

I sympathized awhile, but when the children fell ill of the measles, and I had to tend them, I changed my idea of Heathcliff. He was dangerously sick; however, I will say this, he was the quietest child that I ever watched over. The difference between him and the others forced me to be less partial. Cathy and her brother harassed me terribly; *he* was as uncomplaining as a lamb, though hardness, not gentleness, made him give little trouble." She knotted her thread, threaded her needle once more, and began to hem the lace around the outside of the cap. "It made me certain he was a gypsy brat. They aren't like us, sir. Not even human, perhaps."

"But he recovered," I prompted, wanting to hear more facts firsthand.

"He got through, and the doctor affirmed it was in a great measure owing to me, and praised me for my care. I softened toward Heathcliff, and thus Hindley lost his last ally. Still, I couldn't dote on Heathcliff, and I wondered often what my master saw to admire so much in the sullen boy, who never, to my recollection, repaid his indulgence by any sign of gratitude. He was not insolent to his bene-factor; he was simply unfeeling, but he had only to speak and Mr. Earnshaw would bend to his wishes.

As an instance, I remember Mr. Earnshaw and the chil-dren once met upon a band of gypsies at a parish fair. The gypsies noticed young Heathcliff at once and it came about that they knew him and they knew his poor dead mother. The tale told was that the boy became lost in Liverpool from the others and was thought dead. When Heathcliff learned the tale, he begged that he should go with the gypsies to meet his relations and, at first, Mr. Earnshaw forbid it.

'Gypsy!' taunted Hindley, cuffing him heartily when his father walked away. 'Orphan, gypsy.'

'Tell him to let me go with them,' Heathcliff insisted, al-lowing himself to be pummeled again and again, 'or I will speak of these blows and you'll get them from your father with interest.'

'Off with you, dog!' cried Hindley, threatening him with an iron weight used for weighing potatoes and hay in one of the market stalls.

'Throw it,' Heathcliff replied, standing still, 'and then I'll tell how you boasted that you will turn me out of doors as soon as he dies, and see whether he will not turn you out directly.'

Hindley threw it, hitting Heathcliff on the breast. The boy fell, but staggered up immediately, breathless and white. The master did come along at that very moment and, taking pity, sent young Earnshaw home and allowed Heathcliff to catch up to the gypsies and go along.

I do not know what the boy did that day and night with the gypsies, but I can tell you he returned a different boy. He somehow seemed darker, but carried a confidence I sometimes found frightening. As he entered the barn upon his return, Hindley demanded to know where he had been and what the gypsies had told him of his parentage. When Heathcliff did ignore the request, Hindley knocked him off his feet. I was surprised to witness how coolly the child gathered himself and sat down on a bundle of hay to overcome the qualm which the violent blow occasioned, before he entered the house to announce his return. I persuaded him easily to let me lay the blame of his bruises on a new horse purchased only the day before at the fair: he minded little what tale was told since he had gotten what he wanted in going with the strangers. He complained so seldom, indeed, of such stirs as these with Hindley that I really thought him not vindictive."

Again, Mrs. Dean met my gaze. "I was deceived completely, as you will later hear."

# Chapter 5

In time, of course, Mr. Earnshaw began to fail. He had been active and healthy, yet his strength left him suddenly, and when he was confined to a chair in the corner, he grew grievously irritable. He became preoccupied by the growing number of vampires in the countryside and worried what would become of his children. We understood that the vampires were flooding into England and Scotland from their native land of Transylvania, where human blood was becoming scarce, but none knew what to do about it. Mr. Earnshaw could not sleep or eat for his obsession with the bloodsuckers. All day he filled journals with plans for strengthening the defenses at Wuthering Heights, and at night he burned candle after candle to the nub. By then, he was barely able to walk without the steady arm of a companion. His temper flared over the smallest things, and even though his body had grown weak, he could still rage with the roar of a charging bull. Nothing would make him so furious as some suspected slight of his authority.

This was especially true concerning Heathcliff. He had come to believe that the orphan lad could do no wrong, and he believed that the rest of the household was jealous. In his sickness, he became certain that because he liked

Heathcliff, all hated him and longed to do him ill. In truth, the master's favor did more harm to the boy than good. To have peace in the house, we all humored Heathcliff. That is never best for any child. Giving him what he demanded without question turned a gentle, grateful lad to a youth full of pride and black tempers. As expected, Heathcliff and Hindley clashed. Perhaps there was jealousy of the love Mr. Earnshaw showered on the foundling, but denied his own son. We'll never know. But our peaceful home became a battleground as Hindley defied his father again and again, rousing the old man to fury. In a fit of rage, Mr. Earnshaw would seize his cane to strike Hindley, and his son would heap scorn on him, moving out of range of the ivory-handled weapon. More than once, we feared the master's terrible wrath would be the death of young Earnshaw.

It was a bad time for all. Two households of our small church were ravished by the bloodsuckers. The small son of the butler at Grievegate Hall, not fifteen miles from here, was sent to fetch cheese from their well house at twilight. Six years of age was all he possessed. The child had run the distance a thousand times, yet on that night, he was snatched up by a heartless vampire. When they found poor Georgie, he was as pale as clabber, and two great wounds gaped on his throat."

"The child was dead?" I asked, horrified and fascinated in the same blink of an eye. "Murdered by vampires?"

"Worse," the woman hissed. "Shortly after his recovery, he was found sinking his teeth into pigeons. Then it was rats and larger animals. The family did all they could, but little Georgie was lost to the darkness. When he sucked a parlor maid dry and went for his little sister, his own father surrendered him to the authorities."

"To be imprisoned?" I pleaded, although I knew what the penalty for murder was, even for a child.

"Not that." She shrugged her shrunken shoulders. "What else could be done? Once they get the taste of human blood, even a servant's blood, they will hunt. And even a six-year-old vampire has the strength of three human men. Sadly, it is kill or be killed."

"Sadly," I echoed. Then raised my gaze to her again. "Go on."

At last, our curate, who taught the little Lintons and Earnshaws their numbers and letters, advised that Hindley should be sent away to college to be educated and to learn skills in fighting the vampires. All knew the threat would be greater as time passed, and this was becoming a necessary part of a young man's education. Mr. Earnshaw agreed, though with a heavy spirit, for he said—

'Hindley will never succeed no matter how many schools we send him to. It isn't in his nature to defend those who cannot defend themselves. He is my son and it shames me to utter such words,' the old man muttered. 'But Hindley will be nearly useless should the vampires sweep the moors and invade Wuthering Heights. He doesn't have it in his soul in the manner that Heathcliff does,' he insisted, rapping his stick. 'Heathcliff is the one who will save our immortal souls in the end!'

With the boy gone, I hoped heartily we would have peace. It hurt me to think the master would regret his own good deed by bringing the gypsy orphan home. And we might have got on tolerably, notwithstanding, but for two people, Miss Cathy and Joseph. You saw old Joseph, I dare say, up yonder. He was more religious in those days. He used the word of God to heap praise on his own head and flung curses on his neighbors.

Mrs. Dean waggled her finger. "I was suspicious of him, even then. There was something about Joseph's manners that smelled of the undead. The way he never seemed to fear the beasties the way the rest of us did. The way the

animals began to regard him, too. It was if he knew what
was to come."

"What was to come?" I echoed.

Mrs. Dean shook her head, ignoring my question, pressing on. "Joseph was relentless about ruling the children
rigidly. He encouraged Mr. Earnshaw to regard Hindley as
a reprobate, and, night after night, he regularly grumbled
out a long string of tales against Heathcliff and Catherine.
He took care to flatter the master's weakness for the gypsy
by heaping the heaviest blame on Catherine.

Certainly, the girl tried our patience fifty times a day.
From the hour she came downstairs till the hour she went
to bed, we had not a minute when we didn't suspect she
was into mischief. She was always speaking nonsense,
stuff I think Heathcliff secretly poured into her head. She
spoke of a day when women would defend their homes
and children against the vampires at their places beside the
men. Her spirits were always high, her tongue always
going—singing, laughing, and plaguing everybody who
would not do the same. A wild, wicked slip she was, and
as daring as the devil himself, but she had the bonniest
eyes and the sweetest smile.

She was much too fond of Heathcliff, even then. All day
long they were about in the moors. They were seen fighting with wooden swords, she playing a victim strayed
from the path, attacked by a vampire, and he was always
the savior. It was then that young Heathcliff began to slip
away some nights. Gone a day or two at a time, and her
worrying herself sick over his whereabouts."

Mrs. Dean leaned closer. "With the gypsies is where I
think he was. Taking up training far superior to what the
young master was learning in college. And learning not
just ways to fight them, but to outsmart them, to command them, to coax them into doing his bidding. But Miss
Cathy didn't like Heathcliff gone, not even for a night. The

greatest punishment we could invent was to separate them, yet she got chided more than any of us on his account.

Now, Mr. Earnshaw did not understand jokes from his children; he had always been strict and grave with them. His peevish reproofs wakened in her a naughty delight to provoke him. She was never so happy as when we were all scolding her at once, and she defying us with her bold, saucy look and her ready words. She would turn Joseph's religious curses into ridicule, baiting me, feigning to have been chased by vampires, or worse, bitten by them. She would pretend to be possessed by the spirit of them, be one of them. Back then, we barely even knew such a curse was possible; all remembered the fate of the butler's son at Grievegate Hall. We knew all too well that if you were misfortunate enough to be caught and fed on for too long, you died or were turned into one of them. And as was with poor Georgie, who could know if our dear Catherine had been bitten? She was a constant handful and a worry. After behaving as badly as possible all day, she sometimes came sweetly to make it up at night. And who could deny her . . . who but her own father?

'Nay, Cathy,' the old man would say. 'I cannot love thee; thou'rt worse than thy brother. Go, wipe the blood that I know is not really blood from your neck, say thy prayers, child, and ask God's pardon. I doubt thy mother and I must rue that we ever reared thee!' That made her cry, at first; and then, being continually rejected hardened her, and she laughed if I told her to say she was sorry for her faults.

But the hour came, at last, that ended Mr. Earnshaw's troubles on earth. He died quietly in his chair one October evening, seated by the fireside. A high wind blustered round the house and roared in the chimney. It sounded wild and stormy, yet it was not cold. We were all together—I, a little removed from the hearth, busy at my knitting, and Joseph reading on vampires near the table. Miss Cathy had been sick, and that made her still; she leant against her father's knee, and Heathcliff was lying on the floor with his head in her lap.

I remember the master, before he fell into a doze, stroking her bonny hair—it pleased him rarely to see her gentle—and saying, 'Why canst thou not always be a good lass, Cathy?'

And she turned her face up to his, and laughed, and answered, 'Why cannot you always be a good man, father?'

But as soon as she saw him vexed again, she kissed his hand and said she would sing him to sleep. She began singing very low, till his fingers dropped from hers and his head sank on his breast. Then I told her to hush, and not stir, for fear she should wake him. We all kept as mute as mice a full half-hour; and should have done longer, only Joseph, having finished his reading, got up and said that he must rouse the master for prayers and bed. He stepped forward, and called him by name, and touched his shoulder, but he would not move, so he took the candle and looked at him.

I thought there was something wrong as Joseph set down the light, and seizing the children each by an arm, whispered them to go upstairs.

'I shall bid Father good night first,' said Catherine, putting her arms around his neck before we could stop her.

The poor thing discovered her loss directly and she screamed out, 'Oh, he's dead, Heathcliff! Father's dead!'

And they both set up a heartbreaking cry.

I joined my wail to theirs, loud and bitter, but Joseph asked what we could be thinking of to roar in that way over a saint in heaven.

He told me to put on my cloak and run for the doctor and the parson, taking care. Vampires had been seen lurking at dusk, and the previous night a goat had gone missing. I could not guess of what use either the doctor or the parson would be then. However, I went, through wind and rain, looking forever over my shoulder, praying I would not be devoured, and brought the doctor back with me. The parson said he was not traveling the roads with the vampires flying about and that he would come in the morning.

Leaving Joseph to explain matters, I ran to the children's room. Their door was ajar. I saw they had never lain down, though it was past midnight, but they were calmer and did not need me to console them. The little souls were comforting each other with better thoughts than I could have offered. No parson in the world ever pictured heaven so beautifully as they did, in their innocent talk of slaying vampires all over the world until there were none left to bedevil good folk. And, while I sobbed and listened, I could not help wishing we were all there in their make-believe world, safe together.

# Chapter 6

Mr. Hindley came home to the funeral and set the neighbors gossiping right and left. He brought a wife with him. What she was, and where she was born, he never informed us, but she probably had neither money nor a name, or he would never have kept the union from his father.

The wife didn't disturb the house much on her own account. Every object she saw and every circumstance that took place around her appeared to delight her—except the preparations for the old master's burial, and the presence of so many mourners to be fed and entertained. It seemed like everyone in the county came to the funeral, mostly neighbors, and a few strangers. The strangers were the ones I kept an eye on. It was just around that time that enterprising vampires began to take the part of Godly folk; one mistake and you could wind up having a new acquaintance for afternoon tea, and them having a sip of your blood for supper.

But back to the young missus. In my opinion, sir, I thought the woman half silly in her behavior. She ran into her chamber, and made me come with her, and there she sat shivering and clasping her hands, and asking repeatedly, 'Are they gone yet?'

Then she began describing with hysterical emotion the effect it produced on her to see black, and she fell a-weeping. I asked what was the matter and she said she was afraid of dying herself. She greatly feared death at the hands of the vampires that she had heard plagued the moors! Her dear mother warned her not to come, forbidding her to marry young Earnshaw, and now she feared her good mother might have been right.

I imagined her as little likely to die of an attack as myself. The wife was rather thin, but young, and fresh complexioned, and her eyes sparkled as bright as diamonds. We could both run, if it was a dire necessity. In those days, it was only the sickly or elderly or feeble-minded the vampires preyed upon. Would that were the case now, for these are a cunning, diabolical race of bloodsuckers that hunt us now.

Why, only three Sundays past, the strangest case did unfold in the village of Crumpton-on-Ween, not two days' walk from here. I had the whole tale from my sister Bess, who had it from the butcher's wife, who had the misfortune to live in the town. She's not a Quaker, you understand, but good Church of England, but there are Quakers in Crumpton-on-Ween. 'Tis said that the Quakers have an odd sort of service. Mostly they sit in silence and pray, on occasion rising to speak aloud some thought that has come to them.

"Do you not think it unnatural, Mr. Lockwood?"

"No, I do not," I piped in. "I have in my scope of acquaintances several men of the Quaker persuasion, and I find them quite sensible and pious gentlemen."

"Perhaps these be a different lot," Mrs. Dean suggested diplomatically. "In any case, the butcher's wife's niece said that two strangers in black entered a service whilst it was in progress and took seats on the back bench near the door. The meeting house lay in shadows that day, the weather being inclement and the Quakers quite sparing of their candles, so the congregation was unable to see their visitors clearly. And by and by, an elderly gentleman sitting on the very same bench, a wool merchant by trade, was seen to fall into a deep sleep. Then the two strangers moved forward, taking places directly in front of the slumbering wool merchant."

"Mrs. Dean, I don't see how—"

"Did I mention they were all in black?" She bunched up the nightcap she was stitching in her hands in her excitement to tell the story. "Black hats, black cloaks, black boots and trousers. Their hair, their eyes, the deepest black. Anyway, the service was a long one, and halfway through, after the visitors had moved up three rows, another stranger entered the meeting house. He took a seat at the back of the room, near to the sleeping wool merchant, but within the space of two minutes, he gave a cry that brought the worshipers to their feet. Down went the elderly wool merchant, a Mr. Uriak Wittlebalm by name, not sleeping but dead. Every drop of his blood drained out of him! Out came the most recent arrival's sword, and he—a gypsy vampire slayer in disguise—fell upon the two strangers with great shouts and the flashing of blades."

"My word," I breathed. "So the two visitors were—"

"How clever you are, sir, to see at once what they were," she said, not allowing me to voice my deduction. "They'd not have pulled the wool over your eyes, had you been there, I'm certain. But as I was saying, the strangers leapt up and sprang at the gypsy slayer, fangs bared. A terrible battle ensued, and before the end came, it was discovered that not one, but five of the Quakers had been murdered by the two fiends. Five dead, including Mr. Wittlebalm, and a master thatcher near to dead from loss of blood."

"And did this slayer succeed? Did he destroy the foul villains?"

"Such strength they had! Only by a stroke of luck that the wool merchant was oft to take a drop of spirits for his health did the slayer have a chance. The vampires had drunk so much of his blood and the blood of other parishioners who must have had a nip or two to fight the cold that the creatures became so in their cups that they could not put up their usual show of strength."

"So the gypsy slayed them both?"

Mrs. Dean rose to shovel more coal into the fire. "One through the heart with his silver-bladed sword. The second, he would have but the beastie leapt from a window and vanished into the chestnut woods. The slayer tried to assemble a group to go after him, but none of the parishioners had the fortitude."

"The nerve of them, to enter a house of worship," I observed. "Five dead in such a short time."

She peered at me over her shoulder from where she crouched before the fire. "Aye, sir, come to dinner, as it were. If not for the gypsy slayer, they might have drained the entire congregation."

"And you take this tale to be the truth?" Mrs. Dean, being the sort she was, I wondered if her stories needed to be taken with a grain of salt.

"True as earth, word for word as I heard it." She settled back in her chair and picked up her stitching again.

"Frightening that the vampires should be so bold as to invade a place of worship on a Sunday," I pronounced.

"Indeed. It makes me nervous to sit through service ever since." She snipped a bit of thread between her sharp little incisors and I took note that she seemed to have unusually fine teeth for a woman her age. None blackened or broken, and none missing that I could see. It was a rare condition among those of her class.

"I'll sit by no strangers, I wager that." She touched her

throat. "Sad, indeed, that one cannot even feel safe in church."

"But you were telling me about Mr. Hindley's new wife." I redirected her back to the tale that interested me most. "When she first arrived at Wuthering Heights."

That I was. I must say I had no impulse to sympathize with her. We don't take to foreigners, here, Mr. Lockwood, unless they take to us first. If that's one thing we've learned from the infestation, and the tales that come from towns like Crumpton-on-Ween, it's that the unknown should not be welcomed. That's how they first got in, you know, though few care to admit it. From their own ravaged countryside they came, making noises of changed ways and feeding off animals. But it's still humans they prefer, though in a pinch they will take a sheep or two, even dogs.

Young Earnshaw was altered considerably in the three years of his absence. He had grown sparer, and lost his color, and spoke and dressed quite differently, so differently that some whispered with wonder if he had already fallen under the spell of the beasties. They were in the cities as well, you know, despite what the young missus might have said. But I never thought he had been made vampire. Nor did I think he had followed with the training to fight them that his good father—God rest his soul—had sent him to obtain.

On the very day of his return, Hindley told Joseph and me we must thenceforth quarter ourselves in the kitchen, and leave the house for him. The young missus expressed pleasure, at the beginning, at finding a sister among her new acquaintance. She prattled to Catherine and ran about with her, and gave her all sorts of presents. Her affection tired very soon, however, when she learned how the young miss traipsed about the moors, near daring the vampires to take her, even lifting a sword, on occasion. Eventually the wife withdrew her affection from Catherine and grew peevish, and then Hindley became tyrannical. A few words from her were enough to rouse in him all his old hatred he held for Catherine and Heathcliff. He drove the boy from their company to the servants', deprived him of his school books, and allowed him only pease porridge, the rinds of cheese, and stale crusts at supper. The lad who had led the life of a gentleman's favored child was put to coarse labor outside, compelled to muck stalls, skin and butcher livestock, clear fields of stones, and dig fresh pits for the necessary. From dawn until night, poor Heathcliff had to work harder than any other lad on the farm, and him not fed more table scraps than would keep a stoat alive.

"And did he accept this turn of fate, poor lad?"

Heathcliff bore his degradation pretty well at first because Cathy taught him what she learnt, and worked or attended him in the fields when he practiced his arts of defense and attack. They both promised fair to grow up as rude as savages, the young master being entirely negligent how they behaved and what they did, so they kept clear of him. I do not believe Mr. Hindley even suspected the boy was training to defend the manor. I know for a fact that he did not take notice the days when the boy disappeared to be among his gypsy relatives, returning with even sharper skills.

It was one of Heathcliff and Catherine's chief amusements to run away to the moors on a Sabbath morning and remain there all day, playing vampire or lost maid and slayer, and the after punishment if caught grew a mere thing to laugh at. The teacher might set as many chapters as he pleased for Catherine to memorize, and Joseph might thrash Heathcliff till his arm ached, but they forgot everything the minute they were together again.

One Sunday evening, they were banished from the sitting room for making a noise or some other light offense, and when I went to call them to supper, they were nowhere to be found. We searched the house, the yard, and the stables; they were invisible. At last, Hindley told us to bolt the doors against the night, and swore nobody should let Cathy and Heathcliff in until morning for fear they might bring the beasties with them.

The household went to bed, but too anxious to lie down, I opened my shutters and put my head out to hear them, should they return. I would have let them in. I knew Heathcliff would not let the vampires inside. I had already seen how they feared him, respected him, or both. Only days before, I had seen him talk a vampire down, getting him to turn over a calf and walk down the lane without so much as a mouthful of blood.

In a while, that night, I distinguished running steps coming up the road, and the light of a lantern glimmered through the gate, a trail of vampires howling near behind. I threw a shawl over my head and ran to prevent them from waking Mr. Earnshaw with their snarls and howls. Heathcliff fought them off at the gate and sent them flying into the night, and he did enter then, by himself. It gave me a start to see him alone.

'Where is Miss Catherine?' I cried hurriedly, stanching the blood that ran from a wound on his arm. 'No accident, I hope?'

'She's at Thrushcross Grange,' he answered, wiping clean the black blood from a long-bladed sword. I did not know where the sword had come from and I did not dare ask. 'I would have been there, too, but they had not the manners to ask me to stay.'

'Well, you will catch it!' I said. 'You'll never be content till you're sent away for good. What in the world led you to wandering to Thrushcross Grange in the dark? You know the vampires congregate between here and there.'

'I'm not afraid of them,' he boasted. 'They are afraid of me.'

'And so they were chasing you down the lane,' I muttered. Either he did not hear me or he chose to ignore my jibe.

'Let me get off my wet clothes, and I'll tell you all about it, Nelly,' he replied, handing me the deadly sword.

I bid him beware of rousing the master, and while he undressed and I waited to put out the candle, he continued.

'Cathy and I escaped from the wash-house to have a ramble at liberty and, getting a glimpse of the Grange lights, we thought we would just go and see whether the Lintons passed their Sunday evenings standing shivering in corners, while their father and mother sat eating and drinking, and singing and laughing.

'We ran from the top of the Heights to the park, without stopping—Catherine completely beaten in the race, because she was barefoot. You'll have to seek her shoes in the bog tomorrow. We crept through a broken hedge, groped our way up the path, and planted ourselves on a flowerpot under the drawing-room window. The light came from there; they had not put up the shutters, and the curtains were only half closed. Both of us were able to look in by clinging to the ledge, and we saw—ah! it was beautiful—a splendid place carpeted with crimson, and crimson-covered chairs and tables, and a pure white ceiling bordered by gold, a shower of glass-drops hanging in silver chains from the center, and shimmering with little soft tapers. Old Mr. and Mrs. Linton were not there; Edgar and his sister had it entirely to themselves. Shouldn't they have been happy? We should have thought ourselves in heaven! And now, guess what the children were doing? Isabella—I believe she is eleven, a year younger than Cathy—lay screaming at the farther end of the room, shrieking as if the vampires were sinking their fangs into her. Edgar stood on the hearth weeping silently, and in the middle of the table sat a little dog, shaking its paw and yelping, which, from their mutual accusations, we understood they had nearly pulled in two between them. The idiots! That was their pleasure! To quarrel who should hold a heap of warm hair, and each began to cry because both, after struggling to get it, refused to take it. We laughed outright at the petted things; we did despise them! When would you catch me wishing to have what Catherine wanted? I'd not exchange, for a thousand lives, my condition here, for Edgar Linton's at Thrushcross Grange—not if I might have the privilege of tying Joseph to the front gate and painting the house-front with Hindley's blood to lure the beasties to him!'

'Hush, hush!' I interrupted, fearing the master might hear him. 'Still you have not told me, Heathcliff, how Catherine is left behind?'

'I told you we laughed,' he answered. 'The Lintons heard us, and they shot like arrows to the door; there was silence, and then a cry, "Oh, Mamma, Mamma! Oh, Papa! Oh, Mamma, come here. Oh, Papa, oh!" They really did howl out something like that. We made frightful noises to terrify them still more, trying to sound like vampires scratching at the window and then we dropped off the ledge, thinking we had better flee. I had Cathy by the hand, and was urging her on, when all at once one of the blood-suckers, a particularly ugly fellow I had encountered in the moors earlier in the week, fell upon her, dragging her down.

' "Run, Heathcliff, run!" she cried. "He holds me!"

'The devil had seized her ankle, Nelly. I heard his abominable snorting. But Cathy did not yell out—no! She would have scorned to do it, if she had been spitted on the horns of a mad cow. I did, though. I vociferated curses enough to annihilate any fiend in Christendom, regretting that I had left my sword at the edge of the drive that leads up to the Grange. Without a weapon, I got a stone and thrust it between her attacker's jaws, and tried with all my might to cram it down his throat. A servant came up with a lantern, at last, swinging a hoe, shouting, "Keep fast, beast of Satan, keep fast!"

'He changed his note, however, when he saw the vampire's game, which was not to kill, but maim. The beast was throttled off, his huge purple tongue hanging half a foot out of his mouth, and his pendant lips steaming with bloody slaver. Then another servant threw a bowl of ground garlic at the creature and it fled.

'The manservant picked Cathy up. She was sick, not from fear, I'm certain, but from pain. Fortunately, the crude beast had bitten her ankle, not her neck, and had barely fed upon her! The servant carried her in; I followed, grumbling vengeance. I had let the vampire live that week, only to have him attack my Catherine! He would die, and those he cared for with him!

' "What prey, Robert?" hallooed Linton from the entrance.

' "The gap-toothed vampire that lurks at the gate has caught a little girl, sir," he replied. "And there's a lad here," he added, making a clutch at me. "He looks dangerous. It's likely robbers were for putting them through the window to open the doors to the gang after all were asleep, that they might murder us at their ease. Hold your tongue, you foul-mouthed thief, you! You shall go to the gallows for this. Mr. Linton, sir, don't lay by your gun."

' "No, no, Robert," said the old fool, Linton. "Oh, my dear Mary, look here! Don't be afraid, it is but a boy—yet the villain scowls so plainly in his face."

'He pulled me under the chandelier, and Mrs. Linton placed her spectacles on her nose and raised her hands in horror. The cowardly children crept nearer also, Isabella lisping, "Frightful thing! Put him in the cellar, Papa. He looks exactly like the son of the gypsy slayer that stole my tame pheasant. Doesn't he, Edgar?"

'While they examined me, Cathy came round. She heard

the last speech and laughed. Edgar Linton, after an inquisitive stare, recognized her. They see us at church, you know, though we seldom meet them elsewhere.

' "That's Miss Earnshaw!" he whispered to his mother, "and look how the vampire has chewed on her—how her foot bleeds!"

' "Miss Earnshaw? Nonsense!" cried the dame. "Miss Earnshaw scouring the country with a gypsy! And yet, my dear, the child is in mourning—sure it is—and she may be lamed for life!"

' "How careless is her brother!" exclaimed Mr. Linton, turning from me to Catherine. "I've understood from neighbors that he lets her grow up in absolute heathenism, running about the moors with gypsy vampire slayers. But who is this? Where did she pick up this companion? Oho! I declare he is that strange acquisition my late neighbor made, in his journey to Liverpool."

' "A wicked boy, at all events," remarked the old lady, "and quite unfit for a decent house! Did you notice his language, Linton? I'm shocked that my children should have heard it."

'I recommended cursing—don't be angry, Nelly—and so Robert was ordered to take me off. I refused to go without Cathy, but he dragged me into the garden, pushed the lantern into my hand, and sent me on my way.

'I ran back for my sword, should the vampire return, and I resumed my station as spy. If Catherine had wished to return, I intended shattering their great glass panes to a million fragments to reach her.

'She sat on the sofa quietly. Mrs. Linton took off the gray cloak of the dairy maid, which we had borrowed for our excursion, shaking her head and expostulating. She was a young lady, and they made a distinction between her treatment and mine. Then the woman-servant brought a basin of warm water and washed Cathy's feet, and Mr.

Linton mixed a tumbler of negus, and Isabella emptied a
plateful of cakes into her lap, and Edgar stood gaping at a
distance. Afterward, they dried and combed her beautiful
hair, and gave her a pair of enormous slippers, and
wheeled her to the fire. I left her, as merry as she could be,
dividing her food between herself and a little dog whose
nose she pinched as she ate. I saw her eyes full of stupid
admiration; she is so immeasurably superior to them—to
everybody on earth, is she not, Nelly? Why would she admire them?'

'There will more come of this business than you reckon
on,' I answered, covering him up and extinguishing the
light. 'You are incurable, Heathcliff, and Mr. Hindley will
have to proceed to extremes, see if he won't.'

My words came truer than I desired. The luckless adventure made Earnshaw furious. And then Mr. Linton, to
mend matters, paid us a visit himself on the morrow and
read the young master such a lecture on the road he guided
his family.

Heathcliff received no flogging, but he was told that the
first word he spoke to Miss Catherine should see him driven
from Wuthering Heights. Mrs. Earnshaw undertook to keep
her sister-in-law in due restraint when she returned home,
employing art not force, for with force she would have
found it impossible.

# Chapter 7

Cathy stayed at Thrushcross Grange five weeks, until Christmas. By that time her ankle was thoroughly cured, and her manners much improved. The mistress visited her often, and began a plan of reform with fine clothes and flattery, which Cathy took readily. So, instead of a wild, hatless little savage jumping into the house and rushing to squeeze us all breathless, a very dignified person with brown ringlets falling from the cover of a feathered beaver hat lighted from a handsome pony.

Hindley lifted her from her horse, delighted. 'Why, Cathy, you are quite a beauty! I should scarcely have known you. You look like a lady now.'

I removed Catherine's coat and beneath she wore a grand plaid silk frock, white trousers, and burnished shoes, and, while her eyes sparkled joyfully when the dogs came bounding up to welcome her, she hardly touched them, fearing they might soil her splendid garments.

She kissed me gently. Then she looked round for Heathcliff. 'Is Heathcliff not here?' she demanded, pulling off her gloves and displaying fingers wonderfully whitened from staying indoors.

'Heathcliff, you may come forward,' ordered Mr. Earnshaw. 'You may come and wish Miss Catherine welcome, like the other servants.'

Cathy, catching a glimpse of her friend, flew to embrace him. She kissed him seven or eight times on his cheek and then drawing back, burst into laughter. 'How very black and cross you look! Heathcliff, have you forgotten me?'

Shame and pride threw double gloom over his countenance and kept him immovable.

'Shake hands, Heathcliff,' said Mr. Earnshaw, condescendingly.

'I will not,' replied the boy, finding his tongue at last. 'I will not stand to be laughed at.'

Miss Cathy seized him again before he could escape. 'I did not mean to laugh at you,' she said. 'Heathcliff, shake hands, at least! What are you sulky for? It was only that you looked odd. If you wash your face, and brush your hair, it will be all right, but you are so dirty!'

I must tell you that if Heathcliff was careless and uncared for before Catherine's absence, it was ten times worse now. His clothes were dirty and covered with dry blood from wandering the moors. I could not say when he had last bathed. Truthfully, he had been gone from Wuthering Heights more than he had been there—where, I didn't know, but I could guess. Gypsy slayers had been camping in the area, and while the vampires had been bold only weeks before, they were quieter again, keeping to themselves and the shadows.

Catherine gazed at Heathcliff's soiled fingers and then at her dress, which he had dirtied where he touched her.

He snatched his hand away. 'I shall be as dirty as I please, and I like to be dirty, and I will be dirty.'

With that he dashed out of the room, leaving Catherine unable to comprehend how her remark had made him so angry.

After playing lady's maid to the newcomer, and putting my cakes in the oven, and making the house and kitchen cheerful with great fires, befitting Christmas Eve, I sat down to amuse myself by singing carols. Mr. and Mrs. Earnshaw were engaging Missy's attention by gay trifles bought for her to present to the little Lintons, as an acknowledgment of their kindness.

They had invited them to spend the next day at Wuthering Heights, and the invitation had been accepted, on one condition: Heathcliff must be banned from coming in contact with the Linton offspring.

Smelling the rich scent of heating spices in the kitchen, I remembered how old Earnshaw used to come in when all was tidied, and call me a cant lass, and slip a shilling into my hand as a Christmas gift. From that I went on to think of his fondness for Heathcliff. That naturally led me to consider the poor lad's situation now, and I got up and walked into the court to seek him.

He was not far; I found him in the stable, cornering a young female vampire with the aid of a pitchfork. It hissed and bared ivory fangs, but the gleam in its eyes was more of lust than fierceness, and the amount of white ankle and shapely leg it revealed beneath its gown and cloak bordered on indecent.

'Stay back, Nelly,' he warned, thrusting the tines of the fork in the beastie's direction.

It squealed, cowering, its arms thrust out in an attempt to protect its face.

I drew back, pulling my cloak around me, horrified and yet oddly intrigued at the same time.

'What did I tell you?' Heathcliff demanded of the creature. Her long, stringy black hair was the color of pitch, her eyes black holes, her lips blood red, and when she shrieked, I could see her fangs.

'I told you, you could not pass beyond the outer walls! You take advantage of my Christmas cheer!' he bellowed. 'I throw you and yours a perfectly good sheep and then you dare come after my horses?'

It shrilled in response, almost as if it could speak, but if it could, its language was beyond me.

'I should kill you,' Heathcliff threatened. 'Christmas cheer be damned.' But then he lowered the pitchfork. 'Go, before I change my mind.'

With a hiss, the vampire scurried past me and out into the darkness.

Heathcliff returned the pitchfork to its place along the wall. He said nothing about the vampire, so I said nothing. Instead, I said, 'The kitchen is so comfortable, and Joseph is upstairs. Let me dress you smart before Miss Cathy comes out, and then you can sit together, with the whole hearth to yourselves, and have a long chatter till bedtime.'

I waited, but getting no answer, left him. Catherine supped with her brother and sister-in-law; Joseph and I joined at an unsociable meal, seasoned with his reproofs on one side and sauciness on the other. He seemed in even a fouler mood than usual, though why, I did not know. He kept glancing at the door, as if expecting a visitor. What I would not know until later was that he *had* been, the very same unfortunate *visitor* Heathcliff had just run off. But that is another story.

Cathy sat up late, preparing for the reception of her new friends; she came into the kitchen once to speak to her old one, but Heathcliff was gone. She only stayed to ask what was the matter with him, and then went back.

In the morning he rose early and disappeared into the moors. Seeking the female vampire I had seen the night before? I wondered. He did not reappear till the family were departed for church. Heathcliff's time away from the house seemed to have brought him to a better spirit. He hung about me for a while, and having screwed up his courage, exclaimed—

'Nelly, make me decent. Make me acceptable in appearance so I do not distress Cathy any further.'

'High time, Heathcliff,' I said. 'You *have* grieved Catherine; she's sorry she ever came home, I dare say! It looks as if you envied her because she is more thought of than you.'

The notion of *envying* Catherine was incomprehensible to him, but the notion of grieving her he understood clearly enough.

'Did she say she was grieved?' he inquired, looking very serious.

'She cried when I told her you were off again this morning.'

'Well, *I* cried last night,' he returned, 'and I had more reason to cry than she.'

'Yes, you had the reason of going to bed with a proud heart and an empty stomach,' said I. 'Proud people breed sad sorrows for themselves. And now, though I have dinner to get ready, I'll steal time to arrange you so that Edgar Linton shall look quite a doll beside you. You are younger, and yet, I'll be bound, you are taller and twice as broad across the shoulders. You could knock him down in a twinkling.'

Heathcliff's face brightened a moment, then it was overcast afresh, and he sighed. 'But, Nelly, if I knocked him down twenty times, that wouldn't make him less handsome or me more so.'

'Perhaps you could defend us from a vampire so as to demonstrate your admirable skills and make a fool of Edgar Linton. You could bid return that woman creature you had in the barn and then send her on her way again with a fine thrust of a pitchfork, or your sword. Surely Edgar does not have such skills. One shriek from that beastie and I dare say he would be shaking in his boots.'

'I cannot lure vampires here just to fight them.' He scowled and lowered his head. 'It would not be right.' He sighed. 'Dear Nelly, I wish I had light hair and a fair skin, and was dressed and behaved as well, and had a chance of being as rich as Edgar Linton will be!'

'And cried for mamma, at every turn,' I added. 'And trembled if a vampire so much as crossed his path. Oh, Heathcliff, you are showing a poor spirit! All you must do is clean up and not look so much like a vicious cur. Smooth the lines of your frown. Let the goodness in your soul shine through your black eyes.

'A good heart will help you to a bonny face, my lad,' I continued, 'and now that we've done washing, and combing, and sulking—tell me whether you don't think yourself rather handsome?' I looked into the mirror before him. 'I'll tell you, I do. You're fit for a prince in disguise.'

So I chattered on, and Heathcliff gradually lost his scowl and began to look quite pleasant, when all at once our conversation was interrupted by a rumbling sound moving up the road and entering the court. He ran to the window and I to the door, just in time to behold the two Lintons descend from the family carriage, smothered in cloaks and furs, and the Earnshaws dismount from their horses.

I urged Heathcliff to hasten now and show his amiable humor, and he willingly obeyed, but ill luck would have it that as he opened the door leading from the kitchen on one side, Hindley opened it on the other. They met, and the master, irritated at seeing him clean and cheerful, shoved him back with a sudden thrust, and angrily bid, 'Keep out of the room. You'll be cramming your fingers in the tarts and stealing the fruit.'

'Nay, sir,' I could not avoid answering. 'He'll touch nothing, not he. I suppose he must have his share of the dainties as well as we.'

'He shall have his share of my hand if I catch him downstairs again till dark,' cried Hindley. 'Begone, you vagabond!'

But Heathcliff did not move.

'What!' cried Hindley. 'Wait till I get hold of those elegant locks—see if I won't pull them a bit longer!'

'They are long enough already,' observed Master Linton, peeping from the doorway. 'I wonder they don't make his head ache. It's like a colt's mane over his eyes!'

He intended no insult, but Heathcliff's violent nature was not prepared to endure the appearance of impertinence from one whom he seemed to hate, even then, as a rival. He seized a blade from beneath his coat, one no doubt used to defend himself against the vampires, and drew it under Master Linton's white throat. The young neighbor gave such a cry of fright that it brought Isabella and Catherine hurrying in.

'Heathcliff, no,' Catherine cried, grasping his arm before Hindley could reach him. 'He is not the enemy your blade is intended for.'

Heathcliff slowly lowered the knife. 'But I fear he is,' he whispered. Then he dashed out, Hindley following after him and shouting for Joseph.

Master Linton was fine, not even the skin broken, but his sister began weeping to go home, and Cathy stood by, confounded, blushing for all.

'You should not have spoken to him!' she expostulated with Master Linton. 'He was in a bad temper, and now you've spoilt your visit. He'll be flogged. I hate him to be flogged! Why did you speak to him, Edgar?'

'I didn't,' sobbed the youth. 'I promised Mamma that I wouldn't say one word to him, and I didn't.'

'Well, don't cry,' replied Catherine contemptuously. 'You're not killed. You would be dead on the floor and fodder for the beasties by now if he wanted you so. Don't make more mischief; my brother is coming: be quiet! Give over, Isabella! Has anybody hurt you?'

'There, there, children—to your seats!' cried Hindley,

bustling in. 'That brute of a lad has warmed me nicely. Next time, Master Edgar, take the law into your own fists—it will give you an appetite!'

The little party recovered its equanimity at the sight of the fragrant feast I had prepared for them. They were hungry after their ride, and easily consoled, since no real harm had truly befallen them.

Mr. Earnshaw carved bountiful platefuls, and the mistress made them merry with lively talk. I waited behind her chair, and was pained to behold Catherine, with dry eyes and an indifferent air, commence cutting up the wing of a goose before her.

*An unfeeling child,* I thought to myself. *How lightly she dismisses her old playmate's troubles.* I could not have imagined her to be so selfish.

She lifted a mouthful to her lips, then she set it down again. Her cheeks flushed, tears gushed over them. She slipped her fork to the floor, and hastily dived under the cloth to conceal her emotion. I did not call her unfeeling long. She was in purgatory throughout the day, and wearying to find an opportunity of paying a visit to Heathcliff, who had been locked up by the master.

In the evening we had a dance. Cathy begged that he might be liberated then, as Isabella Linton had no partner; her entreaties were in vain, and I was appointed to supply the deficiency.

We got rid of all gloom in the excitement of the exercise, and our pleasure was increased by the arrival of the Gimmerton Band, mustering fifteen strong: a trumpet, a trombone, clarinets, bassoons, French horns, and a bass viol, besides singers. They go the round of all the respectable houses, and receive contributions every Christmas, and we esteemed it a first-rate treat to hear them. This year, I was pleased to see that they had acquired a guard of gypsy slayers to prevent them being devoured as they crossed the moors. A pretty penny they charge, but worth every cent for one's blood, don't you think? But the gypsies were not allowed inside, no matter how much I pleaded. Instead, they had to bide outside in the cold. They didn't seem to mind, but wrapped their cloaks around them and scanned the house and courtyard with dark, suspicious gazes.

After the usual carols had been sung, we set them to songs and glees. Catherine loved it, too, but she said it sounded sweetest at the top of the steps, and she went up in the dark. I followed. She made no stay at the stairs' head, but mounted farther, to the garret where Heathcliff was confined. She called to him, but he stubbornly declined answering for a while. She persevered, and finally he replied.

I let the poor things converse unmolested, till I supposed the songs were going to cease, and the singers to get some refreshment. Then I clambered up the ladder to warn her.

Instead of finding her outside, I heard her voice within. The little monkey had crept by the skylight of one garret along the roof, into the skylight of the other. It was all I could do to coax her out again.

When she did come, Heathcliff came with her, and she insisted that I should take him into the kitchen and feed him. I set him a stool by the fire and offered him a quantity of good things, but he could eat little. 'Come now, I beg you. 'Tis better than stale crusts and blackbird bone soup that usually makes up your feast.' But he ignored my coaxing, rested his two elbows on his knees, and his chin on his hands, and remained wrapped in dumb meditation.

'What are you thinking?' I asked suspiciously.

'I'm trying to settle how I shall pay Hindley back. I don't care how long I wait, if I can only do it at last. I hope he will not die before I do!'

'For shame, Heathcliff! It is for God to punish wicked people.'

'God won't have the satisfaction that I shall,' he returned. 'I only wish I knew the best way! Toss him to the vampires or dangle him in front of them, letting them slowly drip him dry? No, even that seems too kind.'

"But, Mr. Lockwood, I'm annoyed how I should chatter on at such a rate with you nodding and ready for bed. I could have told Heathcliff's history, all that you need hear, in half a dozen words."

Thus interrupting herself, the housekeeper rose, and set aside her sewing. But I felt incapable of moving from the hearth, and I was very far from nodding.

"Do sit still, another half-hour, Mrs. Dean!" I cried. "You've done right to tell the story leisurely. You must continue in the same manner, for I am interested in every character you have mentioned."

"But the clock is on the stroke of eleven, sir."

"No matter—I'm not accustomed to go to bed in the long hours. One or two is early enough for a person who lies till ten."

"You shouldn't lie till ten. Some say that is a vampire's favorite time of day to feed."

"But I thought the vampires only came out after dark."

"But it would be dark in your bedchamber if you slept till ten and the draperies were drawn," she argued. "Such fate was that of the magistrate's third wife in Chelton Town, who never rose from her bed until the sun was high in the sky. Some said the beasties came down the chimney, others claimed a servant left a window casing unlatched, but when they found the poor dame, she was as white and lifeless as whey. Not only had they sucked her dry, but they had drained every drop from her tame popinjay and left its carcass on her silk pillow."

And she had me half convinced, but I was too eager to hear more of my neighbor than to worry about being devoured mid-morning in my bed. "Nevertheless, Mrs. Dean, resume your chair and continue your tale. And please do not leave anything out. You suggested Joseph was waiting that Christmas Eve for the woman vampire, but you said no more of it."

"I cannot tell you every word spoken, every step taken, or we will be here beyond our deaths." She settled back in her chair. "You must allow me to leap over some three years—"

"No, no, I'll allow nothing of the sort!"

She settled back in her chair, her sewing in her hand again. "Very well, sir. Instead of leaping three years, I will be content to pass to the next summer—the summer of 1778. That is nearly twenty-three years ago."

# Chapter 8

On the morning of a fine June day, my first bonny little nursling, and the last of the Earnshaw stock, was born.

We were busy with the hay in a faraway field when the girl who usually brought our breakfasts came running across the meadow and up the lane, calling me as she ran.

'Oh, such a grand bairn!' she panted out. 'The finest lad that ever breathed! But the doctor says the missus is bad off. He says the vampires have been feeding on her in secret for many months.'

'Feeding on her!' I exclaimed. 'How could that be?' I thought about Joseph and his many odd behaviors, even odd for him, but did not dare even consider the possibility that he could somehow be involved. 'How can that be?' was all I could utter.

'No one knows,' the maid declared with excitement. 'But I heard the doctor tell Mr. Hindley, in her weakened state, she'll be dead before winter. You must come home directly. You're to nurse it, Nelly. You must feed it with sugar and milk, and take care of it day and night.'

'But is she very ill?' I asked, flinging down my rake and tying my bonnet.

'I guess she is, yet she talks as if she thought of living to see it grow a man,' the maid replied. 'She's out of her head for joy, it's such a beauty! If I were her, I'm certain I should not die. I would fight the beasties, I would not let them charm me.' She peered at me more closely, her eyes wide. 'They say that is how it is done. The vampire charms you until you know not what you do. Then he can freely seek your blood!'

'And what did the master say to the doctor?' I inquired, scowling.

'I think he swore, but I paid him no attention. I was straining to see the bairn.'

I hurried eagerly home to admire the babe, though I must say I was very sad for Hindley's sake. I couldn't conceive how he would bear the loss.

When we got to Wuthering Heights, there he stood at the front door. As I passed, I asked how was the baby.

'Nearly ready to run about, Nell!' he replied, putting on a cheerful smile.

'And the mistress?' I ventured to inquire. 'What does the doctor—'

'Damn the doctor!' he interrupted, reddening. 'Frances is quite right; she has encountered no vampires! She'll be perfectly well by this time next week. Are you going upstairs? Will you tell her that I'll come, if she'll promise not to talk? I left her because she would not hold her tongue and the doctor says she must be quiet.'

I delivered this message to Mrs. Earnshaw and she replied merrily—

'I hardly spoke a word, Nelly, and there he has gone out twice, crying. Well, say I promise I won't speak, but that does not bind me not to laugh at him!'

Poor soul! Till within a week of her death that gay heart never failed her. Her husband persisted doggedly in affirming her health improved every day. When the doctor warned him that medicines were useless against long-term bloodletting, followed by the weakened condition of giving birth, he retorted—

'She does not want any more attendance from you! No

beastie ever drank of her blood. It was a fever and it is gone; her pulse is as slow as mine now, and her cheek as cool.'

He told his wife the same story, and she seemed to believe him, but one night, while leaning on his shoulder in the act of saying she thought she should be able to get up tomorrow, her face changed, and she was dead. No one ever said if wounds were found on her neck or other body parts; Mr. Earnshaw would not allow anyone to handle her body, save him.

The care of the child Hareton fell wholly into my hands. Mr. Earnshaw saw to his health, but regarded his son no further. Mr. Earnshaw grew desperate. He neither wept nor prayed; he cursed and defied both God and man.

The servants could not bear his tyrannical and evil conduct long, and they were soon gone. Joseph and I were the only two that would stay. I did not have the heart to leave my charge. Joseph said he remained to hector over tenants and laborers, but I wondered if it was something else that held him there.

The master was seen speaking with the cloaked beasties that lurked in the shadows as daylight fell away at Wuthering Heights, for there were some who could appear in all manner and speech as human; it was only their fangs that gave them away. At first, he only talked to them from high above, in a window's ledge, but later, he grew bolder. I sometimes think he wanted them to take his life. Later, he began to play cards and drink with them, or rather drank alone seated beside them, for they ate or drank nothing but human blood.

The master's bad ways and bad companions formed a pretty example for Catherine and Heathcliff. His treatment of the latter was enough to make a fiend of a saint. And, truly, it appeared as if the lad were possessed of something diabolical at that period. He delighted to witness

Hindley degrading himself past redemption, and became daily more notable for savage sullenness and ferocity.

Word got out that the master of the house was entertaining the vampires and nobody decent came near us, unless Edgar Linton's visits to Miss Cathy might be an exception. At fifteen she was the queen of the countryside. What a haughty, headstrong creature she was! I did not like her, after her infancy was past; she never took an aversion to me, though. She had a wondrous constancy to old attachments; even Heathcliff kept his hold on her affections unalterably.

"That is Edgar Linton's portrait over the fireplace. It used to hang on one side, and his wife's on the other, but hers has been removed, or else you might see something of what she was. Can you make that out?" Mrs. Dean raised the candle, and pointed.

I looked closer and discerned a soft-featured face, exceedingly resembling the young lady at the Heights, but more pensive and amiable in expression. It formed a sweet picture. The long light hair curled slightly on the temples, the eyes large and serious; the figure almost too graceful. Looking at him, I did not wonder how Catherine Earnshaw could forget her first friend for such an individual.

"A very agreeable portrait," I observed to the housekeeper. "Is it accurate?"

"Yes," she answered. "But he looked better when he was animated; that is his everyday countenance."

Catherine had kept up her acquaintance with the Lintons, and as she had no temptation to show her rough side in their company, by her ingenious cordiality toward Mr. and Mrs. Linton, she gained the admiration of Isabella, and the heart and soul of her brother. These acquisitions flattered her from the beginning and led her to adopt a double character without exactly intending to deceive anyone.

Here at Thrushcross Grange, Catherine took care not to act like the wild child she could be, but at home she had little inclination to practice politeness and made no attempt to restrain her unruly nature.

Mr. Edgar seldom mustered courage to visit Wuthering Heights openly. He had a terror of Earnshaw's reputation, and shrank from encountering him, especially once the bloodsuckers became frequent visitors. I think his appearance there was distasteful to Catherine; she was not artful, never played the coquette, and had evidently an objection to Heathcliff and Linton meeting at all. Heathcliff expressed contempt of Linton in his presence, and when Linton spoke of disgust toward Heathcliff, she dared not treat his sentiments with indifference.

I've had many a laugh at her perplexities and untold troubles, which she vainly strove to hide from my mockery. That sounds ill-natured, but she was so proud, it became really impossible to pity her distresses. She did bring herself, finally, to confess, and confide in me, though, as there was no other advisor.

Mr. Hindley had gone from home, one afternoon, and Heathcliff presumed to give himself a holiday. He had reached the age of sixteen then, I think, and without having bad features, or being stupid, he gave an impression of inward and outward repulsiveness that his present aspect retains no trace of.

Catherine and he were still often companions when he could get away, but he had ceased to express his fondness for her in words, and recoiled with angry suspicion from her girlish caresses. He was spending more time among the beasties, not always fighting with them, for he did not always come home bloody and covered in their foul black stench, but doing what, I never knew.

On the before-named occasion, Heathcliff came into the house to announce his intention of doing nothing, while I was assisting Miss Cathy dressing. She had assumed Heathcliff would go to the moors to do whatever it was he did with the beasties, and she imagined she would have the whole place to herself. With this thought in mind, she managed, by some means, to inform Mr. Edgar of her brother's absence, and was preparing to receive him.

'Cathy, are you busy this afternoon?' asked Heathcliff. 'Are you going anywhere?'

'No, it is raining,' she answered.

'Why have you that silk frock on, then?' he said. 'Nobody coming here, I hope?'

'Not that I know of,' stammered Miss. 'But you should be in the moors now, Heathcliff.'

'I'll not work anymore today. I'll stay with you.'

So saying, he went to the fire and sat down. Catherine reflected an instant, with knitted brows. 'Isabella and Edgar Linton talked of calling this afternoon,' she said, after a minute's silence. 'As it rains, I hardly expect them; but they may come, and if they do, you run the risk of being scolded for no good.'

'Order Nelly to say you are engaged, Cathy,' he said. 'Don't choose to spend the afternoon with those silly friends of yours instead of me! I'm on the point, sometimes, of complaining that they—but I'll not—'

'That they what?' cried Catherine, gazing at him with a troubled countenance. 'What are you on the point of complaining about, Heathcliff?'

'Nothing—only look at the almanac on that wall.' He pointed to a framed sheet hanging near the window, and continued. 'The crosses are for the evenings you have spent with the Lintons, the dots for those spent with me. Do you see? I've marked every day.'

Catherine took on a peevish tone. 'And where is the sense of that?'

'To show that I *do* take notice,' said Heathcliff.

'And should I always be sitting with you?' she demanded, growing more irritated. 'What good do I get? What do you talk about? Nothing but the vampires and how you will control them and how you will reign over them one day and other such nonsense. You might be dumb, or a baby, for anything you say to amuse me, or for anything you do, either!'

'You never told me before that you disliked my company, Cathy!' exclaimed Heathcliff with agitation.

'It's no company at all, when people know nothing and say nothing but for boring talk of vampires,' she muttered.

Her companion rose, but he hadn't time to express his feelings further, for a horse's feet were heard on the flagstones, and having knocked gently, young Linton entered, his face brilliant with delight at the unexpected summons he had received.

Doubtless Catherine marked the difference between her friends as one came in and the other went out. The contrast resembled what you see in exchanging a bleak, hilly, coal country for a beautiful, fertile valley, and his voice and greeting were as opposite as his aspect.

'I'm not come too soon, am I?' he said, looking at me. I had begun to wipe the plate and tidy some drawers in the dresser at the far end, for Mr. Hindley had given me instructions that she and Linton were not to be left alone.

'No,' answered Catherine. 'What are you doing there, Nelly?'

'My work, miss,' I replied.

She stepped behind me and whispered crossly, 'When company are in the house, servants don't commence cleaning in the room where they are!'

'It's a good opportunity, now that the master is away,' I answered aloud. 'I'm sure Mr. Edgar will excuse me.'

'I hate you to be fidgeting in *my* presence,' exclaimed the young lady.

'I'm sorry for it, Miss Catherine,' was my response, and I proceeded with my occupation.

She, supposing Edgar could not see her, snatched the cloth from my hand, and pinched me, with a prolonged wrench, very spitefully on the arm.

I've said I did not love her and besides, she hurt me, so I screamed out.

'Oh, miss, that's a nasty trick! You have no right to nip me.'

'I didn't touch you, you lying creature!' she cried, her fingers tingling to repeat the act, her ears red with rage. She never had power to conceal her passion; it always set her whole complexion in a blaze.

'What's that, then?' I retorted, showing a decided purple welt on my arm.

She stamped her foot, wavered a moment, and then slapped me on the cheek, a stinging blow that filled both my eyes with water.

'Catherine, love! Catherine!' interposed Linton, greatly shocked at the violence that his idol had committed.

'Leave the room, Nelly!' she repeated, trembling all over.

Little Hareton, who followed me everywhere, and was sitting near me on the floor, commenced crying himself, and sobbed out complaints against 'wicked Aunt Cathy,' which drew her fury. She seized his shoulders and shook him, and when Linton reached out to interrupt, she boxed him in the ear.

He drew back in consternation. I lifted Hareton in my arms and walked off to the kitchen with him, but still watched through the doorway.

Linton moved to the spot where he had laid his hat.

'Where are you going?' demanded Catherine, advancing to the door.

He swerved aside and attempted to pass.

'You must not go!'

'I must and shall!' he replied in a subdued voice.

'No," she persisted. 'Not yet, Edgar Linton!'

'How can I stay after you have struck me?' asked Linton. 'Next thing I know, you'll be setting your companion beasties after me.'

Catherine was mute.

'You've made me afraid and ashamed of you,' he continued. 'I'll not come here again!'

Her eyes began to glisten. 'Well, go, if you please—get away! And now I'll cry—I'll cry myself sick!' She dropped down on her knees by a chair, and set to weeping in serious earnest.

Edgar persevered in his resolution as far as the court; there he lingered. But then, still hearing her weeping, he turned abruptly, hastened into the house again, and shut the door behind him.

When I went in a while after to inform them that Earnshaw had come home rabid drunk with several *acquaintances* in black cloaks bearing fangs, I saw the quarrel had merely instigated a closer intimacy. Linton had broken the outworks of youthful timidity, and that enabled them to forsake the disguise of friendship, and confess themselves lovers.

# Chapter 9

Hindley entered hurling oaths dreadful to hear, and caught me stowing his son away in the kitchen cupboard. Hareton possessed a wholesome terror of encountering either his father's excessive fondness or his madman's rage. In one, he ran a chance of being squeezed and kissed to death, and in the other, of being flung into the fire or dashed against the wall. Knowing how peculiar his father was and having a bairn's inborn sense of self-preservation, the child was always quiet wherever I chose to put him.

'There, I've found you out at last!' cried Hindley, pulling me back by the skin of my neck, like a dog. 'By heaven and hell, you'll murder that child! I know how it is, now that he is always out of my way. With the help of Satan, I shall throw you to my guests and let them make a meal of you.'

'But I don't like the thought of being sucked dry, Mr. Hindley,' I answered. 'I'd rather be shot, if you please.'

'Wait! Is that my son, Nelly?' Seeming to forget completely his thought of feeding me to the rambunctious guests I could hear in the other room, snarling and hissing, he released me. 'Boy, come here! Let me see your teeth. Are they normal or do you bear fangs like the cloaked ones? Have they put a changeling in place of my son and heir? The teeth will tell.'

Foolishly having come out of the protection of the cupboard, the boy now clung tightly to my skirts.

'Kiss me,' Hindley ordered, grabbing him up. 'Kiss me, Hareton! Damn it, kiss me! By God, as if I would rear such a monster! As sure as I'm living, I'll break the brat's neck.'

Poor Hareton was squalling and kicking in his father's arms with all his might as he carried him upstairs and lifted him over the banister. I cried out and ran to rescue the boy. As I reached them, Hindley leaned forward on the rails to listen to a noise below, forgetting what he had in his hands.

'Who is that?' he asked.

I leaned forward, too, intending to sign to Heathcliff not to come farther. At the instant when my eye left Hareton, he gave a sudden spring, broke free of his father's careless grasp, and tumbled over the railing.

There was scarcely time to experience a thrill of horror before Heathcliff arrived underneath just at the critical moment. By natural impulse, he caught the boy in his arms and set him on his feet. 'There, there, brat, none the worse.' Then he looked up to discover the culprit.

Hindley descended leisurely, sobered. 'This is your fault, Nelly,' he said. 'You should keep the lad out of my sight! You know how he sets my nerves afire. But I've no wish to harm him, just teach him not to act like a wild thing. Is he injured anywhere?'

'Injured!' I cried angrily. 'If he's not killed, he'll be a blithering idiot! It is a wonder his mother does not rise from her grave! You're worse than any of those beasties in the sitting room awaiting your attendance—treating your own flesh and blood in that manner! You might take a lesson from them! At least they protect their little creatures! A pretty state you've come to!'

'I shall come to a prettier, yet, Nelly,' laughed Hindley,

recovering his hardness. 'Convey yourself and the brat away. And you, too, Heathcliff! Else I'll serve all of you to my guests.' He took a pint bottle of brandy from the dresser and poured some into a tumbler.

'Have mercy on your own soul!' I said, trying to snatch the glass from his hand.

But he thwarted me and he drank the spirits and then he was gone.

'It's a pity he cannot kill himself with drink,' observed Heathcliff as the door shut.

'I don't know why those vampires he calls his friends have not sucked him dry,' I remarked. 'Perhaps his blood is too foul for them to digest.'

'They do not harm him because I have forbidden it,' Heathcliff said under his breath. 'It would be too pleasant a death for the likes of him. No, I have better plans.'

For a moment, I stared into Heathcliff's black eyes, and what I saw so frightened me that I clutched the child to my breast and hurried to the kitchen. I didn't know what the gypsy meant by *better plans* and I did not want to know.

In the kitchen I sat down to lull my little lamb to sleep. Unbeknownst to me, Heathcliff, I later realized, had flung himself on a bench by the wall, removed from the fire and out of my sight, where he remained silent. I was singing to the child when Miss Cathy put her head in and whispered—

'Are you alone, Nelly?'

'Yes, miss,' I replied, thinking I was.

She entered and approached the hearth. 'Where's Heathcliff?'

'I don't know. About his work in the stable, I suppose.'

There followed another long pause, during which I perceived a trickle of tears from Catherine's cheek to the flagstones. 'Oh, dear!' she cried at last. 'I'm very unhappy!'

'A pity,' I observed, still rocking the boy.

'Nelly, will you keep a secret for me?' She knelt down by me, lifting her winsome eyes to my face.

'Is it worth keeping?' I inquired, less sulkily.

'Yes, and it worries me, and I have to let it out! I want to know what I should do. Today, Edgar Linton has asked me to marry him, and I've given him an answer. Now, before I tell you whether I consented or not, I want you to tell me which it should have been.'

'Really, Miss Catherine, how can I know?' I set the sleeping boy before the fire on an old blanket where I could keep an eye on him. 'Considering the exhibition you performed in front of him this afternoon, he must be either hopelessly stupid or a venturesome fool to still want you. You can be as mean as a snake some days, miss. And that's God's honest truth.' I raised a hand in oath. 'Not that all in this cursed house are not as mad as May butter.'

'If you talk like that, I won't tell you any more,' she returned, peevishly, rising to her feet. 'I accepted him, Nelly. Be quick, and say whether I was wrong!'

I sat in my place again. 'You accepted him!' I cried. *The fat's in the fire now,* I thought with a sinking heart. *Heathcliff will be neither to hold nor to bind.* 'Then what good is it discussing the matter if you've already told Linton you'll marry him?'

'But you haven't said whether I should have done it!' she exclaimed, rubbing her hands together and frowning.

A shiver ran down my spine as I wondered what would become of us all now. But remembering my place, I tried to keep my tone of voice properly servile and said, 'There are many things to be considered before that question can be answered properly. First and foremost, do you love Mr. Edgar?'

'Of course I do,' she answered.

'Why do you love him, Miss Cathy?'

'I do—that's sufficient.'

Foxes love chickens and devour as many as they can catch. Why did I fear Linton might suffer the same fate in the hands of Miss Cathy? 'You must say why.'

'Well, because he is handsome, and pleasant to be with.'

'Bad!' was my commentary. 'Faces sag and hair slips away. If he takes after his kin, he'll be bald as Dame Setter by the time he's forty.'

'And because he is young and cheerful.'

'Bad, still. If you think he will not age, you are mistaken. That is, if he isn't sucked dry by St. Swithun's Day!'

She ignored my commentary. 'And because he loves me.'

I folded my arms over my bosom. 'Indifferent. You are the prettiest girl for three days' ride.'

'Only three days?'

'I've never been farther than that from my hearth, so how would I know if any be lovelier a day farther off?'

Miss Cathy pouted. 'And he will be rich, and I shall like to be the greatest woman of the neighborhood, and I shall be proud of having such a husband.'

'Worst of all,' I groaned. 'And now say how you love him.'

'As everybody loves—You're silly, Nelly.'

'Not at all. I am the most sensible person I know.' I pointed at her. 'Answer.'

'I love the ground under his feet, and the air over his head, and everything he touches, and every word he says. I love all his looks, and all his actions.'

'And why?'

'You're making fun of me! It's no jest to me!' said the young lady, scowling and turning her face to the fire.

'I'm very far from jesting, Miss Catherine,' I replied. 'You love Mr. Edgar because he is handsome, and young, and cheerful, and rich, and loves you. The last, however, goes for nothing. You would love him without that, probably, and with it you wouldn't, unless he possessed the other four attractions.'

'No. I should only pity him—hate him, perhaps, if he were ugly, and a clown.'

'What of his ability to keep you safe? The beasties remain relatively quiet for now at Wuthering Heights, even while they are mad feasting elsewhere, perhaps because your brother keeps them entertained, perhaps because Heathcliff commands them so, but what if the situation changes? Can Mr. Linton protect you if the vampires decide to take up residence at Thrushcross Grange? I imagine they should like such a fine house with many plump servants to keep them healthy and fat. Some of these vampires have become quite civilized in their behavior, attending teas and balls and sponsoring hunts. Occasionally human guests even escape their invitations without so much as a drop of bloodletting. But they are not to be trusted. Not for a moment,' I warned vehemently.

'Edgar is not a man of weapons. You know that. Not all men are.'

'But there are other handsome, rich young men: handsomer, possibly, and richer than he is, who are well trained in defense against the devils. What should hinder you from loving them?'

'I've seen none like Edgar.'

'You know he won't always be handsome, and young, and may not always be rich.'

'He is now, and I have only to do with the present.'

'Well, that settles it. If you have only to do with the present, marry Mr. Linton. Your brother will be pleased. The old lady and gentleman won't object, for I'm sure they're anxious to see an heir born before they enter the pearly gates. You will escape from this disorderly, comfortless home into a wealthy, respectable one. All seems smooth and easy. So where is the obstacle?' I asked, peering into her pretty face.

'*Here,* and *here!*' replied Catherine, striking one hand on her forehead, and the other on her breast. 'In my soul and in my heart, I fear it's wrong!'

'And why is that, do tell?'

She seated herself by me again, her countenance growing sadder and graver as her clasped hands began to tremble. 'Nelly, do you ever dream queer dreams?' she said, suddenly.

'Yes, now and then.'

'And so do I, and this is one I must tell.'

'Oh, don't, Miss Catherine!' I cried. 'We're dismal enough without conjuring up ghosts and visions to perplex us.' I was superstitious about dreams then, and still am, and Catherine had such an unusual gloom in her eyes that made me foresee a fearful catastrophe. 'I will not hear it,' I repeated, my own hands shaking.

She was annoyed with me, but she did not proceed and instead took up another subject. 'You know, Nelly, if I were in heaven like Papa and Mamma and Hindley's dear departed wife, I would be extremely miserable.'

'Because you are not fit to go there,' I answered. 'All sinners would be miserable in heaven. Tortured, probably.' I rose from my chair, careful not to wake the sleeping child, for the boy had thankfully drifted off in the midst of our conversation. I wrapped him in a blanket, tucked him into the storage compartment of a high-backed bench near the hearth, and closed the lid. Neither mad sire nor bloodsucking guest would think to look for the child there. To conclude my deception, I set a basket of knitting on the seat.

'You are heartless,' Miss Cathy cried. 'You care more for that child than my future.'

'Not true. Have I not cared for you since you were a babe, as if you were my own?'

'And you don't love Heathcliff, either.'

'Who could love him? He's as tortured a creature as the vampire that lives in the attic of the dovecote.'

'You will not listen to me. I must tell you this. It is important.'

'Tell, then, Miss Cathy.'

'Heaven. I dreamt once that I was there.'

'I tell you I won't harken to your dreams, Miss Catherine! I'll walk away and leave you to make your own supper,' I interrupted again.

'This is nothing,' she cried. 'I was only going to say that heaven did not seem to be my home in this dream, and I broke my heart with weeping to come back to earth, and the angels were so angry that they flung me out into the middle of the heath on the top of Wuthering Heights, where I woke sobbing for joy. That will explain my secret. I've no more business marrying Edgar Linton than I have to be in heaven, and if that wicked brother of mine had not brought Heathcliff so low, I would never have considered marrying Edgar. But it would degrade me to marry Heathcliff now, so he will never know how I love him. And I say that not because he's handsome, Nelly, but because he's more myself than I am. Whatever our souls are made of, his and mine are the same and Edgar's is as different as a moonbeam from lightning, or frost from fire.'

As her speech ended, I became aware of Heathcliff's dark presence. Having noticed a slight movement, I turned my head, and saw him rise from the bench and steal out noiselessly. He had listened till he heard Catherine say it would degrade her to marry him, and then he stayed to hear no more.

Cathy, sitting on the ground, was prevented by the back of the bench from noting his presence or departure, but I started, and bid her hush!

'Why?' she asked, gazing around nervously.

'Joseph is here,' I answered, opportunely hearing the roll of his cartwheels up the road. 'Heathcliff will come in with him.'

'Oh, he couldn't overhear me at the door!' said she. 'When supper is ready, ask me to join you. I want to be sure Heathcliff has no idea what has happened to me today. He does not, does he? He does not know what being in love is.'

'I see no reason that he should not know,' I returned. 'And if you were his choice, he'd be a most unfortunate creature! As soon as you become Mrs. Linton, he loses friend, and love, and all! Have you considered how you'll bear the separation, and how he'll stand to be so deserted in the world?'

'He won't be deserted or separated!' she exclaimed, with indignation. 'Who is to separate us, pray? Not as long as I live, Nelly, not for any mortal creature will we ever be separated. Every Linton on the face of the earth could be devoured by the vampires and turned into the heartless creatures before I could consent to forsake Heathcliff. Surely you didn't think that's what I intend to do by marrying Edgar? Heathcliff will be as much to me as he has been all his lifetime. Edgar will have to tolerate him, and he will, when he learns my true feeling toward him. Nelly, I know you think me a selfish wretch, but did it never occur to you that if Heathcliff and I married, we would be gypsy beggars? Him selling his service of escorting fat women to church so their husbands do not have to fret they'll be eaten on their way? We'd be living like the other gypsy slayers, town to town, sleeping in the woods and in deserted barns. I should have to dance barefoot and ragged for fat rich men with bad breath and learn to cheat at tarot. But if I marry Linton, I can help Heathcliff rise and place him out of my brother's power.'

'With your husband's money, Miss Catherine?' I asked. 'I think that's the worst motive you've given yet for being the wife of young Linton.'

'It is not,' she retorted. 'It's the best! My great miseries

in this world have been Heathcliff's miseries. If all else perished, and *he* remained, I would still continue to be. If all
else remained, and he were annihilated, I would no longer
be a part of the universe. My love for Linton is like the fo-
liage in the woods; time will change it, I'm well aware, as
winter changes the trees. My love for Heathcliff resembles
the eternal rocks beneath, a source of little visible delight,
but necessary. Nelly, I *am* Heathcliff! So don't talk of our
separation again; it is impracticable.'

She paused and hid her face in the folds of my gown,
but I jerked it forcibly away. I was out of patience with her
folly! 'If I can make any sense of your nonsense, miss,' I
said, 'it only goes to show me that you are ignorant of the
duties of a wife, or else that you are a wicked, unprinci-
pled girl. Trouble me with no more secrets. I'll not promise
to keep them.'

'You'll keep that?' she asked, eagerly.

'I'll not promise,' I repeated.

She was about to insist, when Joseph entered, ending
our conversation.

'Where's Heathcliff?' demanded the old man, looking
around.

'I'll call him,' I replied. 'He's in the barn, no doubt. Miss
Cathy, do sit here on this settle and mind my knitting.'

'Since when does knitting need minding?' Joseph asked
suspiciously.

'Just last week the dogs did seize a jumper I had near
complete. They tore and unraveled it until there was nothing to do but throw away good wool.' I motioned to
Cathy, and she came without protest and sat on the seat
that hid the boy. I did not trust Joseph. I did not like the
darkness I saw in his eyes, a darkness that had not always
been there. Leaving the child to his mercy might have been
the poor babe's undoing.

So Cathy protected the boy and I went and called for

Heathcliff, but got no answer. Returning, now frightened, I whispered to Catherine that I feared Heathcliff had heard a good part of what she said, and told how I saw him leave the kitchen when she said she could not marry him.

Hearing that, she ran to seek him. She was absent so long that I made supper and Joseph proposed we should wait no longer and dine without her. We had just sat down when the young mistress returned and ordered him to run down the road and find Heathcliff and bring him back. Joseph objected at first, but she was so upset that he finally placed his hat on his head and walked out.

Meantime, Catherine paced up and down the floor.

'I wonder where he is—I wonder where he *can* be!'

'It's surely no great cause of alarm that Heathcliff should take a moonlight saunter on the moors, or even lie in the hayloft too sulky to speak. I bet he's lurking there,' I said. 'See if I don't ferret him out!'

I departed to renew my search, but did not find him.

'I don't know where he's gotten!' observed Joseph on his return. 'He's left the gate open and the miss's pony has trodden down two rows of corn!'

'I don't care about the corn! Have you found Heathcliff, you ass?' demanded Catherine. 'Have you been looking for him as I ordered?'

'Be better I look for the horse,' he replied. 'Before it's as drained of every drop of blood as the dun cow.'

It was a very dark evening for summer, and I suggested we all sit down to eat. I was certain the approaching rain would bring Heathcliff home. Catherine, however, kept wandering back and forth from the gate to the door, in a state of agitation.

Every once in a while, she would throw a look over her shoulder in the direction of the closed parlor where her brother and his fiendish friends kept company. 'Why does he bring them here?' she demanded. 'Does he realize he plays with fire? One day one of them will lose patience with him and his cards and devour him and then the rest of us.'

'Not so long as he continues to lose, I think,' I suggested, trying to put a bit of humor in the bad situation.

But Catherine saw no humor in the day and returned again and again to the gate, and soon great raindrops began to splash around her. About midnight, while we still sat up, the storm came rattling over the Heights in full fury. There was a violent wind, as well as thunder and lightning. A huge bough fell across the roof and knocked down a portion of the east chimney stack, sending a clatter of stones and soot into the kitchen fire.

Having not seen Mr. Earnshaw since he locked himself away with his gory playmates, I shook the door handle of his den, trying to ascertain if he was still alive or if they had finally done him in. Almost to my surprise, he replied, sending me back to the kitchen. There, I found Cathy, who got thoroughly drenched, standing bonnetless and shawl-less to catch as much water as she could with her hair and clothes. She lay down on the kitchen bench, all soaked as she was, turning her face to the back, and curling into a fetal position.

'Well, miss!' I exclaimed, touching her shoulder. 'Intent on getting your death, are you? Do you know what time it is? Half past twelve. Come to bed! There's no use waiting longer on that foolish boy. He's probably gone to Gimmerton or run off with his gypsy cousins.'

'Nay,' she murmured, her back still to me. 'He's gone. And the vampires shall fall upon him and devour him.'

'Not Heathcliff,' I said. 'I would put my last penny on him to come out best in a fight with a nest of the worst.'

'You only say so to comfort me.'

'I say so because it is the truth. He has some sort of power over them and you know it.'

'I know nothing of the sort,' Missy Cathy flung back at me.

Giving one last try to get her up and change out of her wet clothes, I retrieved the boy from the settle compartment and took him and myself to bed. In the morning, I found Miss Catherine still seated near the fireplace and Hindley just entering. He looked haggard and drowsy, but still alive after another night of gambling with the beasties.

'What ails you, Cathy?' he was saying when I entered. 'You look as dismal as a drowned whelp. Why are you so pale, child?'

'I've been wet,' she answered reluctantly, 'and I'm cold, that's all.'

'She got soaked in the rain last night, and there she has sat the night through.' I didn't want to mention Heathcliff's absence, as long as I could conceal it, so I said nothing of why the miss had gotten herself rained on.

The morning was fresh and cool and I threw back the shutters, but Catherine protested peevishly. 'Nelly, shut the window.' And her teeth chattered as she shrank closer to the almost extinguished embers.

'She's ill,' said Hindley, taking her wrist. 'I suppose that's the reason she would not go to bed. Damn it! I don't want to be troubled with more sickness here. Why were you in the rain?'

She looked at me, then addressed her brother. 'Edgar Linton came yesterday, Hindley. I told him to be off because I knew you wouldn't like him here with you gone.'

'You are a confounded simpleton, Cathy! Never mind Linton. Tell me the truth, were you with Heathcliff last night? You don't have to be afraid of me harming him. Though I hate him as much as ever, he has done me several good turns lately that will prevent me from offering his blood or yours to my companions in exchange for my debts. To prevent it, I shall send him from Wuthering Heights for good.'

'I never saw Heathcliff last night,' answered Catherine, beginning to sob bitterly. 'And if you do turn him out, I'll go with him. But, perhaps, you'll never have the opportunity now. I think he's already gone.' Then she burst into uncontrollable grief, and the rest of her words were lost to her sobs.

Hindley bid her get to her room immediately or he would give her reason to cry, and I encouraged her to obey. I will never forget how she behaved when we reached her chamber. She terrified me, wailing and thrashing about. I thought she was going mad, fearing the worst. What if she had been bitten when she was outside in the rain? One never knew how or why the devils chose one person over another to become one of their own. Keeping clear of her teeth, I begged Joseph to run for the doctor.

The doctor pronounced her dangerously ill. She had a fever and he said she was delirious. He bled her, and told me to feed her whey and water gruel and a little powdered bat bone, if I had any, and take care that she did not throw herself down the stairs or out the window. It wasn't until we stepped outside that I dared ask, 'Do you think she's infected?' All I could think of was little Georgie and the parlor maid he supped on.

'Has she come in contact with them?' the good doctor asked. Never once in our exchange did he speak the word *vampire*. It was always *them* or *they*. Rather odd for a man of such education, I thought.

'Come in contact?' I exclaimed, wondering if he had gone daft. 'Haven't we all?'

'If they have, there's naught we can do about it now. All we can do is keep a close watch,' he whispered.

*Watch for what?* I wanted to ask. *Dead pigeons and*

*parlor maids?* But I didn't say it. Instead, I let him out of the house and returned to my charge after stopping off in my bedchamber to add an extra circlet of garlic to my neck. At least if Miss Cathy became one of the beasties, she would not take me by the neck.

I cannot say I made a gentle nurse, but slowly, with time, my patient recovered, showing no signs of possession beyond her usual wearisome and headstrong self. Old Mrs. Linton paid us several visits, and scolded and ordered us around, and when Catherine was well enough to travel, she insisted on conveying her to Thrushcross Grange. I for one was glad to see her go, but the poor dame should have been more careful where she laid her kindness. She and her husband both took the fever, and died within a few days of each other.

Catherine returned to us, saucier and more passionate, and haughtier than ever. Heathcliff had never been heard of since the night of the thunderstorm, and one day when I was missing the young man, I made the mistake of laying the blame of his disappearance on her. She knew very well I was right, but for several months after that, she didn't speak to me beyond the manner a mistress would speak to her lowest servant.

She kept herself aloof from Mr. Earnshaw and his bloody-toothed companions, who came and went all time of day and night as if the door were a turnstile. I have never seen the likes of it! So many vampires that the cloak rack was weighed down and their black, stinking garments littered the staircase railing, yet in that time that Heathcliff was gone, not one human at the Heights was harmed by the slinking creatures. Oh, a goat here, a calf there, and piles of rodents were sucked dry, but never one of us.

Catherine became so known for her rages that her brother allowed her whatever she pleased to avoid aggravating her fiery temper. He was too indulgent in humoring her, not from affection, but from pride. It was his wish to see her bring honor to the family by marrying Edgar Linton, and I think he had an eye on the young man's cash box, for I suspected his own was dwindling.

Edgar Linton was infatuated with Catherine as all men are infatuated with that which has yet to be plucked. He believed himself the happiest man alive on the day he led her to Gimmerton chapel, three years after his father's death.

Much against my inclination, I was persuaded to leave Wuthering Heights and accompany her here to Thrushcross Grange. Little Hareton was nearly five years old, and I had just begun to teach him his letters. When I refused to go, Mr. Linton offered me generous wages and Mr. Earnshaw declared he wanted no women in the house, now that there was no mistress. He didn't give a beggar's rotten fig about Hareton. So I had no choice but to leave Wuthering Heights.

At this point of the housekeeper's story, she glanced toward the clock over the chimney and was amazed to see it was half past one. She would not hear of staying a second longer and vanished to her bed, leaving me no choice but to seek mine. Before I went, however, I was careful to latch the door and, having no garlic to spare in my bedchamber, I carried the tin of garlic tea from the table and sprinkled it liberally in front of the doors and windows. To my bed, I took the new sleep cap Mrs. Dean had made me, and my tiny silver dagger.

# Chapter 10

What a charming introduction I've had to a hermit's life! I've been sick in bed for four weeks, so miserable, I wished some vampire would slip beneath my door and kill me while I sleep, sending me on to my great reward. I have never in my life seen such bleak winds and bitter northern skies. The roads are impassable and the doctor warns that I may not be outside again until spring! Dying at the teeth of a bloodsucker could not be more painful than slowly suffocating from boredom and lingering affliction.

After four weeks of lying on my deathbed, I find myself bored. I'm too weak to read, but I'm desperate for a little enjoyment in celebration of the fact that I may survive my illness. Why not have up Mrs. Dean to finish her tale? She left off when the hero Heathcliff had been gone three years with no word from him, and the heroine had just married the man she did not love. I was eager to hear the remainder of the tale.

I rang for Mrs. Dean. "Come and take your seat here," I begged when she thrust her head through the open doorway. "Take your knitting from your pocket and continue your story of Mr. Heathcliff, from where you left off. Leave nothing out," I told her with the first excitement I've felt in weeks. "I must know how the rogue went from the outcast gypsy lad to the man of wealth and prominence he is today. Did he finish his education on the Continent, and come back a gentleman? Make a fortune on the English highways? He was on his way to becoming a great vampire slayer before he took his leave. Surely his abilities must somehow be connected to his current wealth!"

"He could have done a little of each for all I know, Mr. Lockwood. No one knows how he gained his money or how he was able to become educated."

"It's certainly not the path of the gypsy slayers," I interjected.

Mrs. Dean made herself comfortable in the chair beside my bed and assumed a canny expression. "I'll tell what happened, sir, but in my own words, in my own time. Are you sure you're feeling up to this?"

"I am very much up to it, Mrs. Dean," I said, settling myself back on a mound of goose-down pillows.

Well, after the wedding, I went with Miss Catherine to Thrushcross Grange, and, to my surprise, she behaved infinitely better than I expected. In those early days, she almost seemed fond of Mr. Linton, and his sister, too. The Lintons were very attentive to Miss Catherine's comfort. Of course, it was not the thorn bending to the honeysuckles, but the honeysuckles embracing the thorn. But there were no mutual concessions; Miss Catherine stood erect, while the other two always yielded. Who *can* be ill-natured and bad-tempered when they never encounter opposition?

From the beginning, Mr. Edgar was afraid of rousing Miss Catherine's temper. You know how willful she was, and marriage had not softened her. If he heard me or any other servants speak sharply to her or deny her any whim, he had no trouble showing his displeasure to us. Many times he spoke sternly to me about my pertness; nothing pained him more than to see his lady vexed.

But he was a good master, so I learned to hold my tongue, and for six months there was peace in the house. Catherine had seasons of gloom and silence occasionally, but they were respected with sympathizing silence by her husband. He seemed to think it was her illness after the big thunderstorm that produced the occasional melancholy. And when she smiled again, he met her with a smile. I have to say that in those early days of the marriage, I almost convinced myself they were truly happy together.

The happiness ended. On a mellow evening in September, I was coming from the garden with a heavy basket of apples I'd picked. Dusk had fallen upon me rather quickly and I was in a hurry to make it beyond closed doors with my full volume of blood. The vampires had been relatively quiet those years, but they were always there, always lurking, always ready to snatch a field hand too slow in returning to the barn or a granny who roamed from her parlor into the garden after dark. Some nights, I vow, I would hear the squeak of their nails on the windowpanes or catch a glimpse of ivory fangs in the darkness.

As I hurried through the garden at twilight, I saw undefined shadows lurking in the corners of the house and I touched the tin ball of garlic I wore around my neck. The basket of apples was heavy, so when I reached the relative safety of the kitchen door, I set it down. I swear, I only lingered for a moment, but as I righted myself, I heard a voice behind me say—

'Nelly, is that you?'

My first thought, of course, was that one of those devils had slipped through the garden gate and was preparing to devour me. But what vampire addressed its victim first? By first name?

Then I realized I recognized the deep voice and I spun

around. I saw no one, and the hair rose on the back of my neck. Something stirred on the porch, and, moving nearer, I distinguished a tall man dressed in dark clothes, with dark face and hair. He held his fingers on the latch as if he intended to enter.

I reached for a rake, abandoned by someone at the door. I feared it wouldn't be enough to fight off a bloodsucker, but it was the only weapon within my grasp unless I attempted to pummel the beastie with apples.

'I have waited here an hour,' he said. 'And the whole time I've been here, the house was as still as death. I dared not enter.'

I raised the rake to threaten him.

He stared at me in the darkness. 'What's the matter, Nelly? Don't you know me?'

A ray of silvery moonlight fell on his features; the cheeks were sallow, and half covered with whiskers; the brows low, the eyes deep set and singular. It was his eyes I recognized.

I flung the rake into the bushes and raised my hands to my face in amazement. 'You've come back? Is it really you? Is it?'

'Yes, it's Heathcliff,' he replied, glancing from me up to the windows, which did not glow with light. 'Are they at home? Where is she? Don't look so disturbed. Is she here? Speak! I want to have one word with her—your mistress. Please go, and tell her a person from Gimmerton desires to see her.'

'How will she take it?' I exclaimed. 'What will she do? You *are* Heathcliff! But a changed man! I can't comprehend it.' I stared at him, for he was the same and yet not. 'Where have you been for the last three and a half years?'

'Go carry my message,' he insisted impatiently. 'I'm in hell till you do!'

I entered the house, but when I got to the above-stairs

parlor where Mr. and Mrs. Linton were, I hesitated in the doorway. They sat together in a window whose lattice lay back against the wall, and displayed, beyond the garden trees and the wild green park, the valley of Gimmerton, with a long line of mist winding nearly to its top. Wuthering Heights rose above this silvery vapor.

The scene in the parlor, husband and wife, seated in the window together, looked so peaceful that I considered lighting a few candles and then leaving the room without saying a word of Mr. Heathcliff's presence outside. But I knew he would not leave until he saw her. 'A person from Gimmerton wishes to see you, ma'am,' I muttered.

'What does he want?' asked Mrs. Linton.

'I didn't ask.' I hated to deceive her, but I dared not cross him. Somehow, I realized this new Heathcliff was even more formidable than the reckless ruffian gypsy of his youth.

'Well, close the curtains, Nelly,' she said, 'and bring up tea. I'll be back in a moment,' she said to her husband.

She left the room and Mr. Edgar inquired, carelessly, who it was.

'Someone the mistress doesn't expect,' I replied. 'That Heathcliff—you remember him, sir—who used to live at Mr. Earnshaw's.'

'The gypsy plough-boy?' he asked. 'The one who was always sparring with the vampires on the moors? Why did you not say so to Catherine?'

'You shouldn't speak of him that way, sir. She'll be very upset if she hears you. She was nearly heartbroken when he ran off. I'm sure seeing him now will make her very happy.'

Mr. Linton walked to a window on the other side of the room that overlooked the court. He unfastened the window and leaned out. 'Don't stand there in the dark, love! It's not safe,' he called down. 'Bring your guest in.'

A few moments later, Catherine flew up the stairs, breathless and wild. 'Oh, Edgar!' she panted, flinging her arms around his neck. 'Edgar, darling! Heathcliff's come back!'

'Well, don't strangle me,' her husband chided crossly. 'I never found him that impressive. There's no need to be frantic!'

'I know you didn't like him,' she said, stepping back. 'But, for my sake, you must be friends now. Should I tell him to come up?'

He looked vexed, and suggested the kitchen as a more suitable place for him.

Mrs. Linton eyed him with a droll expression—half angry, half laughing at his fastidiousness. 'No,' she said. 'I will not sit in the kitchen. Set two tables here, Nelly, one for your master and Miss Isabella, being gentry, the other for Heathcliff and myself, being of the lower orders. Will that please you, dear?' She was about to dart off again, but Edgar stopped her.

'Stay here and let Nelly go for him. And please calm down. I don't like the idea of the whole household witnessing the sight of you welcoming a runaway servant as if he were your brother.'

I escorted Heathcliff to the parlor where the master and mistress waited, and when he entered, Catherine sprang forward, took both his hands, and led him to Linton.

Seeing him for the first time in full light, I have to say, Mr. Lockwood, I was amazed, more than ever, to behold Heathcliff's transformation. He had grown a tall, athletic, well-formed man; beside him, my master seemed quite slender and youth-like. His posture suggested the idea of his having been in the army, but I wondered if that was the result of further training in vampire slaying. His countenance was much older in expression; he looked intelligent and retained no marks of former degradation. There was still that half-civilized ferocity lurking in his dark brows and eyes that were full of black fire, but his manner was dignified.

My master's surprise equaled or exceeded mine, and for a minute he didn't know how to address the *plough-boy*, as he had called him.

'Sit down, sir,' Mr. Linton finally said. 'Mrs. Linton is pleased to see you.'

Heathcliff took a seat opposite Catherine, who stared at him as if she was afraid he might vanish. He did not raise his gaze to hers often, but a quick glance now and then sufficed.

As time passed, Mr. Edgar grew pale with annoyance. His displeasure reached a climax when his wife rose and seized Heathcliff's hands again, and laughed.

'I still think I'm dreaming!' she cried. Together they walked over to the window. 'I can't believe you're here! But you've been so cruel, to be absent more than three years and never to think of me. You don't deserve this welcome.'

'I've thought of you more than you've thought of me, apparently,' he murmured. 'I heard of your marriage, Cathy, not long since, and, while waiting in the yard below, I meditated my plan. I just wanted one glimpse of your face and then afterward, I was going to settle my score with Hindley and then kill myself so the law didn't have to. But now that I've seen you and you've welcomed me this way, my plan will have to be altered. You really did miss me, didn't you? And I you. My time away has not been an easy one, but my struggles have been for you!'

'Catherine, unless we are to have cold tea, please come to the table,' interrupted Linton, striving to preserve a due measure of politeness. 'Mr. Heathcliff will have a long walk, wherever he may be lodging tonight, and I'm thirsty.'

Miss Isabella joined them and they all sat down. The

meal hardly lasted ten minutes. Catherine could neither eat nor drink, and Edgar scarcely swallowed a mouthful.

Mr. Heathcliff didn't stay an hour longer and I asked, as he departed, if he went to Gimmerton.

'No, to Wuthering Heights,' he answered. 'Mr. Earnshaw invited me to stay.'

Mr. Earnshaw invited *him!* And *he* called on Mr. Earnshaw! I pondered this sentence long after he was gone, and had a feeling, in the bottom of my heart, that it would have been better had he never come home.

In the middle of the night, that night, Miss Catherine woke me. 'I cannot rest, Nelly, and I need you to keep me company. Edgar is sulky, because I'm happy to have Heathcliff home and he couldn't care less. I barely said a word to Edgar about him and Edgar began to cry, so I left.'

'Why praise Heathcliff to him?' I answered sleepily. 'Keep quiet about him. You want them to openly quarrel? It's only human nature. Neither man wants to hear about the other.'

'That's ridiculous,' she said, settling on the edge of my bed. 'I'm not envious of the brightness of Isabella's yellow hair and the whiteness of her skin. It pleases her brother to see us cordial, and that pleases me. But they are very much alike; they are spoiled children, and I find I must humor them both.'

'You're mistaken, Mrs. Linton,' said I. 'They humor you. You can afford to indulge their passing whims as long as they are trying to please you. There might, however, be something someday that is important to both you and Mr. Linton.'

'Then we would have to fight to the death, wouldn't we, Nelly?' she returned, leaping up and grabbing my hairbrush off the bedside table. She used it as if it were a dagger, sweeping it this way and that as she danced in the darkness. 'Just the way Heathcliff taught me when I was a girl. You know he taught me how to defend myself, should a vampire attack me.' She laughed at the thought. 'I won't listen to your nonsense. I have such faith in Linton's love that I believe I might kill him, and he wouldn't wish to retaliate.'

I plucked my hairbrush from her hand and advised her to value her husband more for his affection toward her.

'I do,' she answered. 'But why must he whine? It's childish. Why should he melt into tears just because I suggested that Heathcliff was now worthy of regard? He might as well get used to him; he might even find he likes him.'

'What do you think of Heathcliff going to Wuthering Heights?' I inquired, giving up all hope of going back to sleep any time soon. 'I was quite surprised myself, remembering how he and your brother got along.'

'Heathcliff explained it,' she replied. 'He said he went to Wuthering Heights to ask about me, and Hindley invited him in. There were some vampires there playing cards with my brother, and Heathcliff joined them. Apparently, my brother lost some money to him, and, finding him plentifully supplied, he requested that Heathcliff return again tonight.'

'Hoping to win back his money,' I offered.

'I worry about Hindley. He puts his trust in the wrong people. Look at who he plays cards with. It's a wonder he hasn't been sucked dry. Anyway, I think Heathcliff means to offer liberal payment to lodge at the Heights, and doubtless my brother will accept. I think he's throwing money away with both hands, between the drink and the gambling losses to the vampires.'

'And you have no fear, the two of them residing under one roof?'

'None for my friend,' she replied. 'A little for Hindley, but he can't be made any morally worse than he already is.

Don't tell me keeping company with vampires all day, even if they are gentlemen vampires, isn't dangerous to one's soul.'

'I'm not sure it's my place to say,' I said, but between you and me, Mr. Lockwood, I wondered if Master Hindley's soul had not fled that den of iniquity long ago.

'Well, I suppose I'll go make my peace with Edgar.' She rose from my bed. 'Good night! I'm an angel!'

The success of her making up with Mr. Linton was obvious the next day when he made no objection to her taking Isabella with her to Wuthering Heights in the afternoon. She rewarded him with sweetness and affection in return.

Heathcliff—Mr. Heathcliff, I should say in future—visited Thrushcross Grange cautiously, at first. Catherine, also, deemed it judicious not to express too much pleasure in receiving him. He visited more and more often, until his presence was expected.

My master's new source of trouble sprang from Isabella Linton evincing a sudden and irresistible attraction toward the tolerated guest. She was at that time a charming young lady of eighteen, infantile in manners but quite expressive in her emotions. Her brother, who loved her tenderly, was appalled by her infatuation. I think somehow he comprehended Heathcliff's disposition and knew that even though his exterior was altered, his mind was unchangeable, and unchanged.

He would have recoiled had he known that his sister's attachment rose unsolicited, and there was no reciprocation of sentiment. Heathcliff barely tolerated her. I know not what caused my lady Isabella's strange behavior. Perhaps the Lintons had married first cousins too many times, but word among the servants was that Isabella was no better than she should be.

"Twice Cook had caught her playing pinch and tickle with one of the young footmen, and she was wont to linger in the stables with the grooms, if you can believe that, Mr. Lockwood! Once the gardener saw her allowing Doole Flath the huntsman to use his teeth to remove a thorn from her bare foot and he a swarthy, unwashed rogue twice her age with a taste for unnatural pleasures."

"Unnatural pleasures?" I asked, eager to improve my knowledge of the local inhabitants. "I'm sure a mere huntsman could hardly . . ."

The good woman leaned closer and lowered her voice. "Oh, yes, sir. Talk was that he would take his ease with anything with four legs or two. He sells his rabbits and deer at more than one kitchen door, but as often at Knevel Hall as any. The vicar said that his housekeeper told him that a two-headed calf was born at Knevel Hall, and that one grotesque head bore the swarthy face and bulging eyes of Doole Flath."

"I . . . I'm not certain how . . ." I began.

Mrs. Dean held up a hand. "I make no judgments, and I'm not one to carry gossip. I only mention the sad case of Doole Flath the huntsman so that you can see how she might be drawn to Master Heathcliff—he himself being of a swarthy nature, but somewhat cleaner. It was said Flath never touched water, not to bathe or drink, and that the only moisture that touched him was the honey-mead he brewed himself of a careless raindrop." She shook her head. "He did stink awful, sir. When he brought rabbits to the door, Cook wouldn't let him in the kitchen. No, sir. Took too many days to air it out after he was there. I'd not want such a foul creature to nibble my bare foot, not if I'd stepped on a pitchfork."

"I'm sure you wouldn't," I agreed. "But of Heathcliff and Isabella, you were saying . . ."

She sighed. "Aye, sir, I was."

In time, knowing Heathcliff did not care for her, Isabella became more and more cross, crying and complaining over nothing. The friendship between her and Miss Catherine also began to fade. One day, Isabella accused Catherine of being harsh to her.

'How can you say I am harsh?' cried the mistress, amazed at the unreasonable assertion. 'When have I been harsh, tell me?'

'Yesterday,' sobbed Isabella. 'And now!'

'Yesterday?'

'When we walked along the moor. You told me to go where I pleased, while you sauntered on with Mr. Heathcliff!'

'And that's your notion of harshness?' Catherine laughed. 'I thought I was being kind. You would have had no interest in the conversation.'

'How do you know that?' she pouted.

'Have you developed an interest in the manner in which we control the vampire population?'

'Control? There is no controlling them. They should all be killed!' Isabella shook her head. 'No, you cannot fool me. You didn't want me to walk with you because you know how much I enjoy Mr. Heathcliff's company.'

'You are an impertinent little monkey!' exclaimed Catherine. 'You cannot possibly be saying you have feelings for him.'

'It's true,' said the infatuated girl. 'I love him more than ever you loved Edgar, and he might love me, if you would let him!'

'I wouldn't be you for a kingdom, then!' Catherine declared. 'Nelly, help me to convince her of her madness. Tell her what Heathcliff is: an unreclaimed creature, without refinement, without cultivation. He's the son of a gypsy slayer and only God knows who! Pray, don't imagine that he conceals depths of benevolence and affection beneath a stern exterior! He's not a rough diamond. He's a fierce, pitiless, fiendish man. I know he could never love you, yet he would be quite capable of marrying your fortune. I'm his friend and I tell you the truth.'

Isabella regarded her sister-in-law with indignation. 'For shame!' she said angrily. 'You're worse than twenty foes, you poisonous friend!'

'You think I speak from wicked selfishness?'

'I'm certain you do,' retorted Isabella. 'And I shudder at you!'

'Good!' Catherine said, and she left the room.

'She uttered falsehoods, didn't she?' Isabella begged, turning to me. 'Tell me, Nelly. Mr. Heathcliff is not a fiend. He has an honorable soul, and a true one.'

'Banish him from your thoughts, miss,' I said. 'He's a bird of bad omen, no mate for you. Much too unrefined, to my notion.'

"Mind you, Mr. Lockwood, I said nothing to Miss Isabella about her own unrefined taste for the hired help. Such is not my place to comment on. Still, I do notice."

"I'm sure," I said, motioning her to continue the tale.

"Mrs. Linton spoke strongly, and yet I can't disagree with her. She's better acquainted with his heart than anyone else on God's earth. Ask yourself this, how has he been living? How has he gotten rich? Good men do not hide their deeds. And why is he staying at Wuthering Heights with a man who abhors him? They say Mr. Earnshaw is worse and worse since he came. They sit up all night together continually with the vampire riffraff coming and going, and Hindley has been borrowing money on his land, and does nothing but play cards and drink.'

'You are leagued with the rest, Nelly!' Miss Linton replied. 'I'll not listen to your slanders!'

Whether she would have got over her infatuation if left to herself, and taken up with the coachman, or whether she would have persevered in nursing it perpetually, I can't say. She didn't have much time to reflect. The next day,

Mr. Heathcliff, aware of Mr. Linton's having gone to town, called rather earlier than usual.

Catherine and Isabella were sitting in the library, hostile, but silent. I was sweeping the hearth when Mr. Heathcliff passed by the window, and I noticed a mischievous smile on Catherine's lips. Isabella, absorbed in a book, remained till the door opened, and then it was too late for her to attempt an escape.

'Come in!' exclaimed the mistress, gaily, pulling a chair to the fire. 'Come sit between us and thaw the ice between us. Heathcliff, I'm proud to show you, at last, somebody who dotes on you more than myself. I expect you to feel flattered. My poor little sister-in-law is breaking her heart merely by thinking about how handsome you are, how good-hearted. No, no, Isabella, don't run off,' she continued with feigned playfulness, grasping her wrist so she could not take her leave of the room. 'We were quarrelling like cats over you, Heathcliff, and I was fairly beaten. I was told that if I would just stand aside, Isabella here would capture your heart for all of eternity. However long that may be, in your case,' she added mysteriously.

'Catherine!' said Isabella, calling up her dignity. 'I insist you adhere to the truth and not slander me, even in jest! Mr. Heathcliff, please bid your friend release me.'

'No, no, you must stay. Heathcliff, why don't you tell us how happy you are to know Isabella's feelings for you. She swears that the love Edgar has for me is nothing compared to the love she holds for you.'

Heathcliff stared hard at Isabella, as one might stare at a strange, repulsive creature like a human infant in its cradle, sprouting vampire fangs.

Isabella couldn't bear his scrutiny, and she grew white and red in rapid succession, tears beading her lashes. She closed her fingernails down on Catherine's hand, trying to force her to let her go.

'There's a tigress!' exclaimed Catherine, freeing her and shaking her hand with pain. 'Begone, for God's sake! How foolish to reveal those talons to *him*. Don't you know what conclusions he'll draw? Look, Heathcliff, you must beware of your eyes.'

'I'd take her hands off, if they ever menaced me,' he answered brutally, when the door had closed after her. 'But why are you teasing her in such a manner, Cathy? Surely you weren't telling the truth. She hasn't really fallen in love with me.'

'She's been pining for you for weeks, the foolish jade, raving about you this morning, and pouring abuse on me because I had the nerve to state your failings in a plain light. But don't worry, I like her too well to allow you to seize her and devour her.'

'And I like her too ill to attempt it,' said he, 'except in a very ghoulish fashion. That waxen face of hers, she looks like she's already dead. And those eyes, they detestably resemble Linton's.'

'He says they are doves' eyes—angels'.'

'But she's her brother's heir, is she not?' Heathcliff asked, after a brief silence.

'I would hope not. A dozen nephews would erase her title, would they not? But let's not talk about her anymore. Let's just dismiss the subject.'

And they did dismiss it. Catherine, probably, never thought about it again. But Heathcliff, I am certain, continued to contemplate Isabella's position, and I became determined to keep an eye on him. His visits were a continual nightmare to me, and also to my master, I suspected. His presence at the Heights was an oppression past explaining.

At the same time, a nest of particularly vicious bloodsuckers rose from their sleep in the moor and began a war against the righteous, snatching one child after another from Goody Blether's cottage until she had lost some seven or eight of her brood through a broken window that her worthless husband could not bother to repair.

"Shocking," I said.

"It was most shocking, Mr. Lockwood. When the eighth of her twenty-three was taken, poor Goody made to mend the shutter herself!"

"And did she succeed?"

"Alas, she was found at daybreak with every drop of her blood drained out of her, dead as a coffin nail, and her a decent and hardworking woman."

"So she tried to mend the shutter after dark?"

"I said she was a good wife and mother, sir, not that she was bright. She had accidentally struck her thumb with the hammer whilst nailing the shutter, made herself bleed, and . . ." Mrs. Dean shrugged. "Once blood began to flow, the creatures' appetites were whetted."

"Murdered," I breathed.

"Not just Goody Blether, but her hapless offspring, her husband, the butcher, a peddler passing through, and three guinea hens. Dead, every one."

"There's a lesson here, I'm certain of it," I pronounced, glancing anxiously at the window.

"There is," she agreed. "Keep your shutters mended and the windows closed at night."

"I was thinking more of Miss Isabelle and her reckless nature."

"That, too," the housekeeper agreed, drawing herself up. "Keep your shoes on whilst walking in the garden."

# Chapter 11

While meditating on these things in solitude, I one day became so frightened that I put on my bonnet to go and see how all was at Wuthering Heights. Just before I reached the gates, I spotted a boy seated on the withered turf: his dark, square head bent forward, and his little hand scooping out the earth with a piece of slate. I knew who it was at once, even though he looked quite different than he had when I left him a year before.

'God bless thee, darling!' I cried, quite relieved to see him. 'Hareton, it's Nelly! Nelly, your nurse.'

He picked up a large flint.

'Don't be afraid,' I said, thinking perhaps he didn't remember me. 'I've come to see your father, Hareton, is all.'

He raised his missile to throw it. I tried to speak to him soothingly, but he hurled the stone anyway. The missile struck my bonnet and was followed by a string of curses from the little fellow. I don't know if he comprehended what he said, but the foul words distorted his baby features into a shocking expression of malignity.

Hareton's actions grieved me more than angered me, and I took an orange from my pocket and offered it to him.

He hesitated, and then snatched it from my hold.

I showed him another, keeping it out of his reach.

'Who has taught you those fine words, my bairn?' I inquired.

'Heathcliff.'

I put the orange in his hand, and bid him tell his father that a woman called Nelly Dean was waiting to speak with him, by the garden gate.

He went up the walk and entered the house. I followed but stopped short when I spotted Heathcliff standing in the distance in a circle of vampires. Skin white as death, they had, and fierce, inhuman eyes, fair to make the hair stand on the back of your neck. And here it was broad daylight! My first instinct was to scream and run, but I was so intrigued by the gathering, which seemed so . . . civilized for a swarm of vampires that I stood my ground. Heathcliff was speaking quietly to them and though I couldn't hear what was being said from my distance, I was intrigued. It was quite obvious that the gypsy boy, now a man, was in full command of the situation. Oh, I heard the occasional hiss or snarl from the beasties, but for the most part they behaved better than most human men I know when gathered with other men. Curious as to what was being said, I crept closer, and hid behind a crumbling stone wall.

'Are my instructions clear?' Heathcliff demanded.

There were murmurs of agreement and I was surprised by how well spoken the beasties were. When they had first come to these parts, they only spoke Transylvanian blather, but they were indeed becoming fine English gentlemen.

"Well, not exactly English gentlemen, Mr. Lockwood," Mrs. Dean injected, cutting her eyes at me. "But well spoken, nonetheless."

"But what did the vampires say?" I begged, rising off my pillow. "Please, Mrs. Dean, do carry on."

They didn't say much of anything. Only agreed to Heathcliff's instructions, which I had not been able to hear. I tried to move in closer, but as luck had it, the toe of my shoe caught on a rock and in my desire to catch myself be-

fore I fell headlong, I made a terrible commotion. Good
heavens! Startled by a mere housekeeper, the gentlemen
vampires jerked and twisted and bared their fangs. Fortunately for me, Heathcliff recognized me.

'No,' he ordered, raising his hand. 'You're dismissed.'

And just like that, they walked off, the whole lot of
them. As if they were out for a stroll in the country. Why,
one had a walking cane!

I was quite relieved, I must say, for I was not ready to
meet my Maker that day, but then Heathcliff turned his
gaze on me, his scowl so dark and frightening, his eyes so
penetrating, that I turned and ran down the road as hard
as ever I could race, making no halt till I reached the gates
of the Grange.

Not long after that day, Heathcliff came to the Grange.
When he arrived, my young lady Linton chanced to be
feeding some pigeons in the court. Heathcliff wasn't in the
habit of even speaking to her unless he was forced to, but
that day he stopped to watch her. I was standing by the
kitchen window, but I drew out of sight. He stepped across
the pavement to her and said something. She seemed embarrassed and tried to walk away, but he laid his hand on
her arm. She averted her face; he apparently put some
question to her which she had no mind to answer. He
glanced at the house, checking to see if anyone was watching, I'm sure, and not seeing me, embraced her.

'Judas! Traitor!' I ejaculated. 'You are a hypocrite, too,
are you?'

'Who is, Nelly?' said Catherine's voice at my elbow. I'd
been so intent on what I was seeing that I had never heard
her enter the kitchen.

'Your worthless friend!' I answered warmly. 'The sneaking rascal. Ah, now he's caught a glimpse of us. Here he
comes. What excuse do you think he'll give for making
love to Miss, when he told you he hated her?'

Catherine brought a finger to her lips, warning me to

keep quiet as Heathcliff came in through the door. 'Heathcliff, what are you doing? You had best leave Isabella alone unless you no longer wish to keep my company. Linton will order you off the property if he sees you with her!'

'God forbid that he should try!' answered the black villain.

'Hush!' said Catherine, shutting the inner door. 'Don't vex me. Did she approach you?'

'What is it to you?' he growled. 'I have a right to kiss her, if she chooses, and you have no right to object. I'm not your husband; you needn't be jealous of me!'

'I'm not jealous of you,' replied the mistress; 'I'm jealous for you. Don't scowl at me! If you like Isabella, you shall marry her. But do you like her? Tell the truth, Heathcliff! I'm certain you don't!'

'I could do so without his permission. And as to you, my jealous Catherine, if I imagined you really wished me to marry Isabella, I'd cut my throat!'

'Quarrel with Edgar, if you please, Heathcliff, and deceive his sister. You'll hit on exactly the most efficient method of revenging yourself on me.'

'It's not you I seek revenge upon.'

With that, the conversation ceased. Mrs. Linton sat down by the fire, while Heathcliff stood on the hearth with folded arms, brooding on his evil thoughts. There I left them to seek the master, who was wondering what kept Catherine below so long.

'Nelly,' said he, when I entered, 'have you seen your mistress?'

'Yes, she's in the kitchen, sir,' I answered. 'She's sadly put out by Mr. Heathcliff's behavior.' I related the scene in the court, and, as near as I dared, the whole dispute that followed between Catherine and Heathcliff. I was tempted to tell him about the scene I had witnessed a few days before with Heathcliff and the vampires, but unsure what one could have to do with the other, I stopped myself.

'This is insufferable!' Edgar Linton exclaimed. 'It is disgraceful that she should call him a friend and force his company on me! Catherine shall linger no longer to argue with the low ruffian—I have humored her enough.'

He walked, followed by me, to the kitchen, where we found that its occupants had recommenced their angry discussion. Catherine was scolding with renewed vigor. Heathcliff had moved to the window and hung his head, somewhat cowed by her violent ranting, apparently, which surprised me. How could a man speak with such self-assurance to a gaggle of vampires and yet be intimidated by a mere woman?

Heathcliff saw the master first, and made a hasty motion to Catherine.

'What is going on here?' said Linton, sitting and addressing his wife.

'Have you been listening at the door, Edgar?' asked the mistress, in a tone implying both carelessness and contempt.

Heathcliff gave a sneering laugh, intentionally drawing Mr. Linton's attention to him.

'I have so far been forbearing with you, sir,' he said quietly, 'but no longer. Catherine has wished to keep up your acquaintance and I have acquiesced—foolishly. Your presence is a moral poison that would contaminate the most virtuous, and for this reason, I shall deny you hereafter admission into this house.'

Heathcliff measured the height and breadth of the speaker with an eye full of derision. 'Cathy, this lamb of yours threatens like a bull!' he said. 'It is in danger of splitting its skull against my knuckles. By God! Mr. Linton, I'm mortally sorry that you are not worth knocking down!'

My master glanced toward the passage, and signed me to fetch the men. He had no intention of putting himself in danger at Heathcliff's hands.

I moved to obey, but when I attempted to call them,

Miss Catherine pulled me back, slammed the door to, and locked it.

'If you have not the courage to attack him,' she ranted, 'make an apology, or allow yourself to be beaten. Edgar, I was defending you and yours. I wish Heathcliff would flog you sick for daring to think an evil thought of me!'

'Have no fear, I will not touch him,' Heathcliff said, turning on her. 'I wish you joy of the coward, Cathy! I compliment you on your taste. I cannot believe you would prefer him over me. Wait, tell me. Is he weeping, or is he going to faint for fear?'

Heathcliff gave the chair Linton rested in a push, and my master quickly sprang up and struck him full on the throat a blow that would have leveled a slighter man.

At that instant what I can only explain as a snarl came out of Heathcliff's mouth, a sound so frightening, so sinister that I fell to my knees and gripped my hands in prayer. I swear, for a blink of an eye, I thought I saw fangs protrude from his mouth. But no one else in the kitchen saw, or maybe cared. Mr. Linton walked out by the back door into the yard, slamming the door hard.

'There! You've done it now. You'll never be permitted to return,' cried Catherine. 'You've played me an ill turn, Heathcliff! But, go—make haste!'

'Do you suppose I would allow him to strike me?' Heathcliff thundered. 'By hell, no! I'll crush his ribs in like a rotten hazel-nut before I cross the threshold!'

By then, I had risen from my knees and glanced out the window. 'There's the coachman, and the two gardeners coming, each with a bludgeon.'

'Please,' Miss Catherine begged him.

With that plea, Heathcliff seized the poker, smashed the lock from the inner door, and made his escape as the men with weapons tramped in.

With Heathcliff gone, Mrs. Linton bid me accompany

her upstairs. 'This is all Isabella's fault, Nelly!' she exclaimed, throwing herself on the sofa. 'You'd best warn her to stay away from me. And, Nelly, if you see Edgar tonight, tell him I'm in danger of being seriously ill. I hope I do fall ill! He has startled and distressed me shockingly! I want to frighten him. Will you tell him, my good Nelly? You know none of this is my fault. What possessed him to listen in on our conversation? Heathcliff's talk was outrageous after you left us, but I could have convinced him that any intentions he had for Isabella were absurd. Had Edgar never gathered our conversation, he would never have been the worse for it. Well, if I cannot keep Heathcliff for my friend—if Edgar will be mean and jealous, I'll try to break their hearts by breaking my own.'

I said nothing when I met the master coming toward the parlor, but I took the liberty of turning back to listen when he joined my mistress.

'Remain where you are, Catherine,' he said without any anger in his voice, but with much sorrowful despondency. 'I shall not stay. I haven't come to fight nor be reconciled. I wish only to learn whether, after this evening's events, you intend to continue your intimacy with—'

'Oh, for mercy's sake,' interrupted the mistress, stamping her foot. 'For mercy's sake, let us hear no more of it now! Your cold blood cannot be worked into a fever. Your veins are full of ice water. But mine are boiling, and the sight of such chillness makes them dance.'

'Answer my question,' persevered Mr. Linton. 'Will you give up Heathcliff, or will you give up me? It is impossible for you to be my friend and *his* at the same time; and I absolutely *require* to know.'

'I require to be let alone!' exclaimed Catherine furiously. 'I demand it!'

She rang the bell and I entered leisurely. It was enough to try the temper of a saint, such senseless, wicked rages!

There she lay dashing her head against the arm of the sofa, and grinding her teeth.

Mr. Linton stood looking at her in sudden compunction and fear. He told me to fetch some water. She had no breath for speaking.

I brought a glassful and when she would not drink, I sprinkled it on her face. In a few seconds she stretched herself out stiff.

Linton looked terrified.

'She has blood on her lips!' he said, shuddering.

'Never mind!' I answered, tartly. And I told him how she had resolved, previous to his coming, on exhibiting just such a fit so as to frighten him.

I gave the account aloud, and she heard me for she sat up, her hair flying over her shoulders, her eyes flashing, her arms standing out preternaturally. She stared for a moment and then rushed from the room.

The master directed me to follow and I did, but she locked me out of her bedchamber. When she didn't come down for breakfast the next morning, I went up to ask whether she would have some brought to her.

'No!' she replied.

The same question was repeated at dinner and tea and again the next day. Each time, I received the same answer.

Mr. Linton spent his time in the library, and did not inquire as to how his wife was. Isabella and he talked for an hour, during which he tried to elicit from her some sentiment of horror for Heathcliff's advances. She gave him nothing but short replies. In the end, he responded with a solemn warning that if she were so insane as to encourage that worthless suitor, it would dissolve all bonds of relationship between herself and him forever.

# Chapter 12

While Isabella moped about the house, always silent, and almost always in tears, her brother shut himself up in his study. He waited, expecting Miss Catherine would come to him and ask his pardon. But Miss Catherine continued to fast, expecting Mr. Linton would throw himself at her feet and beg her forgiveness. I went about my household duties, convinced that the Grange had but one sensible soul in its walls, and that was me.

Mrs. Linton, on the third day, opened her door and requested fresh water and a bowl of gruel; she believed she was dying. I was certain her declaration was meant for Mr. Linton. I believed no such thing; I knew what dying women looked like. I had seen them on the road to the market, lying in the ditch, the blood drained from their veins. It seemed no one died anymore of the good pox or influenza; it was always from vampire attacks. Knowing Miss Catherine to be nowhere close to death, I kept her opinion to myself, and brought her some tea and dry toast.

She ate and drank eagerly, and sank back on her pillow again, clenching her hands and groaning. 'Oh, I will die,' she exclaimed, 'since no one cares anything about me.'

Then a good while after, I heard her murmur, 'No, I'll not die—he'd be glad—he does not love me at all—he would never miss me!'

'Did you need anything, ma'am?' I inquired, still preserving my composure, in spite of her ghastly countenance and strange, exaggerated manner.

I began to wonder if I was wrong. What if she *was* dying . . . no, suffering from the fate worse than death? What if she had been feasted on by vampires? What if she was becoming one of them? That would certainly account for her odd behavior. There seemed never to be any rhyme or reason as to who they merely murdered and who they made into one of their own. Only the week before I had run into an old friend of mine from my younger days. Gertude Putty told me that her sister's parson had behaved perfectly normally one week on the pulpit, then quite mad the following week. A week after that, he was discovered in the parsonage, hanging upside down from the rafters, feasting on a young altar boy. Later, they discovered half the choir, dead and sucked dry, hanging like salted hams in the belfry.

'What is my husband doing?' Miss Catherine demanded, pushing the thick, entangled locks from her pale, thin face. 'Has he fallen into lethargy, or is he dead?'

'Neither,' replied I, keeping my distance just in case my fears turned out to be correct. Once a human turned, they would feast on anyone, even a faithful servant. 'He's tolerably well, I think.' I had my garlic necklace and a stiffly starched white collar, but I was taking no chances with my throat.

'Among his books in his study, I suppose!' she cried. 'And I dying! I on the brink of the grave! My God! Does he know how I'm altered?' she continued, looking at her haggard reflection in a hand mirror. 'Can this be Catherine Linton?' She looked back at me. 'Is he actually so utterly indifferent for my life?'

'Why, ma'am,' I answered, 'the master has no idea of you being deranged, and of course he doesn't fear that you will let yourself die of hunger.'

'You think not? Can you tell him I will?'

'You forget, Mrs. Linton,' I suggested, 'that you have eaten some food and should be feeling better by tomorrow.'

She flung the mirror on the bed. 'If I were only sure it would kill him, I'd kill myself directly! These three awful nights, I've never closed my lids—and oh, I've been tormented! I've been haunted, Nelly!'

I took a step back. 'Haunted?' I asked, clutching at the garlic round my neck. Gooseflesh pricked along my spine. *Haunted* was not a word I cared to hear beneath this roof.

'Nelly, what's wrong with you? Why do you withdraw from me? I'm beginning to think you don't like me. That none of you like me. And I thought while others hated and despised each other, they could not avoid loving me!'

I stayed out of her reach as I watched her tossing about until she increased her feverish bewilderment to madness, and tore the pillow with her teeth. I tried not to let her see me staring. Had her teeth grown longer? Had they always been so pointed?

Both the expressions flitting over her face, and the changes of her moods, began to alarm me terribly. A minute previously she was violent. Now, supported on one arm, she seemed to find childish diversion in pulling the feathers from the tears she had just made in the pillowcase, and arranging them on the sheet.

'That's a drop of blood,' she murmured to herself. 'And this is a coffin, and this . . . this a little vampire baby.' She peered up at me now pressed against the door with fright. 'I have never seen a vampire infant, but surely they must exist, don't you think?'

'I . . . I think no such thing,' I stammered. 'They don't need to make babies, not when they have the opportunity to turn perfectly useful kitchen maids and parsons into vampires! Now give me that!' Braving drawing closer to her, I dragged the pillow away and held it at arm's length.

'Lie down and shut your eyes. You don't know what you're saying.'

'I see in you, Nelly,' she said dreamily, 'an aged woman. You have gray hair and bent shoulders. You are walking among the graves. And there is mine. Why do you weep for me so, Nelly?'

'There will be no grave,' I said, thinking the alternative, a ghoulish life-without-end, even more tragic. 'Now hush and sleep,' I told her, taking a seat on the far side of the room.

'Do you see them?' she went on, staring into the empty air. 'Oh! Nelly, the room is haunted! They come for me, only he is not among them. Only with him would I go. Nelly, please don't leave me alone with them!'

Her cry was so pitiful that I forced back my own fears. Once I ascertained we were alone in the room, I rose from my chair and took her hand in mine.

'There's nobody here!' I insisted.

Her fingers clutched her nightdress, then she covered her eyes with them.

'Oh, dear! I thought I was at home,' she sighed. 'I thought I was lying in my chamber at Wuthering Heights. I thought he had come for me at last.'

I didn't know for sure who *he* was, but I guessed it wasn't Mr. Linton she was pining for.

'Stay with me, Nelly. I dread sleeping; my dreams appall me, for *they* come to me in my dreams. And worse yet, I consider going with them, for I think they might lead me to him.'

'Go with who?' I asked, feeling both fearful for her and pitying her at the same time.

But she didn't seem to hear me. 'Oh, if I were but in my own bed in the old house!' she went on bitterly, wringing her hands. 'And that wind sounding in the fir trees. Do let me feel it—it comes straight down the moor—they bring it

with them. Oh, Nelly, do let me have one breath of that
wind!'

To pacify her, I held the casement ajar a few seconds. A
cold blast rushed through, and fearing I might let one of
the beasties in with it, I closed it and returned to my post
beside the bed.

She lay still now, her face bathed in tears. 'How long is
it since I shut myself in here?' she asked.

'It was Monday evening,' I replied. 'This is Thursday
night, or rather Friday morning.'

'Has Heathcliff called on me? Sent a message?'

I did not answer her, for what would have been the
sense in it? Of course the blackguard hadn't called on her.
He didn't even know she was ill, as if it would have mat-
tered. Too busy congregating with the vampires, I imagined.

'Open the window again wide,' Miss Catherine ordered,
not seeming to notice that I had not answered her. 'Fasten
it open! Quick, why don't you move?'

'Because I won't give you your death of cold,' I answered.

'You won't give me a chance of life, you mean,' she said
sullenly. 'You will not let him in. However, I'm not helpless yet. I'll open it myself.'

And sliding from the bed before I could hinder her, she
crossed the room, walking very uncertainly, threw it back,
and bent out, careless of the frosty air that cut about her
shoulders as keen as a knife.

I entreated, and finally attempted to force her to retire.
But I soon found her delirious strength much surpassed
mine.

There was no moon, and everything beneath lay in
misty darkness. Not a light gleamed from any house, far
or near.

'Look!' she cried eagerly. 'That's my room with the candle in it, and the trees swaying before it . . . and the other candle is in Joseph's garret . . . Joseph sits up late, doesn't he? He's waiting till I come home that he may lock the gate. Well, he'll wait awhile yet. We've braved its ghosts often together, you and I, Heathcliff. And dared each other to stand among the vampires and ask them to come. . . . But Heathcliff, if I dare you now, will you venture out? If you do, I'll wait for you. I won't rest until you are with me. I never will!'

She paused, and resumed with a strange smile. 'He's considering it—but he'd rather I'd come to him! Find a way, then! he tells me.'

Perceiving it vain to argue against her insanity, or the silly notion that she could see a candle from so far away, I looked about for a quilt to wrap around her to keep her from catching her death. I kept hold of her, not quite trusting her alone in the open window, half afraid she would let something in or fly out to join them. At that moment, I heard the rattle of the door handle, and Mr. Linton entered.

'Oh, sir!' I cried. 'My poor mistress is ill, but she is quite strong still and I cannot get her into bed.'

'Catherine ill?' he said, hastening to us. 'Shut the window, Nelly! Catherine! Why . . .' He went silent, the haggardness of his wife's appearance making him speechless.

'She's been fretting here,' I continued, 'and eating scarcely anything.'

He took his wife in his arms and looked at her with anguish.

At first she gave him no glance of recognition, but slowly it seemed to come to her who he was. 'Ah! you are come, are you, Edgar Linton?' she said with angry animation. 'You are one of those things that are ever found when least wanted, and when you are wanted, never found! I suppose we shall have plenty of lamentations now . . . I see we shall . . . but they can't keep me from my grave, where

I'm bound before spring is over! There it is, not among the Lintons, mind you, but in the open air, outside the fence, where people of my ilk must be buried. Who will you come with, Edgar? Your parents or me?'

'Catherine, what have you done?' begged my master. 'Am I nothing to you anymore? Do you love that wretch Heath—'

'Hush!' cried Miss Catherine. 'Hush, this moment! You mention that name and I will throw myself out that window!' She looked toward the window I had closed. 'He didn't come. I waited, but he did not come.'

'Her mind wanders, sir,' I interposed. 'She has been talking nonsense the whole evening, but a little garlic tea and I'm sure she'll rally.'

'I desire no further advice from you,' answered Mr. Linton. 'The doctor. She has need of Mr. Kenneth.'

Feeling no reason to tarry longer, I quit the chamber and went in haste to get the doctor, making the gardener take me in the wagon so I would be less likely to be ravaged by the beasties of the night.

I found Mr. Kenneth just coming from seeing a patient in the village, and my account of Catherine Linton's malady induced him to accompany me back immediately, despite the hour.

'Nelly Dean,' said he, 'I can't help fancying there's something behind this illness. What's been going on at the Grange? We've odd reports up here. A stout, hearty lass like Catherine does not fall ill over nothing. You must tell me, have you seen more vampires than usual lurking about the place?'

Obviously he was thinking the same as I, that she had not just been bled, but put under the spell of the vampires, but hearing it come from his mouth made me deny such a possibility vehemently.

'Certainly not. Some. Every house has some, but you know very well, even before the vampires came to these moors, the Earnshaws were taken to violent dispositions. All madness cannot be lain at the feet of the undead. I may say this: It commenced in a quarrel. She was struck during a tempest of passion with a kind of fit. That's her account, at least; for she flew off in the height of it, and locked herself up. Afterward, she refused to eat, and now she alternately raves and remains in a half-dream. She knows everyone around her, but her mind is filled with all sorts of strange ideas and illusions.'

'Mr. Linton will be sorry?' observed Kenneth, interrogatively.

'Sorry! It'll break his heart should anything happen!' I replied. 'Don't alarm him more than necessary.'

'Well, I told him to beware,' said my companion. 'Hasn't he been thick with Mr. Heathcliff lately?' The good doctor lifted a straggly brow. 'I have heard in the village that Mr. Heathcliff treats the vampires differently, now that he has returned. They say the beasties come to him for advice, financial and otherwise, and that he is invited to their social gatherings, an honored guest. Some call him the king of the vampires.'

'Some in that village also call themselves the Queen of England, Scotland, and Wales. It does not make it true.'

'But you have seen much of Mr. Heathcliff?'

'Heathcliff frequently visits at the Grange,' answered I. 'Though more on the strength of the mistress having known him when a boy, than because the master likes his company.' Whatever thoughts I might have in private, I would do naught to injure my mistress or her family in public. And the doctor was a known gossip and a carrier of tales. Did I give the slightest hint of what I suspected, he would have us all in league with the bloodsuckers, myself included. 'At present, Mr. Heathcliff is not in the best favor of the master. Some minor disagreement that will no doubt be soon mended.'

'And does Miss Linton turn a cold shoulder on him?' was the doctor's next question.

'I'm not in her confidence,' returned I, reluctant to continue the subject.

'No, she's a sly one,' he remarked, shaking his head. 'She keeps her own counsel! But I have it from good authority that last night she and Heathcliff were walking in the plantation at the back of your house, and he pressed her not to go in again, but just mount his horse and away with him! My informant said she could only put him off by pledging her word of honor to be prepared on their first meeting after that. When it was to be, he didn't hear, but you urge Mr. Linton to look sharp!'

This news filled me with fresh fears. What a devil Heathcliff was to leave one woman ranting for want of him while strolling with another. With this thought heavy on my mind, the doctor and I returned to the Grange. He went one way in the front hall, and I the other.

On reaching Isabella's room, my suspicions were confirmed; it was empty. But what could be done now? There was little possibility of overtaking them, even if I pursued them at once. Of course *I* could not pursue them; I dared not rouse the family and fill the place with confusion.

The doctor and I found Catherine in a troubled sleep. Her husband hung over her pillow, watching every shade and every change of her painfully expressive features.

'Tell me what is wrong with her,' my master begged. 'Tell me she has not been bitten.'

Kenneth drew back the collar of her nightgown, and I stifled a gasp. Mr. Linton did not breathe.

Our Catherine was marked. Two perfect puncture marks; I had seen them too many times not to know exactly what they were.

'But this is not possible,' Mr. Linton cried, falling to his knees, his hands clasped as if in prayer. 'When could such a thing have happened?'

All those days and nights that she wandered from the Grange on Heathcliff's arm, I thought, but kept to myself. For all we knew, he could have given her to the beasties himself!

'How bad?' Linton croaked.

'No way to tell,' said the doctor with the least bit of emotion in his voice. 'If she begins to grow fangs, tie her to the bed so as to protect yourself and your household.' He stepped back from the bed, now seeming eager to take his leave. 'Then call the authorities.'

'But perhaps she is just bitten and her soul not taken?' Mr. Linton begged.

'Perhaps,' agreed the doctor. But he sounded unconvinced to me. 'Though I rarely see derangement with cases where the victim has only been bitten and fed upon.'

'Derangement?' Mr. Linton threw me a warning glance that I should keep my opinions to myself. 'There has been no derangement.'

'Of course there has not.' Kenneth took up his hat. 'Keep her calm. I'll leave a sleeping draught in case she has need,' he said and then he was gone from the bedchamber.

I did not close my eyes that night, nor did Mr. Linton, me fearing for my life should she turn on us, and him for worry. We never went to bed, and the servants were all up long before the usual hour, moving through the house with stealthy tread and exchanging whispers as they encountered each other in their vocations. Everyone was active but Miss Isabella, and they began to remark how sound she slept. I feared he was going to send me to call her, but I was spared the pain of being the one to tell him of his sister's flight. One of the maids, a thoughtless girl who had been on an early errand to Gimmerton, came panting upstairs, open-mouthed, and dashed into the chamber, crying—

'Oh, dear, dear! What will happen next? First vampires in the dairy and now this. Master, master, our young lady—'

'Speak softly, Mary. What is the matter?' said Mr. Linton. 'What ails your young lady?'

'She's gone, she's gone! The king of the vampires has run off with her!' gasped the girl.

'That is not true!' exclaimed Linton, rising in agitation. 'What is this talk? Mr. Heathcliff is king of nothing, and my sister would certainly not go anywhere with the rogue. Nelly, go and seek her.'

As he spoke, he took the servant to the door and demanded to know her reasons for such an assertion.

'Why, I met on the road a lad who fetches milk here,' she stammered. 'He was the one who told me that snaggletooth vampire was hanging in the dairy again. He asked whether we weren't in trouble at the Grange. I thought he meant the vampires in the dairy again, so I answered, yes. Then says he, 'They's somebody gone after 'em, I guess?' I stared. He saw I knew nothing about it, and he told how a gentleman and a lady had stopped to have a horse's shoe fastened at a blacksmith's shop, two miles out of Gimmerton, not very long after midnight! He said the blacksmith's lass had got up to spy who they were and she knew them both! It was Mr. Heathcliff and our miss, and they was accompanied by another carriage, filled to the top with vampires. The lass said nothing to her father, but she told it all over Gimmerton this morning.'

'Are we to try any measures for overtaking and bringing Miss Linton back?' I inquired when the maid had gone.

'She went of her own accord,' answered the master. 'She had a right to go if she pleased. Trouble me no more about her. Hereafter, she is only my sister in name, not because I disown her, but because she has disowned me.'

# Chapter 13

For two months the fugitives remained absent, and in those two months, Miss Catherine was diagnosed, at Mr. Linton's insistence, with a *brain fever*. In all honesty, as time passed, I began to wonder if my original fatal diagnosis was incorrect. It was obvious she had been bitten, and she had shown the telltale signs of a poor soul in transition from human to vampire, but the illness had not developed as it should have. In two months' time, she should have become a full bloodsucking vampire, and after feasting on a few family members, would have been hauled off by the authorities to be disposed of by now.

But Miss Catherine fought the illness. Was it possible to prevent the vampires from making you one of their own, if you were stubborn enough? For if there was one thing certain under the sun, she was stubborn. And her husband fought the battle with her. Day and night he stayed with her, and he rejoiced when Catherine's life was declared out of danger by the rather surprised doctor. Hour after hour Mr. Linton would sit beside her, tracing her gradual return to good health, and flattering his hopes that she had never been bitten at all, that we were all mistaken, and that her mind would settle back to its right balance, and she would soon be entirely her former self. Whistling in the graveyard, as it were. I knew the worst had happened, but I didn't want to believe it.

The first time she left her chamber was early March. Mr. Linton had put a handful of golden crocuses on her pillow that morning. She saw them the moment she awoke and she gathered them eagerly together.

'These are the earliest flowers at the Heights,' she exclaimed. 'They remind me of soft thaw winds, and warm sunshine, and nearly melted snow. Edgar, is there not a south wind, and is not the snow almost gone?'

'The snow is quite gone down here, darling,' replied her husband. 'The sky is blue, and the larks are singing, and the becks and brooks are all brim full. Catherine, last spring at this time, I was longing to have you under this roof. Now I wish you were a mile or two up those hills; the air blows so sweetly, I feel that it would cure you.'

'I shall never be there, but once more,' said the invalid. 'And there I shall remain forever. Next spring you'll long again to have me under this roof, and you'll look back and think you were happy today.' And I must tell you, sir, that she looked so strange when she spoke those words that a shiver ran down my spine.

The master told me to light a fire in the parlor and to set an easy chair in the sunshine by the window. Then he brought her down and she sat a long while enjoying the genial heat and, as we expected, was revived by the objects around her. By evening, she seemed greatly exhausted, yet no arguments could persuade her to return to her bedchamber, and I had to arrange the parlor sofa for her bed.

To alleviate the fatigue of mounting and descending the stairs, we made up this chamber where you lie at present, Mr. Lockwood, on the same floor with the parlor. Soon, she was strong enough to move from one room to the other, leaning on Edgar's arm.

"I actually hoped she might recover," Nelly said with a

sigh. "I knew it could not be, but that didn't stop me from praying for her."

And there was double cause to desire it, for another now depended on her existence. We cherished the hope that in a little while, Mr. Linton's heart would be gladdened, and his lands secured from a stranger's grip, by the birth of an heir.

"A child?" I asked, clasping my hands with pleasure.

"A child," Nelly agreed.

I should mention that Isabella sent to her brother, some six weeks from her departure, a short note, announcing her marriage to Heathcliff. At the bottom was an apology and an entreaty for reconciliation.

Linton did not reply, and two weeks later, I got a long letter. I'll read it, for I still keep it. Any relic of the dead is precious, if they were valued living.

It begins:

> Dear Nelly,
> I came last night to Wuthering Heights, and heard, for the first time, that Catherine has been very ill. I must not write to her, I suppose, and my brother is either too angry or too distressed to answer what I send him. Still, I must write to somebody, and the only choice left is you.
> Please tell Edgar that I'd give the world to see his face again—that my heart returned to Thrushcross Grange in twenty-four hours after I left it. I fear I have made a terrible mistake, an error in judgment so great that I may never live to rectify it. The remainder of the letter is for you alone. I want to ask you two questions. The first is—
> How did you ever survive this place?
> The second question is this—

Is Mr. Heathcliff a man? If so, is he mad?
And if not, is he a devil? I won't speak of my
reasons for making this inquiry beyond telling
you these questions are in regard to the
relationship he has with the vampires. I don't
understand what is happening here. I cannot
reason who my husband is to them and they to
him. Once, he fought them on the moors. I have
gathered that he made a great deal of his money
while away by killing them for pay, but he
seems to be almost friendly with them now. No,
it's worse than that. He seems to experience a
camaraderie with them that I have never seen
between man and vampire, and it appears they
hold a great deal of respect for him. Almost
worship him. I beseech you to explain, if you
can, what I have married. Don't write but come,
and bring me a message from Edgar.

He vanishes from my hearth and side night
after night, claiming to walk the moors, but
when he returns . . .

"Ink stained the paper here, sir, and I knew my lady was
in some awful distress."

When he returns, she continued. When he
returns from these journeys he looks more beast
than man, with eyes so haunted that I cannot
bear to look into them. His clothes are
briar-torn and his hands, covered in soil, are as
cold as any gravestone in the dead of winter.
When I asked what had happened, he gave me
such a look that I would not ask again, not to
save my soul. He is, I vow, more demon than
man, after such a night.

"Again, sir, the shaky hand and the smudged paper. I would think that my lady's tears have watered the ink and wrinkled the parchment."

"What more did she say, Nelly?" I would hear more of this, although I too, I must admit, was frightened. What could Heathcliff be doing all night on the vampire-infested moors? How could any human survive? Or was I mistaken? Could my neighbor no longer be counted among our kind? Had the shadows swallowed him?

Now, you shall hear how I have been received in my new home at Wuthering Heights. It was dark when we dismounted in the paved yard of the farmhouse, and your fellow servant, Joseph, issued out to receive us by the light of a dip candle. His first act was to elevate his torch to a level with my face, squint malignantly, project his under-lip, and turn away. He was never of friendly face, but Nelly, he is ghastly now. As pale as whey, his eyes red-rimmed, and he wears a ridiculous soiled red neckerchief tied high around his neck.

Joseph took the two horses and led them into the stables, reappearing to lock the outer gate. Why lock it? I would ask later. Why bother with locks when Heathcliff and Hindley allow the vampires to come and go so freely?

Heathcliff stayed to speak to Joseph, and I entered the kitchen—a dingy, untidy hole. I dare say you would not know it, it is so changed since it was in your charge.

By the fire stood a ruffian child, strong in limb and dirty in garb, with a look of Catherine in his eyes and about his mouth.

*This is Edgar's legal nephew*, I thought. *I*

*must kiss him.* 'How do you do, my dear?' I said.

He replied in a jargon I did not comprehend.

'Shall you and I be friends, Hareton?' I asked.

An oath and a threat to set *Fang* on me if I did not 'frame off' rewarded my perseverance.

'Hey, Fang!' called the little wretch, rousing a half-bred bulldog from its lair in a corner. 'Keep an eye on her,' he warned the beast authoritatively.

Watching the unearthly looking canine, I stepped over the threshold to wait till the others should enter. Mr. Heathcliff was nowhere visible, so I asked Joseph to accompany me inside, but he stared and muttered to himself and wandered off. I then walked round the yard, and to another door, at which I took the liberty of knocking, in hopes some more civil servant might show himself.

After a short time, it was opened by a tall, gaunt man without a neckerchief, and otherwise extremely slovenly. His features were lost in masses of shaggy hair that hung on his shoulders, and his eyes were like a ghostly Catherine's, but with all their beauty annihilated. The man was paler than a corpse.

'What's your business here?' he demanded grimly. 'Who are you?'

'My name *was* Isabella Linton,' I replied. 'You've seen me before, sir. I'm lately married to Mr. Heathcliff, and he has brought me here.'

'Is he come back, then?' asked the hermit, glaring like a hungry wolf.

'Yes—we came just now,' I said. 'But he left me by the kitchen door. I would have gone in but your little boy frightened me off by the help of a bulldog.'

'It's well the hellish villain has kept his word!' growled my future host, searching the darkness looking for Heathcliff. He then indulged in a soliloquy of swearing and threats of what he would have done had the 'fiend' deceived him.

I regretted having tried this second entrance and was almost inclined to leave, but before I could do so, he ordered me in and refastened the door.

There was a great fire in the apartment, whose floor had grown a uniform gray. The brilliant pewter dishes, which used to attract my gaze when I was a girl, were equally gray, now tarnished and dusty.

I asked if I might call the maid and be conducted to a bedroom. Mr. Earnshaw offered no answer. He walked up and down, with his hands in his pockets, apparently quite forgetting my presence.

You'll not be surprised, Nelly, at my feeling particularly cheerless, seated alone on that inhospitable hearth, and remembering that four miles distant lay my delightful home, containing the only people I loved on earth. But there might as well be the Atlantic between us, instead of those four miles. I could not cross them!

I sat until nine that night, and still my companion paced to and fro, his head bent, and perfectly silent, unless a groan or a bitter ejaculation forced itself out at intervals.

I listened for a woman's voice in the house, and filled the interim with wild regrets and

dismal anticipations, which, at last, I must have
uttered without realizing it.

I was not aware I was weeping until
Earnshaw halted in his measured walk and gave
me a stare of newly awakened surprise. Taking
advantage of his attention, I exclaimed—

'I'm tired with my journey, and I want to go
to bed! Where is the maid-servant?'

'We have none,' he answered. 'You must wait
on yourself!'

'Where must I sleep, then?' I sobbed. I was
beyond regarding self-respect, weighed down by
fatigue and wretchedness.

'Joseph will show you Heathcliff's chamber,'
said he. 'Open that door—he's in there. But
mind you, be so good as to turn your lock, and
draw your bolt. Don't forget!'

'But why, Mr. Earnshaw?' I asked, not
relishing the notion of deliberately fastening
myself in with Heathcliff. 'Why would I lock
the door? Must I fear the vampires might
enter?'

He gave something akin to a cackle. 'It's not
the bloodsuckers I warn you against. You'd be
better off if they would simply kill you now. I
know I would be. Look here!' he grunted,
pulling from his waistcoat a pistol with a
double-edged spring knife attached to the
barrel. 'I cannot resist going up with this every
night, and trying his door. If once I find it open,
he's done for!'

As I stared at the weapon, a hideous notion
struck me. How powerful I would be, not only
against the bloodsucking devils, but the humans

as well, if I possessed such an instrument! Was the blade silver? Was that the sweet reek of garlic I smelled? I took it from his hand and touched the blade. Seeing the covetousness in my eyes, he snatched the pistol back and returned it to its concealment.

'I don't care if you tell him,' he said. 'He won't let them kill me. I don't know why, but he won't.'

'What has Heathcliff done to you?' I asked, fascinated and horrified at the same time. 'Why don't you just throw him out if you hate him so?'

'And lose *all,* without a chance of retrieval?' he thundered. 'Make Hareton to be a beggar? Oh, damnation! I *will* have it back, and I'll have *his* gold, too, and then his blood. I will feed him to his own vampires and hell shall have his soul! It will be ten times blacker with that guest than ever it was before!'

Earnshaw was clearly on the verge of madness, and I went in search of Joseph, thinking him the lesser of the evils that night. I found the servant in the kitchen, where he was bending over a large pan that swung above the fire. I cannot tell you what was in that pot, Nelly, but it appeared to be blood and gore and body parts.

'What is that?' I begged, trying not to gag.

'Supper,' was his answer. 'Want some?'

'That's not my supper! Get it off the hearth this minute.' Famished, I took off my hat. 'Mr. Earnshaw,' I continued, 'directs me to wait on myself, and I will.'

'Good Lord!' Joseph muttered, carrying away

the pot that slopped entrails as he loped. 'The boy complains of my cooking, too.'

I went briskly to work, sighing when I remembered a time when this might have been fun. The porridge I made wasn't much, but it was better than starvation. I added chunks of a rather sad-appearing head of garlic to the pot, which did nothing for the taste but helped my spirits immensely. 'I shall have my supper in another room,' I said when it was done. 'Have you no place you call a parlor?'

'*Parlor!*' he echoed, sneeringly, '*parlor!* Nay, we've no *parlors*.'

'Then I will go upstairs,' I answered. 'Show me a chamber.'

With great grumblings, Joseph rose and led me up the steps, opening a door now and then to look into the apartments we passed. At one door, he opened it, peered in, and slammed it shut before I could see clearly into the darkness. Had that been female vampires I saw, hanging upside down from the rafters, sleeping soundly?

I opened my mouth to question Joseph, but he shook his head. 'Look the other way. Best way to keep drawin' breath, I find.' He flung the next door back and indicated I should enter, which, from the superior quality of its dusty furniture, I conjectured to be the best one.

There was a carpet, a good one, but the pattern was obliterated by dust and mold. A fireplace hung with wallpaper, falling off in strips. Spiderwebs clung to the ceiling and draped from the bedposts to the window frame. A handsome oak bedstead stood with ample crimson curtains of rather expensive material and modern make, but they had evidently experienced rough usage. The chairs were also damaged, many of them severely; and deep indentations deformed the panels of the walls, decorated as they were with paintings of long-dead residents of Wuthering Heights, each with great staring eyes that seemed to follow me.

My supper by this time was cold, my appetite gone, and my patience exhausted. 'This is Heathcliff's room?'

'Nay. His room is kept locked. No one has the key but him.'

I peered into the dingy room. 'I can't sleep in this filth.'

'Yer married. Where would yah go?' He plucked at the neckerchief he wore around his neck. 'Accept yer lot. It's what I done. Goes down a lot easier that way.'

*Accept my lot!* I am a bride. I should be queen here, not a prisoner! I was so vexed, I flung my tray and its contents on the ground, seated myself on the stairs, hid my face in my hands, and cried.

'Well done, Miss Cathy! Well done, Miss Cathy!' Joseph clapped his wizened hands together as he retreated down the steps, taking the candle with him, leaving me in the dark.

After some time, I dried my tears and rose to my feet, realizing I had to smother my pride and choke my wrath and do something about laying my weary head down to rest.

An unexpected aid appeared in the shape of Fang, whom I now recognized as a son of our old Skulker, who had spent its puppyhood at the Grange. He acted almost as if he knew me

as he pushed his nose against mine by way of
salute, and then hastened to devour the
porridge I had splattered all over the steps while
I collected the shattered earthenware.

Our labors were scarcely over when I heard
Earnshaw's tread in the passage. My assistant
tucked in his tail and pressed to the wall; I stole
into the nearest doorway. The dog's endeavor to
avoid him was unsuccessful, I guessed by a
scuttling downstairs and a prolonged, piteous
yelping. I had better luck. He passed on, entered
his chamber, and shut the door.

Directly after, Joseph came up with Hareton,
to put him to bed. I had found shelter in
Hareton's room, and the old man, on seeing me,
said—

'There's room for both of you here, if you
like.'

Gladly did I take advantage of this
intimation, and the minute I flung myself into a
chair by the fire, I slept.

My slumber was deep and sweet, though over
far too soon. Mr. Heathcliff awoke me and
demanded, in his loving manner, what I was
doing there?

I told him the cause of my staying up so
late—that he had the key of our room in his
pocket.

The adjective *our* gave mortal offense. He
swore it was not, nor ever should be mine; and
he'd—but I'll not repeat his language, nor
describe his habitual conduct. He is ingenious
and unresting in seeking to gain my abhorrence.
He told me of Catherine's illness, and accused
my brother of causing it, promising that I

should be Edgar's proxy in suffering, till he could get hold of him.

I do hate him—I am wretched—I have been a fool! Beware of uttering one breath of this to anyone at the Grange. I shall expect you every day—don't disappoint me!

Isabella

# Chapter 14

As soon as I read this letter, I went to the master and informed him that his sister had arrived at the Heights. I told him of the letter expressing her sorrow for Mrs. Linton's situation, and her ardent desire to see him, with a wish that he would transmit to her, as early as possible, some token of forgiveness by me.

'Forgiveness!' said Linton. 'I have nothing to forgive her. You may call at Wuthering Heights, if you like, and say that I am not *angry*, but I'm *sorry* to have lost her, especially as I can never think she'll be happy. It is out of the question my going to see her, however. We are eternally divided, and should she really wish to oblige me, let her persuade the villain she has married to leave the country.'

'And you won't write her a little note, sir?' I asked imploringly. Had he no pity for his own flesh and blood, that he could leave her alone to suffer at Wuthering Heights with that monster? If only I could convey to him her true pitiful condition, but I was bound by my lady's privacy. She had written to me, not to her brother, and my lips were sealed.

"'Tis a weighty thing to be a good servant, sir, as you may not realize, but we have our own code of honor and we are bound to it.

'I will not see her,' the master repeated firmly.

'I see,' I said, although in truth I did not, but my curiosity was not satisfied and I urged him to continue listening to her woeful tale.

'It is needless. My communication with Heathcliff's family shall be as sparing as his with mine. It shall not exist!'

Mr. Edgar's coldness depressed me, and all the way from the Grange to the Heights, I puzzled my brains how to console Isabella. I proceeded down the road that ran between the two properties, keeping my eyes and ears keen. When Heathcliff and Isabella ran off, the vampire attacks had increased, but the road was pleasantly serene. I had nearly made it all the way to the Heights without an encounter with any bloodsuckers, when at the gates I spotted a tall, slender, almost handsome beastie wearing a black cloak, and top hat of all things! He stood as if he were waiting for a coach or perhaps a train, completely comfortable in his surroundings.

'Good morning to you, madam,' he called, tipping his hat.

I stopped in my tracks, fingering the dagger I carried in my skirt pocket. It was small, but sharpened to a fine point, I will guarantee you that. I sharpened it every night on a whetting stone soaked in garlic oil as I said my prayers.

My first thought, upon seeing the creature, was to turn and run, of course. But I set out to see poor Isabella and see her I would . . . if I survived to pass these gates. Besides, what would be the point in running? The beasties were lightning quick, quicker than a middle-aged woman, even a beastie wearing a top hat.

'Step aside,' I commanded with all the authority I could muster. 'I have business with Mr. Heathcliff and I carry sufficient protection.' I dug down in my bodice and produced a woollen sack containing more than a pint of crushed garlic.

"Crushed?" I grimaced. "Doesn't it smell awful?"

"Nay, Mr. Lockwood, not when you're used to such measures. Clears the head, it does, and what would a little stench be compared to having every drop of blood drained from your body and having your lifeless body cast upon the moor like an empty husk?"

"I suppose," I agreed with a sigh. "But do go on. This tall and elegant cloaked creature. You got a good look at him? You're certain it was a vampire?"

She snorted. "As certain as I am that two of the beasts are staring through the panes at us." She hurried to the window and drew the drapes. "Off with you!" she cried. "Go suck a dead goat! Beggin' your pardon, sir, but the young beasties do wear upon my nerves. Scraping their fangs on the glass and drooling down it until the window must be scoured with vinegar and dew from a fresh grave to make it fit to see through again." She shook her head. "I vow, they are worse than the grown ones. Four at once did set upon Goody Hedger's mother-in-law. They came down her chimney and pushed through the chain mesh into the old lady's bedchamber. Carried her shrieking from her bed and kept her all night in the church choir loft, passing her back and forth like a bottle of cheap Port-a-gee wine." She shuddered. "They say when they found what was left of her, you could have folded her skin into a gentleman's riding glove. Weighed no more than a new-hatched chick."

I cleared my throat. "A sad story indeed, and much do I pity Goody Hedger."

"Oh, no, sir. No need to pity her. With her mother-in-law's passing, she and her husband came into a fine bedstead, two pewter spoons, a china chamber pot, and a Jersey cow. Of course, the cow was dry. The beasties had sucked her blood until she was in such a state that she wouldn't give a thimble of milk."

"The vampire in the top hat at the gates of Wuthering Heights?" I reminded her. "You were saying . . ."

"Oh, him. I was shaking in my boots, I can tell you that. Handsome, he were, in a gaunt and devilish way, but I was not fooled by his sweet talk.

'Business with Mr. Heathcliff, have you?' he inquired, looking me straight in the eye.

I have to confess to you, Mr. Lockwood, that he possessed a fine jawline and a handsome nose. And spoke quite charmingly, so charmingly that I was tempted to stop and chat. It was frightening how well they were assimilating into English society in such a short period of time. I could easily see from this man how they were making their way into respectable parlors in the countryside.

'Let me pass,' I said, reminding myself of my intention to see Miss Isabella at once. 'Let me pass, sir, or consume me here and now and be done with it.'

'Consume you?' he said, sounding rather convincingly appalled. 'What would make you think I would *consume* you?'

'Your fangs were the first indication.' I lifted my nose haughtily and sallied toward the gates. I would have to pass right by him to proceed any farther.

He smiled down on me, seeming greatly amused. 'And the second?'

'It's broad daylight. Haven't you a crypt you should be attending to?'

He laughed outright, a deep, masculine laugh that, had I been younger or less wise, might have curled my feminine toes.

'It's an overcast day, as most are in the moors,' he continued. 'I've no need for a crypt. It's only the brightest sunlight that vexes us and even then, it is rarely deadly. An

abhorrence to daylight is just another silly human miscon-
ception of us from long in the past.'

'Silly, indeed. Now, go with you,' I ordered, dismissing
him with my hand. 'Mr. Heathcliff would not like you loi-
tering here, scaring off good maids bound on good deeds.'
I patted my sack of garlic, in case he had forgotten.

Just as I was about to pass the creature, he stepped directly in front of me. 'Is Mr. Heathcliff a good friend of
yours, madam?'

I couldn't tell now if he was making fun of me or not.

'Raised him, I did.'

'And did you know what he was, then?'

'What he was?' I looked the handsome beastie right in
his black eyes. 'He was a gypsy orphan boy.'

'Is that what he told you?' He had a queer look on his
face.

'Sir?'

He stepped aside to let me pass and tipped his hat. 'Good
day, madam.'

'Good day, indeed,' I muttered and then hurried on my
way, not even looking over my shoulder as I went. I didn't
know what the bloodsucker was trying to insinuate about
Heathcliff, and my sense of survival told me I did not want
to know.

I dare say Isabella had been watching for me since
morning. I saw her looking through the shutters, as I came
up the garden causeway. I entered without knocking.
There never was such a dreary, dismal scene as the formerly cheerful house presented! I must confess, that if I
had been in the young lady's place, I would, at least, have
swept the hearth, wiped the tables, and chased away the
three mice that were partaking of the morning bread and
cheese. But she already partook of the pervading spirit of
neglect that surrounded her. Her pretty face was wan and

listless, her hair uncurled and carelessly twisted around her head. She looked as if she had slept in her dress.

Hindley was not there. Mr. Heathcliff sat at a table going through some papers, but he rose when I appeared, pushed the nasty little terrier down off his lap, and asked me how I did, quite friendly.

I shuddered myself, remembering how the dog had tormented me when I was last a guest at Wuthering Heights, but what could I expect of that cursed place? "Mr. Heathcliff was the only thing there that seemed decent," Nelly continued, "and I thought he never looked better. So much had circumstances altered their position, that he would have struck a stranger as a born and bred gentleman, and his wife a little slattern!"

She came forward eagerly to greet me and held out one hand to take the expected letter.

I shook my head. She didn't understand the hint, but followed me to a sideboard, where I went to lay my bonnet. The terrier followed, worrying at my stockings, but I gave it such a stare that it fled yipping into a corner.

Heathcliff guessed the meaning of the lady's maneuvers, and said, 'If you have got anything for Isabella, give it to her. You needn't make a secret of it; we have no secrets between us.'

'I have nothing,' I replied, thinking it best to speak the truth at once. 'My master bid me tell his sister that she must not expect either a letter or a visit from him at present. He sends his love, ma'am, and his wishes for your happiness and his pardon for the grief you have occasioned, but he thinks that after this time, his household and the household here should drop inter-communication, as nothing good could come of keeping it up.'

Mrs. Heathcliff's lip quivered slightly, and she returned to her seat in the window. Her husband took his stand on the hearth-stone, near me, and icy fingernails scraped down my spine as he gave as close to a smile as I have ever seen on his graven features. His teeth, sir, his teeth were terrible white. Too white. I shuddered as he began to put to me questions concerning Catherine. I am, good sir, after all, but a meek woman, and what had passed before my eyes in the last few weeks and days would have overcome one much stronger.

I told him as much as I thought proper of her illness, and he extorted from me, by cross-examination, most of the facts connected with its origin. I told him how I had thought she might have been infected by a vampire bite, and he turned quite frightfully furious, but I was quick to explain that I had been wrong as she was still quite human when I left the Grange.

'Mrs. Linton is now just recovering,' I went on quickly. 'She'll never be like she was, but her life is spared, and if you really have a regard for her, you'll not cross her way again. Catherine Linton is different now from your old friend Catherine Earnshaw. Her appearance is changed greatly, her character much more so, and Mr. Linton will only sustain his affection by common humanity, and a sense of duty.'

'That is quite possible,' remarked Heathcliff, forcing himself calm. 'Quite possible that your master should have nothing but common humanity and a sense of duty to fall back upon. But do you imagine that I shall leave Catherine to his *duty* and *humanity*? Can you compare my feelings for Catherine to his? Before you leave this house, I must exact a promise from you, that you'll get me an interview with her.'

'Mr. Heathcliff,' I replied, 'you must not come, and you never shall through my means. Another encounter between you and the master would kill her.'

'With your aid, that will be avoided,' he continued. 'You may not believe me, but I never would have raised a hand against Linton had I not been so provoked. I never would have banished him from her society as long as she desired his. The moment her regard ceased, I would have torn his heart out, and drank his blood!'

I cringed at those words, but he went on.

'But, till then—if you don't believe me, you don't know me—till then, I would have died by inches before I touched a single hair of his head!'

'And yet,' I interrupted, 'you have no scruples in completely ruining all hopes of her recovering by thrusting yourself into her remembrance when she has nearly forgotten you, and stirring in her a new tumult of discord and distress.'

'You suppose she has nearly forgotten me?' he said. 'Oh, Nelly! You know she has not! You know as well as I do that for every thought she spends on Linton, she spends a thousand on me! At a most miserable period of my life, when I was gone from here, I feared she had forgotten me, but only her own words could make me consider the horrible idea again. And then, Linton would be nothing, nor Hindley, nor all the dreams that ever I dreamt. Two words would comprehend my future—*death* and *hell*. Existence, after losing her, would be hell.

'I was a fool to think for a moment that she valued Edgar Linton's attachment more than mine. If he loved with all the powers of his puny being, he couldn't love as much in eight years as I could in a day. Catherine has a heart as deep as I have. He is scarcely a degree dearer to her than her dog, or her horse. It is not in him to be loved like me.'

'Catherine and Edgar are as fond of each other as any two people can be,' cried Isabella, with sudden vivacity. 'I won't hear my brother depreciated, in silence!'

'Your brother is wondrously fond of you, too, isn't he?'

observed Heathcliff scornfully. 'So fond that he turns you adrift on the world.'

'He is not aware of what I suffer,' she replied. 'I didn't tell him that.'

'You have been telling him something. You wrote to him.'

'To say that I was married.'

'And nothing since?'

'No.'

'My young lady is looking sadly the worse for her change of condition,' I remarked.

'She degenerates into a mere slut!' accused Heathcliff. 'She is tired of trying to please me, already. However, she'll suit this house better for not being overnice, and I'll take care she does not disgrace me by rambling abroad.'

'Well, sir,' returned I, 'I hope you'll consider that Mrs. Heathcliff is accustomed to be looked after and waited on. You must let her have a maid to keep things tidy about her, and you must treat her kindly.'

'She abandoned that life of her own free will, under a delusion, I will admit,' he answered, 'picturing in me a hero of romance, and expecting unlimited indulgences from my chivalrous devotion. But, at last, I think she begins to know me. I don't perceive the silly smiles and grimaces that provoked me at first. She knows full well now that I did not love her. She can go if she so wishes.'

'Mr. Heathcliff,' said I, 'this is the talk of a madman, and your wife, most likely, is convinced you are mad. For that reason, she has indulged you, but now that you say she may go, she'll doubtless avail herself of the permission. You are not so bewitched, ma'am, are you, as to remain with him of your own accord?'

'Take care, Nelly!' answered Isabella, her eyes sparkling irefully. 'Don't put faith in a single word he speaks. He's a lying fiend! A monster, and not a human being! I've been told I might leave him before, and I've made the attempt, but I dare not repeat it! Only, Nelly, promise you'll not mention a syllable of this infamous conversation to my brother or Catherine. Whatever my husband may pretend, he wishes to provoke Edgar to desperation. He says he has married me on purpose to obtain power over Edgar, but he shan't obtain it—I'll die first! I just hope, I pray, that he may forget his diabolical prudence, and kill me! The single pleasure I can imagine, is to die, or to see him dead!'

'There—that will do for the present!' said Heathcliff. 'If you are called upon in a court of law, you'll remember her language, Nelly! You're not fit to be your own guardian, Isabella, and I, being your legal protector, must retain you in my custody for your own good. Go upstairs. I have something to say to Nelly in private.'

He thrust her from the room, and returned muttering, 'I have no pity! I have no pity! The more the worms writhe, the more I yearn to crush out their entrails!'

'Do you understand what the word *pity* means?' I said, hastening to take up my bonnet. 'Did you ever feel a touch of it in your life?'

'You are not going yet. Come here now, Nelly. I must either persuade or compel you to aid me in fulfilling my determination to see Catherine without delay. I swear that I intend no harm. I only wish to hear from herself how she is, and to ask if anything I could do would be of use to her. The thought that she could have been bitten pains me beyond words. Last night, I was in the Grange garden six hours, and I'll return there tonight and every night I'll haunt the place—'

'Haunt? That is an interesting choice of words, sir,' I challenged.

He scowled and continued. 'I will go every day, till I find an opportunity of entering. If Edgar Linton meets me, I shall not hesitate to knock him down. If his servants oppose me, I shall threaten them off with pistols. But wouldn't it be better to prevent my coming in contact with them, or their master? And you could do it so easily.'

'The commonest occurrence startles her painfully,' I said. 'She's all nerves, and she couldn't bear the surprise. If you pursue this, I shall be obliged to inform my master of your designs, and he'll take measures to secure his house!'

'In that case, I'll keep you here, woman!' exclaimed Heathcliff. 'You shall not leave Wuthering Heights till tomorrow morning. It is a foolish story to assert that Catherine could not bear to see me. As to surprising her, I don't desire it. You must prepare her—ask her if I may come. You say she never mentions my name, and that I am never mentioned to her. To whom should she mention me if I am a forbidden topic in the house? She thinks you are all spies for her husband. Oh, I've no doubt she's in hell among you! I guess by her silence, as much as anything, what she feels. You say she is often restless and anxious looking. Is that a proof of tranquility? You talk of her mind being unsettled. How the devil could it be otherwise in her frightful isolation? And that insipid, paltry creature attending her from *duty* and *humanity!* From *pity* and *charity!* He might as well plant an oak in a flowerpot, and expect it to thrive, as imagine he can restore her to vigor in the soil of his shallow cares! Let us settle it at once. Will you stay here, and am I to fight my way to Catherine over Linton and his footmen? Or will you be my friend, as you have been hitherto, and do what I request? Decide! Because there is no reason for my lingering another minute, if you persist in your stubborn ill-nature!'

Well, Mr. Lockwood, I argued and complained, and flatly refused him fifty times, but in the long run he forced me to an agreement. To be honest, I feared sleeping there that night; I feared sleeping under the same roof as he.

I engaged to carry a letter from him to my mistress, and

should she consent, I promised to let him have knowledge of Linton's next absence from home, when he might come.

Was it right or wrong? I fear it was wrong, though expedient. I thought I prevented another explosion by my compliance, and I thought, too, it might create a favorable crisis in Catherine's mental illness.

Nelly grew pensive. "Another strange thing, Mr. Lockwood. He followed me out of the house into the yard with the biggest rat I've ever seen clutched in his sharp teeth. Still squealing and squeaking it was, most horrible, dripping blood on the paving stones. He ran after me and dropped the awful thing at my feet. Like a gift!"

I sat up in alarm. "Mr. Heathcliff? A rat in his teeth?"

She clapped a hand over her mouth and giggled girlishly. "Oh, no, sir, not Mr. Heathcliff, not he. 'Twere that devilish wee terrier of his. Mean it is, and dangerous, far worse than the other dogs for all its size. No, 'twas the dog what brought me the rat as if it were a fine prize. I suppose the glare I gave it in the house let it know who won't be trifled with, for I'll have no half-pint of a beast gnawing on my best stockings." She peered at me. "Don't you think it odd, him bringing me his catch, as if I would eat the rat?"

I nodded. "I think it's all odd, Nelly, this whole business of the lady Isabella and Mr. Heathcliff, and above all your Miss Catherine. All most odd."

"Aye, so I think, but then they are my betters and can be expected to have their strange ways and strange pets, and servants must learn to deal and let deal, as we understairs do say.

"Notwithstanding, my journey homeward was sadder than my journey thither, though I did not encounter any vampires in top hats on my way.

"But here is Kenneth, the doctor; I'll go down and tell him how much better you are, Mr. Lockwood. My history is *dree,* as we say, and will serve to while away another morning."

*Dree and dreary!* I reflected as the good woman descended to receive the doctor, and not exactly of a kind which I should have chosen to amuse me. I had more questions than before concerning Mr. Heathcliff, and I must confess, a few spine-tingling fears.

# Chapter 15

Another week over—and I am healthier and spring is nearer! I have now heard all my neighbor's history from the housekeeper, Nelly. I'll continue it in her own words, only a little condensed. Nelly is, on the whole, a very fair narrator, and I don't think I could improve her style.

That night, after my visit to the Heights, I knew, as well as if I saw him, that Mr. Heathcliff was on Grange property, and I was afraid to go outside. Not so much afraid of him—though a little—but afraid of his companions. The same vampires that plagued poor Hindley's card table were now devoted followers of Heathcliff, and I could feel them all around the house. I could almost smell them. A bad omen of what was to come, I know now.

Still carrying Heathcliff's letter in my pocket, I made up my mind not to give it to Catherine until my master went somewhere. As a result of that decision, it was another three days before I was able to deliver the missive. I brought it into her room late in the afternoon when my master went into town to visit a sick friend of the family, a Mr. Jarrel, who had been attacked by a female vampire while helpless in his bath. He had rung for the kitchen lad to bring another bucket of hot water, and who should appear but a cloaked and fanged bloodsucker! Poor Mr. Jarrel was trapped in the tub of cold soapy water. If he tried to flee, he would have had to expose his unclad body to a strange woman, and Mr. Jarrel is known for being a modest man.

A bachelor of some sixty-odd years, he's never been seen in the company of maid, matron, or crone, other than his own dear mother and sisters. He keeps but three servants and those are all male, two of them older than he, and the third, the kitchen lad, a rather slow boy of the albino nature with extremely generous ears and a nose you could hang a hat on. Mr. Jarrel's butler was alerted to the danger by screaming and crashing from the master's bedchamber, and the dripping of water through the dining-room ceiling and onto the mahogany sideboard.

Naturally, the good man assumed that something was wrong. Perhaps robbers had come down the chimney or found a way into the house using a secret passageway. Gypsies may have tunneled into the cellar and sneaked up the back staircase, or mad dogs might have entered the house in a wine barrel. In any case, the quick-thinking butler sent the footman to summon the bailiff, who suspected vampires, as there had been several attacks earlier that day on a neighboring estate. He sent a boy for the sheriff, who came as soon as he finished his breakfast. He came in time to see the shrieking female wearing nothing but a cloak and knee-high boots spring off Mr. Jarrel and leap through an open window to the boxwood hedge below. Naturally, the creature escaped capture.

Poor Mr. Jarrel was barely breathing and there was very little water left in his copper tub. He could not speak, and rumor has it that he has not spoken to this day, but he has an odd smile fixed on his whey-colored face and insists on sleeping with all his bedchamber windows open. Our Mr. Linton had gone to sit with the poor fellow to see if he could coax a few words out of him to clarify the attack. That left us alone here at the house.

We generally made a practice of locking the doors before sunset, especially when the master was not at home. On that occasion, however, the weather was so warm and pleasant that when Catherine asked me to leave the doors and windows wide a little longer, I followed her bidding.

When the master was gone, I went upstairs where I found Mrs. Linton sitting in a loose, white dress, with a light shawl over her shoulders, in the recess of the open window. Her thick, long hair had been partly removed at the beginning of her illness, and now she wore it simply combed in its natural tresses over her temples and neck. Her appearance was altered, as I had told Heathcliff, but when she was calm, there seemed an unearthly beauty in the change.

A book lay on the sill before her, and the scarcely perceptible wind fluttered its pages. I believe Linton had laid it there because she never read anymore, or diverted herself with occupation of any kind. She just sat there, thinking of the past, and of Heathcliff, I suspect. Sometimes she would smile and look up as if gazing into his eyes. At other times, she would turn petulantly away, and hide her face in her hands.

'There's a letter for you, Mrs. Linton,' I said, gently inserting it in one hand that rested on her knee. 'You must read it immediately, because it awaits an answer. Shall I break the seal?'

'Yes,' she answered without altering the direction of her eyes.

I opened it—it was very short.

'Now,' I continued, 'read it.'

She drew away her hand, and let it fall. I replaced it in her lap and stood waiting till it should please her to glance down.

'Must I read it, ma'am? It is from Mr. Heathcliff.'

There was a start and a troubled gleam of recollection, and a struggle to arrange her ideas. She lifted the letter and seemed to peruse it, and when she came to the signature she sighed. Yet still I found she did not understand its content.

'He wishes to see you,' I said, guessing her need of an interpreter. 'He's in the garden by this time, and impatient to know what answer I shall bring.'

'I must go to him,' she said, rising to her feet.

'No, no.' I eased her back into the chair. Light as a feather from a summer bonnet she was. 'I'll fetch him.'

Those were words I will regret until my dying day.

I went downstairs, into the garden, expecting to find him waiting, but he wasn't there. I wandered deeper into the garden, calling his name softly. It was getting dark and I knew I shouldn't be outside, unprotected, but I didn't know how long Mr. Linton would be, and soon the other servants would return from their Sunday family outings and I would not be able to keep Heathcliff's visit a secret.

I walked to the far gate and back to the house. When I entered the kitchen, I was grateful to be alive, but sorely vexed as to what I should do next. Three days he waited in the garden, and now he was not there? I set a pot of beans to boil, with onions and several heads of garlic. Stalling, I suppose. Then I returned to Mrs. Linton's bedchamber to tell her the sorry news.

Only, she wasn't there. She was gone, Mr. Lockwood. Gone. The chamber was empty, so empty that I had the awful sensation of a goose walking over my grave.

I ran down the front stairs, calling her name. In the garden, I called for her and then for Heathcliff and then for Mrs. Linton again until I was hoarse. How could she have gone anywhere? She could barely walk. I checked every building on the property, an hour I looked, until the sun was full set. She was nowhere to be found. I wondered if Heathcliff had come for her, taken her from her room, never to be seen again, but I feared that was too kind an ending to this tale.

Tears running down my cheeks, I returned to the house, thinking I would check my beans and then take a horse to town and seek out Mr. Linton to tell him his little bird had flown the coop.

I was just closing one of the windows in the front parlor when I heard steps traverse the hall. I knew the footsteps.

'Where is she, Nelly?' Heathcliff said at first sight of me.

'Not with you?' I asked, that being my last hope.

He shook his head. 'Trouble in the moors. A small uprising. I came as quickly as I could.'

'I thought she might be with you. She's gone, sir.'

'Gone where?' he begged.

'Not gone. Here,' came a tiny, strangled voice from the open door to the garden.

What I saw, when I turned, Mr. Lockwood, haunts me still today. Our beautiful Catherine, dressed all in flowing white, was covered from head to toe in blood. Her face and her hands were bathed in it.

Heathcliff let out a strangled cry, and in one stride was at her side, his arms around her.

He neither spoke nor loosed his hold for some five minutes, during which period he bestowed more kisses than ever he gave in his life before, I dare say. The blood covering her face, then his, seemed not to matter. But then my mistress had kissed him first, and I plainly saw that he could hardly bear, for downright agony, to look into her eyes.

Something terrible had happened to her in the garden while she was looking for him, and now she was going to die. How I missed her going when I was coming, I do not know to this day. I'd heard not a sound, no cries of pain, no wail of distress, but the blood could only be the result of one terrible thing. Bitten. My lady was bitten, and not once, but dozens of times. Fed upon, she was. Feasted upon, more like it. Did they fly up to the open window and take her? Did she, out of her head as she was, walk into their arms? Will we ever know?

As Heathcliff looked down at Catherine, the same conviction struck him as me, that there was no prospect of ultimate recovery there—she was fated, sure to die.

'Oh, Cathy! Oh, my life! How can I bear it?' were the first strangled words he uttered, in a tone that did not seek to disguise his despair. And now he stared at her so earnestly that I thought the very intensity of his gaze would bring tears into his eyes.

'What now?' said Catherine, leaning back and returning his look with a sudden clouded brow. Blood puddled at her tiny feet. 'You and Edgar have broken my heart, Heathcliff! I wish I could hold you,' she continued, bitterly, till we were both dead! I shouldn't care what you suffered. I care nothing for your sufferings. Why shouldn't you suffer? I do! Will you forget me? Will you be happy when I am in the earth? Will you say twenty years hence, "That's the grave of Catherine Earnshaw. I loved her long ago, and was wretched to lose her; but it is past." Will you say so, Heathcliff?'

'Don't torture me till I'm as mad as yourself,' he cried. He cradled her in his arms. I could do nothing but stand there, frozen in the inner doorway, watching the event unfold. 'Are you possessed with a devil,' he pursued, savagely, 'to talk in that manner to me when you are dying? Do you reflect that all those words will be branded in my memory, and eating deeper eternally after you have left me? Catherine, you know that I could as soon forget you as my existence! Is it not sufficient for your infernal selfishness that while you are at peace I shall writhe in the torments of hell?'

'Peace! I shall not be at peace,' moaned Catherine. 'I shall never be at peace. Look at me! Look at what the beasties have done.' She clawed at the shredded flesh of her neck. 'They tormented me too long, but did not kill me, those fine companions of yours. Those same kind gentlemen you told me, whilst on our long walks, had souls worth saving.'

'No,' he moaned. 'It cannot be true. They would not betray me so.'

'I'm not wishing you greater torment than I have, Heathcliff. This is not your doing. You couldn't control them, not ever, not really. I only wish us never to be parted, and should a word of mine distress you hereafter, think I feel the same distress underground, and for my own sake, forgive me!'

'Here, bring her here,' I managed, spreading a cloth on the settee so that her blood would not stain it. 'Lie her here, Heathcliff.'

Heathcliff carried her in his arms to the settee, laid her down gently and leaned over her, but not so far as to let her see his face, which was livid with emotion. She bent round to look at him, but he would not permit it and he stood abruptly and walked to the fireplace, where he stood, silent, with his back toward us.

Mrs. Linton's glance followed him suspiciously. After a pause, and a prolonged gaze, she resumed addressing me in accents of indignant disappointment—'Oh, you see, Nelly, he would not relent a moment to keep me out of the grave. *That* is how I am loved! Well, never mind. Heathcliff, dear! You should not be sullen now. Surely there is still some way we can be together for eternity, a better chance now that I have been feasted on. Do come to me, Heathcliff!' She raised up, her hand out to him.

At that earnest appeal he turned to her, looking absolutely desperate. His eyes wide, and wet at last, flashed fiercely on her, his breast heaved convulsively. An instant they held asunder, and then they were locked in an embrace from which I thought my mistress would never be released alive.

He fell to his knees, and on my approaching hurriedly to ascertain if she had fainted, he gnashed at me, and foamed like a mad dog, and gathered her to him with greedy jealousy.

A movement of Catherine's relieved me a little. She put up her hand to clasp his neck, and bring her cheek to his as he held her, while he, in return, covering her with frantic caresses, said wildly—

'You teach me now how cruel you've been—cruel and false. *Why* did you despise me? *Why* did you betray your own heart, Cathy? I would not have one word of comfort. You deserve this. The vampires have not killed you; you have killed yourself. Yes, you may kiss me, and cry, and wring out my kisses and tears, but they'll blight you—they'll damn you. You knew what I was. You loved me—then what *right* had you to leave me? What right—answer me—for the poor fancy you felt for Linton? Because misery, and degradation, and death, and nothing that God or Satan could inflict would have parted us, *you,* of your own will, did it. I have not broken your heart—*you* have broken it, and in breaking it, you have broken mine. So much the worse for me, that I am strong. Do I want to live? What kind of living will it be when you—oh God! Would *you* like to live with your soul half in the grave, half out?'

'Let me alone. Let me alone,' sobbed Catherine. 'If I've done wrong, I'm dying for it. It is enough! I forgive you. Forgive me!'

'It is hard to forgive, and to look at those eyes, and feel those wasted hands,' he answered. 'Kiss me again, and don't let me see your eyes! I forgive what you have done to me. I love *my* murderer—but *yours!* How can I?'

They were silent—their faces hid against each other, and washed by each other's tears. At least, I suppose the weeping was on both sides, as it seemed Heathcliff *could* weep on a great occasion like this.

I don't know how much time passed before I heard the sound of the first servants returning up the lane, followed soon by the creak of carriage wheels. 'My master returns!'

Heathcliff groaned a curse, and strained Catherine closer. She never moved.

'Now he is here,' I exclaimed. 'For heaven's sake, hurry out. Go through the window into the garden. Be quick and stay among the trees till he is inside.'

'I must go, Cathy,' said Heathcliff, seeking to extricate himself from his companion's arms. 'But if I live, I'll see you again before you are asleep. I won't stray five yards from your window.'

'You must not go!' she answered, holding him as firmly as her strength allowed. 'You shall not, I tell you.'

'For one hour,' he pleaded earnestly.

'Not for one minute,' she replied.

'I *must*—Linton will be in immediately.'

He must have risen, and unfixed her fingers by the act— she clung fast, gasping. There was mad resolution in her face.

'No!' she shrieked. 'Oh, don't, don't go. It is the last time! Edgar will not hurt us. Heathcliff, I shall die! I shall die!'

'Damn the fool! There he is,' cried Heathcliff, sinking back to the floor in front of her. 'Hush, my darling! Hush, hush, Catherine! I'll stay. If he shot me so, I'd expire with a blessing on my lips.'

'Are you going to listen to her ravings?' I said passionately, hearing my master's footsteps and the whining of his dogs. 'She does not know what she says. Will you ruin her, because she has not wit to help herself? Get up! You could be free instantly. That is the most diabolical deed that ever you did. We are all done for—master, mistress, and servant.'

I wrung my hands and cried out, and Mr. Linton hastened his step at the noise. In the midst of my agitation, I was sincerely glad to observe that Catherine's arms had fallen relaxed, and her head hung down.

*She's fainted, or dead,* I thought. *So much the better. Far better that she should be dead, than lingering a burden and a misery-maker to all about her.*

Edgar entered the parlor and sprang to his unbidden guest, blanched with astonishment and rage. What he meant to do, I cannot tell, but Heathcliff stopped him by lifting Catherine and placing the lifeless-looking form into her husband's arms.

'Look there!' Heathcliff said. 'Unless you be a fiend, help her first—then you shall speak to me!'

Mr. Linton summoned me and we took her up the stairs. We managed to restore her to consciousness, but she was bewildered. She sighed, and moaned, and knew nobody. Edgar, in his anxiety for her, forgot her hated friend. I did not. I went downstairs, at the earliest opportunity, and besought him to depart, affirming that Catherine was better, and he should hear from me in the morning.

'I shall not refuse to go out of doors,' he answered, 'but I shall stay in the garden.'

'Ye'd be better off chasing down the beasties who did this to her and putting silver stakes in their black hearts,' I flared, unable to control my emotion.

'I will see to them,' he vowed blackly. 'But not tonight. Tonight I wait in the garden and you, Nelly, mind you keep your word tomorrow. I shall be under those larch trees. Mind! Or I pay another visit, whether Linton be in or not.'

He sent a rapid glance in the direction of the staircase still stained with her blood, and, ascertaining that what I stated was apparently true, delivered the house of his luckless presence.

# Chapter 16

"That night, the young Catherine you saw at Wuthering Heights was born a puny, seven months' child. Two hours later, her mother of the same name died, a terrible, clawing, screaming death, a forewarning of what was to come."

"What was to come?" I asked. I half expected Nelly to tell me that infant had been born with fangs and a tail, neither of which I had noticed on the young woman.

"What was to come, Mr. Lockwood. You see, Master Linton's lady was dead, but not dead. The beasties had done such a measure upon her that she could not fully die as human because she was not fully human. She was caught somewhere between heaven and hell."

I stared at her, I know, mouth gaping, with eyes as round as tea saucers.

"But I'll get to that in my own time." Nelly folded her hands and continued the story.

Catherine never recovered sufficient consciousness to miss Heathcliff or know Edgar. The widower's bereavement is a subject too painful to be dwelt on; its aftereffects showed how deep the sorrow sank. A great addition, in my eyes, was his being left without an heir. As I gazed on the feeble orphan, I mentally abused old Linton for leaving his estate to Isabella and her offspring, should Edgar not have a son. This wretched infant was to be penniless as well as bereft of a mother's love.

The next morning—bright and cheerful out of doors—Edgar Linton lay with his head on the pillow and his eyes shut. His young and fair features were almost as deathlike as those of the form beside him, and almost as fixed as the dead wife beside him.

With the master asleep, I ventured outside soon after sunrise to steal a breath of refreshing air. I'd gone out to shake off my drowsiness, but in reality, my chief motive was seeing Mr. Heathcliff. If he had remained in the garden all night, he would have heard nothing of the stir at the Grange.

I wished, yet feared, to find him. I felt the terrible news must be told, and I longed to get it over, but *how* to do it, I did not know.

He was there, leant against an old ash tree, his hat off and his hair soaked with the dew that had gathered on the budded branches. He had been standing a long time in that position, for I saw a pair of ouzels passing and repassing scarcely three feet from him, busy in building their nest, and regarding his proximity no more than that of a piece of timber. They flew off at my approach, and he raised his eyes and spoke:

'She's dead!' he said. 'I've not waited for you to learn that. Put your handkerchief away—don't snivel before me. Damn you all! She wants none of your tears!'

I was weeping as much for him as her, for when I first looked into his face, I perceived that he had already sensed she was gone. A foolish notion struck me that his heart was quelled and he prayed, because his lips moved and his gaze was fixed on the ground.

'Yes, she's dead!' I answered, checking my sobs and drying my cheeks. 'Gone to heaven, I hope where we may, everyone, join her, if we take due warning and leave our evil ways to follow good!'

'How did—' He endeavored to pronounce her name, but could not manage it. Compressing his mouth in inward agony, he resumed. 'How did she die?'

*Poor wretch!* I thought. *You really do have a heart and nerves the same as others!* I'll not say that I haven't wondered, sir, but I could see his genuine grief. *Why should you be anxious to conceal them? Your pride cannot blind God!*

'Quietly as a lamb!' I answered aloud. 'She drew a sigh, and stretched herself, like a child reviving, and sinking again to sleep. Five minutes later, I felt one little pulse at her heart, and nothing more!'

'And—did she ever mention me?' he asked, hesitating, as if he dreaded the answer to his question.

'Her senses never returned. She recognized nobody from the time you left her,' I said. 'She lies with a sweet smile on her face. Her life closed in a gentle dream—may she wake as kindly in the other world!'

'May she wake in torment!' he cried, with frightful vehemence, stamping his foot and groaning in a sudden paroxysm of ungovernable passion. 'Why, she's a liar to the end! Where is she? Not *there*—not in heaven—not perished—where? I pray one prayer—I repeat it till my tongue stiffens—Catherine Earnshaw, may you not rest as long as I am living! You said I killed you—haunt me, then! The murdered *do* haunt their murderers. I believe—I know that ghosts *have* wandered on earth. Be with me always—take any form—drive me mad! Only *do* not leave me in this abyss, where I cannot find you! Oh, God! It is unutterable! I *cannot* live without my life! I *cannot* live without my soul!'

He dashed his head against the knotted trunk, lifting up

his eyes, and howled, not like a man, but like a savage beast getting goaded to death with knives and spears.

I observed several splashes of blood about the bark of the tree, and his hand and forehead were both stained. It hardly moved my compassion—it appalled me. This was beyond decent mourning; this was something unclean. The moment he recollected himself enough to notice me watching, he thundered a command for me to go, and I obeyed.

Back upstairs I went to prepare her body, and that was when I really noticed something was amiss.

"Amiss?" I asked, unable to stop myself from interrupting even though I knew Nelly preferred I did not.

"Mr. Linton had awoken, you see, and I urged him to go and wash and dress and prepare for the day. He moved like a man asleep with his eyes open, but did as I suggested. When I was left alone with what remained of the lady, I went to her with a basin of water and washrag, thinking to bathe her. It was the wounds on her neck that I first noticed. Healed. Healed they were! Closed up!

At first, I thought I was mistaken. The lack of sleep, the anguish of the night. I thought my eyes deceived me, but they did not. Everywhere I looked upon her still, pale body, I found that the wounds of her previous night's attacks had healed over. Then I saw the fangs."

Again, I could not help myself. I gulped. I sat straight upright on the seat of my chair. "The fangs?"

Mrs. Dean lifted her upper lip for me to view yellowed, but solid teeth. "Fangs, Mr. Lockwood. Little budding fangs where they had not been before."

"Frightened by the sight," she continued, "I rose from the bed, backing away in horror. When Mr. Linton entered a moment later, I was unable to speak, only point. He sat gently on the edge of the bed and observed the healed wounds.

'What . . . what is wrong with her?' I cried, clasping the belt of garlic I wore round my waist.

He drew up the nightdress, adjusting the white lace ruffle around her neck just so, so that the white lines of wounds were no longer visible. 'Nothing is wrong with her, Nelly.'

'But . . . but the fangs, sir! Don't you see them?'

He didn't even look! He only smoothed her brow, kissed it, and rose from the bed. 'I see no fangs, Nelly, and you will say no more of this.' And with that he walked out of the room! Now, Master Linton was a gentleman, and I knew my place. 'Tis not for such as me to argue with him over what we saw, but fangs is fangs, and I tell you, sir, what I saw was fangs on that corpse, fangs that had not been there while she breathed.

"Go on," I urged.

Mrs. Linton's funeral was appointed to take place on the Friday following her decease. Till then, her coffin remained uncovered, and strewn with flowers and scented leaves, in the great drawing room. Can you imagine? Her lying right there in the house with her little fangs! I did not sleep a wink those days for fear she would rise from her coffin and take me in my bed . . . for fear I should hear the gnawing of those little fangs on the coffin lid. Linton seemed not to fear her and spent his days and nights there, a sleepless guardian.

The babe spent its days in screaming, such a noise from such a wrinkled and skinny scrap of flesh. It wailed at dawn; it wailed through the nooning. It wailed through supper and into the night, such a high-pitched squeal, half between that of a pig caught in a fence and a screech owl.

Heathcliff spent his days and nights far more violently. Only I knew the reason for his unbridled rage. Hip and thigh he did smite those vampires. They say he moved across the moors beheading them, splattering their black blood over half the properties in the county. Took him less than the week, and when he was done, what local vampires he had not killed had fled for safer ground. We poor folk were the safest we had been in years.

I held no communication with him as he rained terror upon the county, but on the night before she was to be buried, Mr. Linton took himself to bed and I went and opened one of the windows. I could feel Heathcliff out there in the garden, and moved by his perseverance, and thankful for his mowing of the vampires, I gave him the chance of bestowing on the fading image of his idol one final adieu.

He did not show himself that night. Indeed, I shouldn't have discovered that he had been there, except for the disarrangement of the drapery about the corpse's face, and for observing on the floor a curl of light hair, fastened with a silver thread. On examination, I ascertained it to have been taken from a locket hung round Catherine's neck. Heathcliff had opened the trinket and cast out its contents, replacing them with a black lock of his own. I twisted the two, and enclosed them together.

So caught up in his grief was Mr. Heathcliff that he apparently did not take notice of the healed wounds on her body, nor the little fangs. Too bad the parson was more observant, else to this day, I think we might have gotten away with burying her in the churchyard, and all might have been different had she been covered with holy ground.

"They didn't bury her in the churchyard?" I inquired, horrified and fascinated at the same time.

"They did not. Apparently others had tried to pull the same sleight of hand as Mr. Linton. Only weeks before, the high sheriff's brother's sister-in-law had attempted to have her nephew buried in the same churchyard, a Willy Rigby by name and smuggler by trade. This Rigby spent most of his time tearing around the country in the dead of night trying to dispose of his ill-gotten gains and had, as a matter of course, fallen in with a nest of young vampires. They'd buried him to his waist in a cave and feasted on him for weeks. When his wife finally realized that he was not off drunk with some tavern slut or taken aboard one of the Royal Navy ships as a swabby, she insisted on a search. To make a long story short, sir, they found him, still alive by the grace of God, but as white as cat puke. Beggin' your pardon, sir. Once they dug him up, he died. Sometimes that happens. Before they're full vampire, I think, they're still vulnerable to earthly ailments. Anyway, the aunt, having ties to the high sheriff, they made up this story for the blacksmith and tried to have the fellow pull out the telltale fangs, so that Willy could be buried in the family plot. Alas, it did not work."

"Why not?" I demanded, fascinated by another of Nelly's tales.

"The teeth would not come out. Rather, fangs, I should say. When the blacksmith seized the fangs with his horse-shoe tools, the fangs only got longer. They then tried to hold the man's wake with a cheese in his mouth, to cover the fangs. A farmers cheese it were, one of Dame Mildred's, and she makes the most foul cheese you have ever tasted, so 'twas no waste of good food. But the good cleric was too wily for them. He snatched the stinky cheese out of Willy's mouth, and all the funeral party were party to viewing the fangs—which were now longer and sharper than before. So poor Willy was packed off to the paupers' field and buried with the contents of Farmer Doug's pigsty piled on top of his grave to keep away any other vampires that might come to investigate. So the good cleric was prepared to watch for deception, you see.

"The parson walked right up to Catherine's coffin at the funeral, lifted the lid, opened her mouth, and slammed the coffin shut! He ordered the pallbearers to carry her outside the churchyard at once and then went off to have his tea."

"And Mr. Linton did not protest?" I asked.

"What good would it have done him? The fangs were plain to see. Fortunately, since she was, or rather had been, born gentry, there was no question of mutilating the corpse, so she was packed away as she was, fangs and all."

Mr. Earnshaw was, of course, invited to attend the remains of his sister to the grave. He sent no excuse, but he never came. Isabella was not asked. Besides her husband, the mourners were wholly composed of tenants and servants, so off we trudged to the plots reserved for those poor souls who met the unfortunate fate of being killed by the bloodsuckers. They were considered unholy, whether they had grown fangs or not, and could not rest on hallowed ground.

The place of Catherine's interment was dug on a green slope off the far west corner of the kirkyard. There, the heath and bilberry plants have crept down from the moor. Quite a pretty place for a damned soul to rest.

# Chapter 17

That Friday she was buried—the last pleasant day for a month. Just as Catherine was laid in her grave, the weather broke, the wind shifted from south to northeast, and brought rain, then sleet and snow.

After the burial, my master kept to his room and I took possession of the lonely parlor, converting it into a nursery. There I was sitting, with the moaning doll of a child laid on my knee, rocking it to and fro, watching the still-driving flakes behind the uncurtained window, when the door opened and some person entered, out of breath and laughing!

My anger was greater than my astonishment for a minute. I supposed it was one of the maids, and I cried— 'How dare you show your giddiness here? What would Mr. Linton say if he heard you?'

'Excuse me!' answered a familiar voice. 'But I know Edgar is in bed, and I cannot stop myself.'

With that, the speaker came forward to the fire, panting and holding her hand to her side. 'I have run the whole way from Wuthering Heights!' she continued, after a pause. 'I couldn't count the number of falls I've had. Oh, I'm aching all over! Don't be alarmed! There shall be an explanation as soon as I can give it. Just have the goodness to step out and order the carriage to take me on to Gimmerton, and tell a servant to seek up a few clothes in my wardrobe.'

Nelly paused for effect. "The intruder was Mrs. Heathcliff."

"Mistress Isabella? Heathcliff's wife?" I asked.

Nelly nodded. She certainly seemed in no laughing predicament. Her hair streamed on her shoulders, dripping with snow and water. The frock she wore was of light silk, and clung to her, wet. Though she wore a thin silk scarf around her neck, she could not hide the telltale signs of bites on her neck, but I could not tell how recent they were.

'Were you bitten, my dear young lady?' I exclaimed, rising to place the babe in an egg basket, for she was still too small to be left floating around in a proper bassinet.

"No eggs remained, you understand, sir, just a nice bed of straw. Saved on the nappies, you see."

"Yes, yes," I said, impatiently, "but what of Mistress Heathcliff?"

But Nelly went on, telling the story in her own way, scarce seeming to hear my question.

I questioned the bites on Isabella's neck because from what folks in the village said, there were presently no vampires for miles around. Heathcliff had slaughtered them all. I had heard from the fishmonger's wife that her cousin had seen a place along the road to Gimmerton where the heads of dozens of vampires had been put on pikes for all to see, human and vampire, but I had not had the opportunity to go see for myself yet.

But when I asked Isabella about the bites, she adjusted the scarf at her neck and replied, 'Mind your station and see about the carriage.'

I tried not to stare at her throat, sir. If Master Heathcliff had done in the bloodsuckers, who had savaged the dear lady? I tried to remember my place, but it did worry me some. I'd walked out to that church that past week without my garlic poultice. Was it possible some new infestation had swept over our moors? But bitter or not, she was a lady and sister to the master of this house, and I knew my duty to my betters.

'I'll go nowhere till you have removed every article of your clothes, and put on dry things. And certainly you shall not go to Gimmerton tonight, so it is needless to order the carriage.'

'I shall go,' she said. 'Walking or riding. My husband has gone mad and I wish to get as far from him as possible, as quickly as possible.'

'Mad?' I asked. 'So it is true? What I've heard?'

'I don't know what you've heard, Nelly. All I know is that day after day he has returned to the Heights soaked in the bloodsuckers' gore. He is more terrifying now than he was previously. He does not sleep, he does not eat. He only paces, crying out, moaning, and sometimes scratching at his face. Even Joseph fears him. Now see to my carriage, else I'll not speak another word to you.'

They were orders, you see, orders I could think of no way to get around, so I instructed the coachman to get ready and sent a maid to pack up some necessary attire, and then returned to Isabella. I found her staring down at the poor infant with such a look in her eyes that it sent icicles sliding down my spine. I vow, sir, did I not know her and how gentle a lady she was, I would have thought she meant harm to the motherless mite.

'Could you not put poor Catherine's baby away?' she asked when I returned. 'I don't like to see it! You mustn't think I care little for Catherine; I've cried, too, bitterly— yes, more than anyone else has reason to cry. We parted unreconciled, you remember, and I shan't forgive myself. But, for all that, I was not going to sympathize with him— the brute beast! Give me the poker!'

I stepped between her and the wailing babe, for it had

awakened and was screaming or as close to screaming as it could manage. Mrs. Heathcliff reached around me and grabbed the poker, and I threw up my arms to protect my head from certain doom, but she meant neither me, nor the wee scrap, harm.

'This is the last thing of his I have about me,' she cried. She slipped the gold ring from her third finger and threw it on the floor. 'I'll smash it!' she continued, striking it with childish spite, 'and then I'll burn it!' She dropped the mis-used article among the coals.

'He shall buy another, if he gets me back again. He'd be capable of coming to seek me, to tease Edgar—I dare not say, lest that notion should possess his wicked head! And besides, Edgar has not been kind, has he? And I won't come suing for his assistance. Necessity compelled me to seek shelter here; though, if I had not learnt my brother was upstairs, I'd have just kept running, running any-where out of reach of my accursed—of that incarnate gob-lin! Ah, he was in such a fury last I saw him! If he had caught me! It's a pity Earnshaw is not his match in strength. I wouldn't have run till I'd seen him done for, had Hindley been able to do it!'

'Don't talk so fast, miss!' I interrupted. 'Drink your tea, and take a breath.'

'Listen to that screeching, more hedgehog than child! It maintains a constant wail—send it out of my hearing for an hour. I shan't stay any longer.'

I rang the bell and committed the babe to a servant's care, and then I inquired how she escaped from Wuthering Heights, and where she meant to go.

'I wish I could remain,' answered she. 'To cheer Edgar and take care of the baby, and because the Grange is my right home. But I tell you, Heathcliff wouldn't let me! Do you think he could bear to see me grow fat and merry? When I enter his presence, the muscles of his countenance are involuntarily distorted into an expression of hatred. It is strong enough to make me feel pretty certain that he would not chase me over England, and therefore I must get quite away. I've recovered from my first desire to be killed by him. I'd rather he'd kill himself! He has extinguished my love effectually, and so I'm at my ease. Even if he had doted on me, the devilish nature would have revealed its existence somehow. Catherine had an awfully perverted taste to esteem him so dearly, knowing him so well. Knowing what a monster he was!'

'Hush, hush! He's a human being,' I said. I don't mind saying that by then, I had my doubts, but none I would put to words.

'He's *not* a human being,' she retorted. 'There is your mistake. I don't know what he is, but it's not human!'

'Is . . . has he become a vampire?'I questioned.

'I do not know what he is, for he slays them one minute, then talks of pitying them the next. It is enough to make one mad. Nelly, you asked what has driven me to flight at last? I was compelled to attempt it because I had succeeded in rousing his rage a pitch above his malignity.

'Yesterday, you know, Mr. Earnshaw should have been at the funeral. He kept himself sober for the purpose—tolerably sober. He did not play cards with the beasties, because they, of course, are dead or have fled. Consequently, he rose, in suicidal low spirits, as fit for the church as for a dance, and instead, he sat down by the fire and swallowed gin or brandy by tumblerfuls.

'Yester-evening I sat in my nook reading some old books near midnight. It seemed so dismal to go upstairs, with the wild snow blowing outside, and my thoughts continually reverting to the new-made grave! I dared hardly lift my eyes from the page before me, that melancholy scene so instantly usurped its place.

'Hindley sat opposite, his head leant on his hand, perhaps meditating on the same subject. He had ceased drinking at a point below irrationality, and had neither stirred nor spoken during two or three hours. The doleful silence was broken at length by the sound of the kitchen latch. Heathcliff had returned from his vampire hunting earlier than usual, owing, I supposed, to the sudden storm. That entrance was fastened, and we heard him coming round to get in by the other.

' "You, and I," Hindley said, "have each a great debt to settle with that man. You, perhaps more than me, for he has done so foul to you. But, if neither of us are cowards, we might combine to discharge it. Are you as soft as your brother? Are you willing to endure to the last, and not once attempt a repayment?"

' "I'd be glad of a retaliation that wouldn't recoil on myself, but treachery and violence wound those who resort to them, worse than their enemies."

' "Treachery and violence are a just return for treachery and violence!" cried Hindley. "Mrs. Heathcliff, I'll ask you to do nothing but sit still and be dumb. Tell me now, can you? I'm sure you would have as much pleasure as I in witnessing the conclusion of the fiend's existence. He'll be *your* death sooner rather than later from the looks of you—" '

'From the looks of you!' I interrupted her, eyeing her neck again. I was completely confused by what she was saying and wondered if she was, indeed, already half mad.

'Hush, and listen, Nelly. Hindley said, "Unless you overreach him and he'll be *my* ruin. Damn the hellish villain! He knocks at the door as if he were master here already! Promise to hold your tongue, and before that clock strikes, you're a free woman!"

'He took the weapon that I described to you in my letter from his breast, and would have turned down the candle. I snatched the candle away, however, and seized his arm.

' "I'll not hold my tongue!" I said. "You mustn't touch him. Let the door remain shut, and be quiet!"

' "No! I've formed my resolution, and by God, I'll execute it!" cried the desperate being. "I'll do you a kindness in spite of yourself, and Hareton justice!"

'I might as well have struggled with a bear, or reasoned with a lunatic, Nelly. The only resource left me was to run to a window and warn his intended victim of the fate that awaited him.

' "You'd better seek shelter somewhere else tonight!" I exclaimed in a rather triumphant tone. "Mr. Earnshaw has a mind to shoot you, if you persist in endeavoring to enter."

' "Shoot me? And he thinks that will kill me? I wish it were only so."

'I don't know what he meant by that, Nelly, but I did not care. I only did not want to be part of a murder.

' "You'd better open the door, you—" Heathcliff answered, addressing me by some elegant term that I don't care to repeat.

'With that I shut the window and returned to my place by the fire.

'Earnshaw swore passionately at me, affirming that I loved the villain and calling me all sorts of names. And I, in secret heart, thought what a blessing it would be for *him*, should Heathcliff put him out of misery. And what a blessing for *me*, should he send Heathcliff to his right abode! As I sat nursing these reflections, the casement window behind me was banged onto the floor by a blow from Heathcliff. He thrust his head through the opening. His hair and clothes were whitened with snow, and his sharp cannibal teeth, revealed by cold and wrath, gleamed through the dark.

' "Isabella, let me in, or I'll make you repent!" he threatened.

' "I cannot commit murder," I replied. "Hindley stands sentinel with a knife and loaded pistol."

' "Let me in by the kitchen door," he said.

' "Hindley will be there before me," I answered. "Heathcliff, if I were you, I'd go stretch myself over Catherine's grave and die like a faithful dog. The world is surely not worth living in now, is it? You had distinctly impressed on me the idea that Catherine was the whole joy of your life. I can't imagine how you think of surviving her loss."

'Heathcliff then flung himself through the window, meeting with Earnshaw, who brandished his weapon. The charge exploded, and the knife, in springing back, closed into its owner's wrist. Heathcliff pulled it from Hindley's grasp and thrust it, bloody, into his pocket. His adversary had fallen senseless with excessive pain, and the flow of blood that gushed from an artery or a large vein.

'The ruffian kicked and trampled on him, and dashed his head repeatedly against the flagstones, then tore off the sleeve of Earnshaw's coat and bound up the wound with brutal roughness.

'I rushed to see if I could give aid, but Heathcliff pushed me back.

' "I nearly forgot you," said the tyrant. "You conspire with him against me, do you, viper?"

'He shook me till my teeth rattled, and pitched me beside the unconscious Hindley. To my joy, he then left us, and I departed to my own room, marveling that I had escaped so easily.

'This morning, when I came down about half an hour before noon, Mr. Earnshaw was sitting by the fire, deadly sick. I ventured to draw near the fire, going round Earnshaw's seat, and kneeled in the corner beside him.

'Heathcliff did not glance my way, and I contemplated his features almost as confidently as if they had been turned to stone. His forehead, that I once thought so manly, and that I now think so diabolical, was shaded with a heavy cloud. His basilisk eyes were nearly quenched by sleepless-ness—and weeping, perhaps, for his lashes were wet. His lips, devoid of their ferocious sneer, were sealed in an ex-pression of unspeakable sadness. Had it been another, I would have covered my face in the presence of such grief. In *his* case, I was gratified. I couldn't miss this chance of sticking in a dart; his weakness was the only time when I could taste the delight of paying wrong for wrong.'

'For shame!' I interrupted. 'One might suppose you had never opened a Bible in your life. If God afflict your ene-mies, surely that ought to suffice you.'

'In general, I'll allow that it would be, Nelly,' she con-tinued, 'but what misery laid on Heathcliff could content me, unless I have a hand in it? I'd rather he suffered *less,* if I might cause his sufferings and he might *know* that I was the cause. Oh, I owe him so much. Anyway, Hindley wanted some water, and I handed him a glass, and asked him how he was.

' "Not as ill as I wish," he replied. "Every inch of me is as sore as if I had been fighting with a legion of vampires!" '

' "Yes, no wonder," was my next remark. "Catherine used to boast that she stood between you and bodily harm. She meant that certain persons would not hurt you for fear of offending her. It's well people don't *really* rise from their grave, or, last night, she might have witnessed a repulsive scene!"

' "What do you mean? Did he dare to strike me when I was down?"

' "He trampled on, and kicked you, and dashed you on the ground," I whispered. "And his mouth watered to tear you with his teeth because he's only half a man."

'Mr. Earnshaw looked up at Heathcliff, who, absorbed in his anguish, seemed insensible to anything around him. The longer he stood, the plainer his reflections revealed their blackness through his features.

' "Oh, if God would but give me strength to strangle

him in my last agony, I'd go to hell with joy," groaned Earnshaw, writhing to rise, and sinking back in despair.

' "Nay, it's enough that he has murdered one of you," I observed aloud. "At the Grange, everyone knows your sister would have been living now, had Heathcliff not made himself so friendly with the vampires."

'Most likely, Heathcliff noticed more the truth of what was said, for his attention was roused. His eyes rained down tears and he drew his breath in suffocating sighs.

'I stared full at him and laughed scornfully. The clouded windows of hell flashed a moment toward me. The fiend that usually looked out, however, was so dimmed and drowned that I did not fear him.

' "Get up, and be gone out of my sight," Heathcliff said.

' "I beg your pardon," I replied.

' "Get up, wretched idiot, before I stamp you to death!" he cried, making a movement that caused me to start.

' "But then," I continued, holding myself ready to flee, "if poor Catherine had trusted you, and assumed the ridiculous, contemptible, degrading title of Mrs. Heathcliff, as you wished, she would soon have presented a similar picture as I! *She* wouldn't have borne your abominable behavior quietly; her detestation and disgust must have found voice."

'Heathcliff snatched a dinner knife from the table and flung it at my head. It struck beneath my ear and stopped the sentence I was uttering. The last glimpse I caught of him was a furious rush on his part, checked by the embrace of Earnshaw, and both fell locked together on the hearth.

'I flew through the kitchen like a soul escaped from purgatory and down the steep road. I shot across the moor, rolling over banks and wading through marshes toward the beacon light of the Grange. I'd rather be condemned to a perpetual dwelling in the infernal regions than, even for one night, abide beneath the roof of Wuthering Heights again.'

Isabella ceased speaking, and took a drink of tea, then rose and put on the bonnet and shawl I had brought. Turning a deaf ear to my entreaties for her to remain another hour, she stepped onto a chair, kissed Edgar's and Catherine's portraits, bestowed a similar salute on me, and descended to the carriage. She was driven away, never to revisit this neighborhood, though a regular correspondence was established between her and my master when things were more settled.

I believe Isabella's new abode was in the south, near London; there she had a son born, a few months later. He was christened Linton, and, from the first, she reported him to be an ailing, peevish creature.

Mr. Heathcliff, meeting me one day in the village, inquired where she lived. I refused to tell. He remarked that he did not care, so long as she stayed away from her brother. Apparently he had learned from others that his wife had born a son, his heir, the fruit of his loins, a man-child."

Nelly plucked at a hair on her chin. "It was about that time that I began to notice changes in Heathcliff. Paler he was, more drawn. And his hairline seemed to be changing," she remarked, seeming to contemplate the information.

"The child," I urged. "You were telling me about Isabella's son."

Oh, yes. Heathcliff often asked about the infant when he saw me, and on hearing its name, smiled grimly, and observed, 'They wish me to hate it, too, do they?'

'I don't think they wish you to know anything about it,' I answered.

'But I'll have it,' he said, 'when I want it. They may reckon on that!'

"A foreshadowing of what was to come," Nelly explained.

"Time passed those years as time does. I was busy with little Cathy. At first I would go to Catherine's grave, but the earth was always upturned, as if she was freshly buried, and the heath and bilberry that grew down from the moors wove its way around the site, but never over it. It frightened me to the point that I was afraid to go, no matter how much garlic I wore in my underdrawers or braided into the moppet's hair and sewed into her petticoats."

"What did Mr. Earnshaw think of the upturned earth?" I asked.

"I've no idea! I'm not sure he ever knew. He never went to the place where she was laid, and certainly no one would ever have mentioned the matter, though there was plenty of talk among the servants and in the village."

"What did they say?" I asked.

She shrugged. "Some said she came forth from the grave regularly to feed, having become a vampire, but I thought that unlikely, else she would have come to her babe and I'd have known it, wouldn't I? She'd not have been able to easily hide. In those years there were few vampires in the moors due to Heathcliff's massacre. The ones we did see were just passing through. The ones foolish enough to stay were hunted down by Heathcliff and their heads added to the pikes. So many heads, so many fangs gleaming in the moonlight, 'twas said that other than a rainy night or in the dark of the moon, you'd need no lantern to pass that way, the fangs did reflect the light so. Boys liked to take their girls there, to scare them, and maybe get a kiss. Sometimes we had coach-loads of curious folk from the bigger towns, come just to see the heads that Master Heathcliff had taken. Queer what some folks do find interesting, don't you think, sir?"

I cleared my throat, thinking that with the proper company, I might have satisfied my curiosity by going to ob-

WUTHERING BITES 189

serve the collection myself, not out of morbid desire but because a gentleman of the world should observe what he can of the underbelly of life.

"They didn't stink, not like regular heads of them what's been hanged or come to no good ends," Mrs. Dean continued. "They just hung there and stared with their fangs all bared."

"So if she wasn't rising from the grave, what was your theory of the loose earth on Mrs. Linton's grave?" I asked, almost fearing her answer.

Nelly drew herself up indignantly. "I'm a servant, sir. It's not my place to have an opinion on such matters."

"But you *did* have an opinion?"

"Perhaps, but I wasn't about to prove my thoughts. I will tell you this; Mr. Heathcliff was seen often walking to the kirkyard at night. He never slept at night anymore to anyone's knowledge."

"I thought Catherine wasn't buried in holy ground."

"No, sir, she weren't, but just outside the churchyard wall. That's how I think Mr. Linton let himself pretend she was inside the fence, her soul safe."

"I see." I rolled those thoughts over in my head and looked back at Nelly. "What of Heathcliff's child? He never laid eyes on him?"

"Not until some thirteen years after the decease of Catherine, when Linton was twelve, or a little more.

On the day succeeding Isabella's unexpected visit, I told Mr. Linton what had happened and I saw it pleased him that his sister had left her husband, whom he abhorred with an intensity that the mildness of his nature would scarcely seem to allow. So deep and sensitive was his aversion that he refrained from going anywhere he was likely to see or hear of Heathcliff. Grief, and that aversion to Heathcliff, transformed him into a complete hermit. He gave up his office of magistrate, ceased even to attend church, avoided the village on all occasions, and spent a life of entire seclusion within the limits of his park.

But he was too good to be thoroughly unhappy long. He didn't pray for Catherine's soul to haunt him like the other one. Maybe he knew better. Be careful what you ask for, that's what I always say. Time brought resignation, and a melancholy sweeter than common joy. He recalled her memory with ardent, tender love, and hopeful aspiring to the better world, where, he doubted not, she was gone. In his mind, it was as if the circumstances of her death had never existed. In his mind, I think he believed he had buried her inside the kirkyard on holy ground as he had intended and not outside, beyond the pale, as it were.

And he had earthly consolation. It was named Catherine, and his attachment sprang from its relation to his dear departed, far more than from its being his own. After the death of Catherine many whispered that Edgar would not be far behind her, but he did not give in to grief as many expected.

"So the sickly child did live?" I asked, almost ashamed that I'd given little thought to the plight of the innocent babe.

"That she did, but more on her later," Nelly continued.

Now, the end of Earnshaw was what might have been expected; it followed fast on his sister's, scarcely six months between them. We, at the Grange, never got a very succinct account of his state preceding it. The doctor came to announce the event to my master.

'Well, Nelly,' said he, riding into the yard one morning, too early not to alarm me with an instant presentiment of bad news, 'Who's given us the slip now, do you think?'

'Who?' I asked in a flurry.

'Why, guess!' he returned, dismounting, and slinging his bridle on a hook by the door.

'Not Mr. Heathcliff, surely?' I exclaimed, for by then I

was on to him and was beginning to suspect he would never die any more than those bloodsuckers' heads would rot.

'No, Heathcliff's a tough young fellow; he looks bloom-ing today. I've just seen him. He actually had a little color in his cheeks.'

'Who is it, then, Mr. Kenneth?' I repeated impatiently.

'Hindley Earnshaw! Your old friend Hindley,' he replied. 'He died true to his character, drunk as a lord. He's barely twenty-seven, it seems.'

I confess this blow was greater to me than the shock of Mrs. Linton's death; ancient associations lingered round my heart.

I could not hinder myself from pondering on the ques-tion—Had his death involved foul play? Whatever I did, that idea would bother me until finally I thought I should go see for myself and requested that I be allowed to go to Wuthering Heights, and assist in the last duties of the dead. Mr. Linton was extremely reluctant to consent, but I pleaded eloquently for the friendless condition in which he lay. I said my old master and foster-brother had a claim on my services as strong as his own. Besides, I reminded him that the child Hareton was his wife's nephew, and, in the absence of nearer kin, he ought to act as its guardian. I told him he ought to and must inquire how the property was left, and look over the concerns of his brother-in-law.

He was unfit for attending to such matters then, but he bid me speak to his lawyer and permitted me to go. His lawyer had been Earnshaw's also, so I went to the village and asked him to accompany me. He shook his head and advised that Heathcliff should be let alone, affirming, if the truth were known, Hareton would be found little else than a beggar.

'His father died in debt,' he said. 'We all said that play-ing cards with those bloodsuckers would not end well.

They were clever, for the undead. The whole property is mortgaged, and the sole chance for the natural heir is to allow him an opportunity of creating some interest in the creditor's heart, that he may be inclined to deal leniently toward him.'

When I reached the Heights, I explained that I had come to see everything carried on decently. Mr. Heathcliff said I might stay and order the arrangements for the funeral, if I chose.

'Correctly,' he remarked. 'That fool's body should be buried at the crossroads, without ceremony of any kind. I happened to leave him ten minutes yesterday afternoon, and in that interval he fastened the two doors of the house against me, and he has spent the night in drinking himself to death deliberately! We broke in this morning, for we heard him snorting like a horse, and there he was, laid over the settle. Flaying and scalping would not have wakened him. I sent for the doctor, and he came, but he was both dead and cold, and stark. So, there will be no fuss; he doesn't deserve it.'

Despite his words, I insisted on the funeral being respectable. Mr. Heathcliff said I might have my own way, but I was to remember that the money for the whole affair came out of his pocket.

Bathed the body myself, I did. He was marked, of course.

"Marked?" I asked, eyes wide.

"Vampire bites. Here and here." She struck both sides of her neck. "And here and here." She touched her wrists, then her ankles.

"But I thought you said there weren't any vampires left in the county."

"So I was told."

"What did Mr. Heathcliff say about the bites?"

"He didn't say a word."

He maintained a hard, careless deportment, indicative of neither joy nor sorrow. If anything, it expressed a flinty gratification at a piece of difficult work successfully executed. I observed once, indeed, something like exultation in his aspect. It was just when the people were bearing the coffin from the house. He had the hypocrisy to represent himself as a mourner! Just before he and Hareton went, he lifted the unfortunate child on to the table and muttered, with peculiar gusto, 'Now, my bonny lad, you are *mine!* And we'll see if one tree won't grow as crooked as another, with the same wind to twist it!'

The unsuspecting lad was pleased at this speech or at least at the attention, for he played with Heathcliff's whiskers and stroked his cheek.

I, however, divined its meaning, and observed tartly, 'That boy must go back with me to Thrushcross Grange, sir. There is nothing in the world less yours than he is!'

'Does Linton say so?' he demanded.

'Of course—he has ordered me to take him,' I replied.

'Well,' said the scoundrel. 'We'll not argue the subject now, but I have a fancy to try my hand at rearing a young one. Tell your master that I don't engage to let Hareton go, undisputed, and if he presses it, I'll be pretty sure to make the other come! Remember to tell him.'

This hint was enough to bind our hands. If Edgar pressed, Heathcliff would seek out his own son. Edgar did not speak of interfering again. Hareton was left to Master Heathcliff, God forgive us.

The guest was now the master of Wuthering Heights. He held firm possession, and proved to the attorney— who, in his turn, proved it to Mr. Linton—that Earnshaw had mortgaged every yard of land he owned for cash to supply his mania for gaming with the beasties; and he, Heathcliff, was the mortgagee. No one ever expressed aloud the question of whether or not the vampires had been in league with Heathcliff, but we all had our opinions. In that manner poor Hareton, who should now be the first gentleman in the neighborhood, was reduced to a state of complete dependence on his father's enemy.

# Chapter 18

The twelve years, continued Nelly, following that dismal period, were the happiest of my life. Our little lady grew like a larch, and could walk and talk, too, in her own way, before the heath blossomed around (but never directly on) Mrs. Linton's grave.

Cathy was the most winning thing that ever brought sunshine into a desolate house. She was a beauty in face, with the Earnshaws' handsome dark eyes, but the Lintons' fair skin, and small features, and yellow curling hair. Her spirit was high, though not rough, and qualified by a heart sensitive and lively to excess in its affections. That capacity for intense attachments reminded me of her mother. Still she did not resemble her, for she could be soft and mild as a dove, and she had a gentle voice and pensive expression. Her anger was never furious, her love never fierce. It was deep and tender.

However, it must be acknowledged, dearest Cathy had faults to foil her gifts. A propensity to be saucy was one; she possessed a perverse will that indulged children invariably acquired, whether they be good-tempered or cross. If a servant chanced to vex her, it was always—'I shall tell Papa!' And if he reproved her, even by a look, you would have thought it a heartbreaking business. I don't believe he ever did speak a harsh word to her.

He took her education entirely on himself and made it an amusement. Fortunately, curiosity and a quick intellect urged her into an apt scholar. She learnt rapidly and eagerly, and did honor to this teaching.

Till she reached the age of thirteen, she had not once been beyond the range of the park by herself. Mr. Linton would take her with him a mile or so outside, on rare occasions, but he trusted her to no one else. Even though the vampires did not run rampant as they once had, they were still out there, lurking in the shadows, waiting for an unsuspecting good soul from which to make a meal. Gimmerton was an unsubstantial name in Cathy's ears. Wuthering Heights and Mr. Heathcliff did not exist for her. She was a perfect recluse and, apparently, perfectly contented. Sometimes, indeed, while surveying the country from her nursery window, she would observe—

'Nelly, how long will it be before I can walk to the top of those hills? I wonder what lies on the other side—is it the sea?'

'No, Miss Cathy,' I would answer. 'It is hills again, just like these.'

'Is it because of the vampires that I cannot go?'

'Aye. They like to feast particularly on blond little girls,' I warned.

'Funny, but sometimes I think it is something more Papa keeps me from.' She pointed through the window. 'And what are those golden rocks like, when you stand under them?' she once asked.

The abrupt descent of Penistone Crags particularly attracted her notice, especially when the setting sun shone on it and the topmost heights, and the whole extent of landscape besides lay in shadow.

I explained that they were bare masses of stone, with hardly enough earth in their clefts to nourish a stunted tree.

'And why are they bright so long after it is evening here?' she pursued.

'Because they are a great deal higher up than we are,' replied I. 'You could not climb them. They are too high and steep. In winter, the frost is always there before it comes to us, and deep into summer I have found snow under that black hollow on the northeast side!'

'Oh, you have been on them!' she cried, gleefully. 'Then I can go, too, when I am a woman and can fight the vampires off on my own. Has Papa been, Nelly?'

I ignored the comment about the vampires, for my master would never have allowed her to be trained to fight, even in self-defense. He was too tangled in his mental fantasy that the bloodsuckers did not exist, and even if they did, raising a weapon against them would have been entirely too unladylike for his darling. 'Papa would tell you, miss,' I answered hastily, 'that they are not worth the trouble of visiting. The moors, where you ramble with him, are much nicer. Thrushcross Park is the finest place in the world.'

'But I know the park, and I don't know those,' she murmured to herself. 'And I should delight to look round me from the brow of that tallest point. My little pony Minny shall take me sometime. She is far too fast for any bloodsucker to catch.'

One of the maids mentioning the Fairy Cave quite turned Cathy's head with a desire to fulfill this project. She teased Mr. Linton about it, and he promised she should have the journey when she got older. I doubt he meant it, but he would have promised her the moon should she have requested it.

'Now am I old enough to go to Penistone Crags?' was the constant question in her mouth.

The road there ran close by Wuthering Heights. Edgar

had not the heart to pass it, so she received as constantly the answer, 'Not yet, love. Not yet.'

As for what else occurred at that time, Mrs. Heathcliff lived above a dozen years after leaving her husband. I was told she was attacked by a swarm of vampires whilst returning from church one Sunday morning. Fortunately, the child had been suffering from the ague and she had left him home. She was treated by the local doctor, but she never came back around as most folks with just a bite or two did. She wrote to inform her brother of the probable conclusion of the attack and entreated him to come to her, if possible. She said in her letter that she had much to settle, and she wished to bid him adieu and deliver Linton safely into his hands. Her hope was that Linton might be left with him. Somehow, she had convinced herself that his father had no desire to assume the burden of his maintenance or education.

My master didn't hesitate to comply with her request, reluctant as he was to leave home. Commending Catherine to my peculiar vigilance in his absence, he reiterated orders that she must not wander out of the park, even under my escort. He did not calculate on her going unaccompanied.

He was away three weeks. The first day or two, my charge sat in a corner of the library, too sad for either reading or playing. In that quiet state she caused me little trouble, but it was succeeded by an interval of impatient, fretful weariness. Me, being too busy, and too old then, to run up and down amusing her, I hit on a method by which she might entertain herself.

I used to send her on travels round the grounds—now on foot, and now on a pony, indulging her with a patient audience of all her real and imaginary adventures when she returned.

The summer shone in full prime, and she took such a taste for this solitary rambling that she often contrived to remain out from breakfast till tea. Then the evenings were spent in recounting her fanciful tales. I did not fear her breaking bounds because the gates were generally locked and the property was patrolled with guards. I thought she would never pass through the gates, even if they were thrown open.

Unluckily, my confidence proved misplaced. Catherine came to me one morning at eight o'clock, and said she was that day an Arabian merchant, going to cross the desert with his caravan. She asked that I provide plenty of provisions for herself and beasts: a horse and three camels, personated by a large hound and a couple of pointers.

I got together a good store of dainties and slung them in a basket on one side of the saddle. She sprang up as gay as a fairy, sheltered by her wide-brimmed hat and gauze veil from the July sun, and trotted off with a merry laugh, mocking my cautious counsel to avoid galloping, and come back early.

The naughty thing never made her appearance at tea. One traveler, the hound, being an old dog and fond of its ease, returned, but neither Cathy nor the pony, nor the two pointers were visible in any direction. I dispatched emissaries down this path, and that path, and at last went wandering in search of her myself.

There was a laborer working at a fence round a plantation, on the borders of the grounds. I enquired of him if he had seen our young lady.

'I saw her at morn,' he replied. 'She would have me to cut her a hazel switch, and then she leapt over the hedge yonder, where it is lowest, and galloped out of sight.'

You may guess how I felt at hearing this news. It struck me directly she must have started for Penistone Crags.

'What will become of her?' I ejaculated, pushing through a gap which the man was repairing, and making straight to the high-road. I didn't even take the time to go back for a better weapon than the wee dagger I had carried all those years.

I walked mile after mile, till a turn brought me in view of the Heights, but no Catherine could I detect, far or near. I was frantic. What if she'd been eaten by wolves? Snatched up by gypsies and forced to tell fortunes in some far heathen place? What if she'd been set upon by robbers and wandered barefoot and penniless into some town, and there seized by the authorities as a pauper and shipped off to the far side of the world as an indentured wench? Worse, what if she'd wandered to Wuthering Heights and been attacked by Master Heathcliff's wee devil terrier? And then there were the vampires. I did not even want to consider what would become of my master if his little daughter was consumed by the bloodsuckers, not after losing a wife and a sister to them.

The Crags lie about a mile and a half beyond Mr. Heathcliff's place, and that is four from the Grange, so I began to fear night would fall ere I could reach them.

I ran to the door, knocking vehemently for admittance. A woman whom I knew, and who formerly lived at Gimmerton, answered. She had been a servant there since the death of Mr. Earnshaw.

'Ah,' said she. 'You are come a-seeking your little mistress! Don't be frightened. She's here safe, but I'm glad it isn't the master.'

'He is not at home then, is he?' I panted, quite breathless with quick walking and alarm. 'Have the dogs eaten her?'

'No, no,' she replied. 'The master's gone for hours at a time. God knows where and I'm not certain even God cares. Hunting, I suppose. He keeps these roads fairly clean of the bloodsuckers. Step in and rest you a bit.'

I entered, and beheld my stray lamb seated on the hearth, rocking herself in a little chair that had been her mother's when a child. Her hat was hung against the wall and she seemed perfectly at home, laughing and chattering, in the best spirits imaginable, to Hareton. He was now a great, strong lad of eighteen who stared at her with considerable curiosity and astonishment.

'Very well, miss!' I exclaimed, concealing my joy under an angry countenance. 'This is your last ride till your papa comes back. I'll not trust you over the threshold again, you naughty, naughty girl!'

'Aha, Nelly!' she cried gaily, jumping up and running to my side. 'I shall have a pretty story to tell tonight. I saw vampires in the distance whilst I was riding and then I found Wuthering Heights. Have you ever been here in your life before?'

'Put that hat on, and home at once,' said I, glancing first this way and then the other for the Heathcliff hounds. 'I'm dreadfully grieved at you, Miss Cathy. You've done extremely wrong! It's no use pouting and crying; that won't repay the trouble I've had, scouring the country after you. To think how Mr. Linton charged me to keep you in, and you stealing off so! It shows you are a cunning little fox, and nobody will put faith in you anymore.'

'What have I done?' sobbed she, instantly checked. 'Papa charged me nothing. He'll not scold me, Nelly—he's never cross, like you!'

'Come, come!' I repeated 'For shame. You thirteen years old, and such a baby!'

This exclamation was caused by her pushing the hat from her head and retreating to the chimney out of my reach.

'Nay,' said the servant. 'Don't be hard on the bonny lass, Mrs. Dean. We made her stop before she went farther. Hareton offered to go with her and I thought he should. Mr. Heathcliff has warned us to all stay away from there.

I suppose it's one of the places where there are still nests of bloodsuckers.'

Hareton, during the discussion, stood with his hands in his pockets, too awkward to speak, though he looked as if he did not relish my intrusion.

'It will be dark in ten minutes. Where is the pony, Miss Cathy? And where are the dogs? I shall leave you unless you be quick, so please yourself.'

'The pony is in the yard,' she replied. 'The dogs, too. I was going to tell you all about it, but you are in a bad temper, and don't deserve to hear.'

I picked up her hat, and approached to put it on her thick little head, but perceiving that the people of the house took her part, she commenced capering round the room. On my giving chase, she ran like a mouse over and under and behind the furniture, rendering it ridiculous for me to pursue.

Hareton and the woman laughed, and she joined them, and waxed more impertinent still till I cried, in great irritation, 'Well, Miss Cathy, if you were aware whose house this is, you'd be glad to get out.'

'It's *your* father's, isn't it?' said she, turning to Hareton.

'Nay,' he replied, looking down and blushing bashfully. He could not stand a steady gaze from her eyes, though they were just like his own.

'Whose, then—your master's?' she asked.

He colored deeper, with a different feeling, muttered an oath, and turned away.

'Who is his master?' continued the tiresome girl, appealing to me. 'He talked about "our house," and "our folk." I thought he was the owner's son. But he never said Miss. He should have done, shouldn't he, if he's a servant?'

Hareton grew black as a thunder-cloud at this childish speech. I silently shook my questioner and at last succeeded in equipping her for departure.

'Now, get my horse,' she said, addressing her unknown

kinsman as she would one of the stable boys at the Grange. 'And you may come with me. I want to see where the vampires come out of the marsh. What's the matter? Get my horse, I say.'

'I'll see thee damned before I be thy servant!' growled the lad.

'You'll see me *what?*' asked Catherine in surprise.

'Damned—thou saucy witch!' he replied.

'There, Miss Cathy! You see you have got into pretty company,' I interposed. 'Nice words to be used to a young lady! Pray don't begin to dispute with him. Come, let us be gone.'

'But, Nelly,' cried she, staring, fixed in astonishment. 'How dare he speak so to me? Mustn't he be made to do as I ask him? You wicked creature, I shall tell my papa what you said!'

Hareton did not appear to feel this threat, so the tears sprang into her eyes with indignation. 'You bring the pony,' she exclaimed, turning to the woman.

'Softly, miss,' answered the addressed. 'You'll lose nothing by being civil. Though Mr. Hareton, there, be not the master's son, he's your cousin, and I was never hired to serve you.'

'*He's* my cousin!' cried Cathy, with a scornful laugh.

'Yes, indeed.'

'Oh, Nelly! Don't let them say such things,' she pursued in great trouble. 'Papa is gone to fetch my cousin from London. My cousin is a gentleman's son.'

'Hush, hush!' I whispered. 'People can have many cousins and of all sorts, Miss Cathy, without being any the worse for it, only they needn't keep their company, if they be disagreeable and bad.'

'He's not—he's not my cousin, Nelly!' she went on, gathering fresh grief from reflection, and flinging herself into my arms for refuge from the idea.

Hareton, recovering from his disgust at being taken for

a servant, seemed moved by her distress and fetched the pony round to the door. He then took to her a fine crooked-legged terrier whelp from the kennel, and putting it into her hand, apologized haltingly. Pausing in her lamentations, she surveyed him with a glance of awe and horror, then burst into tears again.

I could scarcely refrain from smiling at her reaction to the poor fellow who was a well-made, athletic youth. He was good looking in features, and stout and healthy, but attired in clothing befitting a man on the farm, and lounging among the moors after rabbits and game. Still, I thought I could detect in his character better qualities than his father ever possessed. Mr. Heathcliff, I believe, had not treated him physically ill, though he appeared to have bent his malevolence on making him a brute. The young man was never taught to read or write, never rebuked for any bad habit that did not annoy his keeper; never led a single step toward virtue, or guarded by a single precept against vice.

I don't pretend to be intimately acquainted with the mode of living customary in those days at Wuthering Heights. I only speak from hearsay, for I saw little. The villagers affirmed Mr. Heathcliff was near, and a cruel, hard landlord to his tenants, but the house, inside, had regained its ancient aspect of comfort under female management, and of course, vampires did not come to call as they once had. Mr. Heathcliff had put an end to that the night they attacked his beloved Catherine.

None of this surprised me, however. What did surprise me was the rumor that on occasion villagers swore they saw Heathcliff at night stalking about the town, hiding in the shadows, watching them. And he still returned regularly to Catherine's grave, where they say he sobbed and moaned and put up such a racket that everyone avoided the kirkyard road at night.

This, however, is not making progress with my story.

Miss Cathy rejected the peace offering of the terrier, and we set out for home, sadly out of sorts, every one of us.

I could not wring from my little lady how she had spent the day, except that, as I supposed, the goal of her pilgrimage had been Penistone Crags. When she arrived without adventure (beyond a possible sighting of vampires on horses in the distance, led by a great dark one, she claimed) to the gate of Wuthering Heights, Hareton happened to issue forth, attended by some canine followers, who attacked her dogs.

They had a smart battle before their owners could separate them, and that formed an introduction. Catherine told Hareton who she was, and where she was going, and asked him to show her the way, beguiling him to accompany her.

He opened the mysteries of the Fairy Cave, and twenty other queer places such as old vampire dens and a stray pike or two where Mr. Heathcliff liked to display the heads of those he had murdered. Apparently, Hareton did not disclose who the mighty hero was, only that he was a gypsy slayer of great fame.

I gathered that Hareton and the miss had gotten along well until the very moment she had hurt his feelings by addressing him as a servant and Heathcliff's housekeeper hurt hers by calling him her cousin.

I explained to my charge that her papa objected to the whole household at the Heights, and that he would be quite upset to learn she had been there. I dwelled most on the fact that, if she revealed my negligence of his orders, he would perhaps be so angry that I should have to leave. Fortunately, Cathy couldn't bear that prospect and she pledged her word, and kept it, for my sake. After all, she was a sweet little girl.

# Chapter 19

Aletter announced the day of my master's return. Isabella was dead, and he wrote to bid me get mourning for his daughter and arrange a room, and other accommodations, for his youthful nephew.

Catherine ran wild with joy at the idea of welcoming her father back, and indulged most optimistic anticipations of the innumerable excellences of her 'real' cousin.

The evening of their expected arrival came. Since early morning, she had been busy ordering her own small affairs, and now, attired in her new black frock, she obliged me to walk with her down through the grounds to meet them.

'Linton is just six months younger than I am,' she chattered as we strolled leisurely over the swells and hollows of mossy turf, under shadow of the trees. 'How delightful it will be to have him for a playfellow! Aunt Isabella sent Papa a beautiful lock of his hair. It is very dark and quite fine. I have it carefully preserved in a little glass box and I've often thought what pleasure it would be to see its owner. Oh! I am happy—and Papa, dear, dear Papa! Come, Nelly, let us run!'

She ran, and returned and ran again, many times before my sober footsteps reached the gate, and then she seated herself on the grassy bank beside the path and tried to wait patiently. That was impossible, of course; she couldn't be still a minute.

'When will they be here? May we not go a little way—half a mile, Nelly? Only just half a mile? Do say yes, to that clump of birches at the turn!'

I refused staunchly, and, at length, her suspense was ended. The traveling carriage rolled in sight.

Miss Cathy shrieked and stretched out her arms, as soon as she caught her father's face looking from the window. He descended, nearly as eager as herself, and a considerable interval elapsed before they tore themselves from each other's arms.

While they exchanged caresses I took a peep of Linton. He was asleep in a corner, wrapped in a warm, fur-lined cloak as if it had been winter. A pale, delicate, effeminate boy, with inky black hair, I had no doubt he was Heathcliff's spawn.

Mr. Linton advised me to close the door and leave the boy undisturbed, for the journey had fatigued him. Cathy wanted to see him, too, but her father told her to come on, and they walked together up the park. Meanwhile, I hastened home to prepare the servants.

'Now, darling,' said Mr. Linton, addressing his daughter, as they halted at the bottom of the front steps. 'Your cousin is not so strong or so merry as you are, and he has just lost his mother. Don't expect him to play and run about with you, at first. And don't harass him by talking too much. Let him be quiet this evening, at least, will you?'

'Yes, yes, Papa,' answered Catherine. 'But I do want to see him.'

The carriage stopped, and the boy, being roused, was lifted to the ground by his uncle. 'This is your cousin Cathy, Linton,' he said, putting their little hands together. 'She's fond of you already, and mind you don't grieve her by crying tonight. The traveling is at an end, and you have nothing to do but rest and amuse yourself as you please.'

'Let me go to bed, then.' Young Linton shrank from Catherine's salute and put his fingers to his eyes to remove incipient tears.

'Come, come, there's a good child,' I whispered, leading him in. 'You'll make her weep, too—see how sorry she is for you!'

I proceeded to remove Linton's cap and mantle, and placed him on a chair by the table where tea had been laid out, but he was no sooner seated than he began to cry again. My master inquired what was the matter.

'I can't sit on a chair,' sobbed the boy.

'Go to the sofa, then, and Nelly shall bring you some tea,' answered his uncle, patiently. He had been greatly tried during the journey, I felt convinced, by his fretful, ailing charge.

Linton slowly trailed himself off, and lay down. Cathy carried a footstool and her cup to his side. At first she sat silent, but that could not last, for she had resolved to make a pet of her little cousin. She commenced stroking his shiny black hair, and kissing his cheek, and offering him tea in her saucer like a baby. This pleased him; he dried his eyes and lightened into a faint smile.

'Oh, he'll do very well,' said the master to me, after watching them a minute. 'Very well, if we can keep him, Nelly. The company of a child of his own age will instill new spirit into him soon, and by wishing for strength he'll gain it.'

I must confide to you, Mr. Lockwood, that I did not like the looks of him, not from the time I first laid eyes on him. The color of his flesh, the pinch of his face. There was something about that boy that was unearthly, but most certainly not heavenly. I, of course, kept my thoughts to myself.

'Aye, if we can keep him!' I told Mr. Edgar. Had it been my choice, I do not know if I would have allowed him to sleep one night under my roof, but I did wonder how a weakling like him would ever live at Wuthering Heights, between his father and Hareton? What playmates and instructors they would be.

Our doubts were presently decided—even earlier than I expected. I had just taken the children upstairs after tea and seen Linton asleep. He asked that I extinguish all light, but he did not want me to leave until he was asleep. An odd request, but I fulfilled it.

I had just come downstairs and was standing by the table in the hall, lighting a bedroom candle for Mr. Edgar, when a maid stepped out of the kitchen and informed me that Mr. Heathcliff's servant Joseph was at the door, and wished to speak with the master.

'I shall ask him what he wants first,' I said, in considerable trepidation. 'I don't think the master can see him tonight, not after such a long journey.'

Joseph had advanced through the kitchen as I uttered these words, and now presented himself in the hall. He was donned in his Sunday garments, with his most sanctimonious and sourest face, and, holding his hat in one hand and his stick in the other, he proceeded to clean his shoes on the mat. He was as deathly pale as the boy, and wearing the ridiculous scarf around his neck Isabella had spoken of.

'Good evening, Joseph,' I said, coldly. 'What business brings you here tonight?'

'It's Master Linton I must speak to,' he answered, waving me disdainfully aside.

'Mr. Linton is going to bed. Unless you have something particular to say, I'm sure he won't hear it now,' I continued. 'You had better entrust your message to me.'

'Which is his room?' pursued the fellow, surveying the range of closed doors.

I perceived he was bent on refusing my mediation, so very reluctantly I went up to the library and announced the unseasonable visitor, advising that he should be dismissed till the next day.

Mr. Linton had no time to respond, for Joseph mounted close at my heels and, pushing into the apartment, planted himself at the far side of the table, with his two fists clapped on the head of his stick. 'Master Heathcliff has sent me for his lad.'

I do not know to this day how Heathcliff knew so quickly the boy was there, but I have my suspicions. The vampires, they had a way of communicating among themselves that could not be understood by us humans.

"The vampires!" I remarked, quite shocked. "But, Nelly, how—"

"You said I could tell the tale in my own manner, Mr. Lockwood, and so I shall," she interrupted, raising a forefinger as though to a naughty child.

I sat back, not pleased that I had been chastised by my housekeeper, but too eager to hear the tale to its end to protest further. "Please, Mrs. Dean, go on."

Edgar Linton was silent a minute; an expression of exceeding sorrow overcast his features. He would have pitied the child on his own account, but, recalling Isabella's hopes and fears, he grieved bitterly at the prospect of yielding him up, and searched in his heart how it might be avoided. No plan offered itself; Heathcliff was the child's father. There was nothing left but to resign him. However, he was not going to rouse him from his sleep.

'Tell Mr. Heathcliff,' he answered calmly, 'that his son shall come to Wuthering Heights tomorrow. He is in bed, and too tired to go the distance now. You may also tell him that the mother of Linton desired him to remain under my guardianship, and, at present, his health is very precarious. He looks as if he needs a good platter of meat and tender care.'

'No!' said Joseph, giving a thud with his prop on the floor, and assuming an authoritative air. 'No! Heathcliff will have his lad and I will take him!'

'You shall not tonight!' answered Mr. Linton decisively. 'Walk downstairs at once, and repeat to your master what I have said. Nelly, show him down.' And, aiding the indignant elder with a lift by the arm, he rid the room of him and closed the door.

'Very well!' shouted Joseph as he slowly drew off. 'Till morn, and then my master will come for him himself!'

# Chapter 20

To preclude the danger of this threat being fulfilled, Mr. Linton sent me to take the boy home early, on Catherine's pony, and, said he—

'As we shall now have no influence over his destiny, good or bad, you must say nothing of where he is gone to my daughter. She cannot associate with him hereafter, and it is better for her to remain in ignorance of his proximity. Otherwise, she will be anxious to visit the Heights. Just tell her his father sent for him suddenly, and he has been obliged to leave us.'

Linton was very reluctant to be roused from his bed at five o'clock, and astonished to be informed that he must prepare for further traveling. I softened off the matter by stating that he was going to spend some time with his father, Mr. Heathcliff, who wished to see him so much.

'My father!' he cried. 'Mamma never told me I had a father. Where does he live? I'd rather stay with Uncle.'

'He lives a little distance from the Grange,' I replied. 'Just beyond those hills, so you may walk over here when you get hearty. And you should be glad to go home, and to see him. You must try to love him, as you did your mother, and then he will love you.'

'But why have I not heard of him before?' asked Linton.

'Why didn't Mamma and he live together, as other people do?'

'He had business to keep him in the north,' I answered. 'And your mother's health required her to reside in the south.'

'And why didn't Mamma speak to me about him?' persevered the child. 'She often talked of Uncle, and I learnt to love him long ago. How am I to love Papa? I don't know him.'

'Oh, all children love their parents,' I said. 'Your mother, perhaps, thought you would want to be with him if she mentioned him often to you.'

'Is *she* to go with us?' he demanded. 'The little girl I saw yesterday?'

'Not now,' replied I.

'Is my uncle?' he continued.

'I shall be your companion,' I said.

Linton sank back on his pillow. 'I won't go without Uncle,' he cried. 'I can't tell where you mean to take me.'

I attempted to persuade him of the naughtiness of showing reluctance to meet his father. Still, he obstinately resisted any progress toward dressing, and I had to call for my master's assistance in coaxing him out of bed.

The poor thing was finally got off with several assurances that his absence should be short. I said that Mr. Edgar and Cathy would visit him and made other promises, equally ill-founded, which I invented and reiterated at intervals on the ride over.

The pure heather-scented air, the bright sunshine, and the gentle canter of the horse relieved his despondency after a while. He began to put questions concerning his new home, and its inhabitants, with greater interest and liveliness.

'Is Wuthering Heights as pleasant a place as Thrushcross Grange?' he inquired, turning to take a last glance into the valley, where a light mist mounted and formed a fleecy cloud on the skirts of the blue.

'It is not so buried in trees,' I replied, keeping my eyes peeled for bloodsuckers. Cathy's insistence that she had seen them in the distance the day she escaped had me worried. I was especially concerned that she had noticed one in particular that sounded as if it greatly resembled Heathcliff. *Why would Heathcliff be riding with vampires on the moors?* I wondered as I continued to try to keep Linton calm.

'Wuthering Heights is not so large as the Grange, but you can see the country beautifully, all round. And the air is healthier for you—fresher and dryer. You will, perhaps, think the building old and dark at first, but it is a respectable house. The next best in the neighborhood.'

'And what is my father like?' he asked. 'Is he as young and handsome as Uncle?'

'He's as young,' said I. 'But he has black hair and eyes, just like you, and is taller and bigger altogether than your uncle. He'll not seem to you so gentle and kind at first, perhaps, because it is not his way. Mind you to be cordial with him, and naturally he'll be fonder of you than any uncle, for you are his own.' My words sounded so true, I nearly had myself believing them.

'How strange that he should never come to see Mamma and me!' he murmured. 'Has he ever seen me? If he has, I must have been a baby—I remember not a single thing about him!'

'Why, Master Linton,' said I, 'three hundred miles is a great distance. And ten years seems very different in length to a grown-up person compared with what they do to you. It is probable Mr. Heathcliff proposed going, from summer to summer, but never found a convenient opportunity, and now it is too late. Don't trouble him with questions on the subject; it will do no one any good.'

The boy was fully occupied with his own cogitations for the remainder of the ride, till we halted before the farmhouse garden gate. I watched to catch his impressions in his countenance. He surveyed the carved front and the low-browed lattices, the straggling gooseberry bushes, and crooked firs, with solemn intentness, and then shook his head. It was obvious that he disapproved of the exterior of his new abode, but he had the sense to postpone complaining.

Before he dismounted, I went and opened the door. It was half past six and the family had just finished breakfast. The servant was clearing and wiping down the table. Joseph stood by his master's chair telling some tale concerning a lame horse, and Hareton was preparing for the hay field.

'Hallo, Nelly!' cried Mr. Heathcliff when he saw me. 'I feared I should have to come down and fetch my property myself. You've brought it, have you? Let us see what we can make of it.'

He got up and strode to the door. Hareton and Joseph followed in gaping curiosity. Poor Linton ran a frightened eye over the faces of the three.

Heathcliff, having stared at his son in an ague of confusion, uttered a scornful laugh. 'God! What a beauty! What a lovely, charming thing!' he exclaimed. 'Oh, damn my soul! but this is worse than I expected—and the devil knows I was not optimistic!'

I bid the trembling and bewildered child get down off the pony and enter. He did not thoroughly comprehend the meaning of his father's speech, or whether it was intended for him. Indeed, he was not yet certain that the grim, sneering stranger was his father. He clung to me, and on Mr. Heathcliff's taking a seat and bidding him 'come hither,' he hid his face on my shoulder and wept.

'Tut, tut!' said Heathcliff, stretching out a hand and

dragging him roughly between his knees, and then holding up his head by the chin. 'None of that nonsense! We're not going to hurt thee, Linton—isn't that thy name?'

He took off the boy's cap and pushed back his thick black hair, felt his slender arms and his small fingers. During the examination, Linton ceased crying and lifted his great black eyes to inspect the inspector.

'Any odd behavior?' he asked me.

'Sir?'

'Never the mind. Do you know me?' asked Heathcliff, returning his attention to the lad, having satisfied himself that the limbs were all equally frail and feeble.

'No,' said Linton, with a gaze of vacant fear.

'You've heard of me, I dare say?'

'No,' he replied again.

'No? What a shame of your mother! You are my son, then, I'll tell you, and your mother was a wicked slut to leave you in ignorance of the sort of father you possessed. Now, don't wince and color up! Be a good lad and I'll see you're cared for. Nelly, if you're tired you may sit down; if not, get home. I'll guess you'll report what you hear, and see, at the Grange, and this thing won't be settled while you linger about it.'

'Well,' replied I, 'I do hope you'll be kind to the boy, Mr. Heathcliff, or you'll not keep him long. He's all you have akin in the wide world, that you will ever know—remember.'

'I'll be very kind to him, you needn't fear,' he said, laughing. 'Only nobody else must be kind to him; I'm jealous of monopolizing his affection. And, to begin my kindness, Joseph! bring the lad some breakfast. Hareton, you infernal calf, begone to your work. Yes, Nell,' he added when they had departed, 'my son is prospective owner of your place, and I should not wish him to die till I was certain of being his successor. Besides, he's *mine,* and I want the triumph of seeing *my* descendant fairly lord of their estates. I want to see my child hiring their children to till their fathers' lands for wages. That is the sole consideration that can make me endure the whelp. I despise him for himself, and for the memories he revives! But that consideration is sufficient. He's as safe with me, and shall be tended as carefully as your master tends his own. I have a room upstairs, furnished for him in handsome style. I've engaged a tutor, also, to come three times a week, from twenty miles' distance, to teach him what he pleases to learn. I've ordered Hareton to obey him, and in fact I've arranged everything with a view to preserve the superior and the gentleman in him, above his associates. I do regret, however, that he so little deserves the trouble. If I wished any blessing in the world, it was to find him a worthy object of pride, and I'm bitterly disappointed with the whey-faced whining wretch!'

While he was speaking Joseph returned, bearing a basin of milk-porridge, and placed it before Linton. He stirred round the homely mess with a look of aversion, and affirmed he could not eat it.

I saw the old manservant shared largely in his master's scorn of the child, though he was compelled to retain the sentiment in his heart because Heathcliff plainly meant his underlings to hold him in honor.

'Looks just like ye, God help his soul,' Joseph said, peering in Linton's face. 'Guess we'll know soon enough.'

*Know what?* I wanted to ask, but I bit my tongue, for as my master had said, the matter of the child was already out of our hands.

'I *shan't* eat it!' Linton said snappishly, taking but one look in the bowl. 'Take it away.'

Joseph snatched up the food indignantly and brought it to us. 'Dare I ask 'im what his mother fed 'im?'

'Don't mention his mother to me,' said the master angrily. 'And keep your trap shut, Joseph, or you know the consequences.' He looked at me with a black scowl. 'What is his usual food, Nelly?'

I suggested boiled milk or tea, and the housekeeper received instructions to prepare some. Having no excuse for lingering longer, I slipped out while Linton was engaged in timidly rebuffing the advances of a semifriendly sheepdog. But as I closed the door, I heard a cry, and a frantic repetition of the words—

'Don't leave me! I'll not stay here! I'll not stay here!'

Then the latch was raised and fell and he was barred from following me, and so my brief guardianship ended.

# Chapter 21

Cathy rose that morning in high glee, eager to join her cousin, and such passionate tears and lamentations followed the news of his departure that Edgar was obliged to soothe her. He was so upset by her weeping that he told her Linton would come back soon. He added, however, 'if I can get him,' and he and I both knew there were no hopes of that.

This promise poorly pacified her, but time was more potent, and though she still occasionally inquired when Linton would return, before she saw him again, his features had waxed so dim in her memory that she did not recognize him.

When I encountered the housekeeper of Wuthering Heights while in Gimmerton, I would ask how the young master got on. Linton lived almost as secluded as Catherine, and was never seen outside the walls, making me wonder if a bloodsucker had carried Isabella's child off and no one had bothered to inform us at the Grange. For I believed, by now, that Master Heathcliff had no affection for the boy, and had so far descended from the behavior of any decent father as to permit any atrocity by his fiendish acquaintances.

That was not the case, however, and I gathered from the

Heights housekeeper that Linton continued in weak health, and was a tiresome inmate. She said, as I suspected, that Mr. Heathcliff seemed to dislike him immensely, though he tried to conceal it. According to the housekeeper, Heathcliff and his son rarely spoke. Linton learnt his lessons and spent his evenings in a small apartment they called the parlor, or else lay in bed all day. He always had a cough, a cold, an ache, or pains of some sort.

She said she once heard her master and Joseph in an argument. She only caught the end, but apparently Joseph had a suggestion as to how the boy's health might be improved. Whatever the remedy, Heathcliff was adamantly opposed and ended the conversation warning Joseph that his head would be on a pike on the road to Gimmerton if he ever so much as spoke of his *elixir* again.

Mr. Edgar encouraged me to gain information from the housekeeper whenever I could, for he thought a great deal about his nephew. I fancy he would have run some risk to see him, and he once told me to ask the housekeeper whether the boy ever came into the village, but she said he did not. Two years after Linton's arrival, that housekeeper left, and another whom I did not know was her successor. She lives there still.

Time wore on at the Grange in its former pleasant way, till Miss Cathy reached sixteen. On the anniversary of her birth, we never celebrated because it was also the anniversary of my late mistress's death. Her father invariably spent that day alone in the library. I think he would have liked to have gone to Gimmerton Kirkyard, but my late mistress's grave still lay as fresh-turned as the day she was buried, so he did not go.

The twentieth of March of that year was a beautiful spring day, and when Miss Cathy's father retired to mourn alone, my young lady came down dressed to go out. She said her papa had given her leave to have a ramble on the edge of the moors with me, if we went only a short distance and were back within the hour.

I considered the safety of going out, just the two of us, but to tell the truth, the bloodsuckers seemed mostly an annoyance by then. Cows and horses were in constant danger of being sucked of their life's force, and hunting dogs often went missing. Worse, a huntsman or a tanner was occasionally attacked, and once or twice a month a child was carried off into the night, but the vampires seemed under control, or at least there seemed some control to their ravaging the countryside. There seemed to be rules such as no killing on Sundays, before All Hallows' Eve, or on full moons just before mid-winter and summer's solstice. And the rules were being enforced—by whom, I could not say, though I had my suspicions. Except for the case of Squire Shoteshaw's young wife, and that may or may not be laid at the feet of beasties, in my opinion.

'Twas a full moon on the night she vanished. An odd one, the squire's lady was a flothery piece who wore scarlet petticoats and swam mother-naked in the goose pond on a warm night. Word had it the jade had been born a butcher's daughter and had only married the squire for what she could get out of him.

"But the vampires," I reminded Nelly. "You were telling me of their strange rules. Did you mean that you thought it had something to do with Mr. Heathcliff?"

"The squire's lady, you understand, disappeared on the night of a full moon only two days from summer solstice, but . . ." Here, she paused and nodded firmly.

"And Dame Dumble said the gardener's wife said that a ruby ring, a pearl necklace, and a garnet pin, all that had been handed down in the family since the time of the wicked King Richard, vanished with her, along with twenty-two silver coins and a bottle of the squire's finest. So if the lady was taken by beasties, she was taken with all her gowns and the family heirlooms. Not to mention one of the grooms—and him half a Frenchman." She waited for me to make some response.

"Seems highly unlikely," I mused. "My understanding is that it's blood they seek, not jewels or coin."

"Except for the ones fond of cards," Nelly reminded me.

"Except for those with a penchant for gambling," I agreed.

"Exactly, so you can hardly accuse them, for all their dastardly customs, of making off with the squire's wife on a full moon. Mayhap she and her lover used the light of that moon to make their way to France or America or some other heathen place."

"Pray continue your tale," I urged. "I'm most interested in Mr. Heathcliff's story. Was it he who set down the rules for bloodsuckers? Was that why it became safe to walk freely about the county again?" I slid forward in my chair. "After he slayed so many after Catherine's death, did he allow those that dared to return to do so, so long as they did not kill everyone in the county?"

Mrs. Dean cut her eyes at me in warning and I slid back, folding my hands, properly contrite. After a moment, she continued her narrative.

I checked to be certain I had my little knife, and that the garlic pomades we wore round our necks were fresh, and out we sallied. She bounded before me, and returned to my side, and was off again like a young greyhound. I found plenty of entertainment in listening to the larks singing far and near, and enjoying the sweet, warm sunshine. She was a delight to watch with her golden ringlets flying loose behind, and her bright cheeks, as soft and pure in its bloom as a wild rose, and her eyes radiant with cloudless pleasure. She was a happy creature, and an angel, in those days. It's a pity she could not be content.

'We should head back,' I called to Miss Cathy after some time.

'Oh, a little farther—only a little farther, Nelly,' was her answer, continually. 'Let's just climb the next hillock, pass the next bank.'

But there were so many hillocks and banks to climb and pass, that, at length, I began to be weary, and told her we must halt and retrace our steps. It still was not wise for the weak or the tired to roam far, for you never knew for certain if there was a ban on bloodletting or not.

I shouted to her as she got out farther in front of me; she either did not hear or did not regard, for she still sprang on, and I was compelled to follow. Finally, she dived into a hollow, and before I came in sight of her again, she was two miles nearer Wuthering Heights than her own home. I could see her, but I could not catch up to her. Then, in the distance, I saw a woman in a dark cloak approaching her. By the time I realized not who it was, but *what* it was, the creature was almost upon my dear Cathy.

I think the bloodsucker intended to lure Cathy close under the guise of being human, but before it reached her, a gust of wind came up and blew her hood back, revealing tentacles of black hair and a deathly white face, black-rimmed eyes, and a cherry mouth. Cathy saw her for the fiend that she was and screamed and threw up both gloved hands to protect herself.

'Grab your garlic! Grab your garlic!' I shouted, fumbling for my knife as I sprinted toward her.

There was only a hand's width between them when, from nowhere, Mr. Heathcliff appeared. I swear, he must have flown in on a broomstick! One moment it was the two of them, Cathy and the she-bitch, and the next there were three. Mr. Heathcliff lifted the bloodsucker up with one hand with a growl and tossed her like a stick of kindling. She screeched like a fiend as she hurtled through the air, then hit a patch of heath, tucked and rolled, and was gone before I reached my charge.

'What are you doing here unescorted?' Mr. Heathcliff demanded. He had not even creased his black coat in the exchange between him and the she-beastie.

Cathy was shaking with fear, but my little charge stood up to him. 'Was that a lady vampire, sir?'

'It was, and both of you trespass upon my land.'

'I didn't mean to disturb anything. It's only that my papa told me that the Heights were beautiful in the spring. As for her, I have no idea what she was doing here. We never spoke.'

By then, I had reached them, huffing and puffing, and quite disheveled from my sprint. Hareton had joined the little group as well. There was no sight of the woman bloodsucker. Heathcliff glanced at me with an ill-meaning smile and asked Miss Cathy who 'papa' was.

'Mr. Linton of Thrushcross Grange,' she replied. 'I thought you did not know me, or you wouldn't have spoken in that tone to me.'

'You suppose your papa is highly esteemed and respected, then?' he said, sarcastically.

'And what are you, besides one who can chase off vampires?' inquired Catherine, gazing curiously on the speaker. 'That man I've seen before. Is he your son?' She pointed to Hareton, who had gained nothing but increased bulk and strength by the addition of two years to his age. He seemed as awkward and rough as ever.

'Miss Cathy,' I interrupted, trying to put myself between them. 'It will be three hours instead of one that we are out. We really must go back. What if that bloodsucker is lurking in wait for us?' I still clutched my knife in preparation, should I need to defend my person or hers.

'No, that man is not my son,' stated Heathcliff, pushing me aside. 'But I have one, and you have seen him before, too. I see your nurse is in a hurry to return, but I think she would be the better for a little rest. Look at her; she's breathing so hard she looks about to collapse. Why not walk to my house and let her rest? You'll receive a kind welcome, I assure you.'

I whispered to Catherine that she mustn't, on any account, agree to go.

'Why not?' she asked aloud. 'You're out of breath, Nelly, from fright and your run. You need to rest, and the ground is dewy. You certainly can't sit here. Besides, he says I have seen his son. He's mistaken, I think, but I can guess where he lives, at the farmhouse I visited in coming from Penistone Crags. Don't you?'

'I do,' Heathcliff answered. 'Come, Nelly, hold your tongue—it will be a treat for her to look in on us. Hareton, get forward with the lass. You shall walk with me, Nelly.'

'No, she's not going to any such place,' I cried, struggling to release my arm, which he had seized, but she was almost at the door-stones already, scampering round the brow at full speed. Hareton did not pretend to escort her; he shied off by the roadside, and vanished.

'Mr. Heathcliff, it's very wrong,' I continued, pushing aside the near attack from my mind to see to the next crisis at hand. 'You know you mean no good. She'll see Linton, and all will be told as soon as we return, and I shall be blamed.'

'I want her to see Linton,' he answered. 'He's looking better these few days. It's not often he's fit to be seen. And we'll soon persuade her to keep the visit secret. Where is the harm of it?'

*The harm,* I wanted to say, is in any contact with you and yours. *The harm* is in that while we all know your reputation for being the famous *gypsy vampire slayer,* none of us really know who you are or who or what you came from. I said none of those things, but instead, '*The harm* of it is that her father would hate me if he found I allowed her to enter your house, and I am convinced you have a bad design in encouraging her to do so.'

'My design is that the two cousins may fall in love and get married. I'm acting generously to your master. His young chit has no inheritance, and should she second my wishes, she'll be provided for at once as joining successor with Linton.'

'If Linton died,' I answered, 'and his life is quite uncertain, Catherine would be the heir.'

'No, she would not,' he said. 'There is no clause in the will to secure it so. His property would go to me, but, to prevent disputes, I desire their union, and am resolved to bring it about.'

'And I'm resolved she shall never approach your house with me again,' I returned, as we reached the gate where Miss Cathy waited.

Heathcliff bid me be quiet, and brushed past me to open the door. My young lady gave him several looks, as if she could not exactly make up her mind what to think of him, but Heathcliff, he was clever. He smiled when he met her eye, and softened his voice in addressing her, and I was foolish enough to imagine the memory of her mother might disarm him from desiring her injury.

Linton stood on the hearth. He had been out, walking in the fields, for his cap was on and he was calling to Joseph to bring him dry shoes.

He had grown tall of his age, still wanting some months of sixteen. His features were pretty; his complexion brighter than I remembered them, though perhaps that was just a temporary luster brought on by the wholesome air and genial sun.

'Now, who is that?' asked Mr. Heathcliff, turning to Cathy. 'Can you tell?'

'Your son?' she said.

'Yes, yes,' answered he. 'But is this the only time you have beheld him? Think! Do you have such a short memory? Linton, don't you recall your cousin, that you used to tease us so with wishing to see?'

'Linton!' cried Cathy, kindling into joyful surprise at the name. 'Is that little Linton? He's taller than I am! Are you Linton?'

The youth stepped forward and acknowledged himself and she kissed him fervently. She then took a step back and they gazed with wonder at the change time had wrought in the appearance of each. Catherine had reached her full height; her figure was slender, elastic as steel, and her whole aspect sparkling with health and spirits. Despite his resemblance to his father, Linton's looks and movements were very languid, and his form extremely slight. But there was a grace in his manner that mitigated these defects, and rendered him not unpleasing.

After exchanging numerous marks of fondness with him, Miss Cathy walked over to Mr. Heathcliff, who lingered by the door. 'And you are my uncle, then!' she cried, reaching up to salute him. 'I thought I liked you, though you were cross, at first. You frightened off that vampire with impressive skill.' She peered at him more closely. 'Why don't you visit at the Grange with Linton? We could use your skills. Only last week one of those beasties slipped through the gates and sucked several guinea hens dry, then left them hanging on the clothesline with the clean sheets.'

'I visited once or twice too often before you were born,' he answered.

'Naughty Nelly!' exclaimed Miss Cathy, setting herself before me. 'Wicked Nelly! How could you hinder me from coming here? But I'll take this walk every morning in fu-

ture. May I, Uncle?' She spun back to him. 'And sometimes bring Papa. Won't you be glad to see us?'

'Of course!' replied the uncle, with a hardly suppressed
grimace. 'But I'd better tell you that I think your papa will
not.'

I felt the hair rise on the back of my neck. Surely he
would not bring up his relationship with her mother, for
that tale would, no doubt, lead to the truth of the unholy
grave outside the kirkyard! My master had seen fit to protect his daughter from knowledge of her mother's last days
on earth, and it was no one's place to tell her, save him.

Fortunately, that was not the path he took, probably because he did not want to admit that it was *his* fault
Catherine went into the garden looking for him. He did
not want her to know it was *his* fault the vampires had
gotten so comfortable in the moors due to his hospitality
that they would waltz in and feed on a half-wit woman in
her own garden.

'Mr. Linton has a prejudice against me,' he told my
young charge. 'We quarreled at one time of our lives, with
un-Christian ferocity, and, if you mention coming here to
him, he'll put a veto on your visits altogether. Therefore,
you must not mention it, unless you do not wish to see
your cousin hereafter. You may come, if you will, but you
must not mention it.'

'Why did you quarrel?' asked Catherine, considerably
crestfallen.

'He thought me too poor to wed his sister,' lied Heathcliff. 'And was grieved that I got her. His pride was hurt,
and he'll never forgive it.'

'That's wrong!' said the young lady. 'Sometime, I'll tell
him so. But Linton and I have no share in your quarrel. I'll
not come here, but he shall come to the Grange and then
no one will be angry.'

'It will be too far for me,' murmured her cousin. 'To

walk four miles would kill me. No, come here, Miss Catherine, not every morning, but once or twice a week.'

'Linton!'

'Yes, Father?' answered the boy.

'Why not show your cousin around? Take her into the garden before you change your shoes, and into the stable to see your horse.'

'Wouldn't you rather sit here?' asked Linton, addressing Cathy in a tone that expressed reluctance to move again.

'I don't know,' she replied, casting a longing look to the door, and evidently eager to be active. 'Might we see another vampire if we go into the garden? I always seem to miss them at the Grange.'

At the word, the weakling boy shrank back.

'Don't be ridiculous, Linton,' Mr. Heathcliff barked. 'You're perfectly safe.' Mr. Heathcliff sent him a warning glance and went into the yard, calling out for Hareton.

Hareton responded, and presently the two re-entered. The young man had been washing himself, as was visible by the glow on his cheeks, and his wetted hair.

'Oh, I'll ask *you*, Uncle,' cried Miss Cathy, recollecting the housekeeper's assertion. 'That is not my cousin, is he?'

'Yes,' Mr. Heathcliff replied. 'Hareton is your mother's nephew. Don't you like him?'

Catherine gave a queer look.

'Well then, Hareton,' Mr. Heathcliff conceded. 'Take her round the farm and behave like a gentleman. Mind you, don't use any bad words, and don't stare. And if you see that she-bitch peering over the walls, remind her she will not be warned again. Next time her head will be on a pike next to her brother's. Be off, now, and entertain Miss Cathy as nicely as you can.'

We watched the couple walking past the window.

'Don't you think Hindley would be proud of his son, if he could see him?' Mr. Heathcliff remarked. 'Almost as proud as I am of mine. But there's this difference; one is gold put to the use of paving-stones, and the other is tin polished to ape a service of silver. *Mine* has nothing valuable about it, yet I shall have the merit of making it go as far as such poor stuff can go. *His* had first-rate qualities, and they are lost, rendered worse than unavailing. And the best of it is, Hareton is damnably fond of me!'

Heathcliff chuckled a fiendish laugh at the idea. I made no reply, because talk of the dead Hindley rising to see his son made me think of Catherine's grave still fresh after all these years. It was on the tip of my tongue to ask Mr. Heathcliff there and then what he knew of that, but if I angered him and he fed me to that female vampire, how would Miss Cathy ever get home in time for the evening meal?

Meantime, our young companion, who sat too removed from us to hear what was said, glanced restlessly toward the window.

'Get up, you idle boy!' Mr. Heathcliff exclaimed with assumed heartiness. 'Away after them! They are just at the corner, by the stand of beehives.'

Linton gathered his energies and left the hearth. The door was open, and, as he stepped out, I heard Cathy inquiring of her unsociable attendant what was that inscription over the door?

Hareton stared up and scratched his head like a true clown.

'It's some damnable writing,' he answered. 'I cannot read it.'

'Can't read it?' cried Catherine. 'I can read it. But I want to know why it is there.'

Linton giggled—the first appearance of mirth he had exhibited.

'He does not know his letters,' he said to his cousin. 'Could you believe in the existence of such a colossal dunce?'

'And why do those cherubs have fangs? The carving looks rather old; the infestation only came to the moors some forty years ago.'

'Crazy relations, the ones who built the house, I suppose,' Linton offered.

'Is Hareton all as he should be, Linton?' asked Miss Cathy seriously. 'Or is he simple, too? I've questioned him twice now, and each time he looked so stupid I think he does not understand me. I can hardly understand him, I'm sure!'

Linton repeated his laugh, and glanced at Hareton tauntingly. 'There's nothing the matter but laziness, is there, Earnshaw?' he said. 'My cousin fancies you are an idiot. There you experience the consequence of scorning "booklarning," as you would say. Have you noticed, Catherine, his frightful Yorkshire pronunciation?'

The two youngsters broke into a noisy fit of merriment, my giddy Miss delighted to discover that she might turn Hareton's strange talk to a matter of amusement.

Hareton raised his fist to Linton, obviously not appreciating the jests, and Linton cowered.

'Papa warned you to try to behave like a gentleman— now do!'

'If thou weren't more a lass than a lad, I'd fell thee this minute, I would, pitiful lath of a crater!' retorted the angry boor, retreating. His face was burnt with mingled rage and mortification, for he was conscious of being insulted.

Mr. Heathcliff smiled when he saw him go, but immediately afterward cast of look of singular aversion on the flippant pair. Cathy and Linton remained chattering in the doorway, he discussing Hareton's faults and deficiencies, and relating anecdotes of his goings-on, and the girl relishing his pert and spiteful sayings, without considering the ill nature they evinced.

We stayed till afternoon, when I was finally able to tear

Miss Cathy away. As we walked home, with Hareton walking behind us, serving as a guard should the female vampire show her hideous face again, I tried to warn her of the character of the people at the Heights, but she would not listen. She had somehow gotten it in her head that I was prejudiced against them, and nothing I said could change her mind.

She did not mention the visit that night because she did not see Mr. Linton. Next day it all came out, sadly to my chagrin, and still I was not altogether sorry. 'Papa!' she exclaimed, after the morning's salutations. 'Guess whom I saw yesterday, in my walk on the moors?'

She gave a faithful account of her excursion, wisely leaving out the incident with the vampire, and my master, though he cast more than one reproachful look at me, said nothing till she had concluded. Then he drew her to him, and asked if she knew why he had concealed Linton's near neighborhood from her? Could she think it was to deny her a pleasure that she might harmlessly enjoy?

'It was because you dislike Mr. Heathcliff,' she answered.

'No, it was not because I disliked Mr. Heathcliff, but because Mr. Heathcliff dislikes me. He is a most diabolical man, delighting to wrong and ruin those he hates, if they give him the slightest opportunity. I knew that you could not keep up an acquaintance with your cousin without being brought into contact with him. I knew he would detest you, on my account, so for your own good, I took cautions that you should not see Linton again. I meant to explain this sometime as you grew older, and I'm sorry I delayed it.'

'And what of our neighbor being an illustrious vampire slayer? Did you also keep that from me to protect me? He was a gypsy orphan, taken in by my grandfather. I cannot believe you kept that from me, knowing full well I've an interest in vampire slaying.'

My master looked to me as if to ask why I would have provided such information on his enemy, but I shook my head, opening my hands to say I had provided no such information. I imagine it was Linton who had told that tale.

'Mr. Heathcliff was quite cordial, Papa,' Miss Cathy continued. 'And *he* didn't object to our seeing each other. He said I might come to his house when I pleased, only I must not tell you, because you had quarreled with him, and would not forgive him for marrying Aunt Isabella. And you won't. *You* are the one to be blamed. He is willing to let us be friends, at least Linton and I, and you are not.'

My master, perceiving that she would not take his word for her uncle-in-law's disposition, gave a hasty sketch of his conduct to Isabella, and the manner in which Wuthering Heights became his property. He could not bear to discourse long upon the topic, however, and he made no mention of Mr. Heathcliff's association with his own departed wife. 'You will know hereafter, darling,' he concluded, 'why I wish you to avoid his house and family. Besides, it is not safe for you to travel these roads. There are still vampires about.'

I saw the look on her face and knew she was tempted to tell her father of her encounter with the vampire, but she held her tongue for once, and I, not wishing at my age to seek new employment, kept mine as well.

'Now, return to your old employments and amusements,' he directed her, 'and think no more about them!'

Catherine kissed her father and sat down quietly to attend her lessons, but that evening, when she had retired to her room and I went to help her undress, I found her crying.

'Oh, silly child!' I exclaimed. 'If you had any real griefs, you'd be ashamed to waste a tear on this little contrariety.'

'I'm not crying for myself, Nelly,' she answered. 'It's for

Linton. He expected to see me again tomorrow, and he'll be so disappointed. He'll wait for me, and I shan't come!'

'Nonsense!' said I. 'Do you imagine he has thought as much of you as you have of him? Hasn't he Hareton for a companion? Linton will conjecture how it is, and trouble himself no further about you.'

'But may I not write a note to tell him why I cannot come?' she asked, rising to her feet. 'And just send those books I promised to lend him? May I not, Nelly?'

'No, indeed! No, indeed!' replied I with decision. 'Then he would write to you, and there'd never be an end of it. No, Miss Cathy, the acquaintance must be dropped entirely. It's what your papa expects, and I shall see that it is done.'

'But how can one little note—'

'Silence!' I interrupted. 'We'll not begin with your little notes. Get into bed.'

She threw at me a very naughty look, so naughty that I would not kiss her good night at first. I covered her up and shut her door in great displeasure, but, repenting halfway, I returned softly, and there was Miss, standing at the table with a bit of blank paper before her and a pencil in her hand, which she guiltily slipped out of sight on my re-entrance.

'You'll get nobody to take that, Catherine,' I said sternly. 'Unless you intend to summon that she-beastie to carry it for you.'

The letter was finished anyway and forwarded to its destination, not by a vampire letter-carrier, but by a milk-fetcher who came from the village, but that I didn't learn till some time afterward. Weeks passed on, and Cathy recovered her temper, though she grew wondrous fond of stealing off to corners by herself. Often, if I came near her suddenly while reading, she would start and bend over the book, evidently desirous to hide it. I detected edges of loose paper sticking out beyond the leaves.

She also got a trick of coming down early in the morning and lingering about the kitchen, as if she were expecting the arrival of something. She had a small drawer in a cabinet in the library, which she would trifle over for hours, and whose key she took special care to remove when she left it.

One day, as she inspected this drawer, I observed that the playthings and trinkets, which recently formed its contents, were transmuted into bits of folded paper.

My suspicions were aroused. I determined to take a peep at their mysterious treasure, so, at night, as soon as she and my master were safe upstairs, I searched and readily found among my house keys one that would fit the lock. Opening it, I emptied the whole contents into my apron, and took them with me to examine at leisure in my own chamber.

Though I'd had my supicions, I was still surprised to discover that they were a mass of correspondence—daily, almost—from Linton Heathcliff. The earlier dated were embarrassed and short; gradually, however, they expanded into copious love letters, foolish as the age of the writer rendered natural, yet with touches, here and there, which I thought were borrowed from a more experienced source.

Some of them struck me as singularly odd compounds of ardor and flatness, commencing in strong feeling, and concluding in the affected, wordy way that a schoolboy might use to a fancied, incorporeal sweetheart.

Whether they satisfied Cathy, I don't know, but they appeared very worthless trash to me. After turning over as many as I thought proper, I tied them in a handkerchief and set them aside, relocking the vacant drawer.

Following her habit, my young lady descended early and visited the kitchen. I watched her go to the door, on the arrival of a certain little boy, and, while the dairy maid filled his can, she tucked something into his jacket pocket and plucked something out.

I went round by the garden and lay wait for the messenger, who fought valorously to defend his trust, and we spilt the milk between us. But I succeeded in abstracting the epistle and, threatening to sell him to the next carriage of vampires traveling through Gimmerton if he did not go home at once, I remained under the wall and perused Miss Cathy's affectionate composition.

It was more simple and more eloquent than her cousin's, very pretty and very silly. She spoke not only of sugarly love, but her desire—no, her passion—to have him join her on a quest one day to seek out vampires and obliterate them from all corners of the earth. What was even more amusing than the thought of my female charge sparring with vampires was the image of the sickly Linton doing so. I shook my head, and went meditating into the house.

The day being wet, Cathy could not divert herself with rambling about the property, so, at the conclusion of her morning studies, she resorted to the solace of the drawer. Her father sat reading at the table and I, on purpose, had sought a bit of work in some fringes of the window curtain, keeping my eye steadily fixed on her proceedings.

Never did any bird flying back to a plundered nest, which it had left brimful of chirping young ones, express more complete despair in its anguished cries and fluttering than she by her single 'Oh!'

Mr. Linton looked up. 'What is the matter, love? Have you hurt yourself?' His tone and look assured her he had not been the discoverer of the hoard.

'No, Papa—' she gasped. 'Nelly! Come upstairs—I'm sick!'

I obeyed her summons, and accompanied her out.

'Oh, Nelly!' she commenced immediately, dropping on her knees, when we were alone. 'Oh, give them to me, and I'll never, never do so again! Don't tell Papa. You have not told Papa, Nelly, say you have not! I've been exceedingly naughty, but I won't do it anymore!'

With a grave severity in my manner, I bid her stand up.

'So,' I exclaimed. 'A fine bundle of trash you study in your leisure hours, to be sure. Why, it's good enough to be printed! And what do you suppose the master will think, when I display it before him? I haven't shown him yet, but you needn't imagine I shall keep your ridiculous secrets. For shame! And you must have led the way in writing such absurdities. Fighting vampires, indeed! Linton would never have proposed such an exploit, I'm certain.'

'I didn't!' sobbed Cathy, fit to break her heart. 'I didn't once think of loving him till—'

'*Loving him!*' cried I, as scornfully as I could utter the word. '*Loving him!* Did anybody ever hear the like! I might just as well talk of loving the miller who comes once a year to buy our corn. Pretty loving, indeed! You have seen Linton hardly four hours in your life! I'm going with these to the library, and we'll see what your father says to such *loving*.'

She sprang at her precious epistles, but I held them above my head, and then she poured out further frantic entreaties that I would burn them—do anything rather than show them. And being really fully as inclined to laugh as scold—for I esteemed it all girlish vanity—I at length relented in a measure, and asked—

'If I consent to burn them, will you promise faithfully neither to send nor receive a letter again, nor locks of hair, nor rings, nor playthings?'

'We don't send playthings!' cried Catherine, her pride overcoming her shame.

'Nor anything at all, then, my lady!' I said. 'Unless you will vow, here I go. And no more talk of being a lady vampire slayer. There is no such thing!'

'I promise, Nelly!' she cried, catching my dress. 'Oh, put them in the fire!'

I unknotted the handkerchief and commenced dropping them in from an angle, and the flame curled up the chimney. When it was done, I stirred up the ashes and interred them under a shovelful of coals, and she mutely, with a sense of intense injury, retired to her private apartment. I descended to tell my master that the young lady's qualm of sickness was almost gone, but I judged it best for her to lie down awhile.

She wouldn't dine, but she reappeared at tea, pale, and red about the eyes, and marvelously subdued in outward aspect.

Next morning, I answered his latest letter by a slip of paper, inscribed, 'Master Heathcliff is requested to send no more notes to Miss Linton, as she will not receive them.' And, thenceforth, the little boy came with vacant pockets.

# Chapter 22

"Summer drew to an end, and early autumn. It was past Michaelmas, but the harvest was late that year and a few of our fields were still uncleared. That was the first year we suspected the vampires were returning to the moors in large numbers, this time under the disguise of ordinary, though pale, citizens. Some came as peddlers bearing creams that would cure baldness and gout and wrinkles, while others sold rare stones from the sands of Araby that added to a pot of turnip peels and wild onion would transform the scraps into a hearty beef soup of the richest taste and strength that might please the pickiest of trenchermen. These stones, the bearers swore, might be used over and over again without losing their power. They also peddled love potions and a cure for unfaithfulness in lovers, but that concoction smelled like skunk cabbage and one would be hard-pressed to slip it into a mug of cider."

Mrs. Dean leaned closer.

"There was also powdered horn from a giant creature that lived only along the Nile in the land of the Pharaohs. That was sold to aging men to give them the vigor of younger, and as to whether or not that was real or a dupe, I cannot say. All I know is that a great deal was sold at a high price."

"So these vampires came as honest peddlers?" I asked.

"Some did, others as 'sin eaters,' those who are paid to attend funerals and eat funeral meats off the coffin and thereby assume the sins of the newly deceased."

"Sin eaters?" I said dubiously.

"Aye, but a poor sort they were, for no one ever saw them actually eat any of the food. Others of the blood-sucking kind came claiming to be agents of the crown, tax collectors, or census takers. And reapers, of course, those who come in gangs to harvest the crops in autumn."

"I see," I observed, sitting back to hear the next segment of Mrs. Dean's story.

Mr. Linton and his daughter would frequently walk out among the reapers; at the carrying of the last sheaves, they stayed till dusk, and the evening happening to be chill and damp, my master caught a bad cold that settled obstinately on his lungs, confining him indoors through the whole of the winter, nearly without intermission.

Poor Cathy, frightened from her little romance, had been considerably sadder and duller since its abandonment, and her father insisted on her reading less and taking more exercise. She had his companionship no longer and I was an inefficient substitute, for I could only spare two or three hours from my numerous household duties to follow her footsteps, and then my society was obviously less desirable than his.

On an afternoon in October, or the beginning of November—a fresh, watery afternoon, when the turf and paths were rustling with moist, withered leaves, and the cold, blue sky was half hidden by clouds—dark gray streamers, rapidly mounting from the west, and boding abundant rain—I requested my young lady to forgo her ramble because I was certain of showers. She refused, and I unwillingly donned a cloak and took my umbrella to accompany her on a stroll to the bottom of the park.

She went sadly on; there was no running or bounding now, though the chill wind might well have tempted her to a race. And often, from the side of my eye, I could detect her raising a hand and brushing something off her cheek.

I gazed round for a means of diverting her thoughts. On one side of the road rose a high, rough bank, where hazels and stunted oaks, with their roots half exposed, held uncertain tenure. The soil was too loose for the latter; and strong winds had blown some nearly horizontal. In summer, Miss Catherine delighted to climb along these trunks, and sit in the branches, swinging twenty feet above the ground. From dinner to tea she would lie in her breeze-rocked cradle, doing nothing except singing old songs—my nursery lore—to herself, or watching the birds, joint tenants, feed and entice their young one to fly. Or she would nestle with closed lids, half thinking, half dreaming, happier than words can express.

'Look, miss!' I exclaimed, pointing to a nook under the roots of one twisted tree. 'Winter is not here yet. There's a little flower, up yonder, the last bud from the multitude of bluebells that clouded those turf steps in July with a lilac mist. Will you clamber up, and pluck it to show to your papa?'

Cathy stared a long time at the lonely blossom trembling in its earthy shelter, and replied, 'No, I'll not touch it. It looks melancholy, does it not, Nelly?"

'Yes,' I observed. 'About as starved and sackless as you. Your cheeks are bloodless.' My own words made my heart patter; surely she had not been bitten! But I knew it wasn't possible. She was with me night and day. 'Let us take hold of hands and run. You're so low, I dare say I shall keep up with you.'

'No,' she repeated, and continued sauntering on, pausing at intervals to muse over a bit of moss, or a tuft of blanched grass and, ever and anon, her hand was lifted to her averted face.

'Catherine, why are you crying, love?' I asked, approaching and putting my arms over her shoulder. 'You mustn't cry because Papa has a cold; be thankful it is nothing worse.'

She now put no further restraint on her tears; her breath was stifled by sobs. 'Oh, it *will* be something worse,' she said. 'And what shall I do when Papa and you leave me, and I am by myself? I can't forget your words, Nelly. They are always in my ear. How life will be changed, how dreary the world will be, when Papa and you are dead.'

'None can tell whether you won't die before us,' I replied. 'It's wrong to anticipate evil. We'll hope there are years and years to come before any of us go. My master is young, and I am strong, and hardly forty-five. My mother lived till eighty, surviving more than a dozen vampire attacks and, in the end, taking one with her. She was a canty dame to the last. And suppose Mr. Linton were spared till he saw sixty—that would be more years than you have counted, miss. And would it not be foolish to mourn a calamity above twenty years beforehand?'

'But Aunt Isabella was younger than papa,' she remarked, gazing up with timid hope to seek further consolation. 'Linton said she died of a single vampire attack.'

'Aunt Isabella had not you and me to nurse her,' I replied, refusing to consider that I had not been able to save my dear Catherine. 'She wasn't as happy as master; she hadn't as much to live for. All you need do is to wait well on your father, and cheer him by letting him see you cheerful, and avoid giving him anxiety on any subject.'

'I fret about nothing on earth except Papa's illness,' answered my companion. 'I care for nothing in comparison with Papa. And I'll never—never—oh, never, while I have my senses, do an act or say a word to vex him. I love him better than myself, Nelly. I pray every night that I may live after him because I would rather be miserable than that he should be. That proves I love him better than myself.'

'Good words,' I replied. 'But deeds must prove it also, and after he is well, remember you don't forget resolutions formed in the hour of fear.'

As we talked, we neared a door that opened on the road, and my young lady, lightening into sunshine again, climbed up and seated herself on the top of the wall. She reached over to gather some hips that bloomed scarlet on the summit branches of the wild rose trees, shadowing the highway side; the lower fruit had disappeared, but only birds could touch the upper, except from Cathy's present station.

In stretching to pull them, her hat fell off, and as the door was locked, she proposed scrambling down to recover it. I bid her be cautious lest she got a fall, and she nimbly disappeared.

But the return was no such easy matter. The stones were smooth and neatly cemented, and the rosebushes and blackberry stragglers could yield no assistance in re-ascending. I, like a fool, didn't recollect that, till I heard her laughing and exclaiming, 'Nelly, you'll have to fetch the key, or else I must run round to the porter's lodge. I can't scale the ramparts on this side!'

'Stay where you are,' I answered. I was about to hurry home as fast as I could, when I heard Cathy's dance stop as she gave a gasp.

'Oh, dear,' she muttered.

'What is it?'

'A visitor.' Her tone was clipped. She sounded like a frightened child, trying to be brave.

'Who, pray tell?' I demanded.

'Good afternoon, ma'am,' I heard her say next.

'Miss Cathy, who is it?' I cried frantically.

'It . . . it is the lady we met that day on the moors on our way to Wuthering Heights. Do you speak English?' she said next, and I knew it was not me she addressed.

'I do.' The feminine voice was so silky smooth that it might be interpreted by some as enchanting.

'Well, I am Catherine Linton.'

'I know who you are,' replied the female.

I did not know what to do. It would have been impossible for me to climb up and over as Cathy had, but I feared if I ran for help, by the time I returned, there would be nothing left of my charge but a flattened skin and fine bonnet. So there I was, left with nothing to do but quake in my sturdy shoes and pray that either Cathy could save herself or the bloodsucker had just fed.

'Do you have a name?' Cathy asked, surprising me and, apparently, the lady vampire.

'Do you know, no human has ever asked me that before.'

'Well, if you didn't drink our blood, perhaps we'd be friendlier,' the naïve young woman offered.

I would have laughed, had the situation not been so grave.

'I am called Mirela.'

'Is that a vampire name?' Cathy inquired.

'Romanian.'

'It's pretty.'

'Thank you.'

'Miss Cathy,' I spoke up from the other side of the wall. 'We should return home before anyone wonders where we are and sends out the boys with silver-tipped—' An approaching sound arrested me. It was the trot of a horse, and in a minute the horse stopped also.

'Who is *that,* now?' I whispered.

'Ho, Miss Linton!' cried a deep voice. It was Heathcliff. 'I'm glad to meet you. Don't be in haste to enter, for I have an explanation to ask and obtain.' I heard the shift of leather in the saddle. 'Mirela,' he said more sharply. 'You try my patience. I have warned you this girl and her nurse are off-limits. Be gone.'

I did not hear her footsteps on the stones as she left the premises, but I was not entirely sure vampires' footsteps made any sound.

'I shan't speak to you, Mr. Heathcliff,' Catherine said. 'Though I thank you for coming along the way you did. Mirela was pleasant enough, but she was eyeing my neck. I can't say I could have trusted her to not take a bite of me.'

'You're a smart girl, then.'

'Thank you, but I still shan't speak with you. Papa says you are a wicked man, and you hate both him and me. Nelly says the same.'

'That is nothing to the purpose,' said Heathcliff. 'I don't hate my son, and it is concerning him that I demand your attention. Yes! You have cause to blush. Two or three months since, were you not in the habit of writing to Linton? Making love in play, eh? You deserved, both of you, flogging for that! You especially, the elder, and less sensitive, as it turns out. I've got your letters, and if you give me any pertness I'll send them to your father. I presume you grew weary of the amusement and dropped it, didn't you? Well, you dropped Linton with it, into a Slough of Despond. He was in earnest in love. As true as I live, he's dying for you. His heart is breaking at your fickleness, not figuratively, but actually. Though Hareton has made him a standing jest for six weeks, and I have used more serious measures and attempted to frighten him out of his idiocy, he gets worse daily. He'll be under the sod before summer, unless you restore him!'

'How can you lie so glaringly to the poor child!' I called from the inside. 'Pray ride on! How can you deliberately get up such paltry falsehoods? Miss Cathy, I'll knock the lock off with a stone. You can't listen to his vile nonsense. It is impossible that a person should die for the love of a stranger.' I then began to work on the gate lock in earnest with a fist-sized stone.

'I was not aware there were eavesdroppers,' muttered the detected villain. 'Worthy Mrs. Dean, I like you, but I don't like your double dealing,' he added, aloud. 'How could you lie so glaringly as to affirm I hated the "poor child," and invent bugbear stories to terrify her from my door-stones? Catherine Linton, my bonny lass, I shall be away from home all this week.'

'Are you going on a vampire-killing journey, because if you are I should love to—'

'That is not your business,' he snapped. But his voice softened at once. 'Go and see if I have not spoken truth. Just imagine your father in my place, and Linton in yours, then think how you would value your careless lover if he refused to stir a step to comfort you, when your father, himself, entreated him. I swear, on my salvation, he's going to his grave, and none but you can save him!'

The lock gave way, and I issued out, hustling toward them.

'I swear Linton is dying,' repeated Heathcliff, looking hard at me. 'And grief and disappointment are hastening his death. Nelly, if you won't let her go, you can walk over yourself. But I shall not return till this time next week, and I think your master himself would scarcely object to her visiting her cousin while I was safely away!'

'Come in,' said I, taking Cathy by the arm and half forcing her to re-enter, for she lingered, viewing with troubled eyes the features of the speaker, too stern to express his inward deceit.

He pushed his horse close and, bending down, observed, 'Miss Catherine, I must tell you that I have little patience with Linton, and Hareton and Joseph have less. I'll own that he's with a harsh set. He pines for kindness, as well as love, and a kind word from you would be his best medicine. Don't mind Mrs. Dean's cruel cautions; but be generous, and contrive to see him. He dreams of you day and night, and cannot be persuaded that you don't hate him, since you neither write nor call.'

I closed the door and rolled a stone to assist the loosened lock in holding it. I then spread my umbrella and drew my charge underneath, for the rain began to drive through the moaning branches of the trees, and warned us to avoid delay. There was no sign of the woman vampire who possessed a name.

Our hurry prevented any comment on the encounter with Heathcliff as we stretched toward home, but I suspected that Catherine's heart was clouded now in double darkness. Her features were so sad, they did not seem hers; she evidently regarded what she had heard as every syllable true.

The master had retired to rest before we came in. Cathy stole to his room to inquire how he was, but he had fallen asleep. She returned and asked me to sit with her in the library. We took our tea together, and afterward she lay down on the rug and told me not to talk, for she was weary.

I got a book and pretended to read. As soon as she supposed me absorbed in my occupation, she recommenced her silent weeping; it appeared, at present, her favorite diversion. I suffered her to enjoy it awhile, then I spoke, deriding and ridiculing all Mr. Heathcliff's assertions about his son, as if I were certain she would coincide. Alas! I hadn't the skill to counteract the effect his account had produced; it was just what he intended.

'You may be right, Nelly,' she answered. 'But I shall never feel at ease till I know. And I must tell Linton it is not my fault that I don't write, and convince him that I shall not change.'

What use were anger and protestations against her silly credulity? We parted that night—hostile, but next day I found myself on the road to Wuthering Heights, by the side of my willful young mistress's pony. I couldn't bear to witness her sorrow, to see her pale, dejected countenance and heavy eyes, and I yielded, in the faint hope that Linton himself might prove, by his reception of us, how little of the tale was founded on fact.

I only hoped we would not encounter a female vampire by the name of Mirela on our way.

# Chapter 23

The rainy night had ushered in a misty morning—half frost, half drizzle—and temporary brooks crossed our path, gurgling from the uplands. My feet were thoroughly wet. I was cross and low, exactly the humor suited for making the most of this disagreeable task.

We saw no sign of our friend the lady vampire on our journey—perhaps because she had the good sense to stay out of the wretched weather. We entered the farmhouse by the kitchen way to ascertain whether Mr. Heathcliff was really absent. Joseph sat beside a roaring fire, a quart of ale on the table near him, his black, short pipe in his mouth, his habitual scarf tied round and round his neck. Although why Joseph needed a muffler when he sat close enough to the hearth to spit in it, I can't imagine. But there he was, paler and more wretched looking than ever. If there ever was a more morose man, I've yet to see him.

The dogs leapt up, growling and snapping, the wicked terrier in the lead, but when they saw who it was, they ceased their snarling and hunkered down on the stone floor. Even the mean little terrier seemed cowed by her presence. His ears flattened onto his skull, he tucked his tail between his legs and crept back to the corner where he'd been devouring a large rat.

'There, there,' Catherine cried as she ran to the hearth to warm herself. 'Didn't I tell you the dogs won't hurt me, Nelly?'

I asked Joseph if the master was in. My question remained so long unanswered that I thought the old man had grown deaf, or died where he sat, eyes open. I repeated it louder.

'Na-ay!' he snarled. 'Na-ay! Yah better go back from where ye come from.'

'Joseph!' cried a peevish voice from the inner room. 'How often am I to call you? There are only a few red ashes now.'' Linton entered the kitchen. 'Joseph! Come this moment.'

Cathy flew to him.

'No—don't kiss me. It takes my breath—dear me! Papa said you would call,' continued he, after recovering a little from his cousin's embrace. 'Will you come in and shut the door? Those *detestable* creatures waltz right in if you let them.'

'The dogs?' I asked.

He shuddered walking into the parlor, ignoring my question and making me wonder exactly which creatures he meant. I looked around cautiously for any sign of bloodsuckers clinging to the rafters or crouched in dark corners, and we followed.

'It's so cold!' he complained, falling into a chair.

I stirred up the cinders and fetched a scuttle of coal from the kitchen myself, taking care to close the door between the two rooms.

'Well, Linton,' murmured Catherine. 'Are you glad to see me?'

'Why didn't you come before?' he said, looking feverish and ill. 'You should have come, instead of writing. It tired me dreadfully, writing those long letters. I'd far rather have talked to you. Now I can neither bear to talk, nor anything else. I wonder where Zillah is! Will you (looking at me) step into the kitchen and see?'

I had received no thanks for my other service, and being unwilling to run to and fro at his behest, I replied, 'You saw for yourself. Nobody is out there but Joseph.'

'Give them time—they'll be by. It's how he keeps them under control.'

'I have no idea what you speak of,' I responded. "Those beastly dogs?"

'It doesn't matter, so long as they stay far from me. I want a drink,' he exclaimed fretfully, turning away. 'Zillah is constantly gadding off to Gimmerton since Papa went. It's miserable! And I'm obliged to come down here—they resolved never to hear me upstairs.'

'Is your father attentive to you, Master Heathcliff?' I asked, perceiving Catherine to be checked in her friendly advances.

'Attentive? He makes *them* a little more attentive, at least,' he cried. 'The wretches! Do you know, Miss Linton, that brute Hareton laughs at me! I hate him! Indeed, I hate them all. They are odious beings.'

Cathy began searching for some water; she lighted on a pitcher in the dresser, filled a tumbler, and brought it. He bid her add a spoonful of wine from a bottle on the table, and having swallowed a small portion, appeared more tranquil.

'And are you glad to see me?' she repeated, pleased to detect a faint dawn of a smile.

'Yes, I am. It's something new to hear a voice like yours!' he replied. 'But I *have* been vexed, because you wouldn't come. And Papa swore it was my fault. He called me a pitiful, shuffling, worthless thing, and said you despised me. He said if he had been in my place, he would be more the master of the Grange than your father, by this time. But you don't despise me, do you, Miss—'

'I wish you would say Catherine, or Cathy,' interrupted my young lady. 'We are kin, after all. It's not necessary for you to call me Miss, dear cousin.'

'But you admit you despise me as much as they all despise me?'

'Despise you? No! Next to Papa, and Nelly, I love you better than anybody living. I don't love Mr. Heathcliff, though. I dare not come when he returns. Will he stay away many days?'

'Not many. But he goes onto the moors frequently, since the vampires have begun moving about the county again. I don't know what he does out there. If he just killed them, they would be gone, wouldn't you think?' It wasn't a question he wished anyone to answer and he continued, 'You might spend an hour or two with me, some days, in his absence. Say you will! I think I should not be peevish with you.'

'Yes,' said Catherine, stroking his long, soft hair. 'If I could only get Papa's consent, I'd spend half my time with you. Pretty Linton! I wish you were my brother! If you were my brother, you would be of stronger countenance and we could go away to be schooled in the arts of fighting the bloodsuckers. The milkmaid tells me that she has a cousin who says there's a fine school in Paris. The teachers there are the best. They come from the far corners of the world to teach the ancient skills of defense with sword and knife and other secret ways. I should like to go to Paris. Don't you think it a noble task, to spend one's life defending mankind against the bloodsuckers?'

'Lose one's life, most likely,' he whined. He pouted for a moment, then looked at my dear Cathy with the slyest of looks. 'Papa says you would love me better than him and all the world if you were my wife, so I'd rather you were that.'

'No!' she returned gravely. 'People hate their wives, sometimes, but not their sisters and brothers. If you were my brother, you would live with us, and Papa would be as fond of you as he is of me.'

'*My* papa scorns yours!' cried Linton. 'He calls him a sneaking fool!'

'Yours is a wicked man,' retorted Catherine. 'And you are very naughty to dare to repeat what he says. He must be wicked to have made Aunt Isabella leave him as she did!'

'She didn't leave him,' said the boy. 'You shan't contradict me!'

'She did!' cried my young lady.

'Well, I'll tell *you* something!' said Linton. 'Your mother hated your father!'

'Oh!' exclaimed Catherine, too enraged to continue.

'And she loved mine!' added he.

'You little liar! I hate you now,' she panted, and her face grew red with passion.

'She did! She did!' sang Linton, sinking into the recess of his chair, and leaning back his head to enjoy her agitation.

'Hush, Master Heathcliff!' I said finally.

'She did, she did, Catherine! She did, she did!'

Cathy, beside herself, gave the chair a violent push, and caused him to fall against one arm. He was immediately seized by a suffocating cough that soon ended his triumph.

It lasted so long that it frightened even me. As to his cousin, she wept with all her might.

I held him till the fit exhausted itself. Then he thrust me away and leant his head down silently. Catherine quelled her lamentations also, took a seat opposite, and looked solemnly into the fire.

'How do you feel now, Master Heathcliff?' I inquired after waiting ten minutes.

'I wish *she* felt as I do,' he whimpered. 'I have never been struck in my life.'

'*I* didn't strike you!' muttered Cathy, chewing her lip to prevent another burst of emotion. 'If I had struck you, you'd know it. I'm quite strong, you know. I exercise every day. I wish I had a sword, but Papa won't buy me one, so I use a fireplace poker to practice my parrying. I can run and climb and jump as well as handle a poker. So don't fuss to me about a little push that wouldn't have troubled a suckling babe.'

He sighed and moaned like one under great suffering, and kept it up for a quarter of an hour, on purpose to distress his cousin, apparently, for whenever he caught a stifled sob from her, he put renewed pain and pathos into the inflections of his voice.

'I'm sorry I hurt you, Linton,' she said finally. 'But *I* couldn't have been hurt by that little push, and I had no idea that you could, either. You're not much, are you, Linton? It's no wonder your father trains Hareton to fight the bloodsuckers and not you.' She paused. 'Linton?'

'I can't speak to you,' he murmured. 'You've hurt me so that I shall lie awake all night, choking with this cough.'

'Must I go, then?' asked Catherine dolefully, bending over him. 'Do you want me to go, Linton?'

'You can't alter what you've done,' he replied pettishly.

'Well, then I must go.' she repeated.

She lingered, then finally made a movement to the door and I followed.

'You must come back, to cure me,' Linton called after her, lifting his head when he realized she was truly taking her leave. 'You ought to come because you have hurt me! I was not as ill when you entered as I am at present—was I?'

She halted in the doorway. 'You've made yourself ill by crying. I didn't do it all. However, we'll be friends now.' She approached him again. 'You would wish to see me sometimes, really?'

'I told you I did,' he replied impatiently, falling back in

his chair. 'Tomorrow, Catherine, will you be here tomorrow?'

'No!' I answered. 'She will not. Nor the next day neither.'

She, however, gave a different response, evidently, for his forehead cleared as she stooped and whispered in his ear.

'You won't go tomorrow, miss!' I commenced as we went out the kitchen door, Joseph nowhere to be seen. The evil little dog ran after us, the rat, now headless, in his teeth.

She smiled. "Isn't that sweet, Nelly. I think he's making a gift of his rat to me. Good dog," she praised. The creature whined and rolled over on the ground, wiggling with joy. Cathy laughed. 'See, I do have more than one friend in this cheerless house.'

'I don't know why the beasties haven't made a meal of that boy,' I said, stepping over the rat and striding ahead. 'But you'll not come back here any time soon, that I vow.' I grabbed her pony's reins, untying him from the hitching post, and led him along. The terrier followed at Cathy's heels.

'And what is this nonsense about you using a poker for a sword? Is that what you're doing in the garden when I can't see you? I ought to tell your papa.'

'You ought not to,' the little lady snapped.

I gave a harrumph. 'I'll have that lock mended, and you can escape by no way else.'

'I can get over the wall,' she said, laughing. 'The Grange is not a prison, Nelly, and you are not my jailer. And besides, I'm almost seventeen. I'm a woman. And I'm certain Linton would recover quickly if he had me to—'

She halted mid-sentence, her mouth falling open, her eyes going round with fright as she caught sight of something in the barnyard. I turned in the direction she gazed and had to clamp my hand over my mouth to prevent myself from crying out and giving away our location.

The terrier's mood changed from jubilant to defensive. Dropping the rat, he sprang in front of Cathy to protect her, his small body crouched, and the hair rose on his back. Baring his teeth, he uttered a low snarl.

Across the barnyard, Joseph stood, his back against the wall of a shed, his arms spread wide, his head wrenched back, his eyes closed, his face convulsing in pain. On each side of him stood a cloaked figure, one male, one female, their mouths pressed against his throat. Blood ran in rivulets down Joseph's shirt and their greedy mouths. He was not struggling and I got the distinct impression this was not the first time this had occurred.

What had Linton said? *Give them time, they'll be by. It's how he keeps them under control.* Was this ghastly occurrence what the boy referred to? And who was *he?* Surely it was not Joseph sacrificing himself to keep the vampires *under control.*

Unable to tear my gaze away from the horrifying sight, I grabbed my charge. 'Keep silent,' I murmured in her ear. 'Draw no attention to yourself.' *Else they may seize upon our throats as well,* I thought, but did not voice.

As I led Miss Cathy away from the house, the terrier followed, never taking his gaze from the bloodsuckers. I looked back once over my shoulder. Joseph's eyes were open this time, and when his gaze met mine, when I saw the pain—no, worse—the *surrender* in them, I actually felt sorry for the miserable wretch.

We made our escape from the Heights without further issue and my charge was quite silent on our return. Whether she was frightened beyond words, or still busy scheming, I did not know. Somewhere between the two houses, the little black dog lay down in the center of the road and watched us go with sad eyes.

Within sight of the gates of the Grange, I said simply, 'The vampires, Joseph, and that terrible dog, *that* is why you cannot return to Wuthering Heights, my dear.' The young miss made no response and I said nothing more. I knew she knew better than to recount what she had seen. We reached home before our dinner-time; my master supposed we had been wandering through the park, and demanded no explanation of our absence.

As soon as I entered, I hastened to change my soaked shoes and stockings, but sitting such a while at the Heights had done the mischief. On the succeeding morning, I found myself ill. Perhaps it was from the fright of seeing the vampires taking so freely from Joseph his life's blood and the knowledge that the moors were not as safe as we thought they had become. Or perhaps it was the wet stockings, I do not know.

For three weeks I remained incapacitated, a calamity never experienced prior to that period, and never, I am thankful to say, since.

My little mistress behaved like an angel in coming to wait on me and cheer my solitude. The moment Catherine left Mr. Linton's room, she appeared at my bedside. Her day was divided between us; she neglected her meals, her studies, and her play. I said her days were divided between us, but the master retired early, and I generally needed nothing after six o'clock, thus the evening was her own.

Poor thing! I never considered what she did with herself after tea. And though frequently, when she looked in to bid me good night, I noticed the fresh color in her cheeks and a pinkness over her slender fingers, instead of guessing the hue was a result of a cold ride across the moors, I laid it to the charge of a hot fire in the library.

# Chapter 24

It was three weeks before I was able to leave my chamber. The ague was such that the rumor went around in Gimmerton that I had been bitten, but of course it was only the dreadful damp and the soaking I'd received. I had not the faintest sign of fang marks. The doctor was quite pleased about that, but concerned about my weakened condition, and prescribed a poultice of dried mouse and graveyard moss from the west side of the church to be steeped in sour milk and applied warm to my chest three times a day. Some physicians don't understand the importance of such modern treatment, but due to his careful and learned advice, I made slow but steady recovery. And on the first occasion of my sitting up in the evening, I asked Catherine to read to me because my eyes were weak. We were in the library, the master having gone to bed. She consented, rather unwillingly I think, because my sort of books did not suit her. But I bid her read anything she liked and she was quick to choose.

She selected a book I did not—nor did her father, I would guess—even know she possessed. I have no idea how she obtained it, but thought maybe it had come from the library at Wuthering Heights. It was called *Modern Vampires, the Lexicon,* written by a scholar turned vampire slayer after his entire family and household in Essex were sucked dry by a family of bloodsuckers passing through on their way to London to see the sights. She read steadily for about an hour, describing the bloodsuckers' origins, what they ate (which was self-explanatory, I would have thought), what they wore, where they slept, and all manner of other details one might be curious about. The book held my attention at once, but as Cathy read, she asked frequent questions of me.

'Nelly, are not you tired? Hadn't you better lie down now? You'll be sick, keeping up so long, Nelly.'

When that did not work to rid herself of me, she began yawning, and stretching, and— 'Nelly, I'm tired.'

'Then stop reading and talk with me,' I suggested. 'I've learned far more about vampires than any housekeeper need know, anyway.'

That was worse. She fretted and sighed, and looked at her watch till eight, and finally went to her room.

The following night she seemed more impatient still, both with me and the *Vampire Lexicon,* and on the third, she complained of a headache, and left me.

I thought her conduct odd, and after leaving her alone for some time, I decided to go up to her room and check on her.

No Catherine could I discover upstairs, and none below. The servants affirmed they had not seen her. I listened at Mr. Edgar's door, but all was silent. I returned to her apartment, extinguished my candle, and seated myself in the window.

The moon shone bright; a sprinkling of snow covered the ground, and I reflected that she might have taken it into her head to walk about the garden. After a time, I detected a figure creeping along the inner fence of the park, but it was only one of the grooms with a shiny pitchfork chasing a wayward bloodsucker back over the wall. My master had ordered that the prongs of all the pitchforks on the property be replaced with those of pure silver—quite expensive, as you can imagine, but what can you do when the beasties grow so bold as to hurl themselves over the walls?

The groom, however, did not return to the stable, and I soon saw him start off at a brisk pace, as if he had detected something. Thinking it might be the vampire trying a different entry onto the property again, I watched closely. We usually gave them one chance, in order to be neighborly, but my master made it clear that bloodsuckers that could not be trusted had to be impaled. Usually the stable hands would corner the trespassers with a pitchfork, injure them with the silver tines, and then run the wooden handle through their hearts once they had successfully knocked them to the ground. The groom disappeared from my view, but soon reappeared, not carrying a vampire corpse on the end of the pitchfork, but leading Miss's pony with her astride.

Cathy dismounted and the man took his charge stealthily across the grass toward the stable. My young miss entered by the casement window of the drawing room, and glided noiselessly up to where I awaited her.

She pulled the door gently to, slipped off her snowy shoes, untied her hat, and was proceeding, unconscious of my espionage, to lay aside her mantle when I suddenly rose and revealed myself. The surprise petrified her an instant; she uttered an inarticulate exclamation, and stood fixed.

'My dear Miss Catherine,' I began, too vividly impressed by her recent kindness to break into a scold. By this point, I was greatly enjoying the book on vampire particulars and did not wish her to cease reading to me in the evenings. 'Where have you been at this hour? Have you become suicidal? Do you not know it will break your papa's heart if he finds your carcass hanging on the gate in the morning? Where have you been? Speak!'

'To the bottom of the park,' she stammered.

'And nowhere else?' I demanded.

'No,' was the muttered reply.

'Oh, Catherine!' I cried sorrowfully. 'You know you have been doing wrong, or you wouldn't be lying to me.'

She sprang forward and, bursting into tears, threw her arms round my neck. 'Please don't be angry with me, Nelly,' she said. 'Promise not to be angry, and you shall know the very truth. I hate to hide it.'

We sat down in the window-seat and I assured her I would not scold, whatever her secret might be. I guessed it, of course, so she commenced—

'I've been to Wuthering Heights, Nelly, and, until three days ago, I've never missed going a day since you fell ill. I was at the Heights by half past six, and generally stayed till half past eight, and then galloped home. It was not to amuse myself that I went, but because I had promised.

'On my first visit alone, Linton seemed in lively spirits. Zillah, their housekeeper, made us a clean room and a good fire, and told us we might do as we like. Hareton Earnshaw was off with his dogs—robbing our woods of pheasants, as I heard afterward. And Joseph was off trapping hedgehogs. Baked hedgehog with garlic stuffing is one dish that dear Linton will eat, so long as the head is removed before serving. He has a delicate stomach. Don't you find that attractive in a young gentleman, Nelly, that he cannot bear to dine on small intact mammals? So . . . so romantic.'

I rolled my eyes but allowed my charge to continue without telling her what I truly thought of Linton.

'She brought me some warm wine and gingerbread, and appeared exceedingly good-natured. Linton sat in the armchair, and I on the little rocking chair on the hearth-stone, and we laughed and talked so merrily, and found so much to say. We planned what we would do when it grew warm again and talked some of the school in Paris. I won't give you the details because I know you will only call me silly.

'One time, however, we were near quarrelling. He said that he agreed with you, that women had no business fighting vampires. I argued that the moors were mine as easily as they were his, but he did not see to my way of thinking. At last we agreed to disagree, at least for the present, and then we kissed each other and were friends. Minny and I then went flying home as light as air, and I dreamt of Wuthering Heights and my sweet, darling cousin, till morning.

'On the morrow, I was sad, partly because you were feeling poorly, and partly that I wished my father knew and approved of my excursions. But there was a beautiful moonlight after tea, and, as I rode on, the gloom cleared.

'*I shall have another happy evening*, I thought to myself, *and what delights me more, my pretty Linton will.* I trotted up their garden and was turning round to the back when Hareton met me, took my bridle, and bid me go in by the front entrance. He patted Minny's neck, and said she was a bonny pony, and appeared as if he wanted me to speak to him. I told him to leave my horse alone, or else it would kick him.

'He answered in his vulgar accent, "It wouldn't do much hurt if it did," and surveyed its legs with a smile.

'I was half inclined to make it try; however, he moved off to open the door and, as he raised the latch, he looked up to the inscription above, and said, with a stupid mixture of awkwardness and elation—

' "Miss Catherine! I can read that."

' "Wonderful," I exclaimed. ' "Pray let us hear you— you are grown clever!"

'He spelt, and drawled over by syllables, the name—"Hareton Earnshaw."

' "And the figures?" I cried encouragingly, thinking that he came to a dead halt.

' "I cannot tell them yet," he answered.

' "Oh, you dunce!" I said, laughing heartily at his failure.

'The fool stared, with a grin hovering about his lips and a scowl gathering over his eyes, and I told him to walk away, reminding him that I had come to see Linton, not him.

'He reddened—I saw that by the moonlight—dropped his hand from the latch, and skulked off, a picture of mortified vanity. He imagined himself to be as accomplished as Linton, I suppose, just because he could read his own name, and was marvelously discomfited that I didn't think the same. Why ever would his name be carved above the doors, anyway? I don't know who the Hareton Earnshaw was, but—'

'Stop, Miss Catherine, dear!' I interrupted. 'I shall not scold, but I don't like your conduct there. If you had remembered that Hareton was your cousin as much as Master Heathcliff, you would have felt how improper it was to behave in that way. At least he is trying to learn how to read! You made him ashamed of his ignorance before, and he wished to remedy it to please you. To sneer at his imperfect attempt was very bad breeding. Had *you* been brought up in his circumstances, would you be less rude? He was as quick and as intelligent a child as ever you were, and I'm hurt that he should be despised now because that base Heathcliff has treated him so unjustly.'

'Well, Nelly, you won't cry about it, will you?' she exclaimed, surprised at my earnestness. 'But wait, and you shall hear if he learned his ABCs to please me, and if it were worthwhile being civil to the brute. I entered; Linton was lying on the settle, and half got up to welcome me.

' "I'm ill tonight, Catherine, love," he said, "and you must have all the talk, and let me listen. Come and sit by me. I was sure you wouldn't break your word, and I'll make you promise again, before you go."

'I knew now that I mustn't tease him, as he was ill, and I spoke softly and avoided irritating him in any way. I had brought some of my nicest books for him; he asked me to read a little of one, and I was about to comply when Earnshaw burst the door open. He advanced directly to us, seized Linton by the arm, and swung him off the seat.

' "Get to thy own room!" he said in a voice almost inarticulate with passion, his face swelled and furious. "Take her there if she comes to see thee; thou shalln't keep me out of this room! Begone wi' ye both!"

'He swore at us, and left Linton no time to answer, nearly throwing him into the kitchen. He clenched his fist as I followed, seemingly longing to knock me down. I was afraid for a moment, and I let a book fall; he kicked it after me, and shut us out.

'I heard a malignant, crackly laugh by the fire and, turning, beheld that odious Joseph standing, rubbing his bony hands, and quivering.

' "Serves ye right! He's a grand lad! He knows who ought to be maister here one day!"

' "Where must we go?" I said to my cousin, disregarding the old wretch's mockery. How could you take a man seriously who would allow vampires to freely feed on him? Why . . . he's nothing more than a paramour, Nelly. A paramour to the bloodsuckers.'

I wanted to ask the young miss how she even knew what a paramour was, but suspecting the information had come from the same shelf as the *Vampire Lexicon*, I allowed her to go on with her story.

'Linton was white and trembling. He was not pretty then, Nelly, for his thin face and large eyes were wrought into an expression of frantic, powerless fury. He grasped the handle of the door and shook it, but it was fastened inside.

' "If you don't let me in I'll kill you!—If you don't let me in I'll kill you!" he rather shrieked than said. "Devil! Devil!—I'll kill you—I'll kill you!"

'I took hold of Linton's hands and tried to pull him away, but he shrieked so shockingly that I dared not proceed. At last his cries were choked by a dreadful fit of coughing, blood gushed from his mouth, and he fell on the ground.

'I ran into the yard, sick with terror, and called for Zillah, as loud as I could.'

'No, Cathy! What about the vampires we saw in the yard?'

'Why would I be afraid of them, Nelly? They have Joseph to feed on, apparently whenever they wish. I had no fear they would bother with me, for I would put up a great fight and maybe even kill one of them if I had a proper wooden spike!' She frowned at me as if I was completely foolish and went on. 'Zillah soon heard me. She was milking the cows in a shed behind the barn, and hurrying from her work, she inquired what there was to do.

'Dragging her in, I looked for Linton. Hareton had come out to examine the mischief he had caused, and he was then conveying the poor thing upstairs. Zillah and I ascended after him, but he stopped me at the top of the steps, and said I must go home.

'Nelly, I was ready to tear my hair off my head! I sobbed and wept so that my eyes were almost blind, and the ruffian you have such sympathy for just stood there, denying that it was his fault. Finally, frightened by my threats that I would tell Papa and that he should be put in prison and hanged, he began blubbering himself, and hurried out to hide his cowardly agitation.

'Still, I was not rid of him. When I tried to leave, I had barely got some hundred yards off the premises when he suddenly appeared from the shadow of the roadside, like some homeless bloodsucker, and checked Minny and took hold of me.

'"Miss Catherine, I'm ill grieved," he began.

'I gave him a cut with my whip, thinking perhaps he would murder me or hand me off to the vampires that lurked watching us. He let go, thundering one of his horrid curses, and I galloped home more than half out of my senses.

'I didn't bid you good night that evening, and I didn't go to Wuthering Heights the next night. I wished to, wanting to know how Linton fared, but shuddered at the thought of encountering Hareton.

'On the third day I found my courage, and stole off once more. I went at five o'clock, and walked, fancying I might manage to creep into the house and up to Linton's room unobserved. However, that little terrier that I cannot decide is friend or foe gave loud notice of my approach. Zillah received me and showed me into a small, tidy, carpeted apartment, where, to my inexpressible joy, I beheld Linton lying on a little sofa, reading one of my books.

'But he would neither speak to me nor look at me, for a whole hour. Nelly, he has such an unhappy temper. And what quite confounded me was that when he did open his mouth, he declared that I was the one responsible for the uproar that had made him ill, and Hareton was not to blame!

'Unable to reply, except passionately, I got up and walked from the room. The next day was the second day that I stayed home, determined to visit him no more.

'But it was so miserable going to bed, and getting up, and never hearing anything about him, that my resolution melted into air before it was properly formed. It *had* appeared wrong to go to Wuthering Heights, at first. Now it seemed wrong to refrain.

'I arrived on Minny without incident and Zillah came out to greet me.

'I went in; Hareton was there also, but he left the room the moment he saw me. Linton sat in the great armchair half asleep and I began in a serious tone, partly meaning it to be true, "As you don't like me, Linton, and as you think I come on purpose to hurt you, and pretend that I do so every time, this is our last meeting. Let us say good-bye, and tell Mr. Heathcliff that you have no wish to see me, and that he mustn't invent any more falsehoods on the subject."

' "Sit down and take your hat off, Catherine," he answered. "Papa talks enough of my defects, and shows enough scorn of me to make it natural I should doubt myself. I doubt I'm as worthless as he calls me, but I feel so cross and bitter, I hate everybody! I *am* worthless, and I have a bad temper, and if you choose, you *may* say good-bye. Only, Catherine, do me this justice: believe that if I might be as sweet, and as kind, and as good as you are, I would be. And believe that your kindness has made me love you deeper than if I deserved your love. I can't help showing my nature to you and shall regret and repent it till I die!"

'I felt he spoke the truth, and I felt I must forgive him. We were reconciled, but we cried, both of us. I was sorry Linton had that distorted nature. He'll never let his friends be at ease, and he'll never be at ease himself!

'I have gone to his little parlor since that night because his father returned the day after. About three times, I think, we have been merry and hopeful, as we were the first evening. The rest of my visits were dreary and troubled with his selfishness and spite, and now with his sufferings, but I've learnt to endure.

'Mr. Heathcliff purposely avoids me; I have hardly seen him at all. Last Sunday, coming earlier than usual, I heard him abusing poor Linton, cruelly, for his conduct of the night before. I can't tell how he knew of it, unless he listened. Linton had certainly behaved provokingly; however, it wasn't his business and I interrupted Mr. Heathcliff's lecture by entering and telling him so.'

'You didn't!' I exclaimed.

'I did, Nelly. He burst into a laugh and went away, saying he was glad I took that view of the matter. Since then, I've told Linton he must whisper his bitter things.

'So, now, Nelly, you have heard all, and I can't be prevented from going to Wuthering Heights.'

'But what of the danger?' I argued. 'You could be attacked at any time.'

'They would not dare.'

Her eyes narrowed, and for a moment, she almost seemed dangerous.

'You'll not tell Papa, will you, Nelly?' she pressed. 'It will be very heartless if you do.'

'I'll make up my mind on that point by tomorrow, Miss Catherine,' I replied. 'It requires some study, and so I'll leave you to your rest, and go think it over.'

I thought it over aloud, in my master's presence. Walking straight from her room to his, I related the whole story with the exception of the vampires, her conversations with her cousin, and any mention of Hareton.

Mr. Linton was alarmed and distressed more than he would acknowledge to me. In the morning, Catherine learnt my betrayal of her confidence, and she learnt also that her secret visits were to end.

In vain she wept and writhed and implored her father to have pity on Linton. All she got to comfort herself was a promise that she could write, and give him leave to come to the Grange when he pleased, but explaining that she could no longer go to see him. Perhaps, had Mr. Linton been aware of his nephew's state of health, and the strange occurrences with the beasties at Wuthering Heights, he would have seen fit to withhold even that slight consolation.

# Chapter 25

"These things happened last winter, Mr. Lockwood," said Mrs. Dean. "Hardly more than a year ago. It is hard to believe that twelve months later I would be amusing a stranger with such intimate family details! Yet, who knows how long you'll be a stranger? You're too young to rest contented, living by yourself." Her eyes twinkled with scheming. "No one could see Catherine Linton and not love her. You smile, but why do you look so lively and interested when I talk about her? And why have you asked me to hang her picture over your fireplace? And why—"

"Stop, my good friend," I cried. "It may be very possible that *I* should love her, but would she love me? And this matter of her thinking women should be fighting vampires is most distressing. No, I think I should steer clear of such temptation. A lady's place is well defined: the hearth, care and raising of children, fine needlework, sketching. No woman of quality concerns herself with fighting bloodsuckers. The eradication of vampires must be left to men of courage. Not that I lack courage," I added. "But one must be trained from childhood for such dangerous pursuits. And remember, my home is not here. I'm of the busy world, and to its arms I must return. But go on. Was Catherine obedient to her father's commands?"

"She was," continued the housekeeper, "for her affection for him was still the chief sentiment in her heart. He said to me, a few days afterward—"

'I wish my nephew would write, Nelly, or call. Tell me, sincerely, what you think of him. Is he changed for the better, or is there a prospect of improvement, as he grows a man?'

'He's very delicate, sir,' I replied, choosing my words carefully. 'And scarce likely to reach manhood. But this I can say, he does not resemble his father much in character, and if Miss Catherine had the misfortune to marry him, he would not be beyond her control.'

Edgar sighed and, walking to the window, looked out toward Gimmerton Kirk. It was a misty afternoon, but the February sun shone dimly, and we could just distinguish the sparely scattered gravestones. We could not see Mrs. Linton's bare grave, but I knew he was thinking of it.

'I've been very happy with my little Cathy. Through winter nights and summer days she was a living hope at my side. But I've been as happy musing of the day when I might lie beneath the earth beside my lady wife.'

I wanted to ask him if he thought it was safe to be buried beside a grave that looked as if either the dead rose from it periodically, or someone was digging into it, but I kept my mouth shut as I always do, that being my place. It's not for me to advise or gossip about the gentry, and I am ever mindful of my duty.

'What can I do for Cathy?' my master asked. 'I'd not care one moment for Linton being Heathcliff's son, nor for his taking her from me, if he could console her for my loss. I'd not care that Heathcliff gained his ends and triumphed in robbing me of my last blessing! But should Linton be unworthy—only a feeble tool to his father—I cannot abandon her to him! And, hard though it be to crush her buoyant spirit, I must persevere in making her sad while I live, and leaving her solitary when I die. These are such frightening times, Nelly, with those creatures forever watching, plotting, taking as they please. I think I'd rather resign her to God, and lay her in the earth before me.'

Spring advanced, and though my master gathered no real strength, he resumed his walks on the grounds with his daughter. To her inexperienced notions, this itself was a sign of convalescence and she felt sure of his recovering.

On her seventeenth birthday, he did not lock himself in his study, as was customary. Instead, he remained in the firelight of the parlor and wrote again to Linton, expressing his great desire to see him.

Had the invalid been presentable, I've no doubt his father would have permitted him to come. As it was, being instructed, he returned an answer, intimating that Mr. Heathcliff objected to his calling at the Grange. His uncle's kind remembrance delighted him, however, and he hoped to meet him, sometimes, in his rambles, and personally to petition that his cousin and he might not remain long so utterly divided.

That part of his letter was simple, and probably his own. Heathcliff knew he could plead eloquently enough for Catherine's company, then—

'I do not ask,' he said, 'that she may visit here, but, am I never to see her, because my father forbids me to go to her home, and you forbid her to come to mine? Do, now and then, ride with her toward the Heights and let us exchange a few words, in your presence! We have done nothing to deserve this separation, and you are not angry with me. You have no reason to dislike me, you allow, yourself. Dear Uncle! Send me a kind note tomorrow, and permission to join you anywhere you please, except at Thrushcross Grange. I believe an interview would convince you that my father's character is not mine. He affirms I am more your nephew than his son, despite my dark looks, and though I have faults which render me unworthy of Catherine, she has excused them, and, for her sake, you should also. You inquire after my health—it is better, but I continue to be most delicate with little appetite. I sleep hardly an hour or two each night due to the constant presence of the undead bloodsuckers that infest my father's holdings, clawing at the windows, hanging from the rafters, and nesting in the attics and wine cellar, but I do not complain, for it is not my nature. While I remain cut off from all hope, and doomed to solitude, how can I be cheerful and well?'

Edgar, though he felt badly for the boy, could not consent to grant his request because he could not bring himself to accompany Catherine.

He said, in summer, perhaps, he would consider it. Meantime, he wished him to continue writing at intervals, and engaged to give his nephew what advice and comfort he was able by letter, being well aware of his difficult position in his family.

Linton complied, and had he been unrestrained, would probably have spoiled all by filling his epistles with complaints and lamentations. His father, however, kept a sharp watch over him and insisted on every line that my master sent being shown. So, instead of penning his peculiar personal sufferings and distresses, Linton harped on the cruel obligation of being held asunder from his friend and love, and intimated that Mr. Linton must allow a meeting soon.

That spring, Cathy killed her first vampire. It was entirely by accident, I think, but—

"She killed a vampire?" I interrupted, certain I had misunderstood. I gazed at her sweet portrait on the wall. "Our Cathy killed?"

"It was kill or be killed, sir." Nelly defended her with annoyance. "Or kill or watch another killed, as was in this case."

"I'm sorry. Go on, Mrs. Dean. Please."

She settled back in her chair, darning on her lap, and spoke again.

"I was not there when it happened, but Cathy gave me a full report when she had the groom drag the body to the incineration pile. Had you not been feeling so poorly these months, you might have had an opportunity to see the place on the far side of the property. Whenever a vampire is killed, the carcass is placed on a stack of hot burning oak and set afire. The stench is worse than that of rotting fish stuffed with bad eggs, but it keeps the other beasties from dragging away the bodies."

"Cathy, Mrs. Dean. You were speaking of how Cathy was forced to kill."

"Oh, yes." She smiled congenially. "It was a chilly day, wet. I had no desire to be out of doors and I had a fresh pot of treacle on the stove, so when Cathy said she was walking out to the stable to visit with Minny, I thought nothing of it. This is how Cathy said the event unfolded—"

'I was headed straight for the barn, just as I said, Nelly, but halfway across the yard, I heard a strange sound. Something akin to a squeak. I had no idea what the sound was, only that I must go to it. I saw several rugs thrown over a line and a rug beater lying in the wet grass. Only then did I remember that you had sent the new maid, Sally, out to air the bedchamber rugs. There was no sign of Sally, only her bonnet. I called to her and heard another squeak. I don't know what made me do it, Nelly, but I picked up the rug beater and wove my way through the walls of rugs. On the far side, leaned against the tool shed, I found the source of the squeaking. It was the maid, Sally, being held against the wall by a bloodsucker who was taking greedily from her neck.

'He was so short a vampire, and Sally was so tall, that I

wasn't entirely sure how he had trapped her, but nonetheless, there he was.

' "Sally!" I cried, lifting my skirts from the mud and running toward her, waving the rug beater. "Get off her!" I ordered the vampire. "Get off her this moment. This girl is our maid and she has duties to attend to."

'The vampire turned to look at me and broke into a grin, Sally's blood dripping from his fangs. "You're next," he warned.

' "Let her go," I warned. "Else you'll surely be sorry."

' "Will I?" he asked in a perfect Yorkshire accent. Then he laughed, and Nelly, he had the nerve to take another drink from her.

'I vow, she was as pale as plaster.'

'So what did you do, my dear?' I asked of my charge as I set a cup of tea before her in the parlor.

'What was I to do? Those rugs needed to be returned to the house before the dampness of the evening set in, and if he killed Sally, I knew it would take days to replace her, as her mother was so difficult to convince sending her after the first four of her daughters were murdered in service here. So I waved the rug beater at that bloodsucker and when he continued to drain the life's blood from her, I struck him squarely on the back of the head!'

'And that killed him?' I asked, wondering if the vampires were changing. If it was easier to kill them than it once had been.

'It barely stunned him,' Cathy remarked, adding several lumps of sugar to her tea. 'By then, I was so annoyed that I broke the rug beater over my knee and ran full at him, thrusting the jagged end like a spear. I hit him dead on through his back, piercing his heart, apparently, and only pinned Sally's apron to the shed. The vampire screamed. Sally screamed. I had to get a groom to remove the vampire from the shed wall in order to set the silly wench free.

She was most grateful, after we revived her from a dead faint. What I don't understand,' said my entirely too practical charge, 'is why she fainted *after* I killed the vampire. Had she forgotten the importance of getting the last of the dust from the rugs and carrying them in before moisture ruined them entirely?'

'And she will live?' I asked.

'So I suspect.' Cathy sipped her tea. 'I insisted she finish up with the rugs first, then said you would see she had a boiled pigeon egg and a poultice for her neck.'

"Mrs. Dean," I interrupted, unable to remain quiet any longer. "This . . . Sally. Does she work here still?"

"Yes, of course. The pretty child who acts as chambermaid." Nelly smiled. "She's a good worker, though as skinny as a rake handle. Skinny Sally, we call her, and the loss of so much blood has done nothing for her color, but what's to be done? As Miss Cathy said, it is not easy to find a maid, especially those over the age of ten." She sighed. "Of course, we had to buy a new rug beater the next time we went to Gimmerton, but it was a minor loss compared to that of a good chamber-maid. There are more sisters, I understand. Her mother seems to bear nothing but puny girls, but the next in line is but nine or ten years old. Sally had a twin but she didn't live long enough for us to hire her."

"What happened to her?"

"Bitten on her way home from the tanner's. Sucked dry as a cornhusk and blown away. They found the remains at Gobbin's Mill, in the pond, floating like a tiny boat. Poor thing. Luckily there are eight more sisters at home, but three still unweaned and they would be of little use to us here in the hall. Not for some space of time. A pity, for Sally and her sisters don't eat much, not like the kitchen girl, who can devour an entire tub of turnips in an afternoon. But back to that spring. *After* Cathy killed the vampire."

The young miss was a powerful ally at home and eventually persuaded my master, who was still declining, to permit her and Linton to have a ride or a walk together, about once a week, under my guardianship, on the moors nearest the Grange. My master had no idea that the boy's health was declining as quickly as his own.

I, for my part, began to fancy my forebodings were false, and that Linton must be actually rallying, when he mentioned riding and walking on the moors, and seemed so earnest in pursuing his object. He even tolerated my charge's constant chatter of the school in Paris they would attend and the world sights they would see when his constitution improved.

"I could not picture a father treating a dying child as tyrannically and wickedly as I afterward learned Heathcliff had treated him, but I will come to that soon enough, Mr. Lockwood." She rose from her chair. "Tea, sir? I can call Sally."

# Chapter 26

Summer was already past its prime when Edgar reluctantly yielded his assent to Catherine and Linton's entreaties, and she and I set out on our first ride to join her cousin.

It was a close, sultry day, devoid of sunshine, but with a sky too dappled and hazy to threaten rain, and our place of meeting had been fixed at the guide-stone, by the crossroads. On arriving there, however, a dark-haired, pale-skinned young man who, though dressed like a herd-boy, looked like a vampire to me, had been dispatched as a messenger from Wuthering Heights. He told us that Master Linton was just on the other side of the Heights and he would be much obliged if we would join him there.

By the time we reached him, we were scarcely a quarter of a mile from his own door. Worse, we found he had no horse, and we were forced to dismount and leave ours to graze. The vampire boy turned herder had followed us and now watched closely from a distance, as if he had been sent to spy.

Linton lay on the heath, awaiting our approach, and did not rise till we came within a few yards. Then he walked so feebly, and looked so pale, that I immediately exclaimed—

'Why, Master Heathcliff, you are not fit for enjoying a ramble this morning. How ill you do look! Have you been bitten?'

'Certainly not,' he grumbled. 'My father will not allow it. Nor will he allow my own partaking of Joseph's cure for my ailment.'

'What nonsense do you speak of?' I asked. 'You cannot mean Joseph wants you to drink human blood?'

'The wretch claims it would make me strong again, but Papa will not allow it.'

'A good thing,' I commented. 'Who would take the word of a man who willingly allows bloodsuckers to feed on him? For all we know, he enjoys it!'

Catherine surveyed Linton with grief and astonishment, not seeming to be disturbed by talk of drinking blood. It's funny how what once seemed beyond reason becomes perfectly reasonable over time. 'Are you worse than usual?' she asked him.

'No—better—better!' he panted, trembling and retaining her hand as if he needed its support. His large dark eyes wandered timidly over her, the hollowness round them transforming to haggard wildness the languid expression they once possessed.

'But you are worse,' persisted his cousin. 'You're worse than when I saw you last—you are thinner, and—'

'I'm tired,' he interrupted hurriedly. 'It is too hot for walking. Do you forget that I have not been born with your robust nature? Let us rest here.'

Cathy sat down, and he reclined beside her. 'This is something like your paradise,' said she, making an effort at cheerfulness. 'You recollect the two days we agreed to spend in the place and way each thought pleasantest? This is nearly yours, only there are clouds, but then they are so soft and mellow, it is nicer than sunshine. Next week, if you can, we'll ride down to the Grange park, and perhaps we'll get lucky and be attacked by a vampire and I will show you the skills I've learned from the books Hareton gave me from your papa's library.'

I had not realized she had more forbidden books, but I did not think that was the time to discuss the matter with her.

Either Linton did not remember what she spoke of or he was ignoring her, having no intention of riding to the Grange to allow himself to possibly be attacked by vampires and risk his life on the chance that Cathy could defend them. In truth, he didn't seem all that pleased to see her. An indefinite alteration had come over his whole person and manner. The pettishness that might be caressed into fondness had yielded to a listless apathy.

Catherine perceived, as well as I did, that he held it rather a punishment than a gratification to endure our company, and she soon proposed we leave.

That proposal unexpectedly roused Linton from his lethargy, and threw him into a strange state of agitation. He glanced fearfully towards the Heights, begging she would remain another half-hour, at least.

I wondered why he was so intent upon our staying and I glanced at the young bloodsucker that still watched us. Had the two of them set up some sort of ambush? Were we to be made into an evening supper?

'I think,' said Cathy, 'you'd be more comfortable at home than sitting here. Obviously I cannot amuse you today by my tales and songs. In the last six months it appears that you have lost your taste for my diversions.'

'So stay to rest yourself,' he replied.

'I am a vampire slayer! I don't need rest.'

'You are no such thing! You are a female. And Catherine, don't think or say that I'm very unwell, for it's only the heavy weather and heat that makes me dull. Tell Uncle I'm in tolerable health, will you?'

'I'll tell him that *you* say so, Linton. I couldn't affirm that you are,' observed my young lady.

'And be here again next Thursday,' continued he. 'And give him my thanks for permitting you to come. And— and, if you *did* meet my father, and he asked you about me, don't lead him to suppose that I've been silent and stupid. Don't look sad and downcast, as you are doing—he'll be angry.'

'I care nothing for his anger,' exclaimed Cathy.

And on my faith, I do believe that she truly did not, for she was a most courageous lass, my Cathy.

'But I do,' said her cousin, shuddering. '*Don't* provoke him against me, Catherine, for he is very hard.'

'Is he severe to you, Master Heathcliff?' I inquired. 'Has he grown weary of indulgence, and passed from passive to active hatred?' He did not answer. 'When last we came we saw evidence that Joseph conspires with the bloodsuckers. Does Joseph mistreat you?'

'He is as mistreated as I. Worse, I think.' Linton turned his sour face on me. 'Do not think he gives himself voluntarily to the bloodsuckers, old woman! It is my father who gives him to them. How else do you think he has been able to control them all these years?'

I did not believe the boy. What he was saying was beyond belief, and I already knew him to be a liar. 'Mr. Heathcliff has controlled them because he is a gypsy vampire slayer by birth. They fear him, that is why they stay in check,' I explained.

Linton did not answer, and eventually his head drooped drowsily and he uttered nothing except suppressed moans of exhaustion or pain. Cathy began to seek solace in looking for bilberries and shared the produce of her researches with me.

'It is half an hour now, Nelly!' she whispered in my ear,

eyeing the herd-boy. 'I can't tell why we should stay. He's asleep, and Papa will be wanting us back.'

'Well, we must not leave him asleep,' I answered. 'That vampire boy might pounce on him, though I doubt he would offer much of a meal considering how puny he is. But let's wait until Linton wakes.'

Linton here started from his slumber in bewildered terror, and asked if anyone had called his name.

'No,' said Catherine. 'Unless in dreams. I cannot conceive how you manage to doze, out of doors, in the morning.'

'I thought I heard my father,' he gasped, glancing at the herd-boy, who now amused himself by picking flowers and braiding them into a chain of blossoms. 'You are sure nobody spoke?'

'Quite sure,' replied his cousin, rising. 'For today, we must part,' she said. 'And I won't conceal that I have been sadly disappointed with our meeting, though I'll mention it to nobody but you. Not that I stand in awe of Mr. Heathcliff!'

'Hush,' murmured Linton. 'For God's sake, hush! He's coming.' And he clung to Catherine's arm, but she hastily disengaged herself and whistled to Minny, who obeyed like a dog.

'I'll be here next Thursday,' she cried, springing to the saddle. 'Good-bye. Quick, Nelly!'

And so we left him, scarcely conscious of our departure, so absorbed was he in anticipating his father's approach.

Before we reached home, Catherine's displeasure softened into a perplexed sensation of pity and regret. She had vague, uneasy doubts about Linton's actual circumstances, physical and social, and I had to agree with her. But for the time being, we both agreed we would say nothing of our fears to her father of the strange visit. A second journey would make us better judges.

# Chapter 27

Seven days glided away and we set off toward the Heights on a golden afternoon in August. Catherine's face was just like the landscape—shadows and sunshine flitting over it in rapid succession, but the shadows rested longer, and the sunshine was more transient.

We found Linton in the same place as the previous week; there was no sign of the vampire herd-boy, but I kept a watch for him. My young mistress dismounted and told me that I had better hold the pony and remain on horseback; she didn't intend to stay long. Just because I didn't see the vampire boy didn't mean he wasn't there, and I refused to let Cathy leave my sight. We climbed the slope of heath together.

Master Heathcliff received us with greater animation than the previous week, but not the animation of high spirits; it looked more like fear.

'It is late!' he said, speaking short and with difficulty. 'Isn't your father very ill? I thought you wouldn't come.'

'*Why* don't you just say you don't want me to come anymore?' cried Catherine, swallowing her greeting. 'And spare us both this pain?'

Linton shivered, and glanced at her, half supplicating, half ashamed.

'My father *is* very ill,' she said. 'So why am I called from his bedside when you wished I wouldn't come? I desire an explanation, and I can't dance attendance on your affections now!'

'My affections!' he murmured. 'For Heaven's sake, Catherine, don't look so angry! Despise me as much as you please. I am a worthless, cowardly wretch, but I'm too mean for your anger—hate my father, and spare me for contempt.'

'Nonsense!' cried Catherine, in a passion. 'Foolish, silly boy. I shall return home; it is folly pretending we still care for each other. Rise, and don't degrade yourself into an abject reptile!'

With streaming face and an expression of agony, Linton threw himself on the ground and seemed convulsed with exquisite terror. 'Oh!' he sobbed, 'I cannot bear it! Catherine, Catherine, I'm a traitor, too, and I dare not tell you! But leave me and I shall be killed! *Dear* Catherine, my life is in your hands. You'll not go, then? Kind, sweet, good Catherine! And perhaps you *will* consent—and he'll let me die with you!'

My young lady, on witnessing his intense anguish, stooped to raise him.

'My father threatened me,' gasped the boy. 'And I dread him—I dread him! I *dare* not tell the truth of him!'

'Oh well!' said Catherine, with scornful compassion. 'Keep your secret. *I'm* no coward—save yourself. I'm not afraid!'

I was considering what the mystery might be, with several choices, each more horrendous than the previous, when I heard the sound of hoofbeats. I looked up and saw Mr. Heathcliff almost upon us, descending on a great black steed looking to be straight from the apocalyptic pages of Revelation. Behind him rode the herd-boy, black hair streaming in the wind, clinging to his waist, a triumphant look on his bloodless face.

'It is something to see you so near my house, Nelly!' He reined in abruptly, allowing the horse to rear and bring its hooves dangerously close to my head. 'How are you at the Grange? Let us hear! The rumor goes,' Heathcliff added in a lower tone, 'that Edgar Linton is on his deathbed.' The horse blew and snorted, prancing on massive legs. 'Perhaps they exaggerate his illness?'

The boy pitched himself off the back of the equine beast of hell. I kept my eye on him and my hand on my silver dagger in my apron pocket as I replied to Mr. Heathcliff. 'My master is dying,' I replied. 'It is true enough. A sad thing it will be for us all, but a blessing for him, for he will soon join his missus.'

'You think so, Nelly? You think he will lie beside her in her restless grave? Do you—'

'Sir!' I interrupted, cutting my eyes toward Catherine. 'This is not a matter to be discussed before gentle ears.'

He frowned, reining his big black horse around me in a circle. He wide-eyed, teeth gleaming, and the horse seemed as fierce as the devil's steed as well. 'How long will Mr. Linton last, do you think?' he asked.

'I don't know,' I said. Again, I had my thoughts, but I'd not share them with him. He might be high and mighty now, but he would never be gentry no matter how many called him master. He was naught but gypsy spawn whose bareness I had bathed, and I'd not forget it.

'Because that lad yonder seems determined to beat me to the kirkyard, and I'd thank his uncle to be quick, and go before him. But first—get up, Linton! Get up!' he shouted, turning on the boy. 'Don't grovel on the ground, there—up this moment!'

As Mr. Heathcliff whirled the monstrous horse around,

Linton sank prostrate in a paroxysm of helpless fear. Miss Cathy put herself between the boy and the man.

'*Damn* you! Get up!' Mr. Heathcliff commanded.

'I will, Father!' Linton panted. 'Only, let me alone, or I shall faint! I've done as you wished. Catherine will tell you that I—that I—have been cheerful. Catherine, give me your hand.'

'You, boy!' Catherine ordered the pale-as-paste herder. 'Help me!'

To my surprise, the little demon came running to do her bidding.

'You would imagine I was the devil himself,' Mr. Heathcliff grumbled, watching Cathy and her self-made servant lift Linton to his feet. 'Miss Linton, be so kind as to walk home with him, will you? He shudders if I touch him.'

'Linton, dear!' whispered Catherine. 'I can't go to Wuthering Heights . . . Papa has forbidden me. Why are you so afraid?'

'I can never re-enter that house,' he answered. 'I'm *not* to re-enter it without you!'

'Fine, I'll respect the young lady's scruples,' cried his father. 'Nelly, take him in.'

'I must remain with my mistress. To mind your son is not my business.'

'Fine. Come then, Linton.' Mr. Heathcliff leaned down, grasping the collar of his son's coat to lift him off the ground by the scruff of his neck. 'Are you willing to return, escorted by me?'

But Linton clung like a leech to his cousin and the herd-boy, screaming that she should accompany him.

'Let him go!' Miss Cathy demanded, looking straight into the black eyes of hell. 'I will escort him to the house.'

'You must not,' I cried, but she silenced me with a look. Determined was she, young or not; she showed her breeding in every line. She was a lady, in spite of her odd ways, and I could not stand against her, not even to please her father.

Mr. Heathcliff released his son and the boy crumpled to the ground, only getting to his feet with Cathy's and the vampire boy's assistance. Together, an odd threesome, they made their way toward Wuthering Heights.

We reached the threshold and the little vampire declared he could go no farther; he was not permitted inside. I stood waiting while Catherine conducted the invalid to a chair, expecting her out immediately. Mr. Heathcliff came from behind me on foot and pushed me forward.

'My house is not stricken with the plague, Nelly. Come in.'

'It's not the plague I worry about, sir,' I said, eyeing the boy vampire.

'I have a mind to be hospitable today,' Mr. Heathcliff continued, quite congenially. 'Come in, sit down, and allow me to shut the door.'

He shut it and locked it also. I started.

'You shall have tea before you go home,' he added. 'I am by myself. Hareton is gone off on one of his journeys and Zillah and Joseph have gone to Gimmerton. And, though I'm used to being alone, I'd rather have some interesting company, if I can get it. Miss Linton, take your seat by *him*. How she does stare!' he said, looking back to me. 'It's odd what a savage feeling I have to anything that seems afraid of me! Had I been born where laws are less strict, and tastes less dainty, I should treat myself to a slow vivisection of those two, as an evening's amusement.' He drew in his breath, struck the table, and swore to himself. 'By hell! I hate them.'

'I'm not afraid of you!' exclaimed Catherine, who could not hear the latter part of his speech.

She stepped close up, leaving Linton's side, her eyes flashing with passion and resolution. 'Give me that key. I will have it!' she said. 'I wouldn't eat or drink here if I were starving.'

Heathcliff had the key in his hand that remained on the table. He looked up, seized with a sort of surprise at her boldness, or, possibly, reminded by her voice and glance, of the person from whom she inherited it.

She snatched at the instrument, and half succeeded in getting it out of his loosened fingers, but he recovered it speedily.

'Now, Catherine Linton,' he said. 'Back off, or I shall knock you down, and that will make Mrs. Dean mad.'

Regardless of this warning, she captured his closed hand and its contents again.

'We *will* go!' she repeated, exerting her utmost efforts to cause the iron muscles to relax, and finding that her nails made no impression, she applied her teeth pretty sharply.

Heathcliff shot a look at me that kept me from interfering. His black eyes were so intense, so frightening, that I expected his teeth to grow into fangs at any moment. Catherine was too intent on his fingers to notice his face. 'I know what you are!' she shouted. 'Linton told me—'

He opened his hand, the key fell, and in one swift movement he slapped her in the face.

At this diabolical violence, I rushed on him furiously, drawing my dagger from my apron. 'You villain!' I began to cry. 'You villain!'

He saw the glint of the dagger and, I swear by all that is holy, moved quicker than humanly possible. He hit my forearm so hard with his fist that I staggered dizzily back.

'No silver in my house!' the fiend raged. 'Pick it up! Pick it up and throw it out the window,' he ordered Cathy.

Trembling like a reed, poor thing, she did as he ordered, tossing my small but mighty weapon into the yard through the tiny opening in the window.

Mr. Heathcliff picked up the key from the floor, and

when he looked at Cathy again, he seemed to have gained control of himself. 'Go to Linton now, as I told you, and cry at your ease! I shall be your father tomorrow—all the father you'll have in a few days—and you shall have plenty of that—you can bear plenty—you're no weakling—you shall have a daily taste, if I catch such a devil of a temper in your eyes again!'

Cathy ran to me instead of Linton, and knelt down, and put her burning cheek on my lap, weeping aloud. As brave as she was, his attack had been a shock. In her life, none had ever struck her, and she knew not how to bear it.

Mr. Heathcliff, ignoring us all, tucked the key into his pocket and made tea. The cups and saucers were laid ready. He poured it and handed me a cup. I took one sniff and looked him in his eye. 'I prefer mine with a heavy dollop of garlic,' I dared to say.

'Well, I do not.' He was silent for a moment, his gaze locked solidly with mine, but then he looked away. 'I'm going out to seek your horses. Do not try to leave.' His black-eyed gaze met mine again as he made his departure. 'You know what lies beyond these doors, Mrs. Dean. I have given them leave to do as they please, should anyone leave this house unescorted by me.'

I had only to peer out the window to spot not just the herd-boy vampire, but two other shady characters in black cloaks, the same two I had seen feeding on Joseph that day. When they caught my eye, the female smiled, baring her fangs, and gave a little wave. I slammed the window shut and turned the latch. 'Master Linton,' I cried, whipping around to face him. 'You know what your diabolical father is after. Tell us or I'll box your ears.'

'Yes, Linton, you must tell,' said Catherine. 'It was for your sake I came, and it will be wickedly ungrateful if you refuse.'

'Give me some tea and then I'll tell you,' he answered. 'Mrs. Dean, go away. I don't like you standing over me.'

Catherine gave him his tea and wiped her face. I felt disgusted at the little wretch's composure, since he was no longer in terror for himself. The anguish he had exhibited on the moor subsided as soon as he entered Wuthering Heights, so I guessed that now that he had done his father's evil bidding, he had no further immediate fears.

'Papa wants us to be married,' he continued, after sipping some of the liquid. 'And he knows your papa wouldn't let us marry now, and he's afraid of my dying if we wait. We are to be married in the morning, and you are to stay here all night. If you do as he wishes, you shall return home the next day, and take me with you.'

'Take you with her, pitiful changeling?' I exclaimed. '*Marry* you? Why, the man is mad! Do you imagine that beautiful young lady, that healthy, hearty girl, will tie herself to a little perishing monkey like you? Are you cherishing the notion that *anybody,* let alone Miss Catherine Linton, would have you for a husband? I've a very good mind to shake you severely, for your contemptible treachery, and your imbecile conceit.'

I did give him a slight shaking, but it brought on the cough, and he took to his ordinary resource of moaning and weeping.

'Stay all night? No!' Cathy said, looking slowly round. 'Nelly, I'll burn that door down, but I'll get out.'

'And let the vampires string you up and suck the blood from your veins until you're nothing but a pretty little shell?' I demanded. 'Your papa will certainly appreciate that. Your grave will need not be deep or wide.'

Linton clasped her in his two feeble arms, sobbing. 'Won't you have me, and save me? Oh! Darling Catherine! You mustn't go, and leave me, after all. You *must* obey my father, you *must! You do not know what he is, what he is capable of doing!*'

Our jailer re-entered at that moment. 'Your beasts have trotted off,' he said. 'Linton! Sniveling again? What has she been doing to you? Come, come, get to bed. Zillah won't be here tonight; you must undress yourself. Hush! Hold your noise! Once in your own room, I'll not come near you, you needn't fear. By chance, you've managed tolerably. I'll look to the rest.'

He spoke these words, holding the door open for his son to pass, and closed it behind him. Mr. Heathcliff then approached the fire, where my mistress and I stood silent. Catherine looked up and instinctively raised her hand to her cheek where he had struck her.

'Oh, you are not afraid of me?' he muttered. 'Your courage is well disguised. You *seem* damnably afraid!'

'I *am* afraid now,' she replied. 'But only because I do not have a sword to run through your black heart. That and because if I stay, Papa will be miserable. Mr. Heathcliff, let me go home! I promise to marry Linton. Papa would like me to, and I love him—and why should you wish to force me to do what I'll willingly do of myself?'

'Let him dare to force you!' I cried. 'There's law in the land, thank God, there is!'

'Silence!' he barked. 'To the devil with your clamor! I don't want *you* to speak. Miss Linton, I shall enjoy myself remarkably in thinking your father will be miserable.'

'At least send Nelly to let Papa know I'm safe!' exclaimed Catherine, weeping bitterly. 'Or marry me now. Poor Papa! Nelly, he'll think we're lost. What shall we do?'

'He'll think you are tired of waiting on him, and ran off for a little amusement,' answered Heathcliff. 'You cannot deny that you entered my house of your own accord, despite your father's warnings. And it is quite natural that you should desire amusement at your age and that you should weary of nursing a sick man. Catherine, his happiest days were over when your days began. He cursed you, I dare say, for coming into the world. And it would just do if he cursed you as *he* went out of it. Weep away. As far as I can see, it will be your chief diversion hereafter.'

'I'll not retract my word, I swear it,' said Catherine. 'I'll marry him, within this hour, if I may go to Thrushcross Grange afterward. Mr. Heathcliff, you're a cruel man, but you're not really the fiend they say, are you? No, don't turn away! *Do* look! I don't hate you. You cannot help what you are any more than I can help what I will be. I'm not angry that you struck me. Have you never loved *anybody*, in all your life, Uncle? *Never?* Ah! You must look once—I'm so wretched—you can't help being sorry and pitying me.'

'Keep your hands off me, or I'll kick you!' cried Heathcliff, brutally repulsing her. 'I'd rather be hugged by a snake. How the devil can you dream of fawning on me? I *detest* you!'

It was growing dark by then, and we heard a sound of voices at the garden gate. Our host hurried out instantly. There was talk for two or three minutes, and he returned alone.

'It was three servants sent to seek you from the Grange,' said Heathcliff. 'You should have opened a shutter and called out, for then I could have turned them over to the beasties. I would have liked that.'

Then he bid us go upstairs, through the kitchen, to Zillah's chamber. I did not know how we could get away, but the less time we spent in Mr. Heathcliff's presence, the safer our necks would be. There was no telling when he might throw open the door and allow a bloodsucker to drag one of us off into the moors.

Once in the room, neither of us lay down, for different

reasons, I think. Catherine took her station by the window and watched anxiously for morning so that the plan could unfold and she could return to her father.

I seated myself in a chair in front of the door, and rocked, to and fro, half expecting a swarm of vampires to crash through at any moment. How I thought I would protect my Cathy without my dagger, I did not know. A bedpost for a spike, perhaps? A well-placed hairpin? As I rocked, I passed harsh judgment on my many derelictions of duty from which, it struck me then, all the misfortunes of all my employers sprang. It was not the case, in reality, I am aware, but in my imagination that dismal night, I thought Heathcliff himself less guilty than I.

At seven o'clock, after a near-sleepless night, he came and inquired if Miss Linton had risen.

She ran to the door immediately and answered, 'Yes.'

'Here, then,' he said, opening it and pulling her out.

I rose to follow, but he turned the lock again. I demanded my release.

'Be patient,' he replied. 'I'll send up your breakfast in a while.'

I thumped on the panels, and rattled the latch angrily, and Catherine asked why I was still shut up. He answered, I must try to endure it another hour, and they went away.

I endured it two or three hours before I heard a footstep, not Mr. Heathcliff's.

'I've brought you something to eat,' said a voice. The door opened and I beheld Hareton, laden with food enough to last me all day.

'Take it,' he added, thrusting the tray into my hand.

'Stay one minute,' I began.

'Nay!' cried he, slamming the door and locking it behind him.

All that day I waited, but no one returned for me. That

night, instead of waiting at the door for the beasties to come for me, I set my chair at the window. To this day, I do not know what possessed me to do so. Did I expect them to fly through the window? Did I wish to see death before it overtook me?

What I saw through the window that night was far more frightening than death. It was close to the witching hour, and I must have drifted off. Something woke me as strong as a nudge on the shoulder and I peered out into the darkness, through the wavy glass. There was a queer half-moon low in the sky that illuminated the yard below where shadows lurked. Drawing closer to the window, my breath fogging on the glass, I squinted. The shadows had shifted. Then, not shadows at all; I realized it was cloaked figures I watched. They came from the corners of the house, from over the stone wall, through the gaps in the eaves of the dovecote . . . crawling, walking, oozing.

Creatures with a purpose, they were. Evil for certain; I could smell it in the air, like the foul breath of Satan's hounds. Toward a tall, cloaked figure they moved, drawn to it. As I watched, my breath caught in my throat and I realized it enticed a part of me, as well. Suddenly, my heart pounded and my palms were slick with sweat. Something deep inside me wanted to squeeze beneath the window sash, slip down the wall, and slink across the shadows to join them in worshipping it.

The tallest of the creatures raised its hands, the hood of its cloak falling, and that was when I saw him. My first instinct was to draw back, to pull the draperies, to hide beneath the bed, and pray for dawn, but I could not look away. You see . . .

It was Mr. Heathcliff!

Frozen I was by fear, by dread, by the knowledge that somewhere deep in my heart, I had known what Linton suggested was true. I had known he was one of them from the beginning. From the day Mr. Earnshaw brought him home.

He was one of the undead—he was vampire!

Before I could contemplate the meaning of such a revelation, I heard the swarm of beasties begin to hiss and growl, spit and snarl. From the midst of them, I saw them thrust something, *someone* forward. A young girl with long, pale hair and a slender, pretty face. The moonlight shimmered off her hair as she was offered to Mr. Heathcliff. I don't think she made a peep; perhaps she was too terrified or perhaps all the hissing and squealing, now near a frenzy, simply drowned out her meager voice.

The shadows-turned-bloodsuckers held the girl by her upper arms and I watched with unspeakable horror as Mr. Heathcliff leaned over her and bared his fangs. One of the beasties grabbed her hair, pulling her head back to expose her pretty, slender neck, and just as Mr. Heathcliff was about to sink his ivory teeth into her, he looked up at the window and his gaze met mine. In those black, hellish eyes I was shocked not by the violence in them, but by what appeared to be remorse. It lasted no more than a blink of an eye and then he took her. She screamed . . . or perhaps it was I. I do not know, for my head was so full of the sound that I fell back in my chair, my hands clasped over my ears.

I did not look out that window again that night. Nor did I watch the door. For some reason, for once, I was not afraid for myself or my charge, and I slept long and hard, a dreamless sleep.

In the morning, I half expected Mr. Heathcliff to come for me, for he knew I had seen the truth of his existence. But he did not come. I remained enclosed, the whole day, and the whole of the next night, and another, and another. Five nights and four days I remained. The bloodsuckers did not congregate again in the courtyard below my window, and I saw nobody but Hareton, once every morning. He was a model of a jailer: surly, and dumb, and deaf to every attempt at moving his sense of justice or compassion.

As time passed with no word of Cathy, I began to wish Heathcliff had sent one of his vampires for me, for that could have been no less cruel than my imprisonment.

# Chapter 28

On the fifth afternoon of my incarceration at Wuthering Heights, a different step approached—lighter and shorter, and this time, the person entered the room. It was Zillah, donned in her scarlet shawl, with a black silk bonnet on her head and a willow basket swung on her arm.

'Eh, dear! Mrs. Dean,' she exclaimed. 'Blessed be to see you! There's been talk of you at Gimmerton. They all said you had been carried off by a swarm of bloodsuckers from Cheshire on their way to a vampire fair, and the miss with you. I didn't believe it; you strike me as too smart for Cheshire beasties, and then the master told me you'd been rescued, and he'd lodged you here! Did you escape from them on your own, or did my master and young Hareton come brandishing swords and rip you from their talons? They say Hareton is a master of the sword already, though mostly he prefers a hoe. He has a way of hooking them with it and then he draws them close, beheads them with the sharp blade, and runs the handle through their black hearts just to be certain the deed is done. I haven't seen it myself, but—'

'Your master is a true scoundrel!' I interrupted. 'But he shall answer for it. He needn't have raised that tale; it shall all be laid bare!'

'What do you mean?' asked Zillah. 'It's not *his* tale. They tell that in the village—about how you were swept off the road to Gimmerton into vampire carriages. Yellow wheels, they said they had. I said to Earnshaw, when I came in, "There's queer things, Mr. Hareton, happened since I went off," I said to him. "It's a sad pity what happened to that young lass, and Nelly Dean. She was a good housekeeper," I told him. From the way he looked at me, I thought he had not heard, so I told him the rumor of the Cheshire bloodsuckers. The master listened, and he just smiled to himself, and said, "If they have been in the hands of vampires, they are free now, Zillah. Nelly Dean is lodged, at this minute, in your room. You can tell her she can go when you go up; here is the key. The fright of her encounter with the beasties got into her head, and she would have run home and perhaps been swept up again, but I kept her here safe till she came round to her senses. You can bid her go to the Grange, at once, if she be able, and carry a message from me, that her young lady will follow in time to attend the squire's funeral."

'My master is dead?' I asked, overwhelmed by the thought of it.

'No, no. Sit you down, Mrs. Dean,' Zillah replied. 'He's not dead. Doctor Kenneth thinks he may last another day. I met him on the road and asked.'

Instead of sitting down, I snatched my outdoor things and hastened below, for the door was now open.

On entering the kitchen, I looked about for someone to give information of Catherine. The place was filled with sunshine and the door stood wide open, but nobody seemed at hand. As I hesitated whether to go off at once, or return and seek my mistress, a slight cough drew my attention to the hearth.

Linton lay on the settle, sole tenant, sucking a stick of

sugar-candy and pursuing my movements with apathetic eyes.

'Where is Miss Catherine?' I demanded sternly, supposing I could frighten him into giving information by catching him thus, alone.

He sucked on like an innocent.

'Is she gone?'

'No,' he replied. 'She's upstairs. She's not to go with you; we won't let her.'

'You won't let her, little idiot!' I exclaimed. 'Direct me to her room immediately, or I'll make you sing out sharply.'

'Papa would make you sing out, if you attempt to get there,' he answered. 'He says I'm not to be soft with Catherine; she's my wife, and it's shameful that she should wish to leave me! He says she hates me and wants me to die, so that she may have my money. But she shan't have it, and she shan't go home! She never shall! She may cry as much as she pleases!'

He resumed his former occupation, closing his eyes as if he meant to drop asleep.

I wanted to snatch the sweet from his hand and stab him with it. But first, I wanted to run it through his father's black, lifeless heart. What kind of turncoat creature was Mr. Heathcliff that he could slay vampires, but also be one of them? Had my first Catherine known what he was? Was that what had driven her so mad in the end? Was that why, to this day, she could not rest in her grave? Or was the truth of her unrest even darker, I wondered, thinking of the little fang buds she had grown. Did Heathcliff still hold some sort of command over her? But I could not contemplate that matter now. I had bigger fields to cut.

I addressed the boy again. 'Have you forgotten all Catherine's kindness to you last winter, when you affirmed you loved her, and when she brought you books, and sang you

songs, and came many a time through wind and snow to
see you? And you join him against her. That's fine gratitude, is it not?'

The corner of Linton's mouth fell and he took the sugar-
candy from his lips.

'Did she come to Wuthering Heights because she hated
you?' I continued. 'Think for yourself! As to your money,
she does not even know that you will have any. And you
say she's crying, and yet you leave her alone, up there in a
strange house! *You*, who have felt what it is to be so neglected! You're a heartless, selfish boy!'

'I can't stay with her,' he answered crossly. 'She cries so
I can't bear it. And she won't give over, though I say I'll
call my father. I did call him once and he threatened to
throw her into the barnyard to the wailing beasties at midnight if she was not quiet. But she began again the instant
he left the room, moaning and grieving all night long.'

'Is Mr. Heathcliff out?' I inquired, perceiving that the
wretched creature had no power to sympathize with his
cousin's mental tortures.

'He's in the courtyard,' he replied. 'He's talking to Doctor Kenneth, who says Uncle is dying, truly, at last. I'm
glad, for I shall be master of the Grange after him—and
Catherine always spoke of it as *her* house. It isn't hers! It's
mine; Papa says everything she has is mine. All her nice
books are mine. She offered to give me them and her pony,
Minny, if I would get the key of our room and let her out,
but I told her she had nothing to give, they were all, all
mine. And then she cried and took a little picture from her
neck, and said I should have the two pictures in a gold
case—on one side her mother, and on the other, Uncle.
That was yesterday—I said *they* were mine, too, and tried
to get them from her. The spiteful thing wouldn't let me.
She pushed me off, and hurt me. I shrieked out and Papa
came and he struck her down.'

'And were you pleased to see her struck?' I asked.

'I was glad at first—she deserved punishing for pushing me, but when Papa was gone, she made me come to the window and showed me her cheek cut on the inside, against her teeth, and her mouth filling with blood. She has never spoken to me since, and I sometimes think she can't speak for pain. I don't like to think so! But she's a naughty thing for crying continually, and she looks so pale and wild, I'm afraid of her!'

'And you can get the key if you choose?' I said.

'Yes, when I am upstairs,' he answered. 'But I can't walk upstairs now.'

'In what apartment is it?' I asked.

'Oh,' he cried, 'I shan't tell *you* where it is! It is our secret. Nobody, neither Hareton nor Zillah, are to know. You've tired me—go away, go away!' And he turned his face onto his arm, and shut his eyes again.

I considered it best to depart without seeing Mr. Heathcliff, and bring a rescue for my young lady, from the Grange. So I retrieved my little knife from where I had been forced to throw it in the yard days before and set off in great haste, looking neither to right or left along the road for bloodsuckers.

How changed I found my master, even in those few days! He lay an image of sadness, and resignation, waiting for his death. Very young he looked, though his actual age was thirty-nine. He thought of Catherine, for he murmured her name. I touched his hand and spoke.

'Catherine is coming, dear master!' I whispered. 'She is alive, and well, and will be here, I hope, tonight.'

I trembled at the first effects of this information. He half rose up, looked eagerly round the apartment, and then sank back in a swoon.

As soon as he recovered, I related our detention at the Heights. I uttered as little as possible against Linton, nor did I describe all his father's brutal conduct—my intentions being to add no bitterness, if I could help it, to his already overflowing cup.

He knew that one of his enemy's purposes was to secure the personal property, as well as the estate, to his son, or rather himself, yet why he did not wait till his decease? It was a puzzle to my master how nearly he and his nephew would quit the world together.

However, he felt that his will had better be altered. Instead of leaving Catherine's fortune at her own disposal, he determined to put it in the hands of trustees, for her use during her life and for her children. This way, it could not fall to Mr. Heathcliff should Linton die.

I dispatched a man to fetch the attorney, and four more, provided with serviceable weapons, to demand my young lady of her jailer. Both parties were delayed very late. The single servant returned first.

He said Mr. Green, the lawyer, was out when he arrived at his house, and he had to wait two hours for his re-entrance. Then Mr. Green told him he had a little business in the village that must be done, but he would be at Thrushcross Grange before morning.

The four men came back unaccompanied, also. They brought word that Catherine was too ill to quit her room and Mr. Heathcliff would not allow them to see her in that state.

I scolded the stupid fellows well, for listening to that tale, but I did not carry it to my master. Instead, in the morning, I resolved to take a whole bevy up to the Heights and storm it, literally, unless the prisoner was quietly surrendered to us.

Her father *shall* see her, I vowed, and vowed again, if that devil be killed on his own door-stones in trying to prevent it!

Happily, I was spared the journey, and the trouble.

It was evening and I was about my duties when I heard a knock at the door and hurried to it, hoping it was Mr. Green. The harvest moon shone clear outside. It was not the attorney. My own sweet little mistress sprang on my neck, sobbing, 'Nelly! Nelly! Is Papa alive?'

'Yes!' I cried. 'Yes, my angel, he is. God be thanked, you are safe with us again!'

She wanted to run upstairs to Mr. Linton's room, but I compelled her to sit down on a chair, and made her drink, and washed her pale face, chafing it into a faint color with my apron. I implored her to say she was happy with young Heathcliff. She stared, but soon comprehending why I counseled her to utter the falsehood, she assured me she would not complain.

I couldn't abide to be present at their meeting. I stood outside the chamber door a quarter of an hour, and hardly ventured near the bed after that.

All was composed, however. Catherine's despair was as silent as her father's joy. She supported him calmly, in appearance, and he fixed on her features his raised eyes, that seemed dilating with joy.

He died blissfully, Mr. Lockwood. Kissing her cheek, he murmured, 'I am going to her.' None could have noticed the exact minute of his death, it was so entirely without a struggle.

Whether Catherine had spent her tears, or whether the grief was too weighty to let them flow, she sat there dry-eyed till the sun rose. She sat till noon, and would still have remained there had I not coaxed her away to rest.

It was well I succeeded in removing her, for at dinner-time appeared the lawyer, having called at Wuthering Heights first to get his instructions on how to behave. He had sold himself to Mr. Heathcliff, it seemed, the foul and despicable dog—may the bloodsuckers drain him!

"Mrs. Dean, did he know what he was?" I asked, unable to keep my thoughts silent another moment. "Did he know he was a vampire?"

Nelly pursed her lips in annoyance. "No one knew, except perhaps his immediate household, and me, Mr. Lockwood! May I continue?"

I slid back in my chair. "Please do," I begged, for though a part of me wished to pack my bags and take leave of this doomed house that very moment, a stronger tide pulled me toward knowing all there was to know of this sad tale.

Mr. Green took upon himself to order everything and everybody about the place, Mrs. Dean continued.

He gave all the servants but me notice to quit. He carried his delegated authority to the point of insisting that Edgar Linton should not be buried beside his wife, but on holy ground inside the gates of the kirkyard with his family. Preparations for the funeral were hurried over; Catherine, Mrs. Linton Heathcliff now, was suffered to stay at the Grange till her father's corpse had been laid to rest.

She told me that her anguish had at last spurred Linton to dare the risk of liberating her after his father turned away the men I sent to retrieve her. The boy fetched the key and unlocked the door before going to bed. Catherine stole out before the break of day by way of the window in her mother's room and ran all the way home as if being chased by a swarm of vampires, even though she saw nary a one those long four miles.

# Chapter 29

The evening after the funeral, my young lady and I were seated in the library musing mournfully. For reasons of perfect logic, I told myself, I had not spoken to her of what I saw from the window that night at Wuthering Heights. As days passed, I half convinced myself that I had fallen asleep and dreamed the hideous nightmare, or I had simply been mistaken in what I *thought* I saw in the shadows of the night. The moors could be like that, like the mirages of the desert, making you think you have seen one thing when you have seen another. But in truth, I think mostly I did not tell her because what would have been the purpose? Her fate was her fate.

We had just agreed the best destiny that could await Catherine would be permission to continue to reside at the Grange. Linton could join her, and I would remain as housekeeper. That seemed rather too favorable an arrangement to be hoped for, and yet I did hope, and began to cheer up under the prospect of retaining my home, and my employment, and, above all, my beloved young mistress. But then a servant—one of the discarded ones, not yet departed—rushed hastily in and said that *that devil Heathcliff* was coming through the court.

If we had been mad enough to dare to attempt to lock

him out, we wouldn't have had the time. He made no ceremony of knocking or announcing his name; he was master, and availed himself of the master's privilege to walk
straight in, without saying a word.

The sound of our servant's voice directed him to the library; Heathcliff entered, and motioning him out, shut the
door.

It was the same room into which Mr. Heathcliff had
been ushered, as a guest, eighteen years before. The same
moon shone through the window, and the same autumn
landscape lay outside. We had not yet lighted a candle, but
all the apartment was visible, even the portraits on the
wall—the splendid head of Mrs. Linton and the graceful
one of her husband.

Heathcliff advanced to the hearth. Time had little altered his person, either. There was the same man, his face
rather sallower, and more composed, his frame thinner,
and no other difference. I saw no sign of the vicious canine
teeth he had bared a few nights before, but since he did
not smile, I could only imagine they were still there.

Catherine had risen, with an impulse to dash out, when
she saw him.

'Stop!' he said, grabbing her arm. 'No more running
away! Where would you go? I'm come to fetch you home,
and I hope you'll be a dutiful daughter and not encourage
my son to further disobedience. I was embarrassed to punish him when I discovered his part in helping you escape.
He's such a cobweb; a pinch would annihilate him. But
you'll see by his look that he has received his due! I
brought him down one evening, the day before yesterday,
and set him in a chair in the courtyard and allowed a couple of our *neighbors* to pay their respects.'

'You fed your son to the vampires?' I demanded, unable
to control my temper.

'I did not,' he said coolly. 'There was no need. We simply *held court*. In two hours' time, I called Joseph to carry

him inside and, since then, my presence is as potent on his nerves as a ghost. I fancy he sees me, or them, or often both, though we are not near. Hareton says he wakes and shrieks in the night and calls you to protect him from me, Catherine. And so, whether you like your precious mate or not, you must come and see to his welfare.'

'Why not let Catherine continue here?' I pleaded. 'You could send Master Linton here. As you hate them both, you'd not miss them. With you, they can only be a daily plague to your unnatural, *lifeless* heart,' I dared to say.

'I'm seeking a tenant for the Grange,' he answered sternly, returning the evil eye I had offered him. 'And I want my children around me. Besides, that lass owes me her services for her bread. I'm not going to nurture her in luxury and idleness after Linton is gone.' He glanced at Catherine. 'Make haste and get ready now. And don't oblige me to compel you.'

'I shall come,' said Catherine, leaping to her feet, her jaw set stubbornly.

'Catherine, no,' I protested, wondering now if I had been mistaken not to tell her what her father-in-law was.

'Hush, Nelly! This is my life, my life that I will control.' She turned her gaze on Mr. Heathcliff. 'Linton is all I have to love in the world, and though you have done what you could to make him hateful to me, and me to him, you *cannot* make us hate each other! And I defy you to hurt him when I am by, and I defy you to frighten me.'

'You are a boastful champion,' replied Heathcliff. 'It is not I who will make him hate you—it is his own sweet spirit. He's as bitter as gall at your desertion and its consequences, so don't expect thanks for this noble devotion now. I heard him draw a pleasant picture to Zillah of what he would do if he were as strong as I. The inclination is there, and his very weakness will sharpen his wits to find a substitute for strength.'

'I know he has a bad nature,' said Catherine. 'He's your

son. How could he not? But I know he loves me, and for that reason I love him. Mr. Heathcliff, you have *nobody* to love you, and, however miserable you make us, we shall still have the revenge that your cruelty arises from your greater misery! You *are* miserable, are you not? Lonely, like the devil, and envious like him? *Nobody* loves you—*nobody* will cry for you when you die! I would not want to be you.'

'You shall be sorry to be yourself presently,' said her father-in-law, 'if you stand there another minute. Begone, witch, and get your things.'

She scornfully withdrew.

In her absence, I began to beg for Zillah's place at the Heights, offering to resign mine to her, but he would not hear of it. He bid me be silent, and then, for the first time, allowed himself a glance round the room and a look at the pictures. 'I'll tell you what I did yesterday.'

'Will you?' I said, my sarcasm thick.

'I got the sexton who was digging Linton's grave to remove the earth off her coffin lid, and I opened it. Do you know, Nelly, that she looked no different than she did the day we buried her? As beautiful, as perfect, as when last I saw her living.'

I shuddered at this monstrous revelation. I wanted to tell him that was impossible, but I knew from my own eyes that the grass would not grow over her grave, and the soil, no matter how many winters passed, still looked freshly turned. So who knew? Perhaps she had not rotted properly as the rest of us would. Why he would not find this odd, I did not know. Unless he already knew the explanation.

'I struck one side of the coffin loose and I bribed the sexton to pull it away when I'm laid there, and slide mine out, too. With the walls of the coffins removed, we will lie side by side for all eternity!'

'You were very wicked, Mr. Heathcliff!' I exclaimed. 'Were you not ashamed to disturb the dead?' What I really wanted to know, though, was how he thought *he* would be *resting* anywhere for eternity, considering the truth of what he was. There was no *resting for eternity* for vampires!

'Disturbed her? No, Nelly! It is she who has disturbed me, night and day, through eighteen years—incessantly—remorselessly—till yester-night, and yester-night I was at last tranquil. I dreamt I was sleeping the last sleep by that sleeper, with my heart stopped and my cheek frozen against hers.' He looked to me. 'I know what she wants now, what she must have to rest peacefully, at last.'

'Indeed?' I said, unable to think of any other comment I could make that would not leave me drained of my blood.

'I expected a transformation on raising the lid, but I'm better pleased that it should not commence till I share the soil with her. You know, I was wild after she died, from dawn to dawn, praying for her to return to me—her spirit. I have a strong faith in ghosts. I have a conviction that they can, and do exist, among us!'

What he was saying made little sense to me, but I let him go on because I could not, for the life of me, think how to stop him.

'The day she was buried, there came a fall of snow. In the evening I went to the churchyard. It blew bleak as winter—all round was solitary. I didn't fear that her fool of a husband would wander up so late, and no one else had business to bring them there.

'Being alone, and conscious that two yards of loose earth was the sole barrier between us, I said to myself— "I'll have her in my arms again! If she be cold, I'll think it is this north wind that chills *me,* and if she be motionless, it is sleep."

'I got a spade from the tool house, and began to delve with all my might.'

'You dug her up the day she was buried?' I asked, surprised anything could shock me anymore. Particularly concerning him. 'Is that why her grave always looks freshly laid? Because you dig her up with regularity?'

'No, I do not dig her up with *regularity*. Listen to me, Nelly. I am trying to tell you what happened that night. My shovel, it scraped the coffin. I fell to work with my hands. The wood commenced cracking about the screws. I was on the point of attaining my object when it seemed that I heard a sigh from someone above, close at the edge of the grave, and bending down. "If I can only get this off," I muttered. "I wish they may shove in the earth over us both!" and I wrenched more desperately still. There was another sigh, close at my ear. I appeared to feel the warm breath of it displacing the sleet-laden wind. I knew no living thing in flesh and blood was by, but as certainly as you perceive the approach to some substantial body in the dark, though it cannot be discerned, so certainly I felt that Cathy was there. She was not under me, but on the earth.

'A sudden sense of relief flowed from my heart, through every limb. I relinquished my labor of agony, and turned consoled at once. Her presence was with me; it remained while I re-filled the grave, and led me home. You may laugh, if you will, but I was sure I should see her there. I was sure she was with me, and I could not help talking to her.

'Having reached the Heights, I rushed eagerly to the door. It was fastened; that accursed Earnshaw and my wife were attempting to keep me out. I remember stopping to kick the breath out of him, and then hurrying upstairs to my room, and hers. I looked round impatiently—I felt her by me—I could *almost* see her, and yet I *could not!* I ought to have sweat blood then, from the anguish of my yearning—from the fervor of my supplications to have but one glimpse! I had not one. She showed herself, as she often was in life, a devil to me! And, since then, sometimes more and sometimes less, I've been the sport of that intolerable torture! Infernal—keeping my nerves at such a stretch, that, if they had not resembled catgut, they would, long ago, have relaxed to the feebleness of Linton's.

'When I sat in the house with Hareton, it seemed that on going out, I should meet her. When I walked on the moors I should meet her coming in. When I went from home, I hastened to return. She *must* be somewhere at the Heights, I was certain! And when I tried to sleep in her chamber, I couldn't lie there; for the moment I closed my eyes, she was either outside the window, or sliding back the panels, or entering the room, or even resting her darling head on the same pillow as she did when a child. And I must open my lids to see. And so I opened and closed them a hundred times a night—to be always disappointed! It racked me!

'Now, since I've seen her, I'm pacified—a little. It was a strange way of killing, not by inches, but by fractions of hairbreadths, to beguile with the specter of a hope, through eighteen years!'

Mr. Heathcliff paused and wiped his forehead. His hair clung to it, wet with perspiration; his eyes were fixed on the red embers of the fire, the brows not contracted, but raised next to the temples, diminishing the grim aspect of his countenance, but imparting a peculiar look of trouble and a painful appearance of mental tension toward one absorbing subject.

Realizing he had reached the end of his mad ranting, I looked at him. 'Sounds to me as if her soul is as tortured as yours,' I observed. When I was dead, I was hoping to enter the pearly gates of heaven. I did not want to roam the moors at night haunting Mr. Heathcliff.

'Tortured, indeed. Caught between the here and the

hereafter,' he said softly, speaking more to himself than to me. 'But I suspect now I know what she needs. What I must do.'

'What she needs?' I asked, thinking back to what he had said earlier. 'You mean to rest peacefully.'

'In time you will know all,' he said.

Questions still dangled on the end of my tongue. First and foremost, I wanted to know how it was that he had come to be both a gypsy slayer and vampire, for I had never heard of such a creature and could only imagine what a tortured soul *that* creature would be. But Catherine entered, announcing that she was ready when her pony was saddled, and I did not have further opportunity to quiz him.

Heathcliff turned to her. 'You may do without your pony; it is a fine evening, and you'll need no ponies at Wuthering Heights. For what journeys you take, your own feet will serve you—Come along.'

'Good-bye, Nelly!' whispered my dear little mistress. As she kissed me, her lips felt like ice.

*Protect her from the beasties,* I prayed silently, half fearing she had already been bitten. What else would make her so cold?

'Come and see me, Nelly. Don't forget.'

'Take care you do no such thing, Mrs. Dean!' said her new father. 'When I wish to speak to you, I'll come here. I want none of your prying at my house!'

He signed her to precede him, and casting back a look that cut my heart, she obeyed.

# Chapter 30

I see Zillah in Gimmerton and she tells me something of what goes on at Wuthering Heights, otherwise I should hardly know who was dead and who living, bitten or still clean. The first time I met up with her, after my dear girl had been taken from me, I asked if she knew her master was not only a vampire slayer, but vampire, too, thinking I might find an advocate for my dear girl. I expected a shocked response, or perhaps one of fear if she had been recruited to guard Mr. Heathcliff's secret, but I did not expect the answer I received.

'Of course I know. I empty chamber pots at the Heights. There is nothing that goes on there that I do not know.'

'And . . . and you do not mind, being under the employment of such a devil, for surely he is worse than a vampire. An even more tortured soul, playing both sides!'

'Safest employment in Great Britain, I say,' Zillah corrected me. 'As his employee, my neck is off-limits to all who seek the nourishment of blood, and he never takes from his servants. Why would he, for then he would constantly have to interview for the positions left vacant.'

'But . . . how did this happen? How can it be? I knew the boy as a child. My previous master brought him into the house as an orphan found on the streets of Liverpool. He was the child of a gypsy vampire slayer.'

'His *mother* was a gypsy slayer, but his *father*,' Zillah explained with far more haughtiness than she had a right to bear, 'his *father* was a vampire. Taken advantage of, his mother was, on a moonless night when she should have kept behind locked doors instead of hunting bloodsuckers. My master was the spawn of that night.'

'No,' I breathed, my eyes widening. 'Vampires do not procreate. That is impossible!'

'Apparently not,' she finished, snub nose high in the air. 'Now, do you wish to hear of the new missus or not?'

I learned that Zillah thinks Catherine haughty, and does not like her. My young lady asked some aid of her when she first arrived, but Mr. Heathcliff told Zillah to follow her own business and let his daughter-in-law look after herself. Zillah, being a narrow-minded, selfish woman, willingly acquiesced. Catherine repaid her unwillingness to aid her with contempt, and thus enlisted my informant among her enemies, as securely as if she had done her some great wrong.

'The first thing Mrs. Linton did,' Zillah explained, on her arrival at the Heights, 'was to run upstairs without even wishing good evening to me and Joseph. She shut herself into Linton's room and remained till morning. Then, while the master and Earnshaw were at breakfast, she entered the house, and asked all in a quiver if the doctor might be sent for. Her cousin was very ill.

' "We know that!" answered Heathcliff. "But his life is not worth a farthing, and I won't spend a farthing on him."

' "But I don't know what to do," she said. "And if nobody will help me, he'll die!"

' "Walk out of the room," cried the master, "and let me never hear a word more about him! None here care what becomes of him. If you do, act the nurse; if you do not, lock him up and leave him."

'How they managed together, I can't tell. I fancy he fretted a great deal, and moaned night and day. She had precious little rest, one could guess by her white face and
heavy eyes. Once or twice, after we had gone to bed, I've
happened to open my door again, and seen her sitting crying, on the stairs' top. But then I've shut myself in, quick,
for fear of being moved to interfere. I did pity her then,
I'm sure. Still, I didn't want to lose my place, you know!

'At last, one night she came boldly into my chamber,
and frightened me out of my wits by saying—

' "Tell Mr. Heathcliff that his son is dying—I'm sure he
is, this time. Get up, instantly, and tell him!"

'Having uttered this speech, she vanished again. I lay a
quarter of an hour listening and trembling. Nothing stirred—
the house was quiet.

'*She's mistaken, I told myself. He's got over it. I needn't
disturb them.* I knew the master didn't like his nights disturbed. He either occupied himself pacing the dead Catherine's bedroom or he roamed the moors, chasing down
vampires, or chasing humans, I suppose, depending on his
mood. So after Mrs. Heathcliff came to me, I began to
doze. But my sleep was marred a second time, by a sharp
ringing of the bell—the only bell we have, put up on purpose for Linton. It turned out the master was indoors that
night, and he called to me to see what was the matter. Too
busy pacing that haunted room to see for himself, I suppose. He said to check on the bell ringer and make it clear
he wouldn't have that noise repeated, else he would send
one of the beasties from the barn rafters to check in on
them.

'I delivered Catherine's message. He cursed to himself,
and in a few minutes came out with a lighted candle and
proceeded to their room. I followed. Mrs. Heathcliff was
seated by the bedside, with her hands folded on her knees,
the devil dog curled at her feet. Her father-in-law went up,

held the light to Linton's face, looked at him, and touched him. Afterward he turned to her.

' "Now—Catherine," he said. "How do you feel?" 'She was silent.

' "How do you feel, Catherine?" he repeated.

' "He's safe, and I'm free," she answered, stroking that terrier's head. "I should feel well—but," she continued with a bitterness she couldn't conceal, "you have left me so long to struggle against death, alone with no companions but the bloodsuckers that peek in the windows, that I feel and see only death! I feel like death!"

'And she looked like it, too! I gave her a little wine. Hareton and Joseph, who had been wakened by the ringing and the sound of feet, and heard our talk from outside, now entered. Joseph was pleased, I believe, of the lad's removal. Hareton seemed a little bothered, though he was more taken up with staring at Catherine than thinking of Linton. But the master bid him get off to bed again; we didn't want his help. He made Joseph remove the body and we all went back to bed.

'In the morning, he sent me to tell Mrs. Heathcliff that she must come down to breakfast. She had undressed and appeared to be going to sleep. She said she was ill. I informed Mr. Heathcliff, and he replied—

' "Well, let her be till after the funeral. Go up now and then to get her what she needs and as soon as she seems better, tell me." '

Cathy stayed upstairs a fortnight, according to Zillah, who visited her twice a day, and would have been rather more friendly, but her attempts at increasing kindness were proudly and promptly repelled.

Heathcliff went up at once, to show her Linton's will. He had bequeathed the whole of his, and what had been her moveable property, to his father. The poor creature was threatened, or coaxed, into that act during her week's absence, when his uncle died. The lands, being a minor, he could not meddle with. However, Mr. Heathcliff has claimed and kept them in his wife's right. I suppose legally, at any rate, Catherine, destitute of cash and friends, cannot disturb his possession.

'Nobody ever approached her door and nobody asked anything about her. The first occasion of her coming down into the house was on a Sunday afternoon.

'She had cried out, when I carried up her dinner, that she couldn't bear any longer being in the cold. I told her the master was going to Thrushcross Grange, and Earnshaw and I needn't hinder her from descending. As soon as she heard Mr. Heathcliff's horse trot off, she made her appearance, donned in black, and her yellow curls combed back behind her ears, as plain as a Quaker.

'Joseph had gone, but I thought it proper to bide at home. Young folks are always the better for an elder's over-looking. I let Hareton know that his cousin would very likely sit with us, so he should leave his guns and swords alone while she stayed.

'He colored up at the news, and cast his eyes over his hands and clothes. The saber he was sharpening was shoved out of sight in a minute. I saw he meant to keep her company and I guessed he wanted to be presentable. Trying not to laugh at the idea of him ever being presentable, I offered to help him and joked at his confusion. He grew sullen, and began to swear.

'Now, Mrs. Dean,' she went on, seeing me not pleased by her manner. 'You might think your young lady too fine for Mr. Hareton and you might be right, but I'd like to see her pride a peg lower. And what will all her learning and her daintiness do for her now? She's as poor as you or I. Poorer.'

Hareton allowed Zillah to give him her aid and she flattered him into a good humor, so when Catherine came he tried to make himself agreeable, by the housekeeper's account.

'Missus walked in,' she said, 'as chill as an icicle, and as high as a princess. I got up and offered her my seat in the armchair. She turned up her nose at my civility. Earnshaw rose, too, and bid her come to the settle, and sit close by the fire. He was sure she was starved.

' "I've been starved a month and more," she answered, resting on the word, as scornful as she could.

'And she got a chair for herself, and placed it at a distance from both of us.

'Having sat till she was warm, she began to look around and discovered a number of books in the dresser, many pertaining to the current vampire infestation. She was instantly upon her feet again, stretching to reach them, but they were too high up. Her cousin, after watching her endeavors awhile, at last summoned courage to help her. She held her frock, and he filled it with the first that came to hand.

'That was a great advance for the lad. She didn't thank him, but he felt gratified that she had accepted his assistance, and ventured to stand behind as she examined them. He even pointed out what struck his fancy in certain pictures which they contained; sketches of vampire anatomy and such. Then he went from looking at the book to looking at her instead of the book.

'She continued reading. His attention became, by degrees, quite centered in the study of her thick, silky curls. And, perhaps not quite aware of what he did, but attracted like a child to a candle, he proceeded from staring to touching. He put out his hand and stroked one curl as gently as if it were a bird. He might have taken a bite from her neck, she pulled away so quickly.

' "Get away, this moment! How dare you touch me!"

she cried, in a tone of disgust. "I can't endure you! I'll go upstairs again, if you come near me."

'Mr. Hareton recoiled, looking as foolish as he could do, and sat down on the settle. He remained very quiet, and she continued turning over her volumes, another half-hour. Finally, Earnshaw crossed over and whispered to me.

' "Will you ask her to read to us, Zillah? I would like to hear what is said of the bloodsuckers that I don't already know, but I can't read myself. Dunnot say I wanted it, but ask of yourself."

' "Mr. Hareton wishes you would read to us, ma'am," I said immediately. "He'd take it very kind—he'd be much obliged."

'She frowned and, looking up, answered, "Mr. Hareton, and the whole set of you, will be good enough to understand that I reject any pretense at kindness you have the hypocrisy to offer! I despise you, and will have nothing to say to any of you! When I would have given my life for one kind word, even to see one of your faces, you all kept off. But I won't complain to you! I'm driven down here by the cold, not either to amuse you or enjoy your society."

' "What could I have done?" began Earnshaw. "I am much a prisoner as you. How was I to blame?"

' "Be silent! I'll go out of doors, or anywhere, rather than have your disagreeable voice in my ear!" said my lady.

'Hareton muttered, she might go to hell, for him! And unsheathing a sword, he began to sharpen it right in front of her. She seemed unexpectedly interested in the weapon, but when he offered to show it, she saw fit to retreat to her solitude.'

At first, on hearing this account from Zillah, I determined to leave my situation, take a cottage, and get Catherine to come and live with me. But Mr. Heathcliff would as soon permit that as he would set up Hareton in an independent house, and I can see no remedy, at present. All I could do was wait and see what would unfold next.

Thus ended Mrs. Dean's story. As strange as it may seem, I believed what she'd told me, or at least I believed that *she* believed what she'd related. For that reason, I made plans for my future. Notwithstanding the doctor's prophecy, I am rapidly recovering strength, and, though it be only the second week in January, I propose getting out on horseback in a day or two, and riding over to Wuthering Heights, with an armed escort, of course. There, I will inform my landlord that I will be taking my leave of the moors and that he may look for another tenant to take the place. At the beginning of Nelly's tale, I did think myself on an adventure, but upon hearing that Mr. Heathcliff is, indeed, a vampire, one that digs up graves, well, I have no intention of renting from any such gentleman, for he is surely no gentleman at all!

# Chapter 31

Yesterday was bright, calm, and frosty. After hiring some strapping men with swords in Gimmerton, I went to the Heights as I proposed. Mrs. Dean entreated me to bear a note from her to her young lady, and I did not refuse.

The front door stood open, but the gate was fastened, as at my last visit. I knocked, and invoked Earnshaw from among the garden beds; he unchained it, glancing at the mounted men carrying various implements used in vampire destruction.

"Won't need them," Earnshaw mumbled. "'Tis safe enough in here."

Glancing back over my shoulder, I nodded, indicating they should stay put, and I then followed Earnshaw inside.

The fellow is as handsome a rustic as need be seen. I took particular notice of him this time, knowing far more about it, and concluded that he did his best to make the least of his advantages.

I asked if Mr. Heathcliff were at home. He answered, no, but he would be in at dinner-time. It was eleven o'clock. I considered simply leaving a note; after all, did a man like me owe a *bloodsucker*, no matter how much land he owned, an explanation for vacating his premises? Then I reminded myself of the same argument I had repeated to myself over the last twenty-four hours since Mrs. Dean had finished her tale. What if it was just that? A *tale?* Some of the things she had said had certainly been far-fetched.

Giving my silver dagger inside my coat a satisfying pat, I made my decision and announced to Earnshaw my intention of waiting for him, at which he immediately flung down his tools and accompanied me as a watchdog, not as a substitute for the host.

We entered together. I did not see Joseph, which was just as well. After what Mrs. Dean had said about him allowing the bloodsuckers to feed off him, I did not care to make his acquaintance again.

Catherine was there, making herself useful in preparing some vegetables for the approaching meal. She looked sulkier and less spirited than when I had seen her first. She hardly raised her eyes to notice me, and continued her employment with the same disregard to common forms of politeness. She never returned my bow or gave my "good morning" the slightest acknowledgment.

*She does not seem so amiable,* I thought, *as Mrs. Dean would persuade me to believe. She's a beauty, it is true, but not an angel.*

With a surly grunt, Earnshaw bid her remove her things to the kitchen.

"Remove them yourself," she said, retiring to a stool by the window where she began to carve figures of birds and beasts out of the turnip parings in her lap.

I approached her, pretending to desire a view of the garden, and, as I did, dropped Mrs. Dean's note onto her knee, unnoticed by Hareton—but she asked aloud, "What is that?" and chucked it off.

"A letter from your old acquaintance, the housekeeper at the Grange," I answered, annoyed at her exposing my kind deed. It was true, my guards were only a shout away, but I did not appreciate her risking my blood, not with me having just come from the sickbed.

Hareton beat her to the letter on the floor and put it in his waistcoat, saying Mr. Heathcliff should look at it first.

Catherine silently turned her face from his, drew out her pocket-handkerchief, and applied it to her eyes. Her cousin, after struggling awhile to keep down his softer feelings, pulled out the letter and flung it on the floor beside her, as ungraciously as he could.

Catherine took up and perused the letter eagerly. She then questioned me about the inmates, rational and irrational, of her former home, and gazing toward the hills, murmured in soliloquy—

"I should like to be riding Minny down there! I should like to be climbing up there—Oh! Can you imagine how well I could train in the open air were I permitted, Hareton?"

I surmised that the *training* she referred to was in reference to the silly notion Mrs. Dean had conveyed to me that the girl thought women should be schooled in vampire slaying. Not wanting to push their already poor excuse for hospitality, I did not ask. In truth, I was beginning to wonder if Mrs. Heathcliff was as mad as all the rest. It would not be beyond belief that imprisonment in this cursed house would drive a sane mind insane. But, then, she had always been an odd child, if all that Mrs. Dean had said was true.

She leaned her pretty head against the sill, with half a yawn and half a sigh, and lapsed into an aspect of abstracted sadness.

"Mrs. Heathcliff," I said, after sitting some time mute, "are you not aware that I am an acquaintance of yours? So intimate, that I think it strange you won't come and speak to me. My housekeeper never wearies of talking about and praising you, and she'll be greatly disappointed if I return with no news of or from you."

"You must tell her," she continued, "that I would answer her letter, but I have no materials for writing, not even a book from which I might tear a leaf."

"No books!" I exclaimed. "How do you contrive to live here without them? Though provided with a large library, I'm frequently very bored at the Grange; take my books away, and I should be desperate!"

"I was always reading, when I had them," said Catherine. "But Mr. Heathcliff never reads, so he took it into his head to destroy my books. His own, as well. He once had a great library on the subject of vampires. But I haven't seen any of my books in weeks. Hareton, I came up on a secret stock in your room, some of the best in Mr. Heathcliff's collection. Apparently, you gathered them, as a magpie gathers silver spoons, for the mere love of stealing!"

Hareton blushed crimson when his cousin made this revelation of his private literary accumulations, and stammered an indignant denial of her accusations.

"I should imagine Mr. Hareton is desirous of increasing his knowledge. The more we understand of the bloodsuckers, the better we can defend ourselves," I said, coming to his rescue. "He'll be a clever scholar in a few years!"

"Yes, I hear him trying to spell and read to himself, and pretty blunders he makes!" Catherine responded, turning to her cousin. "I hear you turning over the dictionary, to seek out the hard words, and then cursing, because you couldn't read their explanations!"

"But, Mrs. Heathcliff," I said, taking pity on the young man, "we have each stumbled and tottered on the threshold. Had our teachers scorned, instead of aiding us, we should stumble and totter yet."

Hareton's chest heaved in silence a minute. He labored under a severe sense of mortification and wrath, which it was no easy task to suppress.

I rose and, from a gentlemanly idea of relieving his embarrassment, took up my station in the doorway, surveying the external prospect as I stood.

He followed my example, and left the room but presently reappeared, bearing half a dozen volumes in his hands, which he threw into Catherine's lap, exclaiming— "Take them! Some of them are not just his, some were yours that you brought with you. I saved them from the fire. I never want to hear, or read, or think of them again!"

"I won't have them now," she answered. "I shall connect them with you, and hate them." She opened one that had obviously been often turned over, and read a portion in the drawling tone of a beginner, then threw it and laughed.

Mr. Hareton's self-love would endure no further torment, and he gathered the books and hurled them on the fire. I read in his countenance what anguish it was to him to destroy the books. I fancied that as they were consumed, he recalled the pleasure they had already imparted, and the triumph and ever-increasing pleasure he had anticipated from them.

"Yes, that's all the good that such a brute as you can get from them!" cried Catherine, watching the conflagration with indignant eyes.

"You'd *better* hold your tongue now!" he answered fiercely.

And his agitation precluding further speech, he advanced hastily to the entrance, where I made way for him to pass. But, before he had crossed the door-stones, Mr. Heathcliff, coming up the causeway, encountered him, and laying hold of his shoulders, asked, "What's to do now, my lad?"

"Naught, naught!" he said, and broke away, to enjoy his grief and anger in solitude.

Heathcliff gazed after him, and sighed. "When I look

for his father in his face, I find *her* every day more! How the devil is he so like her? I can hardly bear to see him."

As I watched, I had difficulty seeing this tormented man as the hideous bloodsucker Mrs. Dean made him to be. He was simply dissimilar to others I'd seen. Had Mrs. Dean embellished her story, wrought in the entertainment of it and her desire to please me?

Mr. Heathcliff bent his eyes to the ground and walked moodily in. There was a restless, anxious expression in is countenance I had never remarked there before. He looked sparer in person.

His daughter-in-law, on perceiving him through the window, immediately escaped to the kitchen, so that I remained alone.

"I'm glad to see you out of doors again, Mr. Lockwood," he said in reply to my greeting. "I've wondered, more than once, what brought you here from the city."

"An idle whim, I fear, sir," was my answer, still watching him closely for the flash of fangs. "I shall set out for London next week, and I must give you warning that I feel no disposition to retain Thrushcross Grange beyond the twelve months I agreed to rent it. I believe I shall not live there anymore."

"Indeed! You're tired of being banished from the world, are you?" he said. Then to himself, "So am I." He looked back at me. "But, if you are coming to plead off paying for a place you won't occupy, your journey is useless. I never relent in exacting my due from anyone."

"I'm coming to plead off nothing about it!" I exclaimed. "Should you wish it, I'll settle with you now." I drew my notebook from my pocket.

"No, no," he replied coolly. "I'm not in such a hurry. Sit down and take your dinner with us. A guest that is safe from repeating his visit can generally be made welcome."

I declined the invitation, however, making a vague excuse, and bid adieu, having no wish to partake of nourishment in that house for fear of what I might be served or to whom I might be served. I would have departed by the back way, to get a last glimpse of Catherine, but Hareton received orders to bring my horse, and my host himself escorted me to the door, so I could not fulfill my wish.

*How dreary life is in that house!* I thought to myself as my companions escorted me safely from Wuthering Heights. What a realization of something more romantic than a fairy tale it would have been for Mrs. Linton Heathcliff, had she and I struck up an attachment, as her good nurse desired, and migrated together into the stirring atmosphere of the town!

# Chapter 32

*1802*

This September, I was invited to hunt the moors of a friend, and on my journey to his abode, I unexpectedly came within fifteen miles of Gimmerton. The hostler at a roadside public house was holding a pail of water to refresh my horses when a cart of very green oats, newly reaped, passed by, and he remarked—

"From Gimmerton, that is! They're always three weeks later than other folk wi' their harvest."

"Gimmerton?" I repeated. My residence in that locality had already grown dim and dreamy, though I did find that Mrs. Dean's tales were handy at the dining table and I was often invited to supper parties on the basis of my entertainment capabilities. Fine society was always interested in vampire anecdotes, for life on the moors where the infestation seemed far removed from the parlors of London. And now that I was safe away and secure in more civilized residence, I often thought fondly on my strange experiences and stranger acquaintances at Wuthering Heights. "How far is it from here?"

"Fourteen mile' over the hills, and a rough road," he answered.

"Vampires thick between here and there?" I inquired.

"Hostile ones? Not too thick," the hostler replied. "You and yer servant armed?"

"Of course."

"And yer mounts look to be quick. You'll be safe enough."

The reason I asked was that a sudden impulse had seized me to visit Thrushcross Grange. It was scarcely noon, and it occurred to me that I might as well pass the night under my own roof as in an inn, as my lease had not run out yet and I had fully paid. Besides, I could spare a day easily to arrange matters with my landlord to end the lease, and thus save myself the trouble of invading the neighborhood again.

Having rested awhile, I directed my servant to inquire the way to the village; we managed the distance in some three hours. I reached the Grange before sunset and rode into the court. Under the porch, a girl of nine or ten sat knitting, and an old woman reclined on the house steps, smoking a meditative pipe.

"Is Mrs. Dean within?" I demanded of the dame.

"Mistress Dean? Nay!" she answered. "She doesn't bide here. She's up at th' Heights."

"Are you the housekeeper, then?" I continued.

"Eea. I keep th' hause," she replied.

"Well, I'm Mr. Lockwood, the master. Are there any rooms to lodge me in, I wonder? I wish to stay here all night."

"Th' maister!" she cried in astonishment. "We heard by way of a fishmonger's sister that ye had been devoured by bloodsuckers two months past whilst on yer way from church with the parson and his sister. Sucked dry as pigs' bladders and found swinging in the bell tower among the pigeons. Yah should have sent word!"

"That I had not been devoured?" I questioned.

The crone thought a moment, lips curled around the stem of her pipe. "Fair 'nough," she finally conceded, rising on old, stiff bones. "Ye do seem live 'nough to me, and they's nothin' dry nor proper 'bout th' place. No, there isn't!"

She threw down her pipe and bustled in; the girl followed, and I entered, too, soon perceiving that her report was true; the house was in no condition for my overnight stay. But I bid the woman stay composed. I told her I would go out for a walk, and, meantime, she must try to prepare a corner of a sitting room for me to sup in, and a bedroom to sleep in. No sweeping and dusting, only good fires and dry sheets were necessary. "All well at the Heights?" I inquired of the woman.

"Fer all I know!" she answered. "As well as might be 'spected."

I would have asked why Mrs. Dean had deserted the Grange, but decided I would ask her myself, so I turned away and made my exit, rambling leisurely along. Behind me, the sinking sun glowed and the mild glory of a rising moon in front—one fading, and the other brightening, as I quitted the park with my armed servant trailing behind me, and climbed the stony byroad branching off to Mr. Heathcliff's dwelling.

Before I arrived in sight of Wuthering Heights manor house, all that remained of day was a beamless, amber light along the west, but I could see every pebble on the path, and every blade of grass, by that splendid moon. Not one sign of the infestation did we come upon, but I knew better than to think they were not out there, watching, waiting.

I had neither to climb the gate, nor to knock—it yielded to my hand. *That is an improvement!* I thought. And I noticed another, by the aid of my nostrils; a fragrance of stocks and wallflowers wafted on the air, from amongst the homely fruit trees.

Both doors and shutters were open, and yet, as is usually the case in a coal district, a fine, red fire illumined the chimney. I could see the residents within and hear them talk before I entered, and so I looked and listened before announcing my arrival.

"Con-*trary!*" said a voice, as sweet as a silver bell. "That for the third time! I'm not going to tell you again!"

"Contrary, then," answered another, in deep but softened tones. "And now, kiss me for minding so well."

"No. Read it over first correctly, without a single mistake."

The male speaker began to read; he was a young man, respectably dressed, and seated at a table, having a book before him. His handsome features glowed with pleasure, and his eyes kept impatiently wandering from the page to a small white hand over his shoulder.

Its owner stood behind, her light shining ringlets blending, at intervals, with his brown locks as she bent to superintend his studies. It was lucky he could not see her face, or he would never have been so steady. I could see her quite well, however, and I bit my lip at having thrown away the chance I might have had of doing something besides staring at its smiting beauty.

The task was done, not free from further blunders, but the pupil claimed a reward, and received at least five kisses, which he generously returned. Then they came to the door, whispering as if they had a great secret. As they took their leave, I was surprised to see that not only the young man picked up a heavy sword from the hearth, but the woman as well, though hers was shorter and appeared light of weight.

After they were gone, I walked around to the kitchen and there sat my old friend, Nelly Dean, sewing and singing a song. When I advanced, recognizing me directly, she jumped to her feet, crying—

"Why, bless you, Mr. Lockwood! How could you think

of returning in this way? All's shut up at Thrushcross Grange. You should have given us notice!"

"I've arranged to be accommodated there," I answered. "I depart again tomorrow. And how are you transplanted here, Mrs. Dean? Tell me that."

"Zillah left, and Mr. Heathcliff wished me to come, soon after you went to London, and stay till you returned. But, step in, pray! Have you walked from Gimmerton this evening?"

"From the Grange," I replied. "I brought an escort who waits in the courtyard. While they make me lodging room at the Grange, I want to finish my business with your master because I don't think of having another opportunity in a hurry."

"What business, sir?" said Nelly, conducting me into the house. "He's gone out at present, and won't return soon."

"About the rent," I answered.

"Oh! Then it is with Mrs. Heathcliff you must settle," she observed. "Or rather with me. She has not learnt to manage her affairs yet, and I act for her; there's nobody else."

I looked surprised.

"Ah! You have not heard, I see!" she continued.

"Heard?" I asked.

"Sit down, and let me take your hat. You have had nothing to eat, have you?"

"I have ordered supper at the Grange. Now you sit down, too. Let me hear what you have to say. You say you don't expect them back for some time—the young people?"

"No—I have to scold them every evening for their late rambles, but they pay me no heed. She has convinced him of her capabilities in fighting the bloodsuckers and now they have become somewhat of a team, as odd as it sounds. At least have a drink of our old ale. It will do you good."

She hastened to fetch it and re-entered in a minute, bearing a reaming pint, whose contents I lauded with becoming earnestness. And afterward she furnished me with the sequel of Heathcliff's history. He had a "queer" end, as she expressed it.

I was summoned to Wuthering Heights, within a fortnight of your leaving us, she said, and I obeyed joyfully, for Catherine's sake.

My first interview with her grieved and shocked me! She had altered so much since our separation. Mr. Heathcliff did not explain his reasons for changing his mind about my coming here; he only told me he wanted me, and he was tired of seeing Catherine. He ordered that I must make the little parlor my sitting room, and keep her with me. It was enough if he were obliged to see her once or twice a day.

She seemed pleased at this arrangement and, by degrees, I smuggled over a great number of books, and other articles, that had formed her amusement at the Grange and flattered myself we should get on in tolerable comfort.

The delusion did not last long. Catherine, contented at first, in a brief space grew irritable and restless. For one thing, she was forbidden to move out of the garden, and it fretted her sadly to be confined to its narrow bounds as spring drew on. For another, in caring for the house, I was forced to quit her frequently, and she complained of loneliness. She said she ever preferred quarrelling with Joseph in the kitchen to sitting at peace in her solitude.

I did not mind the skirmishes between the two, but Hareton was often obliged to seek the kitchen also, when the master wanted to have the house to himself. In the beginning, Cathy quietly joined in my occupations and shunned remarking or addressing him—though he was always as sullen and silent as possible. After a while, she changed her behavior and became incapable of letting him alone, talking at him, commenting on his stupidity and idleness, expressing her wonder how he could endure the life he lived. She remarked time and time again how amazed she was that he could sit a whole evening staring into the fire, and dozing.

'He's just like a dog, is he not, Nelly?' she once observed. 'Or a cart-horse? He does his work, eats his food, and sleeps, eternally! What a blank, dreary mind he must have! Do you ever dream, Hareton? And, if you do, what is it about? But you can't speak to me!'

Then she looked at him, but he would neither open his mouth nor look again. 'He's perhaps dreaming now,' she continued. 'He twitched his shoulder as the terrier twitches hers. Ask him.'

'Mr. Hareton will ask the master to send you upstairs, if you don't behave!'

'I know why Hareton never speaks, when I am in the kitchen,' she exclaimed, on another occasion. 'He is afraid I shall laugh at him. Nelly, what do you think? He began to teach himself to read once, and, because I laughed, he burned his books, and dropped it. Was he not a fool?'

'Were not you naughty?' I said. 'Answer me that.'

'Perhaps I was,' she went on. 'But I did not expect him to be so silly. Hareton, if I gave you a book, would you take it now? I'll try!'

She placed one she had been perusing on his hand. He flung it off, and muttered, if she did not give over, he would break her neck.

'Well, I shall put it here,' she said, 'in the table drawer, and I'm going to bed.'

Then she whispered to me to watch whether he touched it, and departed. But he would not come near it, and so I informed her in the morning, to her great disappointment. I saw she was sorry for his persevering sulkiness and indolence. Her conscience reproved her for frightening him off improving himself; she had done it effectually.

But her ingenuity was at work to remedy the injury. While I ironed, or pursued other stationary employments I could not well do in the parlor, she would bring some pleasant volume and read it aloud to me. Often she read about vampires. Did you know, Mr. Lockwood, there are actually novels now being published with vampires in them? When Hareton was there, she generally paused in an interesting part, and left the book lying about, and she did it repeatedly. But he was as obstinate as a mule, and, instead of snatching at her bait, in wet weather he took to smoking with Joseph, one on each side of the fire, the elder happily too deaf to understand her wicked nonsense, as he would have called it, the younger doing his best to seem to disregard it. On fine evenings the latter followed his bloodsucker hunting expeditions, and Catherine yawned and sighed, and teased me to talk to her, and ran off into the court or garden, the moment I began. Then she began to cry, saying she was tired of living, that her life was useless.

Mr. Heathcliff, who grew more and more disinclined to society, spent long hours sitting at Catherine's unholy grave. He no longer sought out the local vampires, either to congregate with them or kill them. I had heard nothing more of how he knew how to save Catherine or when such salvation would take place. Truthfully, I did not want to know, and I had my own hands full with the young Miss Cathy.

On Easter Monday, Joseph went to Gimmerton fair with some cattle, and in the afternoon I was busy getting up linen in the kitchen. Earnshaw sat, morose as usual, at the chimney corner, and my little mistress was beguiling an idle hour with drawing pictures on the window panes, varying her amusement by bursts of songs, and whispered ejaculations, and quick glances of annoyance and impatience in the direction of her cousin. Earnshaw steadfastly smoked, and looked into the grate.

At a notice that I could do with her no longer, intercepting my light, she removed to the hearth-stone. I bestowed little attention on her proceedings, but, presently, I heard her begin—

'I've found out, Hareton, that I want—that I'm glad—that I should like you to be my cousin, now, if you had not grown so cross to me, and so rough.'

Hareton returned no answer.

'Hareton, Hareton, Hareton! Do you hear?' she continued.

'Get off wi' ye!' he growled, with uncompromising gruffness.

'Let me take that pipe,' she said, cautiously advancing her hand, and abstracting it from his mouth.

Before he could attempt to recover it, it was broken, and behind the fire. He swore at her and seized another.

'Stop,' she cried. 'You must listen to me, and I can't speak while those clouds are floating in my face.'

'Will you go to the devil!' he exclaimed ferociously, 'and let me be!'

'No,' she persisted, 'I won't. When I call you stupid, I don't mean anything. I don't mean that I despise you. Come, you are my cousin, and we should be friends.'

'I shall have naught to do wi' you and your mucky pride and damned, mocking tricks!' he answered. 'I'll go to hell, body and soul, before I look sideways at you again!'

Catherine frowned, and retreated to the window-seat, chewing her lip, and endeavoring, by humming an eccentric tune, to conceal a growing tendency to sob.

'You should be friends with your cousin, Mr. Hareton,'

I interrupted, 'since she repents of her sauciness! It would do you a grand deal of good to have her for a companion.'

'A companion?' he cried. 'When she hates me, and does not think me fit to wipe her shoes! Nay, if it made me a king, I'd not be scorned for seeking her goodwill anymore.'

'It is not I who hate you, it is you who hate me!' wept Cathy, no longer disguising her tears. 'You hate me as much as Mr. Heathcliff does, and more.'

'You're a damned liar,' began Hareton Earnshaw. 'Why have I made him angry by taking your part then, a hundred times?'

'I didn't know you took my part,' she answered, drying her eyes. 'And I was miserable and bitter at everybody, but now I thank you, and beg you to forgive me.' She returned to the hearth, and frankly extended her hand.

He blackened, and scowled like a thunder-cloud, and kept his fists resolutely clenched, and his gaze fixed on the ground.

Catherine then impressed on his cheek a gentle kiss. The little rogue thought I had not seen her, and, drawing back, she took her former station by the window, quite demurely.

I shook my head reprovingly and then she blushed, and whispered, 'Well! What should I have done, Nelly? He wouldn't shake hands, and he wouldn't look. I must show him some way that I like him, that I truly want to be friends.'

Whether the kiss convinced Hareton, I cannot tell. He was very careful for some minutes, that his face should not be seen, and when he did raise it, he was sadly puzzled where to turn his eyes.

Catherine employed herself in wrapping a book called *Vampire Warfare in the New Century* neatly in white paper, and having tied it with a bit of ribbon and ad-

dressed it to 'Mr. Hareton Earnshaw,' she asked me to
convey the present to its destined recipient. 'Tell him, if
he'll take it, I'll come and teach him to read it well,' she
said. 'And if he refuses it, I'll go upstairs, and never tease
him again.'

I carried it, and repeated the message, and was anxiously
watched by my employer. Hareton would not open his fingers, so I laid it on his knee. He did not strike it off. I returned to my work. Catherine leaned her head and arms
on the table, till she heard the slight rustle of the covering
being removed, then she stole away and quietly seated herself beside her cousin. He trembled, and his face glowed;
all his rudeness and all his surly harshness had deserted
him. He could not summon courage, at first, to utter a syllable in reply to her questioning look and her murmured
petition.

'Say you forgive me, Hareton, do! You can make me so
happy, by speaking that little word. And you'll be my
friend?' added Catherine, interrogatively.

'Nay! You'll be ashamed of me every day of your life,'
he answered.

'So, you won't be my friend?' she said, smiling as sweet
as honey, and creeping close up.

I overheard no further distinguishable talk, but on looking round again, I perceived two such radiant counte-
nances bent over the page of the book, that I did not doubt
the treaty had been ratified, on both sides, and the enemies
were, thenceforth, sworn allies.

The work they studied was full of costly pictures and
those, and their position, had charm enough to keep them
unmoved that day. The intimacy thus commenced, grew
rapidly, though it encountered temporary interruptions.
Earnshaw was not to be civilized with a wish, and my
young lady was no philosopher, and no paragon of patience. But both their minds tending to the same point—

one loving and desiring to esteem, and the other loving and desiring to be esteemed—they contrived in the end to reach it.

You see, Mr. Lockwood, it was easy enough to win Mrs. Heathcliff's heart. But now, I'm glad you did not try. The crown of all my wishes will be the union of those two. I shall envy no one on their wedding day. There won't be a happier woman than myself in England!

# Chapter 33

The next day, my charge got downstairs before me, and out into the garden where she had seen her cousin performing some work. When I went to bid them come to breakfast, I saw she had persuaded him to clear a large space of ground from currant and gooseberry bushes, and they were busy planning together an importation of plants from the Grange.

I was terrified at the devastation which had been accomplished in a brief half-hour. The black currant trees were the apple of Joseph's eye, and she had just fixed her choice of a flower bed in the midst of them!

'There! That will be all shown to the master,' I exclaimed, 'the minute it is discovered. And what excuse have you to offer for taking such liberties with the garden? We shall have a fine explosion on the head of it. See if we don't! Mr. Hareton, I wonder you should have no more wit, than to go and make that mess at her bidding!'

'I'd forgotten they were Joseph's,' answered Earnshaw, rather puzzled. 'But I'll tell him I did it. He'll take no revenge. I think he likes me since I ran off the beasties, telling them they could no longer partake of him whenever they please.'

I had been well surprised when that exchange had taken

place a few weeks before. Surprised the bloodsuckers feared Hareton Earnshaw enough to obey, for he was not friendly with them as Mr. Heathcliff had once been. Surprised we heard nothing of it from Mr. Heathcliff. But I, for one, was glad it did not become an event in our lives, though I suppose it was a remarkable one for Joseph.

At that time, it was still Mr. Heathcliff's routine that he would dine with us, though he never ate or drank a morsel. Catherine usually sat by me, but today she stole nearer to Hareton, and I presently saw she would have no more discretion in her friendship than she had in her hostility.

'Now, mind you don't talk with and notice your cousin too much,' were my whispered instructions as we entered the room. 'It will certainly annoy Mr. Heathcliff, and he'll be mad at you both.'

'I'm not going to,' she answered.

The minute after, she had sidled to Earnshaw, and was sticking primroses in his plate of porridge.

He dared not speak to her, there. He dared hardly look, and yet she went on teasing till he was twice on the point of being provoked to laugh. I frowned as she glanced toward the master, whose mind was occupied on other subjects, and she then re-commenced her nonsense. At last, Hareton uttered a smothered laugh.

Mr. Heathcliff started; his eye rapidly surveyed our faces. Catherine met it with her accustomed look of nervousness, and yet defiance, which he abhorred.

'It is well you are out of my reach,' he exclaimed. 'What fiend possesses you to stare back at me continually with those infernal eyes? Down with them! And don't remind me of your existence again. I thought I had cured you of laughing!'

'It was me,' muttered Hareton.

'What did you say?' demanded the master.

Hareton looked at his plate, and did not repeat the confession.

Mr. Heathcliff looked at him a bit, and then his gaze strayed to the window. He immediately spotted the alterations in the garden. 'What is this?' he demanded, rising to get a closer look.

'I've pulled up two or three bushes,' replied the young man.

'And why have you pulled them up?' said the master.

Catherine, of course because it is in her nature, had to put in her tongue. 'We wanted to plant some flowers there,' she cried. 'I'm the only person to blame, for I wished him to do it.'

'And who the devil gave *you* leave to touch a stick about the place?' demanded her father-in-law, much surprised. 'And who ordered you to obey her?' he added, turning to Hareton.

The latter was speechless. His cousin replied, 'You shouldn't grudge a few yards of earth for me to ornament, when you have taken all my land!'

'Your land, insolent slut? You never had any!' said Heathcliff.

'And my money,' she continued, returning his angry glare and, meantime, biting a piece of crust, the remnant of her breakfast. 'You robbed me of all.'

'Silence!' he exclaimed. 'Get done, and begone!'

'And Hareton's land, and his money,' pursued the reckless thing. 'Hareton and I are friends now, and I shall tell him all about you!'

The master seemed confounded a moment. He grew pale, eyeing her all the while, with an expression of mortal hate.

'If you strike me, Hareton will strike you!' she said. 'So you may as well sit down.'

'If Hareton does not turn you out of the room, I'll strike

him to hell,' thundered Heathcliff. 'Damnable witch! Dare you pretend to rouse him against me? Off with her! Do you hear? Fling her into the kitchen! I'll kill her, Nelly Dean, if you let her come into my sight again!'

Hareton tried under his breath to persuade her to go.

'Drag her away!' he cried savagely. 'Are you staying to talk?' And he approached to execute his own command.

'He'll not obey you, wicked man, anymore!' said Catherine. 'And he'll soon detest you, as much as I do!'

'Wisht! Wisht!' muttered the young man reproachfully. 'I will not hear you speak so to him.'

'But you won't let him strike me?' she cried.

'Come then!' he whispered earnestly.

It was too late. Heathcliff had caught hold of her.

'Now *you* go!' he said to Earnshaw. 'Accursed witch! This time she has provoked me when I could not bear it, and I'll make her repent it forever!'

He had his hand in her hair. Hareton attempted to release the locks, entreating him not to hurt her. His black eyes flashed; he seemed ready to tear Catherine in pieces, and I was just worked up to risk coming to the rescue, when of a sudden, his fingers relaxed, he shifted his grasp from her head to her arm, and gazed intently in her face. Then he drew his hand over his eyes, stood a moment to collect himself, apparently, and turning anew to Catherine, said with assumed calmness, 'You must learn to avoid putting me in a passion, or I shall really murder you sometime! You don't know what I'm capable of—what I might do to you. Go with Mrs. Dean, and keep with her, and confine your insolence to her ears. Nelly, take her, and leave me, all of you! Leave me!'

I led my young lady out, and she was too glad of her escape. The other followed, and Mr. Heathcliff had the room to himself, till dinner.

I had counseled Catherine to get herself upstairs, but as

soon as Heathcliff saw her vacant seat, he sent me to call her. He spoke to none of us and went out before we had finished our meal, saying that he should not return before evening.

The two new friends established themselves in the house, busy in their several occupations, of pupil and teacher. I came in to sit with them, after I had done my work, and felt soothed and comforted to watch them. You know, they both appeared in a measure my children. I had long been proud of one, and now, I was sure, the other would be a source of equal satisfaction. His honest, warm, and intelligent nature shook off rapidly the clouds of ignorance and degradation in which it had been bred, and Catherine's sincere commendations acted as a spur to his industry. His brightening mind brightened his features, and added spirit and nobility to their aspect. I could hardly fancy it the same individual I had beheld on the day I discovered my little lady at Wuthering Heights, after her expedition to the Crags.

While I admired, and they labored, dusk drew on, and with it returned the master. He came upon us quite unexpectedly, entering by the front way, and had a full view of the whole three, ere we could raise our heads to glance at him. *Well,* I reflected, *there was never a pleasanter or more harmless sight, and it will be a burning shame to scold them.* The red firelight glowed on their two bonny heads, and revealed their faces, animated with the eager interest of children. Though he was twenty-three, and she eighteen, each had so much of novelty to feel and learn that neither experienced nor evinced the sentiments of sober disenchanted maturity.

They lifted their eyes together, to encounter Mr. Heathcliff. Perhaps you have never noticed that their eyes are precisely similar, and they are those of Catherine Earnshaw. The present Catherine has no other likeness to her, except a breadth of forehead, and a certain arch of the nostril that makes her appear rather haughty, whether she is or not. With Hareton the resemblance is carried further.

I suppose this resemblance disarmed Mr. Heathcliff. He walked to the hearth in evident agitation, but it quickly subsided as he looked at the young man. He took the book from his hand, and glanced at the open page, then returned it without any observation. Shortly, Catherine and Earnshaw slipped out and I was about to depart also, but he bid me sit still.

'It is a poor conclusion, is it not,' Heathcliff observed, having brooded awhile on the scene he had just witnessed. 'An absurd termination to my violent exertions? I get levers and mattocks to demolish the two houses, and train myself to be capable of working like Hercules, and when everything is ready, and in my power, I find the will to lift a slate off either roof has vanished! My old enemies have not beaten me. Now would be the precise time to revenge myself on their representatives. I could do it, and none could hinder me. But where is the use? I don't care for striking. I can't take the trouble to raise my hand! That sounds as if I had been laboring the whole time only to exhibit a fine trait of magnanimity. It is far from being the case—I have lost the faculty of enjoying their destruction, and I am too idle to destroy for nothing.

'Nelly, there is a strange change approaching, and I'm in its shadow. I take so little interest in my daily life that I barely feel present any longer. Those two, who have left the room, are the only objects that retain a distinct material appearance to me, and that appearance causes me pain, amounting to agony. About *her* I won't speak and I don't desire to think, but I earnestly wish she were invisible. Her presence invokes only maddening sensations. *He* moves me differently, and yet if I could do it without seeming insane, I'd never see him again!

'Five minutes ago, Hareton seemed a personification of my youth, not a human being. I felt to him in such a variety of ways, that it would have been impossible to have accosted him rationally.

'In the first place, his startling likeness to Catherine connected him fearfully with her. And what does not recall her? I cannot look down to this floor, but her features are shaped on the flags! In every cloud, in every tree—filling the air at night, and caught by glimpses in every object, by day I am surrounded with her image! The entire world is a dreadful collection of memoranda that she did exist, and that I have lost her!

'I cannot live as I am, Nelly. Born half one and half another.'

'You mean part slayer, part vampire,' I dared to say, for though I wished to keep my full allowance of blood, I could not help but be curious. After all, I had practically raised him.

He eyed me and for a moment I feared I had pushed too far and *was* about to meet my Maker, but he looked away.

'You cannot imagine, Nelly, the torment I suffered when the dark side of me began to emerge. For years, I wanted nothing but to see their black blood spilled, but as I grew older, as I transformed, I found myself caught between hatred and pity for the beasties. With her at my side, perhaps I could have come to find balance in my existence, but it is not possible. Not without her, and so the time has come for a change.'

'But what do you mean by a *change*, Mr. Heathcliff?' I said, alarmed at his manner, though he was neither in danger of losing his sense, nor dying. According to my judgment he was quite strong and healthy; and, as to his reason, from childhood he had a delight in dwelling on dark things and entertaining odd fancies. 'You have no feeling of illness, have you?' I asked.

'No, Nelly, I have not,' he answered. 'And I greatly doubt that I ever shall suffer such weakness of body.'

'Then you are not afraid of death?' I pursued.

'I wish for death, if it is even possible. I cannot continue in this condition, torn between mortal flesh and something more terrible! You cannot know—cannot imagine the torture I suffer with each passing hour . . . each day . . . cannot imagine the torments that devour my soul. I have a single wish, and my whole being and faculties are yearning to attain it. They have yearned toward it so long, and so unwaveringly, that I'm convinced it *will* be reached—and *soon*—because it has devoured my existence. I am swallowed in the anticipation of its fulfillment.'

'What are you going to do?' I asked.

'I will not say, except to tell you that my time has nearly come. I'm weary and I can bear the agony no longer. Her time has nearly come. I only pray I will succeed.'

He began to pace the room, muttering terrible things to himself, till I was inclined to believe that conscience had turned his heart to an earthly hell, and I wondered greatly how it would all end.

# Chapter 34

One night shortly after that, after the family was in bed, I heard Heathcliff go downstairs and out the front door. I did not hear him re-enter, and in the morning I found he was still away.

We were in April then. The weather was sweet and warm, the grass as green as showers and sun could make it, and the two dwarf apple trees near the southern wall, in full bloom.

After breakfast, Catherine insisted on my bringing a chair and sitting with my work under the fir trees at the end of the house. From there, I watched Hareton dig and arrange her little garden under her direction. I was comfortably reveling in the spring fragrance around, and the beautiful soft blue overhead, when my young lady, who had run down near the gate to procure some primrose roots for a border, returned only half laden, and informed us that Mr. Heathcliff was coming in.

'And he spoke to me,' she added, with a perplexed countenance.

'What did he say?' asked Hareton.

'He told me to be gone as fast as I could,' she answered. 'But he looked so different from his usual look that I stopped a moment to stare at him.'

'How?' he inquired.

'Why, almost bright and cheerful. No, *almost* nothing—very *much* excited, and wild and glad!' she replied.

'Night-walking amuses him, then,' I remarked, affecting a careless manner. In reality, I was as surprised as she was, and anxious to see the master looking glad; that would not be an everyday spectacle, and I made an excuse to go in.

Heathcliff stood at the open door. He was pale, and he trembled, yet he certainly had a strange, joyful glitter in his eyes that altered the aspect of his whole face.

'Rambling about all night on the moors?' I asked. I wanted to discover where he had been since he no longer pursued the vampires with much interest, but I did not like to ask directly.

'Don't annoy me, Nelly. Let me alone.'

I obeyed, and in passing, I noticed he breathed as fast as a cat. Something was astir with him, but what, I did not know.

That noon, he did not bother to join us at our meal. We saw him walking to and fro in the garden and Hareton said he'd go and ask why he did not sit with us, as was his custom even though he no longer ate, thinking we had grieved him some way.

'Well, is he coming?' cried Catherine, when her cousin returned.

'Nay,' he answered. 'But he's not angry. He seemed rare and pleased indeed, speaking of the time for endings and beginnings, but then I made him impatient by speaking to him twice and then he bid me be off to you. He wondered how I could want the company of anybody else.'

After an hour or two, Heathcliff re-entered in no degree calmer. He had the same unnatural—it *was* unnatural—appearance of joy under his black brows, the same bloodless hue, and his teeth visible, now and then, in a kind of smile.

'Have you heard any good news, Mr. Heathcliff?' I asked. 'You look uncommonly animated.'

'Where should good news come from, to me?' he said. 'Nelly, once and for all, let me beg you to warn Hareton and the others away from me. I wish to be troubled by nobody. I wish to have this place to myself.'

'Is there some new reason for this banishment?' I inquired. 'Tell me why you are so queer, Mr. Heathcliff. Where were you last night? I'm not putting the question through idle curiosity, but—'

'You are putting the question through very idle curiosity,' he interrupted, with a laugh. 'Yet, I'll answer it. Last night, I was on the threshold of hell. Today, I am within sight of my heaven. I have my eyes on it! And now you'd better go—you'll neither see nor hear anything to frighten you, if you refrain from prying.'

He did not quit the house again that afternoon, and no one intruded on his solitude, till, at eight o'clock, I deemed it proper to carry a candle to him. Why I thought a vampire, even a half-breed vampire, needed light, I do not know. A gesture to the humanity I still hoped was within him, perhaps.

I found him leaning against the ledge of an open window, but not looking out. His face was turned to the interior gloom. The fire had smoldered to ashes. The room was filled with the damp, mild air of the cloudy evening and still, still as a grave, dare I say?

I uttered an ejaculation of discontent at seeing the dismal grate and commenced shutting the casements, one after another, till I came to his. 'Must I close this?' I asked in order to rouse him, for he would not stir.

The light flashed on his features as I spoke. Oh, Mr. Lockwood, I cannot express what a terrible start I got, by the momentary view! Those deep black eyes! That smile and ghastly paleness! He appeared to me, not as Heath-

cliff, but as the vampire I had seen that night in the courtyard and, in my terror, I let the candle bend toward the
wall, and it left me in darkness.

'Yes, close it,' he replied, in his familiar voice. It was as
if he had not even been aware of the brief transformation!

I hurried out in a foolish state of dread, and sent Joseph
up to take him a light and rekindle the fire. I dared not go
in myself again just then, but thought it safe enough for
Joseph to go. After all, he had already seen the worst and
lived to tell the tale.

We later heard Heathcliff mount the stairs; he did not
proceed to his ordinary chamber, but turned into that with
the paneled bed. The same room I believe you said you
slept in. The window, as you recall, is wide enough for
anybody to get through, and it struck me that he plotted
another midnight excursion.

Why the sudden secrecy of his wanderings? I wondered.
After all these years of coming and going at night, which
started in his boyhood, why would he care what any of us
thought or knew?

Dawn came and I rose and went into the garden, as
soon as I could see, to ascertain if there were any foot-
marks under his window. There were none.

*He has stayed at home,* I thought. *He'll be all right
today.*

I prepared breakfast for the household, as was my usual
custom, but told Hareton and Catherine to get theirs before the master came down, for he lay late. They preferred
taking it out of doors, under the trees, and I set a little
table to accommodate them.

On my re-entrance, I found Mr. Heathcliff in the
kitchen at the table. Looking at the opposite wall, he commenced to surveying one particular portion, up and down,
with glittering, restless eyes, and with such eager interest
that he stopped breathing, during half a minute together.

'Something I can get for you, master?' I said, not liking his behavior, which seemed even queer for him whose behavior was most queer in its own right.

He didn't notice me, and yet he smiled. I'd rather have seen him gnash his fanged teeth than smile so. 'Mr. Heathcliff! Master!' I cried. 'Don't, for God's sake, stare as if you saw an unearthly vision.'

'Don't, for God's sake, shout so loud,' he replied. 'Turn round, and tell me, are we by ourselves?'

'Of course,' was my answer. 'Of course we are!'

Still, I involuntarily obeyed him, as if I were not quite sure. When I glanced back at him, I perceived he was not looking at the wall, for when I regarded him alone, it seemed exactly that he gazed at something within two yards' distance. And whatever it was, it communicated, apparently, both pleasure and pain, in exquisite extremes. At least the anguished yet raptured expression of his countenance suggested that idea. The fancied object was not fixed, either; his eyes pursued it with unwearied vigilance, and, even in speaking to me, were never weaned away.

As I watched him, I found myself fascinated that the undead could see visions. There had been no such mention of the matter in the books my Cathy had been reading to me, and I made a note to myself to mention the fact to her later. Perhaps, with all our experience with the bloodsuckers, she and I ought to write a book of our own someday!

After some time with the staring, Heathcliff rose, left the house, slowly sauntering down the garden path, and disappeared through the gate.

The hours crept anxiously by and another evening came. I did not retire to rest till late, and when I did, I could not sleep. He returned after midnight and shut himself into her room again. I listened, and tossed about, and, finally, dressed and descended. It was too irksome to lie up there, harassing my brain with a hundred idle misgivings.

I distinguished Mr. Heathcliff's step, restlessly measuring the floor, and he frequently broke the silence by a deep inspiration, resembling a groan. He muttered detached words, also; the only one I could catch was the name of Catherine, coupled with some wild term of endearment or suffering and spoken as one would speak to a person present: low and earnest, and wrung from the depth of his soul. Whatever matter he was contemplating, it was certain he was vexed.

I had not courage to walk straight into the apartment, but I desired to divert him from his reverie, and therefore fell upon the kitchen fire, stirred it, and began to scrape the cinders. It drew him forth sooner than I expected. He opened the door immediately, and said—

'Nelly, come here—is it morning?'

'It is striking four,' I answered. 'You want a candle to take upstairs?'

'No, I don't wish to go upstairs,' he said. 'When day breaks, I want to send for Green, the lawyer. I wish to make some legal inquiries of him while I can bestow a thought on those matters, and while I can act calmly. I have not written my will yet, and how to leave my property I cannot determine! I wish I could annihilate it from the face of the earth.'

'I would not talk so, Mr. Heathcliff,' I interposed. 'You look well enough to me and surely not grave-bound.'

'Just the same, I put you in charge of my burial. You must take notice that the sexton obeys my direction concerning the two coffins! We shall not be separated. No minister need come, nor need anything be said over me—I tell you, I have nearly attained *my* heaven, and that of others is altogether unvalued and unconverted by me!'

'And supposing they refuse to bury you anywhere near the kirk, but choose to add your head to one of your pikes along the road to Gimmerton?' I said, shocked at his godless indifference, all the time wondering how he proposed he was going to die. Did he mean to have one of his own servants run him through his heart with a sword? Or because he was half human, was he able to succumb as the rest of us would someday? 'How would you like that?'

'They won't do that,' he replied. 'Even in death, they will still fear me. If they did, however, put me upon a pike, you must retrieve my head and body secretly and put them in the grave beside her!'

As soon as he heard the other members of the family stirring he retired to his den, and I breathed freer. But in the afternoon, while Joseph and Hareton were at their work, he came into the kitchen again, and with a wild look, bid me come and sit in the main house. He wanted somebody with him.

I declined, telling him plainly that his strange talk and manner frightened me, and I had neither the nerve nor the will to be his companion, alone.

'I believe you think me a fiend!' he said, with his dismal laugh. 'Something too horrible to live under a decent roof!'

It occurred to me to point out that he *was,* indeed, a fiend and all knew it, but I kept my lips sealed, as was my place.

Then turning to Catherine, who was there, and who drew behind me at his approach, he added, half sneeringly, 'Will *you* come? I'll not hurt you. No! To you, I've made myself worse than the devil. Well, there is one who won't shrink from my company! By God, she's relentless. Oh, damn it! It is unutterably too much for flesh and blood to bear—even mine.'

He solicited the society of no one more. At dusk, he went into his chamber.

The following day was very wet; indeed, it had poured down most of the night, and still a light rain fell. As I took my morning walk round the house, I observed the master's window swinging open; the rain would have driven in all night. *He must either be up or out. But I'll make no more ado, I'll go boldly and look!*

Having succeeded in obtaining entrance with another key, I ran to unclose the panels, for the chamber was vacant. I walked to the window and looked out in the direction of Gimmerton and knew, at once, deep in my soul, where he had gone.

Without haste, for I knew there was no need for it, I put on my best bonnet and cloak and found Hareton, requesting he accompany me into the village. He agreed without question; perhaps he knew why he was going. Perhaps he was just acting as the good soul I knew he had become. I wanted to slip out before Cathy arose, but we had no such luck, and before the three of us passed through the gates, Joseph was trailing behind, as well. On our way, we picked up two herd-boys, a dairymaid, the tanner's son, and an elderly bloodsucker we all knew well because he was too ancient and snaggle-toothed to do us any harm. One by one, they fell into line behind me like a trail of goslings, never asking where we went or why.

Upon reaching the church, I did not pass through the gates, for what would have been the sense in that? Instead, I walked round back, trying to take care not to tread on too many graves, for these days it seemed more were planted outside the walls than within. Upon approaching Catherine's grave, I warned Cathy to stay back, but she refused, and soon enough we all came to stand at Heathcliff's feet.

My heart leapt in my chest at the awful sight.

He was as dead as I have ever seen a man . . . or vampire.

Sometime in the night, he'd laid himself down beside Catherine's unearthed grave and thrust a silver stake through his own heart. But before he had sent himself to heaven or hell, wherever he was bound, he had dug up her coffin and done the same to her corpse.

Cathy gasped and Hareton took her shoulders to steady her. 'Is that my mother dead these eighteen years?' she questioned. 'And a stake through her heart?'

Joseph stepped up to look more closely. ''Pears so, miss.'

The herd-boys, tanner's son, dairymaid, and old vampire joined Joseph along the far side of the grave and, gazing down, agreed in earnest with him. My lady Catherine did, indeed, have a silver stake through her heart; she looked freshly murdered and dead at last, and quite beautiful.

Stooping down beside Heathcliff's body, I combed his long, black hair from his forehead. I then tried to close his eyes, to extinguish, if possible, the frightful, life-like gaze of exultation on his face. They would not shut; they seemed to sneer at my attempts, and his parted lips and sharp fangs sneered, too!

So it appeared, Mr. Lockwood, that my master found a way to release Catherine and himself from their torment of being part vampire, part human (though they reached that state through different circumstances), and to reside with her forever more.

'Should we take the silver stakes?' Hareton questioned after we all stood and stared for a passage of time. 'They must be worth quite a bit.'

'Leave them,' I said, wanting to take no chances that either of them might rise again. 'With him dead and no legal will, you will inherit all, Hareton. Plenty more where these came from, I should guess.'

'Rather pretty, isn't she?' Cathy remarked thoughtfully, gazing down on her mother's corpse. 'Though perhaps not as pretty as I.'

'Most certainly not,' Hareton agreed, kissing her soundly on the cheek.

'Anyone for breakfast?' I asked, looking up at the rag-tag audience.

We buried him later that day, to the scandal of the whole neighborhood, as he had wished. Earnshaw, I, Cathy, Joseph, the sexton, and six men to carry the coffin comprised the whole attendance.

The six men departed when they had let it down into the grave, and we stayed to see both of them covered. Hareton dug green sods and laid them over the brown soil himself. It is as smooth and verdant as its companion mounds inside the gates—and I hope its tenants sleep as soundly.

"As for me, I can say I will sleep more soundly when I am back under the roof of the Grange, for I do not like it here at the Heights, Mr. Lockwood."

"So the household is to move to the Grange once Mr. Earnshaw and Mrs. Heathcliff are married?" I asked.

"So they tell me, although something is afoot on the subject of plans being made," answered Mrs. Dean. "They have been quite secretive the last few days, whispering and giggling. I do not like it one bit, I will tell you."

"And who will live here then?"

"Why, Joseph will take care of the house, and perhaps the old snaggle-toothed bloodsucker will stay to keep him company. They get along quite well now that Joseph is no longer fodder. They will live in the kitchen, and the rest will be shut up."

"For the use of such ghosts as choose to inhabit it," I observed.

"No, Mr. Lockwood," said Nelly, shaking her head. "I believe the dead are truly dead now and at peace."

At that moment the gate swung to; Cathy and Hareton were returning, hands clasped.

"*They* are afraid of nothing," she grumbled, watching their approach through the window. "Together, they would brave Satan and all his legions."

As they stepped onto the door-stones, and halted to take a last look at the moon—or, more correctly, at each other, by her light, I felt irresistibly impelled to escape them again. Pressing a remembrance into the hand of Mrs. Dean, I vanished through the kitchen as they opened the house door.

My walk home was lengthened by a diversion in the direction of the kirk. I sought, and soon discovered, the two headstones on the slope next to the moor, moss creeping over both. I lingered round them, under that benign sky, watched the moths fluttering among the heath and harebells, listened to the soft wind breathing through the grass, and wondered how anyone could ever imagine unquiet slumbers for the sleepers in that quiet earth.

By the light of the moon, I returned to the Grange, dined, and slept so well that I did not wake until I heard an unfamilar voice in my ear.

"Best be quick if ye value yer skin!"

I opened my eyes to see the old woman with the pipe tossing my belongings into my bag. "They's already set fire to the Heights. Grange is next."

"Set fire?" I flew out of the bed, tugging off my nightcap. "Whatever do you speak of?"

"The master, handsome he is. And he's set determined to see both houses burnt to the ground before he and the missus are on their way. Wants to leave no fine manors for the beasties to set up housekeeping, with him gone. Would you care to wear yer pants, sir?" she asked, her lips wrapped round her pipe. She offered my trousers.

I grabbed them and stepped into them, tucking in my nightshirt. I could smell burning wood. "What are you talking about?" I demanded, stepping into my shoes. "You make no sense, woman!"

"Master Earnshaw. Sneaked into town and was wed last night, he and Mrs. Heathcliff. They're set off to Paris to go to some vampire slaying school. He paid us a year salary and gave us two horses and a cow to start anew. Ye best hurry," she urged as she went out the door.

My shoes on, my overcoat flung over my arm, I ran down the grand stairs and out the door to find a gypsy wagon parked in the garden. Cathy sat beside Mrs. Dean on the wagon seat, directing Hareton in the lighting of a pitch torch.

"Mrs. Dean," I gasped, snatching my bag from the old woman.

"That's the last of them," Catherine called to her new husband. "The parlor draperies would probably be the wisest location to start the blaze, my love."

"Of course, my love," Hareton called back to her.

"Mrs. Dean." I hurried to the covered gypsy wagon. "What is happening?"

"My master's set Wuthering Heights on fire, and now the Grange is to see the same destiny. You can spot the flames from here, the blaze is so grand," she told me good-naturedly, pointing in said direction.

Against my inclination, I turned and looked. Sure enough, in the distance, I saw a grand wall of red flames and a great column of smoke. "But why?" I asked, still amazed and so entirely not awake yet that I was not sure that I was not dreaming.

"A cleansing, Mr. Lockwood," the new Mrs. Earnshaw explained, adjusting her traveling bonnet. "Only fire will erase the curse on both these houses. We have been doing family research and have discovered that far in the past, there was a Hareton Earnshaw of Wuthering Heights who was a great vampire slayer in the days when such matters were kept secret. That is the explanation for the vampires carved in stone over the gate and his name inscribed there. And since Hareton and I are both descendants, we see it as our duty to follow our forefather's footsteps. Besides, with us gone, if we do not burn the houses to the ground, the bloodsuckers will be dining on the villagers at our tables."

"You don't say," I said, aghast in shock.

"My husband and I, now wealthy enough to do as we like, are enrolling in a school in Paris where we will learn the finer arts of vampire slaying. We hope to travel the world killing them." She smiled prettily.

"And you, Mrs. Dean?" I asked incredulously. "Do you intend to slay vampires?"

"Certainly not, Mr. Lockwood," she cried, drawing herself up quite haughtily. "I am a housekeeper. I will keep house for Mr. and Mrs. Earnshaw." She glanced at the painted gypsy wagon she sat upon. "Or I will keep a wagon, whichever my master and missus prefer. And Joseph will continue to care for the horses and whatever else is needed."

She nodded, and for the first time I spotted Joseph standing behind the wagon. He appeared to be wearing one of Heathcliff's old coats, for he was quite well dressed, though he still wore a long kerchief tied round his neck, no doubt to cover the scars of years of being fed upon.

Hareton walked out of the house, no longer carrying the torch, and I smelled the acrid odor of burning fabric. Within minutes, flames were shooting from the open parlor windows, and those gathered looking quite satisfied with his work.

"Well, my darling. Should we be off to Paris?" Catherine asked her husband sweetly. "Mayhap kill some bloodsuckers on our way?"

"Indeed, my love," he answered, leaping up in the wagon seat and taking the leather reins in his meaty hands.

I must have been looking a bit forlorn, for as Hareton wheeled the gypsy wagon past me, Mrs. Dean looked out and called to me, "Should you like to join us, Mr. Lockwood? I know not where our journey will lead, but I have no doubt we will see more than a bit of adventure." She gazed at the house now ablaze. "And you will certainly not be sleeping here tonight."

I could not go, of course. Even the thought was preposterous. I was a man of considerable and distinguished responsibilities in London, and I had the hunting party to attend today. I could not leave the country in a gypsy wagon with two young slayer lovebirds, a manservant, and a housekeeper. I was in no way equipped to accompany them on any vampire slaying expedition. I didn't even have a proper weapon.

"Thank you for your offer, Mrs. Dean, but I could not possibly. You understand."

She gave a wave, and I watched the gypsy wagon depart the garden. Feeling the heat of the flames behind me, I gazed over my shoulder at the burning house, then at Wuthering Heights, a ball of fire in the distance. I thought of Heathcliff and Catherine and the moss growing over their graves. The ever-lasting peace they had found.

I looked back to the departing wagon. "A bit of adventure," Mrs. Dean had offered.

And before I knew what I was doing, I was running after the wagon, for I knew there would be much more to her tale, and I was not ready to retire to a quiet and sedate middle age. In truth, it was more than the promised adventure that drew me; it was the seductive and fascinating Mrs. Dean. A gentleman I am, and a man of breeding and quality I do claim to be, but in fact, my own father was born to a family of shipwrights, and I learned honest labor before I was ever tucked off to Cambridge and the life of my betters. My parents and siblings and every last stitch and knob of kin have vanished, and if I wished to take a clever and loving woman to wife, what care I if she began her days below stairs?

"Wait! Wait for me," I cried, and ran after them. Whether I shall have time or inkling to continue an account of my affairs, I cannot say, and that, in any case, would be another story for another evening by the fire. Bid you well, dear readers, and go not out on a moonless night without sufficient quantity of prime garlic, for despite what others may tell you, the bloodsucking vampires do rule the darkness.